Marcia Muller pioneered the contemporary female private investigator novel, with the first Sharon McCone mystery, *Edwin of the Iron Shoes*, in 1977. The Sharon McCone private eye series has since gained huge critical acclaim, an enormous readership, and dozens of imitators.

In addition to her success as a novelist, Marcia Muller is a well-known anthologist and critic. She has co-edited several collections of mystery stories with Bill Pronzini, and the 1986 reference book, *1001 Midnights: The Aficionado's Guide to Mystery and Detective Fiction.*

She lives in northern California.

**Other Marcia Muller titles from
The Women's Press:**

There's Something in a Sunday (1992)
The Shape of Dread (1992)
Trophies and Dead Things (1992)
Pennies on a Dead Woman's Eyes (1993)

MARCIA MULLER

A SHARON McCONE MYSTERY

WHERE
ECHOES
live

The Women's Press

Published in Great Britain by
The Women's Press Ltd, 1992
A member of the Namara Group
34 Great Sutton Street, London EC1V 0DX

First published in the United States of America by
The Mysterious Press, New York, 1991

British Library Cataloguing-in-Publication Data.
A catalogue record for this book is available from the
British Library.

ISBN 0 7043 4315 0

Printed and bound in Great Britain by
BPCC Hazell Ltd.
A member of BPCC Ltd.

While Tufa Lake and Promiseville are fictional locales, the author has drawn inspiration from Mono Lake and Bodie, California. She wishes to express her gratitude to all those individuals who unselfishly labor for the preservation of such natural and historical treasures.

Special thanks to Collin Wilcox and Citabria 11659 for their valuable assistance.

For Virginia and William Campbell Gault

Part One

▲ ▲ ▲

Tufa Lake, California

One

▲▲▲

Tufa Lake lies in the high desert of northeastern California, only miles from the Nevada border. The land there is volcanically formed; dark basalt hills surround the lake basin on three sides, and on the fourth is a chain of pumice and ash-shrouded craters. Between them and the shoreline spreads an alkali plain covered by sagebrush and tundra, and the ghostly white tufa towers that stand as mute testimony to man's greedy abuse of his environment.

These knobby pinnacles of calcified vegetation—created by mineral-rich underground springs, and once completely submerged—have gradually been revealed as the lake's feeder streams are siphoned off for the faucets and swimming pools of southern California. Hundreds of them dot the plain, and others form islands where the migrating gulls, grebes, and plovers come to nest, breed, and feast on the plentiful brine shrimp. More often than not the water from which they rise is eerily still, reflecting the colors of the changeable desert sky.

In spite of the nearby highway and the lakeshore town of

3

Vernon, this is a place of great silence. Standing at the water's edge, as I did the first time I went there one October, it is easy to imagine how it was a hundred years ago, or how it will be a hundred years into the future. And when a gull cries and launches itself on a steep trajectory into the sun, the sounds reverberate like gunshots off the surrounding hills.

This is a place out of time—a place where echoes live.

I turned away from the lake and walked up the rocky slope toward the cabins. There were six of them, plus a main lodge—built of dark brown wood with green composition roofs and shutters, nestled in a grove of cottonwoods and willows. The highway ran between them and a sheer hillside; yellow-leafed aspens grew thick in the hill's deep declivities, like veins of gold that had burst open and spilled down. Although when I'd arrived an hour before it had been warm—much too warm for this altitude in late October—the sun had dipped behind the high peaks and there was now a pronounced chill in the air.

I went up the steps and crossed the porch of the cabin on the far left. The small living room had the look of rustic summer places everywhere: a rattan sofa and chairs whose flowered cushions were faded and flattened; a potbellied wood stove in one corner; a Formica-and-metal dinette set in front of the door leading to the kitchen. The smell was the same, too: musty with dry rot, stale cooking odors, dead fires, and age. I went to one of the windows that opened onto the porch, grasped it, and heaved it upward. It gave a weary groan, and then a slightly fishy but fresh breeze began to filter inside.

When I turned, I saw Anne-Marie's note flutter from the coffee table to the floor. I rescued it, read it again. "Gone down to Lee Vining to talk with some of the Mono Lake Committee," it said. "Be back around 5:30. See you then at Zelda's."

I smiled at the fact that my friend had omitted both an address and an explanation of what Zelda's was. Of course it would never have occurred to her that a private investigator wouldn't be able to figure it out in a town whose population fell short of the 200 mark and whose streets were not numerous. And it was just as well she hadn't wasted the effort: I'd spotted the restaurant earlier on my way through Vernon.

Although it was only a little after four, I decided to check the office Anne-Marie was working out of in case she'd returned early. If she hadn't, I'd do some exploring on my own. I went through the curtained archway to one of the cabin's two bedrooms, pulled my favorite green sweater from my weekend bag, and traded it for the light T-shirt I'd been wearing. After I brushed my hair and refastened it in its ponytail, I grabbed my bag and car keys and climbed the slope to where I'd left my MG in front of the lodge.

Mrs. Wittington, proprietor of Willow Grove Lodge, was cutting back some chrysanthemums that grew in a half barrel next to the door of the main building. She saw me and straightened, pushing a soiled baseball cap back from her forehead and propping the hand that held the clippers on one well-padded hip. As she smiled at me, her suntanned face crinkled pleasantly.

"Everything okay with the cabin?" she asked.

"Yes, just fine."

She nodded in satisfaction. "You won't find better—and certainly not cleaner—cabins than mine around here. And off season they're a steal. Your friend was real pleased with the arrangement we worked out. Of course, I was pleased to have her. They bring their lawyer in, it means those people are serious about keeping this place from going to hell."

"Those people" were the California Coalition for Environmental Preservation; my friend and former colleague, Anne-Marie Altman, had taken an indefinite leave of absence from

All Souls Legal Cooperative in San Francisco to act as their chief counsel.

I said, "I thought the problem of the water diversions to the L.A. Basin had almost been solved, just as at Mono Lake."

"The diversions? Oh, sure. The state's probably going to pay L.A. for the water they planned to steal from us." She snorted derisively. "No, that's not the big problem anymore. It's the gold mining."

"Gold mining?"

"Out Stone Valley way." She waved the clippers to the east, toward Nevada. "Was a boom town there in the late eighteen hundreds—Promiseville. Petered out in the twenties. Since then there've always been a few prospectors in the valley, mainly folks who just want to be left the hell alone. But now some foreign company's got hold of the mineral rights, wants to put in a full-scale operation."

"And the people here don't want that?"

"Hell, no. Do you realize what it would do to this place? The noise. The processes they use—they'd poison the air. Destroy what God has made. Pretty soon it wouldn't matter if we won the fight to preserve the lake for the birds, the people who love it. We'd have nothing, and a bunch of damned foreigners would have the gold." She looked around, her face pulling into mournful lines. "Every night I pray that won't happen, but I'm not sure the Lord hears me. Wouldn't that be a bitch, if we saved the water only to lose everything anyway?"

"It certainly would," I agreed, appreciating both the irony of the situation and her strange conversational mix of religious references and profanity.

Perhaps the incursion of the foreign gold-mining interests was the reason Anne-Marie had asked me to come here this weekend. In her somewhat hurried phone call on Thursday—yesterday—she'd said only that some things were going on that bothered her and she'd feel better if I checked them out. When I told her that I couldn't give her longer than the weekend because I'd used up all my vacation days, she laughed and said, "I'm sure your boss will bend the rules for me if I need you beyond Sunday."

I was sure of that, too: Hank Zahn, who is my nominal boss at All Souls, happens to be Anne-Marie Altman's husband.

Mrs. Wittington was watching me anxiously, as if hoping for some reassurance. I said, "I'm sure the Coalition won't allow Tufa Lake to be destroyed after all the efforts to save it."

"Good intentions . . ." She shrugged and turned back to her chrysanthemums. "Well, if you need anything down at the cabin, just let me know."

I said I would and went on toward my MG.

I'd owned the red MG for years, since I first went to work at All Souls. Its appearance stopped just short of being scabrous, but in September I'd had the engine overhauled as a birthday present to myself. The trip to Tufa Lake was the first long one I'd made since then; all the way—from the Bay Area to Stockton, across the flat Central Valley, into the foothills of the Sierra Nevada, and across Yosemite—I'd carefully monitored the little car's performance. The rebuild had been worth it, I'd decided, just as a new body-and-paint job would not be. In my line of work, a spiffy attention-getting sports car is a definite liability.

As I pulled onto the highway I turned left toward Vernon, a mile and a half away where the ridge of hills curved to the east, creating more flatland between them and the lakeshore. On the outskirts I passed a trailer park and a scattering of small houses, mostly of the prefab variety. Then businesses began to appear on either side of the road: a couple of gas stations, a convenience store, a Laundromat, a take-out pizza parlor, a motel that was closed for the season. Unpaved lanes lined with more small homes meandered toward the hills; a white-steepled church was tucked back at the end of one of them. Beyond a boat-rental yard on the water's edge, a point of land jutted out; on it was Zelda's—cocktails, steaks, seafood. And beyond that was a sort of industrial-business complex—insurance brokerage, bookkeeping service, well drilling, real estate—consisting of wide-bodied trailers parked in a haphazard fashion on a large paved area. I left the MG on the shoulder of the road and went looking for the one that served as temporary headquarters for the Coalition for Environmental Preservation.

It was easy enough to locate, because a banner bearing the Coalition's emblem—a brilliant orange California poppy—hung from one side. An old mint-condition Morgan was pulled up at the opposite end from the steps. Anne-Marie's Subaru was nowhere in sight, but I decided to go inside and ask for her anyway. As I approached, however, loud voices came from within, the words indistinguishable but the tones clearly angry. The door burst open, and a woman came through it so fast that she lost her balance and stumbled down the steps.

She was a little woman in her mid- to late thirties, dressed in rugged denims, work boots, and a heavy wool shirt. Her brown hair was cropped short, and her round face was tanned and coarsened from exposure to the elements. In spite of her lack of stature, the way she gripped the railing and righted herself demonstrated wiry strength. She whirled toward the still-open door, raised a clenched fist, and shouted, "You *asshole!*"

A man appeared in the doorway—very tall, lanky, curly-haired, and amused. He said, "Lily, you're getting too refined for my taste."

"Fuck you, you fuckin' tree hugger!"

The man shook his head. "There you go again, sweet-talking me."

The woman quivered with rage. She stomped her booted foot, then pivoted and strode across the pavement toward the road. As she passed me, I heard her mutter, "Goddamn son of a bitch bastard!"

When I looked back at the trailer, the man was still standing in its door, grinning. He said to me, "You've got to admire her grasp of the English language."

"Uh, yes. Who is she?"

"Ms. Lily Nickles. The Tiger Lily, they call her."

"And what was that all about?"

"Nothing much. Lily's just kind of . . . combative. After you've been around her awhile you realize it's all a front. She figures a prospector has to be tough."

"She's a prospector?"

"Yeah, Lily's the most die-hard miner in Stone Valley."

I glanced toward the highway. Lily Nickles was climbing into a dusty tan Jeep parked a few yards from my car.

The man asked, "You looking for someone?"

"Anne-Marie Altman." I moved over to the foot of the steps. Up close I could see he was about my age and attractive in a hawk-nosed, droopy-mustached way. His dark blond hair curled over the collar of a suede jacket that had seen better days—no, years—and his brown eyes held an intensity that complemented the sharp jut of his profile.

He grinned again. "You must be her detective friend. Sharon McCone, isn't it?" When I nodded, he added, "Anne-Marie's not back from Lee Vining yet."

"I thought she probably wouldn't be."

The man came out of the trailer, shut the door, and locked it. As he loped down the steps he asked, "Do you know Anne-Marie wants you to meet her at Zelda's?"

"Yes, she left a note at the cabin."

"Good. She wants to talk privately with you. Then after dinner we'll all meet back here."

"All?"

"Well, you, her, me, Ned Sanderman. That's as many as are on a need-to-know basis."

Odd way of phrasing it, I thought. He made whatever this business was sound like a covert government operation. "Can't you tell me something about it now?" I asked.

"Anne-Marie should be the one to brief you. Besides, I've got an appointment five minutes ago." He started toward the Morgan in a long, loose stride.

"Hey," I called, "what's your name?"

"Heino Ripinsky."

Jesus, I thought, it's no wonder he didn't introduce himself!

Ripinsky must have been used to reactions like mine, because he stopped beside the car, whirled, and leveled an index finger at me. "Don't laugh," he warned. "Don't you *dare* laugh!"

I controlled the twitching at the corners of my mouth and spread my hands wide. "Me? Why would I do that?"

He laughed then and got into the Morgan. Over the racket of its engine, he shouted, "You can call me Hy."

As I watched it roar off toward the highway, I spotted a sticker on the car's rear bumper: Tufa Lake Is for the Birds.

What next? I wondered. I'd been here only a little over an hour and had already encountered three reasonably eccentric characters. Of course, I didn't know why I persisted in the largely false notion that people in small towns should be ordinary; I'd spent a fair amount of time in such places and had found their residents to be fully as peculiar as those of any big city.

I looked at my watch, saw it was only four-forty. I'd spend the next fifty minutes playing tourist, then meet Anne-Marie and find out about this matter that was so serious that only four people were on a "need-to-know basis."

Two

▲ ▲ ▲

The area I wanted to explore first was the alkali plain at the south end of the lake, where the tufa towers stood. I stopped for directions at the gas station across from the business complex, then followed the highway out of town for about four miles to where an unmarked, unpaved road branched off to the east and looped around the ashy gray craters.

In a recent issue of a California travel magazine I'd read how these "fire mountains," as geologists have dubbed them, are considered the site most likely within the next fifty years to produce an eruption the size of the 1980 Mount Saint Helens disaster. A 1982 hazard notice of potential volcanic activity issued by the U.S. Geological Survey provoked great outcry in the area, mainly from business people, and the threat of an eruption whose magnitude and timing cannot be predicted hovers like a dark cloud above the craters.

After about a mile, the road swung north again and ended in a rocky turnaround about a hundred yards from the lakeshore. I left the MG there and continued on foot. The ground here was covered by white powder, finer than sand; my athletic shoes raised little puffs of it, and soon the legs of my jeans were dusted. I could smell the lake now: fishy, underscored by a not unpleasant acridness. A chill wind had sprung up, rippling the water. I seemed to be the only person around, although the low growl of an automobile engine on the unpaved road came faintly to my ears.

Ahead of me loomed a petrified forest of twisted, surreal shapes. They stood alone, their knobby limbs raised high, some in interlocking groups—eight, ten, twelve feet tall, stained pink and gold by the setting sun. Clumps of dry vegetation clustered at their bases; ground squirrels darted among them. The cold wind rustled the sagebrush and thistles, kicked up white dust devils, whistled and moaned in the towers' chinks and crevices. The tufa was fully as beautiful as I had expected, but also grotesque and eerie. I felt a chill on my shoulder blades that had little to do with the wind.

Like a child entering the enchanted forest in a fairy tale, I began wandering through the tufa. When I touched a squat, gnomelike formation, its calcified surface rasped against my skin. I pulled my hand back quickly, as if I'd been burned, then laughed at my extreme reaction. The sound bounced back at me from all sides—high-pitched, hollow, and much too loud in the great silence.

Soon I reached the shore. The sun had sunk quickly behind the western ridge of hills, and the water was deep indigo now, faintly streaked with pink. Waterfowl bobbed on its rippling surface, mere silhouettes in the gathering dusk. The offshore islands rose like dark turreted castles.

I knelt down and dipped my fingers into the lake; it was cold as ice. When I raised them and touched them to my tongue, they tasted very salty and bitter. I stood and looked around, trying to imagine the landscape as it had been before man, with typical lack of foresight, began diverting the water of the feeder streams. Where I was standing would have been lake bottom; all the pinnacles would have been submerged, the shoreline somewhere around the outer rim of the alkali—

In my peripheral vision I caught a quick motion some fifty feet away, beside a hunchbacked giant. I peered over there, saw nothing in the rapidly fading daylight. At first I heard only the sigh and whine of the wind; then there came another sound—the scuff of feet running away over the soft powdery ground.

I rushed around the pinnacle. Saw no one, nothing but a more massive formation that completely blocked my view. The scuffing noise had stopped. Only the thistles and sage-brush moved, bending to the wind.

Frowning, I told myself I was being too imaginative. Then the scuffing noise came again, farther to the west in the petrified maze.

I listened as the sound died out. When I'd heard nothing but stillness for a full minute I shrugged and started back toward where I'd left my car. Probably a hiker, I thought, who came out here to enjoy the solitude and was surprised to find another person cluttering up the landscape. Perhaps one of those whom Mrs. Wittington had referred to as "folks who just want to be left the hell alone." In an area like this—

The roar of an engine ripped through the silence.

At first I couldn't tell where it was coming from. Then I realized it was to the west, the way the footsteps had gone. A squarish shape—some off-road vehicle or a van?—shot from behind an outcropping and sped across the plain toward the junction of the unpaved road and the highway. Driving blind, without even its parking lights.

I ran toward my car, but by the time I got there, the other vehicle had turned north on the highway and pursuit would have been futile. Besides, I thought, what good would it have done? Whoever had been watching me from behind the tufa tower had done nothing threatening or illegal. And whatever made him or her flee probably had nothing to do with me.

Or was this business Anne-Marie had asked me here to look into more serious than I'd assumed?

Zelda's was a combination tavern and restaurant, housed in an enormous and architecturally undistinguished knotty pine structure on the very tip of the point. Now that darkness had fallen, the flashing red-and-gold neon sign atop its roof had been turned on and the parking area was rapidly filling with cars and jeeps and pickup trucks. I'd noticed no other restaurant in town, so I assumed this had to be Vernon's official hangout.

Inside, the building was cavernous and noisy, with exposed rafters, plate glass overlooking the lake, and illuminated beer-sign decor. To the left was a dining room with a dance floor and covered instruments on the bandstand; to the right was a lounge where people stood three deep around the bar. I found Anne-Marie there, defending the second chair at her table from would-be takers. Her willowy body was clad in jeans and a denim jacket; her long legs were propped on the ledge below the wide window. She'd already gotten me a glass of white wine.

"Hey," she called as I approached, "I'd about given up on you."

"Sorry." I slipped into the empty chair. "I was playing tourist and got carried away."

"I figured as much. How are you?"

"Not bad. You?"

"Tired, but otherwise I feel great. I'm on a crusade, and you know what that does for me."

Anne-Marie is a veteran of both the fledgling women's movement and the poverty law wars of the seventies; she's happiest when plotting to overthrow the status quo. In recent years, however, she'd languished as All Souls' tax attorney—an area of specialization she undertook more because of the co-op's needs than her own desire. This leave of absence had visibly done her good: tonight her pert blond hair was windblown; her elegant, finely sculpted face was flushed with good health; her blue eyes shone. In the past year or so she'd grown gaunt and hollow-eyed; now she'd fleshed out some, and the extra poundage became her. Seeing her this way made me realize that Anne-Marie had been a very depressed woman before taking her leave. Of course, there had been problems early on in her marriage with Hank, but they'd ironed them out, and after he'd been shot and almost died the previous summer, they'd developed a closeness that was rare even among happily married couples.

I said, "So tell me about the crusade. I stopped by the Coalition trailer and met one of the people this afternoon; he made it sound quite mysterious."

"Oh? Who?"

"Heino Ripinsky."

"Ah, Hy. He would." I was about to ask more about Ripinsky, but she added, "We'll talk about all that over dinner. Right now I want to hear how you've been, what's going on at home." Prior to coming to Tufa Lake, Anne-Marie had spent a month at the Coalition's Sacramento headquarters and had only gotten to The City, as we San Franciscans egocentrically call it, for one weekend.

"Well, there's not a great deal to tell," I said. "Hank, of course, has been a grouch with you out of town. We all humor him. Rae—"

"I know what's going on at All Souls; I speak with Hank every other night. What I want to know is what's going on with *you.*"

"You mean with George and me."

She nodded, smiling conspiratorially.

I had been seeing George Kostakos, professor of psychology at Stanford and very possibly love-of-my-life, since July, when he'd returned to me after six months of coping with his estranged—now former—wife's mental breakdown and recovery. The half year before that had been a very bad one: not only had I begun to doubt George's stated intention to come back to me after he put his life in order, but I'd also begun to doubt my willingness to allow him back into mine. But with the resumption of our relationship, my reservations had vanished; I was happier now than I'd been in years. Not that a few dark clouds didn't remain on the horizon. . . .

"Well?" Anne-Marie said.

"Well . . . he wants me to move in with him."

"And?"

"I don't know if I can do that."

"Shar, why not? George is a wonderful man."

"I don't know. . . . I guess I need my own space."

"I'm sure there's plenty of space for both of you in that enormous condo of his."

"But there's my house—I've finally got it fixed up the way I want it. And Ralph and Alice—"

"Cats? You'd sacrifice George for a couple of *cats?*"

I glared at her. One of the few things she and I don't agree on is the merits of the feline species. She's allergic to them and seems to take the wheezing and sneezing they produce in her as a personal affront. "Ralphie and Allie are family," I said firmly.

"So take them along. George is a cat person, isn't he?"

"Yes—unlike some people I know. But we're talking outdoor cats here. George's flat is on the second floor, and there's no place for them to roam but a courtyard where they'd dig up the flower beds. They'd go crazy cooped up inside, and they'd drive *us* crazy."

Anne-Marie raised her eyebrows and sighed. "Why do I feel I'm not getting the whole story?"

"What's that supposed to mean?"

She merely stared at me, waiting.

"All right." I looked down and began fiddling with my

cocktail napkin. "He's also started talking about marriage."

"And what's wrong with that?"

"Nothing, really. I'm not against marriage."

"For other people."

"No, even for myself, if conditions were right. But . . . here's the real problem: I'm pretty sure he would want to have a child, sort of to make up for the daughter he lost."

"Uh-oh." Anne-Marie leaned back heavily in her chair. Her dislike of children is second only to her dislike of cats, and she assumes all other childless adults share in it.

"You see?" I said. "I've grown too old and selfish to have a child. I enjoy my freedom and my work too much. What would I do with a baby? Drag it to All Souls and plunk it down in a corner of my office? Take it along in the car on stakeouts?"

"There's always day care. Or George."

"Don't tell me he could take the primary responsibility; his career is going into high gear now that his book is being published."

"Day care," she repeated.

"Oh, all right, so I'm making excuses! Dammit, it's not as if I don't like children. I've got eleven nieces and nephews, and I love them all, even though they make that extremely difficult at times. Every year I write twenty-two checks for birthdays and Christmas. Periodically they show up and eat me out of house and home and make me take them to Marine World. They call—collect—for advice on problems with their parents, their teachers, their boyfriends and girlfriends. I'm already doing my duty to the next generation!"

Anne-Marie smiled tolerantly. "I'm with you a hundred percent on this. You don't have to justify your feelings to *me*."

"I know," I said. "And I know exactly who I *am* trying to justify them to."

Over dinner—panfried golden trout—Anne-Marie explained the situation that had brought her, and now me, to Tufa Lake.

The California Coalition for Environmental Preservation, as I knew, was a troubleshooting organization funded by some twenty-five advocacy groups. One of their goals was to present a unified front to legislators by formulating a state-wide policy on the environment. Anne-Marie had been engaged in research for the proposed policy up until the previous week, when a call requesting assistance had come from the Friends of Tufa Lake. Since it looked as if a legal problem might be involved, she had been sent to Vernon along with Ned Sanderman, one of the Coalition's crack troubleshooters.

"I take it the problem concerns the foreign gold-mining company that's got hold of the mineral rights in Stone Valley," I said.

She raised her eyebrows. "That's very good, for someone who's been in town only a few hours."

I smiled modestly, unwilling to admit that I'd found out about the mining by pure accident.

"Well," she went on, "that *is* the problem. The mesa above Promiseville hasn't been mined since the twenties, but modern methods of extracting gold have made mining profitable again. And it's not only the mineral rights that Transpacific Corporation controls; they own the land itself."

"I thought most of the land around here was federal," I said, recalling signs I'd spotted for the Toiyabe National Forest.

"Most is. But Transpacific—they're a U.S. corporation, but backed by big-money interests in Hong Kong—bought up some three thousand privately held acres from a descendant of the family who owned the original Promiseville mine. The other seven hundred acres were also under private ownership, but they were bought from the federal government only a year ago."

"How can someone buy federal land?"

"It's a complicated process, having to do with patenting mining claims with the Bureau of Land Management. I won't bore you with the details now; there's a file on the technicalities back at the cabin. Suffice it to say it's completely legal."

"Then what can you do to stop them?"

"My job is to go over the land deal with a fine-tooth comb to see if there's any legal loophole. Or any unethical transaction that might cast a long enough shadow to make Mono County refuse to issue the final mine permits."

"From the way Mrs. Wittington at the lodge spoke, I guess people in the area are pretty much opposed to the mining operation."

"Oh, there're plenty who see it as a boost to the economy, but they're being shortsighted. It would only be a temporary boost and cause more problems than it would solve. Most of the intelligent people here simply don't want large-scale open-pit mining in Stone Valley." Anne-Marie set down her fork, her face flushed, eyes bright; she was on a crusade, all right.

"Not only is open-pit mining noisy and disfiguring to the landscape," she went on, "but the cyanide leaching process they use poisons the air and groundwater. In addition, there're a number of historic buildings where Promiseville once was that the Friends of Tufa Lake are trying to get approved for landmark status. The blasting from the mine would weaken and eventually destroy them."

I nodded, pushing a sprig of parsley around on my plate. "Okay," I said, "but you didn't get me up here to help you research legal issues. What else is going on?"

Anne-Marie glanced around as if she were afraid we would be overheard, then leaned forward, lowering her voice. "In the week I've been here, I've found out some things that just don't compute. Other things have happened that seem downright suspicious. I need someone with a good investigative head to make sense of them."

"All right, fill me in."

She proceeded to tick items off on her fingers.

Item one: When queried by the Coalition, the Bureau of Land Management in Sacramento reported that the 700-acre tract had been purchased from them by a man named Franklin Tarbeaux. Tarbeaux had staked a claim to the mineral rights, then filed the appropriate mineral-survey documents and completed the patenting requirements—paying a mere $10 an acre.

Item two: Mono County records showed that Tarbeaux almost immediately sold the land to Transpacific Corporation for $700,000—or $1,000 an acre. Although his profit margin was significant, the per-acre price was less than a tenth of what similar tracts were currently going for.

Item three: The additional 3,000 acres, which encompassed the original Promiseville mine, had been purchased from Earl Hopwood, a descendant of the family who once owned it. Transpacific had paid Hopwood only $10 an acre—what the BLM charged for federal land and much less than it should have brought on the open market.

Item four: When Anne-Marie and Ned Sanderman queried people in the area about Franklin Tarbeaux, no one admitted to knowing him. The desert rats who lived in Stone Valley claimed they weren't aware that anyone had been mining the 700 acres on the eastern side of the mesa above Promiseville, where the old mine was located.

Item five: Earl Hopwood was something of a hermit; he lived in a cabin at the far end of Stone Valley and prospected up and down the stream that ran through it. When Hy Ripinsky, who had known Hopwood since childhood, went looking for him, he found the old man hadn't been seen for two weeks or more.

"That was after Transpacific moved in with their survey crew, fenced the land, and began taking core samples," Anne-Marie added.

"And that's it?"

"No. This is the really strange stuff: a couple of days after

Ned and I arrived, both Hy's home and the Friends of Tufa Lake trailer—it's next to the one we're using—were broken into. And the next day Ned and I noticed signs of forced entry at our cabins at the lodge."

"What was taken?"

"Nothing, as far as we could tell."

"Lots of crime in this area?"

"Very little—mostly drunk driving or fishing without a license, or so they tell me."

I set down my fork and waited while the waitress cleared our plates. As she bustled around serving coffee, I thought of the person who had been watching me in the tufa forest. More "really strange stuff"?

After the waitress had gone I said, "I suppose in a place like this everybody knows everybody else's business."

"You got it."

I sipped coffee, thought a bit more. "What, if anything, does Lily Nickles have to do with this?"

Anne-Marie looked surprised. "The Tiger Lily? So far as I know, nothing, except that she prospects out in Stone Valley. Where did you run into her?"

"She was having an argument with Hy when I went to the trailer. He didn't seem angry or upset; she did."

"Hy's slow to anger. But when he does, watch out."

"Tell me about him. He kept injecting quasi-military terms into our conversation. And where for God's sake did he get that dreadful name?"

She smiled faintly. "From his parents, as is customary. His mother was German, hence the 'Heino.' His father was a descendant of Russians who emigrated to Alaska via the Aleutians generations ago. Hy was born in the Central Valley but raised here in Vernon after his mother divorced and remarried. He left for a number of years in the seventies. Some claim he was CIA, and from the way he speaks and thinks, I believe it."

"No one asks him?"

"He's not a man you question about the past."

"From CIA operative to environmentalist is a long step. How did that happen?"

"What little I know comes from Rose Wittington. When Hy returned here he was reclusive at first, stayed out on the little sheep ranch on the road to Stone Valley that he inherited from his stepfather. He seemed to have plenty of money: added on to the house, drove an expensive car, owned an airplane. But he didn't socialize, even with old friends, and was rarely seen in town."

"What changed that?"

"He met Julie Spaulding, an environmentalist who'd moved here a few years earlier and founded the Friends. She gradually coaxed him out of his isolation and involved him in the cause. After a year or so they married. Julie died of multiple sclerosis about three years ago. In her will—she'd inherited from her father, a big Kern County grower—she set up a foundation to fund environmental organizations, particularly the Friends, and she named Hy director of it." Anne-Marie paused, looking thoughtful. "Rose Wittington said what you did: that it was quite a transformation from CIA—if that's what he was—to environmentalist. But she hasn't observed Hy the way I have. Underneath that laid-back exterior, he's still dangerous."

"In what way?"

"Well, consider how he operates, even within the framework of environmentalism. He's . . . how can I describe it? Are you familiar with Earth First!?"

I nodded. Earth First! was an organization that relied on direct confrontational tactics—some called them "eco-terrorism"—to get their point across. While those on the radical end of the spectrum saw little wrong with removing survey markers from construction sites or sabotaging oil-drilling equipment, few condoned such practices as spiking trees—inserting hidden nails into forest trees so that chain saws would be shattered and the flying steel would injure or even kill loggers. I'd seen a news item around the time of Earth Day reporting that Earth First! had renounced the tactic, but with my usual cynicism I had wondered what they'd renounced it in favor of. And later reports of an explosion that injured two of their leaders and was suspected of being triggered by a device of their own manufacture had led me to assume my cynical suspicions were justified.

"Is Hy involved with them?" I asked.

"No, he's too much of a maverick to ally himself with any group. The only reason he's on the board of the Friends and cooperating with the Coalition is because of the connection with the Spaulding Foundation. And I doubt he'd have anything to do with the foundation if he didn't feel obligated because of Julie's will. But Hy's like the Earth Firsters in a way: a genuine crazy man who'll go up against anybody in any way in order to make them listen."

"A crusader like you, huh?"

"Much worse; Hy doesn't give a hoot for the law. And he's not afraid of anything—including cops and sheriffs' deputies with clubs and riot guns. When the campaign to save Tufa Lake was at its hottest, he did plenty of time in various jails. As soon as he served one sentence, he'd get into trouble and end up behind bars again. He claims he was influenced by Martin Luther King and Gandhi; I'd add the kamikaze pilots and Genghis Khan to the list."

"Was his wife still alive while this was going on?"

"Some of it, but he got much worse after she died. I think she was a steadying influence on him. Rose Wittington says Julie was confined to a wheelchair most of her life, but that didn't stop her from doing what she wanted. She traveled around the state helping out different groups with both personal efforts and monetary donations; when she came to Tufa Lake she decided it was where she wanted to settle. She was a fighter, like Hy: when the Friends picketed the water department in L.A. she was there. The same for the sit-ins in Sacramento. But Julie was always in control. For a long time after she died, Hy wasn't."

"And now?"

She shrugged. "He's better, but sometimes I think it's only his responsibilities to the foundation that keep him from going off and . . . well, doing God knows what."

"So Julie Spaulding made him director of her foundation for a very good reason."

"I guess she did."

"Has he had any confrontations with Transpacific?"

"No, he went to the mine site only once, on a public relations tour the corporation gave for concerned individuals. Otherwise Transpacific has kept a very low profile and refused to enter into a dialogue with the environmentalists. Until they do, there's nothing *to* confront."

"And then?"

"That's a question I don't want to find out the answer to."

"I wonder what Hy and the Nickles woman were arguing about this afternoon."

Anne-Marie looked at her watch, then pushed back her chair. "We're supposed to meet him and Ned at the trailer right about now. Why don't you ask him?"

Three

▲ ▲ ▲

Ten o'clock. I stifled a yawn
and tried to focus on what Ned Sanderman was saying.

We'd been sitting on the uncomfortable office chairs in the
rented trailer for close to three hours, and he'd talked
almost nonstop the whole time. Right now the subject was
how much Transpacific stood to lose should the environmentalists find a way to block the issuing of the final mining
permits. The cost of the land, plus capital improvements,
plus the cost of whatever core sampling had been done up to
that point, Ripinsky said with an edge of annoyance. No,
Sanderman objected, there were also administrative costs,
legal expenses, plus loss of potential profit. The worth of a
gold mine, he said, was equal to the value of the ore, less the
aforementioned expenses. He then backed up this statement with examples that he punched out on his personal
computer. ("It goes everywhere I go," he'd informed me—not
that I'd asked.)

Ned Sanderman was one of the new breed of environmentalists: logical, unemotional, equipped with the latest tech-
nology, and with an eye for the bottom line. He'd told me

that, too, plus most of his life story, in the first ten minutes after we'd been introduced. I now knew more about Ned Sanderman than I did about some of my own relatives, the primary fact being that he was boring.

Slender and short, with a clean-shaven baby face and blond hair that was styled to cover a bald spot, he'd surprised me when he revealed that he was forty-six. "I had my mid-life crisis seven years ago at thirty-nine," he said. "I was a computer engineer in Silicon Valley. Then one day I woke up to the fact that there was more to life than building a stock portfolio and acquiring expensive toys. I'd made it in my chosen career, and I needed more meaning in my life. I wanted to be connected in a basic way to the end results of my work."

"So he ran away and joined the environmentalists the way some people join the circus," Anne-Marie commented.

Sanderman gave her a puzzled look. He was essentially humorless, and while he suspected the remark was supposed to be funny, it was obvious he didn't know what to make of it. Also obvious was his intense self-absorption. The only question he'd asked me was how I liked the cabin at the lodge. When I said it seemed fine, he disdainfully cataloged the defects of his, especially of its kitchen. "I wouldn't so much as boil water in there. God knows what germs are lying in wait," he complained.

Now he'd somehow gotten off on the heap leach cyanide process and was droning on about the dangers it posed to the environment. The details—poisoned fish, birds, and other wildlife, to say nothing of undrinkable water and unbreathable air—were dismaying, but we'd been over this before. It was at least the dozenth tangent he'd lurched off onto. The first five or six times Anne-Marie and Ripinsky had tried to steer him back to the subject of our meeting. Finally they'd given up.

I glanced at Anne-Marie; her eyes had glazed over. Ripinsky sat tilted back in his chair, feet on one of the cheap metal desks, staring up at the ceiling; from the expression on his face, I gathered that his mind was somewhere in the outer layers of the stratosphere. I shifted uncomfortably on the chair and yawned discreetly.

Ripinsky's gaze shifted from the ceiling to me. He grinned, winked, and took his feet off the desk. Maybe his thoughts hadn't been hovering miles above earth after all.

"Time's up, Ned," he said. "I've got something to brief everybody on."

Sanderman looked flustered, then frowned. He opened his mouth, closed it, and folded his arms. I sensed Ripinsky had interrupted him many times before—and even more abruptly.

Ripinsky went on, "When you came in"—he nodded to Anne-Marie—"you asked about a visit the Tiger Lily paid me this afternoon. I didn't get a chance to go into it, because right away Ned here started presenting his credentials."

Sanderman flushed but didn't say anything.

"Lily and I didn't have a real amiable conversation," Ripinsky continued. "In fact, she ended up getting pretty steamed at me. That's nothing new; woman's had it in for me ever since I rebuffed her advances after Julie died. But that's another story entirely, and not terribly interesting. What *is* interesting is the story she had to tell this afternoon."

"And?" Sanderman asked irritably.

"Seems Lily's been doing some exploring up on the mesa. She claims she noticed it had been quiet there for weeks now—too quiet for them to be taking core samples—so she decided to check it out. And guess what? There's no survey crew, no geologists, just a skeleton crew of security people. And no drill rigs, hydraulic shovels, or trucks, either."

"So they're done with the sampling."

Ripinsky shook his head. "Can't be. They only just started."

"Then the samples showed there wasn't enough ore to make further tests worthwhile. In that case—"

"No way. When I took their little public relations tour right after they announced they'd acquired the property, their supervising geologist told me they were dead sure that with modern mining capabilities they could take a minimum of half a million ounces of gold out of that mesa over the life of the mine. That's twenty million dollars gross at today's prices."

Sanderman got up and went to his computer. He punched a few figures up onto the screen and said, "That's right."

"Yeah, well, I've got a computer, too—it's called a brain. Anyway, Lily tried to find out from the guards what was happening, but she didn't get anywhere. Even tried to bribe one of them with . . . her not inconsiderable charms, but it was no go."

We all were silent for a minute. Then I asked, "Why did she get so angry with you?"

He grinned and ran a finger over his droopy mustache. "Lily's a bit paranoid, and something of a racist, too. Seems a couple of the guards are Chinese. She started in on her Yellow Peril theory—evil Orientals taking over the county. Talk like that is just plain stupid, and I told her so. And that set her off."

"What was it she called you—a tree hugger?"

"Among other things. Lily hates environmentalists."

"I'd think she'd be on your side."

"Not the Tiger Lily. The only thing she wants from the environment is gold. Lacking that, she'll take venison, trout, and firewood. But she doesn't give a damn about nature in its unspoiled state or preserving Promiseville. If she had her way she'd tear down every historic building in the valley except the house she's squatting in and burn them in her wood stove."

"Then why did she come to you?"

He shrugged. "Because she didn't know anybody else to turn to. And underneath all that bravado, she's a little scared."

Anne-Marie was tapping on her desk with a pencil. "What we need is more information about Transpacific."

I asked, "Where are they headquartered?"

"The city."

"Then I'll check up on them when I get back there."

"Good."

Ripinsky stood, stretched his tall, lean body. "I don't know about the rest of you, but it's been a long day. And McCone's had quite a drive; she probably wants to turn in."

Gratefully I stood, and Anne-Marie followed suit. We made plans to meet back there in the morning, so I could outline my plan of action—assuming I'd developed one by then—and Ripinsky, Anne-Marie, and I left together.

As I drove away, I could see Sanderman through the still-lighted window of the trailer; he was once again playing with his computer.

I followed Anne-Marie's Subaru to the lodge and pulled up beside it at the edge of the grove. She got out and said, "Sorry Ned went on like that. I think he may have been trying to demonstrate that he has the situation under control and doesn't really need you."

"I take it he wasn't in favor of an outsider coming in."

"He might have been, if Hy hadn't supported the idea."

"Is there some ill will between them?"

She took a small flashlight from her bag and shone it on the ground as we walked downhill to the cabin. "More like competitiveness, at least on Ned's part. Hy was perfectly civil to him at first, but now relations are definitely strained. All I could think of for the last half hour was how much I'd like to get out of there and have a brandy. Fortunately, I've got some in the cabin. Join me for a nightcap?"

"You're on."

We climbed the steps to the cabin's porch; she got the door unlocked, reached inside, and switched on an overhead fixture—two bare bulbs attached to a horseshoe-shaped piece of hammered metal that cast garish light over the room and accentuated its more obvious flaws.

"Ugh," she said and went to turn on a table lamp. "Switch that overhead off, will you? Brandy's in the kitchen cupboard to the right of the sink. I'll get the wood stove going—it's *cold* in here."

I did as she asked, then went through the swinging door to the kitchen and located a pull chain for the light over the sink. The room had knotty pine cabinets, worn green linoleum, and cracked tile countertops in an unfortunate shade of orange. The appliances were as old as the fifties-vintage ones in the kitchen at All Souls. Still, if Sanderman's kitchen was as clean as this, I had to dispute his claim of germs lurking within. Probably his complaints were merely an indication that he was unhappy at being here.

I found the brandy and two glasses that looked as if they had originally contained olives or maraschino cherries and carried them back to the living room. Anne-Marie stood with her back to me at one of the windows that opened onto the porch. She half turned, and I saw a peculiar frozen expression on her face.

Quickly I set the bottle and glasses on the coffee table. "What's wrong?"

"The window. That's why it's so cold in here."

"Oh, I'm sorry. I opened it earlier and forgot to close it when I left."

"But you didn't take the screen off, did you?" She pointed to where it was supposed to hook at the bottom; the hook was still in the eyelet, it had been ripped off the screen's frame.

She started to say something else, but I held up my hand, listening. It was very quiet in the cabin—but such silences can be deceptive. I crossed to the wood stove and picked up the poker, then moved toward the bedrooms.

I swept the curtain aside from the archway leading to the room I was occupying. Nothing except the cheap maple bureau and single nightstand between twin beds. There was no closet where anyone could hide. My weekend bag sat on the bureau; I glanced at it as I moved toward the bath that connected this room with Anne-Marie's. The bag seemed to be the way I'd left it.

I reached into the bathroom and switched on the light. Pushed the door open, poker poised. Again, nothing—just the chipped white porcelain fixtures. I repeated the same maneuver at the opposite door; only Anne-Marie's neatly made bed and carefully aligned clothing and cosmetics greeted me.

When I went back to the living room and replaced the poker—feeling slightly foolish about the theatrical way I'd been wielding it—Anne-Marie still stood by the window. She said, "Another forced entry."

"Looks like." I went to the door and stepped onto the porch. The missing screen was propped against the railing.

She said through the open window, "I wonder why he didn't put back the screen, to cover up."

"Either he doesn't care that we know or he got scared off by something."

"Did he take anything of yours?"

"I don't think so. We'd both better check, though."

I replaced the screen as best I could and shut and locked the window. Anne-Marie went to her room, emerged shaking her head, and went to tend the fire. I returned to my bedroom and took a closer look at my bag. When I examined the side pocket, I found it unzipped; the envelopes I'd stuffed there earlier at my office had been disturbed. I pulled them out and carried them to the living room.

"What're those?" Anne-Marie asked, pouring two glasses of brandy and taking hers to the rattan chair opposite the couch.

"My mail. You remember how people in my neighborhood were having trouble with kids trashing their mailboxes? Well, they finally got around to mine, so I'm having everything forwarded to All Souls. It looks as if whoever broke in here went through these envelopes."

"Is there anything in them that would identify you as an investigator?"

"The forwarding stickers give All Souls' name, but not my position. Most people would just assume I'm an attorney." I sat down and began checking through the envelopes' contents.

"I don't know exactly why, but I'd rather no one here knew you're an investigator. Maybe Hy's passion for secrecy is contagious."

"Well, what I've got here is my Visa and Macy's bills, a solicitation from the Friends of the Library, and a letter from my mother. No mention of my job in any of those. By the way, this reminds me." I held Ma's letter up. "I have to be back in the city by Tuesday afternoon, latest. She's coming to visit."

Anne-Marie looked surprised; she knew that Ma seldom set foot outside San Diego. "How come?"

"I'm not sure, and neither are my brothers and sisters. Ma seems to have embarked on an odyssey from one of us to the other. It's mystifying—and somewhat nervous-making."

"Maybe she wants to meet George and is using this so-called odyssey to check him out."

"Ma's not that subtle. But she'll have her chance; he's invited us to dinner Tuesday night."

"I can't *wait* for a full report on that!"

"I can wait. I could wait forever." Ma is well meaning and I love her, but she can be very pushy with the men I'm involved with—and even the men I'm *not* involved with. "What I think I'll do," I went on, "is try to cover as much ground as I can here, then check out Transpacific while I'm in the city, and come back here next weekend, if necessary."

She nodded agreement and went to monitor the fire. I relaxed, basking in its warmth and sipping brandy. Then an unsettling thought occurred to me. "Anne-Marie," I said, "you don't suppose whoever went through my mail would call All Souls and try to find out more about me?"

". . . They might. But don't worry about it; as I said earlier, I'm probably being overly cautious."

"Maybe not, though." Briefly I recounted my experience in the tufa forest.

When I finished she was silent for a moment. "I think you should call All Souls and tell them not to give out any information about you."

"Good idea." I stood up, looked for a phone.

"Isn't one," she said, "but you can use Mrs. Wittington's."

I glanced at my watch. "Isn't eleven-thirty a little late to bother her?"

"No way—she's a late-night movie buff like me. A couple of times this week I've gone up to the lodge and watched till two with her. She loves anything bloody or with truckers in it."

"Truckers?"

"Uh-huh. *They Drive by Night, Smokey and the Bandit.* Don't matter who's in it, how bad it is, or from what era so long as there's a truck and a hairy guy driving it. Rose is a bundle of contradictions: talks salty as can be and enjoys a stiff bourbon, but she's also a born-again and attends a Bible-study group up in Bridgeport every Saturday night."

"Interesting woman. Well, if it won't disturb her, I'll go up and call right now."

When Rose Wittington admitted me to the lodge she wore a pink quilted bathrobe and fleece-lined slippers, and a glow that I suspected was bourbon-induced on her round face. Over by the stone fireplace was a grouping of chintz-covered furniture and a big-screen TV that showed not one but two hairy guys leaning against a semi truck. The pillow and afghan on the settee told me Anne-Marie was right about how Mrs. Wittington was spending her evening. She showed me to a phone behind the reception desk and went back to her movie.

I placed a credit-card call to All Souls. No problem there about the late hour, either: Ted Smalley, our secretary, is a night owl, as well as one of those rare and much-treasured individuals who considers his job a twenty-four-hour proposition.

"Hi, Shar," he said, recognizing my voice. "If you're calling to check on Ralph and Alice, they're fine. I went over to your place around six, herded them inside, fed and played with them. They should be sacked out by now." My cats—still kittens, really—originally belonged to a friend of Ted's who died of AIDS. Ted takes a very proprietary interest in them, to the point of willingly pet-sitting whenever I go out of town. He would have been horrified to know that I had scarcely given them a thought since leaving them in his capable hands.

"Thanks, Ted," I said. "I've got another reason for calling: has anybody phoned there tonight to ask about me?"

"You mean messages?"

"No, an actual inquiry, possibly about my job title."

"I don't . . . Wait a minute. Some guy called a while ago. Rae answered because I was in the can. Hey, Rae!"

He set the receiver down with a clunk, and in a few seconds my assistant, Rae Kelleher—who, like Ted, lives as well as works in the co-op's big Bernal Heights Victorian— came on the line. "Hi, how's it going?"

"Fine, so far. Tell me about this guy who called. Did he give a name?"

"Mr. Something-or-other. He sort of mumbled, and I didn't quite catch it. I guess I should have asked, but I was watching TV and distracted."

"What did he want?"

"Well, he asked for you, and when I said you were out of town, he said maybe I could help him. All he wanted, he told me, was to get your exact job title so you could be approved for your new Discover Card. It struck me as odd for him to be calling so late, but a lot of these credit centers work around the clock and, like I said, I was trying to watch Arsenio. And I know how important good credit is, so I told him you were our head investigator."

I was silent for a moment. "What did he sound like? Anything distinctive about his voice.?"

". . . No. It was just . . . normal." She paused, then asked, "Shar, did I do something wrong?"

"No, of course not."

"Well, that's a relief. For a second there . . . but you know what Willie says about good credit."

"I know." How well I knew: Willie Whelan, Rae's boyfriend, is probably the world's foremost authority on deficit spending. His chain of cut-rate jewelry stores is making him rich by extending credit to anyone at any time—and at usurious rates. "Listen," I added, "I'll be back on Tuesday at the latest. Can you manage till then?"

"Sure. They don't call me 'Nero' Kelleher for nothing."

"Nero?"

"As in Wolfe."

"Ah, of course." Rae had recently become enamored of mystery fiction and was rapidly working her way through one of All Souls' numerous bookcases.

After I hung up, I called my thanks to Mrs. Wittington and trudged back downhill toward the cabin. What would Hy Ripinsky, alleged former CIA agent, call this? Having one's cover blown?

Up until a little while ago, I hadn't seen any need to *have* a cover. Now I felt vulnerable without it.

Four

▲ ▲ ▲

The unpaved road to Stone Valley climbed into rocky sagebrush- and mesquite-covered hills; a creek paralleled it—narrow, shallow, bordered by rusty gold aspens. In the distance rose barren snowcapped mountains, made blue by a high haze. Above them a jet out of Fallon Naval Air Station over in Nevada laid lazy contrails across the noonday sky. They were the only evidence of life as we know it in the late twentieth century.

I kept a sharp eye out for potholes and held the MG's speed below twenty. After more than four miles, the road flattened out on a high meadow of dry brown grass. The land was fenced with sticks topped by a single strand of barbed wire; to my right a rough board fence enclosed a pen. Two men in denims—from their appearance, I guessed they were descendants of the Paiutes who had lived in this country long before the Euro-Americans arrived—were rounding up a flock of sheep. Hy Ripinsky's ranch hands, I thought, remembering he'd said that I would come to his place about five miles beyond the intersection where this road branched off the highway east of Vernon.

The ranch house appeared around the next bend—sprawling, but with no apparent architectural plan, constructed of pine and native stone. The Morgan was in town, where I'd left Ripinsky at the Coalition's trailer half an hour ago, but a Land Rover stood between a huge satellite TV dish and a dilapidated barn. I eyed the Rover suspiciously as I drove past, thinking of the off-road vehicle that had sped away across the alkali plain the evening before. Then I shrugged; my suspect pool would be large indeed if I chose its members on the basis of their owning a vehicle tough enough to withstand the terrain in the Tufa Lake area. Besides, Ripinsky would have had to drive like a demon—impossible on this road in a low-slung car like the Morgan—to get the Land Rover and return to the tufa forest.

After another mile or so the road began climbing again, in switchbacks this time, with cliff face to one side and a sheer rock-strewn drop-off to the other. The stream meandered below, glinting silver where it tumbled over rapids. I steered carefully around a particularly sinuous curve, and then the whole of Stone Valley lay before me.

I pulled onto the shoulder and studied the vista, unsure of what I'd expected but knowing this wasn't it. The valley was depressingly barren. Not a tree, not a blade of grass grew there; the only living things were the sagebrush and mesquite that clung to the dark hills. It was easy to spot the site of the proposed mine by the new chain-link fence on the flat top of a high eastern mesa. Nothing moved up there or in the valley; even the waters of the stream looked stagnant. And scattered across the valley floor were husks of the buildings of what had once been called Promiseville.

No promise here now. Just some two dozen small weathered pine structures with rusted iron roofs. Most clustered in a central area, but a few others straggled haphazardly up the eastern slope toward the remains of an old stamp mill. The mill had caved in, was nothing more than a heap of splintered wood and twisted metal; debris from it spilled down the hillside. The road that led past it to the chain-link fence showed evidence of recent grading.

I eased the MG back onto the road and continued the descent to the valley floor, past a hillside cemetery with wind-scoured tombstores and a sagging iron fence. A red-tailed hawk perched on one of the stones; it regarded me with flinty eyes as I drove by. The air was hot and still here, the silence unnatural and oppressive. I didn't know which would have gotten to me first had I lived there: the seasonal extremes of heat and cold or that terrible silence. Much as I often deplore the fog and noise of the city, I'm a San Franciscan at heart and function best in a temperate urban environment.

When Anne-Marie and I had met with Ripinsky at the trailer at ten-thirty that morning—Ned Sanderman being unaccountably absent—I questioned him about the people in the valley and got a rough idea of where to find them, plus directions to the claim of the missing prospector, Earl Hopwood. Then I set out to recheck the stories they'd told previously. In particular I was interested in Lily Nickles's tale of the strange lack of activity at the mine site; if necessary I'd go up there and look around myself.

After I guided the MG onto what I assumed must have been the main street of Promiseville, I stopped by a burned-out ruin and consulted my list. According to Ripinsky, Nickles had been squatting for more than three years in a house on the hill below the stamp mill. I left my car where I'd stopped and proceeded on foot, unable to resist peering through the dust-covered windows of the buildings I passed.

What I saw further deflated my spirits: caved-in ceilings, wallpaper hanging in great peeling swaths, broken floor-boards, exposed lathe. Ripinsky had told me that many of Promiseville's residents had remained after the boom days, eking out whatever living they could, until fire destroyed most of the town in the late 1920s. Then all had fled, taking with them only their most portable and cherished possessions. This was borne out by the pathetic assortment of objects remaining in the little houses: corroded iron bedsteads; once-fancy curtains hanging in tatters at the windows; a cookstove with a skillet still standing on one burner; rodent-gnawed armchairs; the smashed porcelain head of a child's doll.

As I turned and trudged up the hill, I wondered about the people of Promiseville. Why had they remained so long after the boom days ended? Life here had to have been extremely arduous, given the blizzards of winter and the searing dryness of summer. While in the 1920s the rest of the country had taken for granted electric lights, indoor plumbing, motorcars, and silent movies, I saw no evidence that any of those improvements had made it to this remote outpost. But something had encouraged the people to stay—perhaps inertia, or simply the fact that Promiseville was home.

And then fire had dealt the town a final devastating blow. Many people had been forced out; those who hadn't had fled with them. There had been panic, despair, and—in those who might have stayed anyway—a fear of isolation and loneliness. But Promiseville had been home to all of them, and I wondered if in the ensuing years many hadn't regretted their hasty departure, even come to miss this place.

Ripinsky had told me Lily Nickles's house was the largest on the hillside, with a front porch positioned so it commanded a view of the valley. I identified it easily by the tan Jeep parked beside it. It faced west, away from the tumble-down stamp mill and the mine site. The front steps had been mended with new lumber that seemed raw next to the weathered pine; a sagging wicker rocker stood by the door. As I stepped onto the porch I saw a mud-caked and rusting assortment of prospecting gear—picks, shovels, pans that looked like my wok—jumbled in one corner. I knocked at the door but received no answer. The windows were draped in burlap, so I couldn't see inside.

If Nickles wasn't home, Ripinsky had said, I'd be likely to find her prospecting half a mile to the north where the stream took a sharp bend around a field of boulders. From Nickles's porch I surveyed the terrain and decided against risking the MG's tires and suspension. Then I went back down the hill and followed the streambed. The water was shallow and rock-filled, as torpid as it had looked from the road above. Debris littered the banks: artifacts of the past such as rusted containers and tools mingled with modern-day refuse, including beer cans, shotgun shell casings, and Styrofoam cups. I passed a couple of other ruins—one merely a crumbling brick wall and foundation—and then saw the boulder field on the opposite side of the stream. From behind an outcropping the size and shape of a sleeping elephant came the chug of a gasoline-powered engine and a gush of water so strong it couldn't have been the stream itself. I quickened my pace until the rock no longer blocked my view.

The Tiger Lily stood knee-deep in water. Floating beside her on the inner tube of a truck tire was a peculiar-looking machine. Two hoses extended from it into the stream, and next to the engine compartment was an aluminum contraption resembling a sluice box, which spewed water. Nickles wore a turquoise tank top and faded cutoff jeans; both were dark with moisture, and her cropped brown hair was plastered to her head. The machine made so much noise that she didn't hear me when I called out to her.

I sat down on the bank, took off my athletic shoes and socks, and rolled up my jeans. When I stepped into the stream, its iciness was a shocking contrast to the noonday heat; the rocks under my bare feet were slick with moss. Nickles noticed me as I began wading toward her.

Above the chug of the engine she yelled, "Hey, you, get out of there!"

I kept going.

"You heard me, dammit! Get outta my stream!" She made a fist and shook it angrily.

"Take it easy, Lily."

She frowned, clearly surprised that I knew her name. Then she rolled her eyes in exasperation, reached down, and shut off the engine. In the sudden quiet, the gush of water from the aluminum trough was very loud.

"What the hell do you want?" Nickles demanded.

"To talk about what you told Hy Ripinsky you saw up at the Transpacific mine site."

Her eyes narrowed. "That fuckin' tree hugger sent you?"

"Right." I told her my name and that I was associated with the Coalition.

"Wait a minute," she said. "You were there yesterday—at the trailer."

"Yes." I waded over to her, pointed at the machine on the inner tube. "What's that?"

"Hydraulic concentrator. Works like a dredge."

"And does what?"

"Sucks up gravel and sorts it."

"Why?"

She glared at me. "You don't know anything, do you? Must be one of those city tree huggers. Why do you think it sorts it? For gold. Gold's heavy, heaviest metal you're likely to find; it sinks and gets trapped in the hopper. The rest gets washed out again."

"I thought you panned for gold."

"Panning's for sampling, helps you read the stream, see which gravel bars're worth working. Or it's for weekend prospectors—assholes, most of them. This baby"—she patted the concentrator—"it can process fifty times the material in a single day, plus I can haul it around on my back."

Nickles was still eyeing me narrowly, a disagreeable twist to her dry cracked lips. But something in her tone told me she was secretly pleased at an opportunity to show off her expertise. I said, "You're a high-tech miner, then."

"No, *they're* high-tech." She jerked a thumb over her shoulder at the eastern mesa. "Me, I'm just lucky I scored enough nuggets last year so I could afford this baby."

"Can we talk about them?" I nodded in the direction that she'd mentioned.

She hesitated, then said, "Ah, what the hell? I can use a break. You want a beer?"

"Sure. Thanks."

Nickles seized the plastic line that anchored the inner tube to a rock and gently towed the concentrator to shore. I helped her boost it onto the high bank, and then she gave me a hand up. "Sit down over there," she told me, motioning at the sleeping-elephant rock. "And get into the shade—the sun's a killer today."

While I picked my way through the boulder field, Nickles squatted down, pulled on another plastic line, and fished a six-pack of Coors from the stream. She broke out two cans and lowered the rest back into the water. When she came over and handed one to me, I thought of how the fervent liberals at All Souls would cringe to see me drinking a brand they boycotted. Well, the fervent liberals had never been in Stone Valley in the blistering early afternoon heat. . . .

Nickles and I sat on a flat slab of granite at the base of the elephant, our backs against its cool flank. The shade was welcome, the icy beer more so. I drank deeply, then said, "First off, the Coalition people tell me you never heard of Franklin Tarbeaux, the man who sold the seven hundred acres to Transpacific."

She swigged beer and shook her head. "Name like that I'd remember. Plus the guy's got to be loaded now; sure as shit I'd make it my business to get to know him."

"Were you aware that the land on the eastern side of the mesa belonged to a private individual?"

"Well, no, I wasn't *aware* that any *private individual* had got his hands on it—or even that it was being mined." Her voice mimicked mine, but she smiled to take the sting out of it. "I thought it was BLM land, like most of it around here."

"And the missing prospector, Earl Hopwood—"

"Who says he's missing?"

"Hy Ripinsky says no one's seen him for over two weeks."

"So? Knowing Earl, I'd say he's over in Reno or Carson City, shacked up with some whore and losing all his profit from that land deal at the blackjack tables."

"Does he disappear like that often?"

"Often enough. Earl's sixty-nine years old, but he's still randy as a billy goat. Except for me—and I wouldn't let that old bag of bones touch me if his pole was ten feet long— there's nobody around here for him to get randy *with*."

"But would he take off for two weeks?"

"If he was flush enough—and he had to be, after selling that land."

It was possible, I supposed, that Hopwood had simply gone off on a spree, but I still intended to take a look around his claim. "Hopwood is a descendant of the people who originally owned the Promiseville mine?"

She nodded. "Family came over here from England or some such goddamn place in the mid-eighteen hundreds, staked their claim, got rich." Nickles's eyes became surprisingly soft and dreamy. "The house I live in—it was theirs. Nothing fancy the way we think today, but it still looks down on the whole valley. . . .

"That's why I picked it," she added after a moment. "For luck. Figured if I lived in the rich folks' house, maybe one of these days I'd get rich, too."

The woman interested me, so I deviated from my line of questioning. "What about you, Lily? How'd you come to be a prospector?"

She finished her beer, crumpled the can, and pitched it toward the stream. It landed on the bank with a faint ping. "Wasn't much else I could do; didn't have much schooling. My mama, she was a dealer at one of the crummy casinos over in Reno. Never knew my dad. We lived with my grandparents, and they was always on me—stick to your schooling, get a good job, marry a nice fellow who'll take care of you." She grinned wickedly. "Trouble was, I liked to party too much.

"I was just in the eighth grade when I hooked up with this guy who was working the Strip, trying to get a stake together for his prospecting gear. We took off for the Mother Lode, found a lot of gold around Jamestown, even ran our own bar for a while. Had a couple of kids, too."

After a long pause she continued softly, "He's dead, years now. I don't want to talk about that. My kids—I don't know. The county welfare took them away from me." Her eyes misted, and she swiped angrily at them. "Why the hell am I telling you all this, anyway?"

I shrugged, drained my beer can. "Maybe it's this place—Stone Valley, Promiseville. It makes you lonely for someone to talk to."

"It's lonesome, yeah. Nights, it's so quiet out here, it near drives me crazy. I sit on my porch and look out, and you know what I see? That cemetery. It's full of people whose dreams all died. Some nights the only thing I can think of is those people who came to get rich and never got nothing but a pine coffin. And I worry that someday that might be me."

"But you don't leave."

"I got no place to go. No place I want to be, now." She bit her lip, looked away from me.

I sensed she'd had all she could handle of this kind of talk, so I said, "Tell me about what you saw at the mine site."

Nickles had slumped against the rock. Now she sat up straighter, shook her head as if to clear it. "Up there," she said. "Well, I'd been wondering for a while, on account of there was nothing going on. No big trucks on the access road, no blasting, nothing that told me they was taking core samples. So I thought I'd go up and have a look. . . ."

That had been two days ago. She'd climbed the mesa at

first light, taking a circuitous route from the north, where the granite was fractured into large outcroppings that provided cover. She wasn't sure why she felt compelled to stay hidden, but some instinct had told her it was a good idea.

"Turned out I was right, too," she said.

The sun had just cleared the far mountains of Nevada that morning. In its spreading light she saw that the land had been freshly graded and terraced on the side of the mesa that faced away from town. The property appeared to be completely surrounded by a high electrified chain-link fence. Four trailers stood near the gate to the access road, and several vehicles were parked near them.

Nickles "slithered snakelike" to a good vantage point and used her binoculars to study the property. There was no evidence of the workings of the old mine, nor did she see any equipment to suggest sampling had begun. As she watched, a man came out of one of the trailers and walked to a shed next to the gate. He called to someone inside, and another man came out and went to the trailer.

"That's when I realized they had guards on the land," she said. "Why did they need to guard it when there wasn't nothing there? I decided I better find out."

She'd also decided the direct approach was best, so she started around to the access road, keeping an eye on what went on at the guard station. "I figured I could wander up there and act real neighborly. Say something like 'I was just out for a stroll and thought I'd stop in and see what a real mining operation's all about.' Only when I got closer I saw that the guy on the gate had a big Magnum on his hip, and a high-powered rifle besides. And—this really gave me a turn—damned if he wasn't Chinese."

When I didn't react, Nickles glowered impatiently. "You hear what I said? Chinese."

I remembered what Ripinsky had told us about Lily's Yellow Peril theories. In order to preserve the rapport between us, I did my best to look shocked.

Nickles nodded, as if we shared some special knowledge. "Haven't been any of those in these parts since they hung the Chinaman back in the eighteen-fifties. When I saw that one, I decided I better rethink things. And while I was busy doing that, a third guy came out of the trailer and went over to the Chink. The Chink took one of the jeeps and drove off—patrolling, I guess. The other guy got out a folding chair and sat down in the sun. When I took a close look, I saw he was a Chink, too. And had a rifle."

"So what did you do?"

"What any sensible person would—got the hell out of there."

"I thought you spoke with one of the guards."

"Who told you that?"

"Hy Ripinsky."

She looked blank for an instant, then bellowed with laughter. "Son of a bitch believed me! I told him I offered to fuck the guy if he would tell me what was going on, and Ripinsky believed me!"

"Why did you say that?"

"Because Ripinsky hands me a pain. I kind of like to shock him. Besides, it made for a better story."

"And why were you yelling at him when I saw you leave the trailer?"

Her mouth pulled down and hardened. "Son of a bitch called me a bigot."

"Because of what you said about the guard being Chinese?"

"Uh-huh. Something weird's going on up there, and for all we know it could be a commie plot. You'd think Ripinsky would worry; he's been out in the world, he knows how things are. But no, all he says is that I'm talking stupid and that I shouldn't be calling them Chinks."

I was silent for a while, thinking over what she'd told me. Nickles took it as disapproval, said defensively, "I'm *not* a bigot. I just don't like Chinks—or Japs or slopes. Indians, now—I can see in your face that you got some Indian blood. I grew up with Indians, think they're just as good as me."

"But you didn't grow up around Asians."

"Shit, no." But she smiled. Lily Nickles was bright enough to have long ago figured out for herself what I was hinting at. I wondered how much of her racist talk was a put-on, of the same sort she'd pulled on Ripinsky.

I thought some more about the situation with the land on the mesa and isolated a fact that had been bothering me. "Lily, since Earl Hopwood's a prospector, why didn't he mine that acreage he owned on the mesa rather than sell it?"

"You got to know Earl to understand that. First of all, what he prospects for—*when* he bothers—are placer deposits, like me. That's gold that's been moved away from its source by erosion. But to get at what veins are left up there"—she gestured at the mesa—"you got to do hard-rock mining. Dig, blast, tunnel. Costs more. And it's damned hard, dangerous work. Earl Hopwood's lazy as they come."

"Okay, I can understand why he didn't mine it, but why sell it for a price so far below market value?"

"Sold it cheap, did he? Well, what can I tell you?" She shrugged. "Earl's stupid. All the brains in that family got used up generations ago. It probably looked like a lot of money to him."

"He must have realized—"

"Earl don't realize nothing. I tell you, we're talking *stupid* here. That cabin of his? He went and built it on land where there hasn't ever been so much as a nugget."

"Ripinsky said the stream runs through there. Isn't that where you find placer gold?"

"Sure, but it runs too fast. You need slow-moving water— where there's a bend in the streambed, deep pools, gravel bars—for the gold to settle."

"Is looking for signs like that what you meant when you talked about 'reading the stream'?"

"Partly. It's simple; any fool can do it. But not Earl

Hopwood. Instead he goes and builds his cabin on land he can't ever cla m, much less own."

Early that morning I'd read the file Anne-Marie had put together for me on staking claims to mineral rights; one of the requirements was proof of discovery of the mineral within the boundaries of the claim. To purchase land from the federal government under the patenting process, the requirements were even more stringent. Maybe we *were* talking stupid here; Hopwood certainly hadn't shown good sense in building his cabin on federal land where at any time the government could insist he demolish the structure.

Nickles said, "What's your name—McCone?"

I nodded.

"McCone, what do you think is going on up there?"

"I have no idea."

"Me neither. But whatever it is, it scares the shit outta me."

Five

▲▲▲

Two of the prospectors I
tried to locate after I left Nickles weren't around; a third ran
me off with a shotgun. By the time I reached Hopwood's
so-called claim, it was late afternoon and the temperature—
thank God—had dropped slightly.

The claim was at the far end of the valley, in a boulder-
clogged box canyon where the stream cascaded over a high
granite ledge. I'd had to walk the whole way—better than
three miles by my estimation—and was glad I was in even
better shape than usual, thanks to the long vigorous walks
on the beach George and I had been taking. Still, I was
weary and parched, and it was with considerable relief that
I spotted Hopwood's cabin.

It was fairly substantial, set back from the streambed
under a jagged overhang. From the weathered look of the
pine and the wavy window glass I guessed that Hopwood
had scavenged his building materials from Promiseville.
The reinforced plank door was secured by a hasp and
padlock, but I went up to it and knocked anyway. After the
unsurprising lack of an answer, I checked the windows; like

those at Nickles's house, they were draped in cloth. The cabin—in fact, the entire little canyon—held that hushed stillness that said no one was there, had not been for a while now.

Before taking a more thorough look around, I went to the stream's edge and cupped up some of the icy water in my hands to drink; it had a pleasant metallic tang. My thirst slaked, I took off my shoes and socks and dangled my feet in the eddying coolness. I closed my eyes for a bit and listened to the rush of the falls. Thought of the long walk back to my car and sighed.

What had I found out today? Only that there was a perfectly reasonable explanation for why no one in the town or valley had seen Earl Hopwood for more than two weeks. I'd confirmed that Lily Nickles had never heard of Franklin Tarbeaux, and that the Transpacific people weren't sampling the ore on their land but were cautious to the point of employing armed guards. Well, what of it? The company was under foreign management who didn't understand this part of the country. In the locations of most of their other operations guards were probably a routine necessity. My day's work had told me nothing helpful.

So why did I have this heightened sense of wrongness?

Well, for one thing, Nickles had said she was afraid, and she didn't strike me as a woman who frightened easily—or would normally admit to it. And there were the still-unexplained break-ins at Ripinsky's home, the trailers, and the lodge. Plus the person who'd spied on me in the tufa forest, the additional break-in last night, the call to All Souls.

Besides, the sense of wrongness was particularly strong in this little box canyon—too strong for a place whose only resident had simply gone on a gambling-and-womanizing spree in Nevada.

I don't believe in the supernatural, but I do believe that sometimes places can absorb the emotions surrounding events that have happened there. A house where people have been happy has a good feel. A place of misery never seems quite right. Crime scenes—especially those of homicides—are the worst of all, filled with an aura of rage and desperation and pain.

I got up and began looking around. The area behind the cabin, between it and the cliff face, was full of rusted prospecting gear, tools, and cast-off automotive parts. I circled the building, trying the windows, but they were securely locked. I might have been able to justify going inside had one been left open, but in no way did the circumstances warrant an illegal forced entry. Turning away, I covered the surrounding area foot by foot in widening semicircles; then I crossed the stream, stepping from rock to rock, and began to search the opposite bank.

And smelled something putrid.

It didn't take long to pinpoint the source of the smell: behind a pair of man-sized boulders near the cliff face. My stomach lurched as I moved closer, and I thought, *Oh, no* . . .

Reluctantly I made myself step around one of the boulders. And felt a flash of both revulsion and relief at what I saw.

Earl Hopwood's garbage dump. Its mounds of refuse looked as if they'd been years in the making, and were compacting and decaying just as slowly. Flies buzzed around them. The stench was bad enough to make me breathe shallowly through my mouth. I started to turn away, sure I couldn't stomach any further investigation.

But something caught my eye, a few feet away on top of the rotting mass. It was a jagged piece of wood that looked as if it had once been part of a crate. With a red-lettered word on it, not at all faded by the elements: "Dynamite."

Above that was the bottom of another line of letters. "Red Devil," it looked like. A brand name.

I glanced around, found a broken broom handle, and used

it to pull the piece of crate toward me. It was slimy with some kind of decayed food, so I picked it up gingerly, carried it to the stream, and washed it. I wanted to take it with me as evidence—but of what, I hadn't a clue.

Dynamite, I thought. Dynamite was used by hard-rock miners to blast into hillsides. Dynamite was used by high-tech commercial miners like Transpacific.

It was *not* used by prospectors for placer gold—prospectors like Lily Nickles and Earl Hopwood.

So what had Hopwood been doing with an entire case of it?

I decided to run this one by the Tiger Lily.

The sun had sunk behind the hills by the time I got back to Promiseville; the derelict buildings were wrapped in purple shadow that made them look like ghosts of a romantic past rather than reminders of an era fraught with hardship and disappointment. The windows of Nickles's house showed no light, and the Jeep was nowhere in sight.

I stood on her front porch listening to the silence for a minute, and the feeling of lonesomeness she'd described stole over me. The headstones on the barren knoll across the valley caught the rays of the rising moon, seemed to glow phosphorescently through the encroaching darkness. I thought of Nickles sitting here night after night, looking out at the place where so many dreams were buried and perhaps going a little crazy. Although I was anxious to talk with her, I was glad she'd gotten out of here, if only for a little while.

Back at my car, I locked the fragment of the dynamite crate in the trunk before I started for Vernon. When I passed Hy Ripinsky's ranch house, I saw the lights were on and the Morgan parked next to the Land Rover. On impulse, I pulled off the road and knocked on his door.

Ripinsky answered at once, a book in hand, his tall figure clad in faded jeans, a badly frayed sweater, and scuffed moccasins. He blinked in surprise, but seemed glad to see me.

The house's living room was more attractive than its exterior suggested: Woven Indian rugs covered the pegged-pine floor, the sectional sofa and chairs were deeply cushioned and comfortable looking, on shelves flanking the stone fireplace sat hundreds of colorfully jacketed books, and on the wall above the mantel was a display of antique rifles. Ripinsky offered me a beer and went to fetch it. I crossed to one of the bookcases and studied the titles.

Justice Rides Alone; *Horses, Honor, and Women*; *Wear a Fast Gun*; *Hell on the Pecos*; *Bitter Sage*; *The Last Days of Horse-Shy Halloran*. Westerns, apparently. I picked up a volume that lay horizontally on top of some others: *Hopalong Cassidy and the Trail to Seven Pines*, by someone called Tex Burns. Leering wickedly, Hoppy crouched over the recumbent figure of a man while Topper gazed on placidly. Hoppy was—so help me!—dressed prettily in lavender. This book, I thought, could easily become a hot collector's item in San Francisco's predominantly gay Castro district.

Ripinsky returned and handed me a Bud. "I see you're interested in my westerns."

"This in particular." I held up Hopalong.

He grinned. "Bet you never suspected about old Hoppy. I bought that one strictly for the dust jacket—the book is unreadable. Actually I bought a lot of my collection for the jackets; they were wonderful, particularly on westerns, in the thirties and forties."

He spent a few minutes showing me some of the better ones, many by an artist named Nick Eggenhofer. Then he took me to the shelves on the other side of the fireplace and pointed out a book on Eggenhofer's life and art—appropriately titled *Horses, Horses, Always Horses*—as well as other reference works on the Old West.

"I've got to confess I haven't read half the nonfiction," he said. "I prefer fiction. My wife claimed the little boy in me was trying to make up for never getting to be a gunfighter."

But according to local gossip, I thought, he *had* become a gunfighter of sorts. I wanted to ask him about his rumored connection with the CIA, but his face had grown melancholy after he spoke of his dead wife. This was not the time to question him about personal matters. I sensed there might never be a good time for that.

"So," he said, motioning for me to sit on the couch, "brief me on what you found out in the valley."

"Very little, I'm afraid." I filled him in, ending with my discovery of the fragment of dynamite crate on Earl Hopwood's garbage heap.

"Odd," he commented. He took a briar pipe from the table next to his easy chair and began filling it. "Earl doesn't prospect much anymore, and he never did go in for anything as ambitious as hard-rock mining, even though he owned that acreage on the mesa. I can't imagine what he'd be doing with dynamite."

"Lily says she doubts there's ever been any gold near his cabin. What do you suppose he lives on?"

Ripinsky lit his pipe. Through the curling smoke he said, "I'm sure he's found a fair amount of gold up and down that stream over the years, and he's bound to have Social Security. You forget—it doesn't cost much to live in this part of the state, particularly in the manner Earl's become accustomed to."

"Become?"

"Earl hasn't always been a prospector. Up until twenty years ago he ran the filling station across from where the office park is. Then his daughter, Peggy—she was my age, we went to school together—left town and Earl didn't see much reason for staying. So he gave up the station, moved out to the valley."

"Lily says he's just squatting on that land."

"She's probably right. To tell the truth, I never thought about it. Earl calls it his claim, but now that you mention it,

I don't see how there could be enough gold in that canyon for him to file. And even if there was, I doubt he'd bother; after Peggy left, Earl lost whatever ambition he had to start with."

"She was his only child?"

"Yeah. Earl was widowed young, raised her himself from when she was just a baby. Pretty Peggy, we called her. She was too pretty to waste her life in Vernon."

"What happened to her?"

"She went to Berkeley, got some kind of job and attended the university. Married well—two or three times."

"What are the chances Hopwood's been with her the past two weeks?"

"Not good; the longest I ever remember him visiting Peggy was over the weekend one Christmas."

"Still, I should check it out. What's her married name?"

Ripinsky thought, then shook his head. "If I ever knew any of her husbands' names, I've forgotten them."

"Who would know?"

"Maybe Rose Wittington. She used to take care of Peggy when she was a little girl, and they were fond of each other. I can't think of anyone else—she cut all her ties to Vernon when she left."

Like you, I thought. But you came back.

I asked, "What do you think of Lily's idea that Hopwood's over in Nevada living it up on the proceeds of his land sale?"

"On the surface it sounds reasonable, but it feels wrong to me."

"To me, too. And then there's the other man involved in the Transpacific deal—Franklin Tarbeaux. Why doesn't anyone know anything about him?"

Ripinsky frowned. "You know, the name bothers me. Sounds familiar, has all along. But I can't place it."

"Are you sure you haven't met him at some time?"

"Given my own name, other distinctive ones make an impression on me. If I'd met Tarbeaux, I'd remember."

"That's what Lily said. I went by her place on the way back from Hopwood's, to ask her if she's ever known him to use dynamite or heard any blasting going on while he was still in the valley, but she wasn't home. Any idea where she'd go on a Saturday night?"

He smiled. "You city folks lead complicated lives, given your options. Here, on the other hand . . . unless Lily ran into town for a six pack or to do her laundry, there's only one place she'd be—Zelda's."

"Of course. I think I'll stop by there and talk with her."

Ripinsky emptied his pipe into the ashtray and stood, stretching. "If you want, I'll follow you in, keep you company."

"I've already interrupted your evening." I motioned at the book he'd been carrying when I arrived.

"That's okay. I need to get out of here." Briefly he glanced around the room, as if searching the shadows for someone no longer there. "Memories," he added with a rueful half smile.

"I know." Oh, yes, I did. Bittersweet memories hadn't plagued me recently, but up until a few months ago, they'd seemed to be the only sort I had.

By eight o'clock the parking lot at Zelda's was so crowded that I had to leave the MG on the shoulder of the road. I waited until Ripinsky's Morgan pulled up behind me, then got out and walked back to meet him. The night was cold now; the full moon spilled an icy path of light across Tufa Lake. I zipped my suede jacket and stuffed my hands in its pockets, glad I'd thought to bring it along this morning.

Zelda's red-and-gold neon sign flashed a welcome against the black sky. Music boomed from the building—country music with a hard-driving beat. Although I grew up on rock, in recent years my taste has shifted to classical and country. Classical because it soothes and inspires me; country because it's either upbeat and humorous or so emotionally down-and-out that I know my life can never possibly get that bad. Lonesome whistles and lost weekends and prison sentences and all varieties of broken hearts—now *that* can lift the spirits. Besides, I have a family connection with the C-and-W world: my sister Charlene's husband, Ricky Savage, broke into the big time with his "Cobwebs in the Attic of My Mind" and has followed it up with such hits as "My Library of Memories" and "The Cellar of Despair." (If there's a theme to Ricky's songs, it's more or less architectural.)

Ripinsky held the door open for me, and we stepped inside. The noise was deafening; people shouted in order to be heard over the band, and in the lounge a crowd was cheering on a pair of arm wrestlers. The temperature and humidity were close to tropical; the smoke level rivaled L.A. smog on a bad day.

I glanced up at Hy. He gave me a "What can I say?" look and nudged me toward the lounge. A howl went up from the spectators as one of the wrestlers forced his opponent's arm to the table. The loser groaned loudly, then shouted that the next round of drinks was on him.

We found places at the end of the bar near the lakeside windows and ordered a couple of Buds. When they came we leaned with our backs against the plank, looking for Nickles. We had seen her Jeep outside, but there was no sign of her. It was too noisy for conversation, so we merely sipped beer and I noshed on pretzels—I'd had nothing to eat since eleven that morning. When we finished, Ripinsky leaned toward me and shouted, "Maybe she's dancing. Let's you and I give it a whirl."

I hesitated—it had been a couple of years since I'd done much dancing—then said, "Why not?" and followed him from the bar. While I hooked my jacket on a coatrack near the door, he scanned the crowd on the floor for Nickles. The bobbing and dipping mass of humanity was tightly packed; individual faces were indistinguishable in the dim light and low-hanging haze of smoke. Hy shrugged, grabbed my hand, and pulled me after him.

At first I felt awkward but soon found his lead easy to follow. He moved with agility and a certain western flair without trying anything fancy that might have tripped me up. His lean, hard body fit comfortably against mine; it seemed natural to be close to him.

George, I reminded myself. George.

And my inner voice retorted, *Don't be an idiot—you're only dancing!*

The band segued into "Cobwebs in the Attic of My Mind." I put my lips close to Hy's ear and admitted my relationship by marriage to its author. That amused him, and he told me about his teenage cousin who was trying to be another Dolly Parton. "Looks like her, big tits and all," he said, "but the only gigs she can get are singing the national anthem at Little League games." The band played another Ricky Savage hit—"You Can Leave My Bedroom but Not My Heart"—and then I spotted Nickles.

She was at the far side of the floor near the windows, draped against a short fellow in western wear. Her close-cropped head lolled on his shoulder, and the arm he had slung around her pulled up the back of her sweater, exposing a few inches of bare skin. The man nuzzled her neck, and Lily giggled and stumbled. I tapped Ripinsky on the shoulder and pointed them out.

He glanced their way and grimaced. "I doubt we'll get much information out of her in that condition. Shithoused, both of them—and it's early, too."

I nodded, watching the man whisper in Nickles's ear. She giggled some more, and he began to dance her toward a side door. When they stepped off the floor, she lurched and he had to steady her. The two went outside, leaving the door open behind them.

"Where does that go?" I asked Hy.

"Balcony, and then down to the dock." He was frowning

now. "Normally I wouldn't butt in, but I know that guy. Tank-truck driver who delivers to the filling station that Earl Hopwood used to run. Mean son of a bitch, for a little guy. And I've never seen Lily so drunk she could barely stand up."

"Why don't we get some air ourselves? You go ahead. I'll grab my jacket and join you."

When I caught up with him on the balcony, there was no sign of Nickles and her friend. We walked along the plank flooring to the stairway that descended to the dock. At first I could make out nothing but the swath of moonlight on the lake; then I spotted Nickles's light-colored sweater and the man's hat. They were at the end of the dock.

I touched Hy's arm and pointed to them.

He nodded and quickened his pace.

And then the man with Nickles yelled. It wasn't a drunken whoop, mere noisemaking; the sound held an element of horrified surprise.

Ripinsky and I began to run. Down on the dock, Nickles sank into a crouch. The man yelled again.

On the steps I bumped into Ripinsky and stumbled, missed two before I righted myself. I could see Nickles's partner standing behind her, frozen now. They were staring over the dock's edge into the water.

I raced down the dock, Ripinsky behind me. It bucked and swayed under our weight. I pushed past the still-frozen man, grabbed Nickles by her hunched shoulders.

"Lily, what's wrong?"

She twisted around, her face shocked and bewildered. I dropped down and put my arms around her.

Ripinsky moved past us. I heard him grunt in surprise.

Nickles remained very still. She smelled of beer and smoke. I held her and looked over her shoulder at Hy.

He stepped back from the dock's edge and motioned down. I leaned out, peering into the blackness.

A body floated in the water. Bumped against the dock on

the waves its bucking had set in motion. A man's body, from the size of it, clad in light-colored clothing. Face down, shoulders humped. Bumping and bumping . . .

I looked away, said to Nickles's dancing partner, "Take her back to the restaurant. Get somebody to call the sheriff's department."

He snapped out of his frozen state and stepped forward, pulling Nickles to her feet. Shock had sobered him up; it seemed to have turned her to jelly. He had to support her as they moved slowly along the dock.

Ripinsky was squatting down, trying to get a grip on the body. Reluctantly I went to help him. At first it floundered out of reach, then drifted back. Together we grasped it, hauled it onto the dock. I recoiled as it hit the planks.

My eyes met Ripinsky's. His were as black and glittering as the water. He hesitated, then took hold of the corpse's shoulder and heaved it onto its back.

The man's face stared up at us, blank with death. It was round, handsome in a pug-nosed way, and much too youthful for the abundance of white hair that was slicked to the skull and forehead. He couldn't have been in the water long; there was no odor or bloating. Two dark holes marred his pale shirtfront—the entry holes of small-caliber bullets.

I asked, "Do you know him?"

"I've never seen him before."

Ripinsky squatted again and began going through the corpse's pockets. When he reached inside the tan jacket, he came up with a wallet. He stood, took matches from his own pocket, and handed them to me. I lit one and held it so he could examine the wallet's contents.

"Driver's license," he said after a few seconds, "issued to Michael M. Erickson. Address in Barbary Park in San Francisco. Lots of plastic: American Express, Visa, Master Card, department stores. Blue Shield health plan I.D."

"Have you ever heard of him?"

"No." He continued to search the wallet.

The match I held burned my fingers. I dropped it into the water, lit another, and stared down at the dead man's face.

Michael M. Erickson. A San Franciscan, like me. Barbary Park was a newish residential development in the financial district—town houses perched atop a few floors of offices and shops and linked to the nearby Golden Gateway and Embarcadero Center by pedestrian walkways. Perhaps not a prestigious address by the standards of the city's social mavens, but an expensive one. Here in Vernon, Erickson was about as far from his usual milieu as he could get. As far from life as anyone gets . . .

I shuddered, feeling the sense of horror and futility that violent death brings.

Ripinsky whistled suddenly. Said, "He*llo!*"

I dragged my gaze away from the dead man. "What have you found?"

"Hidden pocket inside the cash compartment. Second set of I.D."

"Whose?"

He looked at me. In the instant before the match in my fingers went out, I saw his amazement.

"Ask and ye shall receive," he said. "Meet Mr. Franklin Tarbeaux."

Six

▲▲▲

The sheriff's detectives who came down from the Mono County seat at Bridgeport were Dwight Gifford and Kristen Lark. Gifford, a taciturn man in his mid-thirties who had the look of a bodybuilder, seemed to be compensating for premature baldness with his boar's-bristle mustache. Lark was younger—late twenties—and possessed of incredible nervous energy. Her slender frame was in constant restive motion; when she spoke she barely paused for breath. Her blond curls looked as if they were charged with static electricity; even the freckles across the bridge of her upturned nose appeared as if they might suddenly shift alignment. At first I thought the partners badly mismatched, but as I watched them work I realized they functioned exceptionally well together.

The man from the county medical examiner's office determined that Michael M. Erickson, a.k.a. Franklin Tarbeaux, had been shot twice in the chest at close range with a small-caliber weapon. He couldn't yet accurately estimate the time of death, but he did confirm that the body had not been in the lake very long. "And it didn't drift far, either," he added. "There's not enough current, even at night when the wind kicks up." While the lab crew set up floodlights on the dock, the two detectives, Ripinsky, and I pushed through the crowd that deputies were holding at bay on the balcony and went into the restaurant.

The band had taken an enforced break, and the dining-and-dancing section had emptied. The lounge was still full of drinkers who watched the proceedings below through the windows. The owner—Bob Zelda, a chubby little man who bore not the slightest resemblance to the exotic Fitzgeraldesque creature I'd vaguely imagined—had offered Lily Nickles and her dancing partner asylum in his office. Gifford went back there to question them, and Ripinsky and I talked with Lark at a table in a corner of the dining room.

She asked good questions, homing in on the salient facts with precision; in an interview situation, she managed to restrain her natural restiveness, and she listened well, catching nuances and probing when necessary. While Hy explained about the second set of I.D. the dead man carried and about Franklin Tarbeaux's connection to the Transpacific land deal, she took careful notes. Then she looked at me.

"You're here in a professional capacity?"

"Yes."

"Working for who?"

"The Coalition for Environmental Preservation." I went on to tell her about the events that had prompted Anne-Marie to ask me to come, plus what had happened since I'd been here.

"These break-ins," Lark asked, "were they reported to us?"

"Not the one last night. Nothing was taken and, given the call to my office, it was obvious what the person was after."

Hy said, "Deputies came out to my house, as well as to the Friends' and Coalition's trailers. I don't know about the lodge."

Lark looked thoughtful, tapping her fingers on the table. "What I'm thinking," she said after a moment, "is that this Erickson, or Tarbeaux, is connected with those. He also might have been the person with the off-road vehicle who was prowling around in the tufa. One of my deputies found a Bronco up the road a ways; papers show it was rented four days ago in Modesto under the Tarbeaux name." She held up a hand before either of us could speak. "That's what I'm thinking—but there's a danger in that kind of reasoning.

"A county like this with a small population, you tend to want to blame what crime happens on outsiders, but that's not always a proper assumption. We've got a lot of wild territory here, mountains to desert, that attracts . . . well, weirdos. Folks like your prospector woman in there. Used-up hippies. Loners who have good reasons for wanting to be left alone. So while I'd like to think this Erickson/Tarbeaux is our perp because he's from San Francisco where things like that happen all the time, I've got enough sense to know that's only because it would make my job easier."

Ripinsky and I nodded.

"Well," Lark added, shutting her notebook, "we'll know more about that when we compare the victim's prints with any that were lifted from the house and the trailers—the lodge, too, if we were called. Is there anything else I should know?"

I said, "Not that I can think of. Hy?"

He shook his head.

Lark glanced at the doorway; Gifford was emerging from the lounge. She stood. "You remember anything, give one of us a call."

I said, "I'm planning to drive back to San Francisco by way of Nevada on Monday, so I'll have to pass through Bridgeport. Okay to stop in and see what you've got?"

"Okay by me. I hope you're not planning to follow up on this yourself."

"Only as far as it affects my case—and then only with your permission."

She shrugged. "You got it, as long as you keep us posted."

Gifford came up behind her, stroking his bristly mustache. "Either of you a friend of Ms. Nickles?"

Hy and I exchanged glances.

"The reason I ask, the boyfriend—if that's what he is— took off, and she's in bad shape. Not drunk so much as upset, but I still wouldn't want her driving."

I said, "We'll take care of her."

As the two of them left the room, Hy grabbed my arm. "*We'll* take care of her?"

"It'll probably require both of us."

"Probably." He sighed. "What are we going to do with her? We can't just dump her off at her place in Stone Valley."

I thought of the awful loneliness of the valley night. "God, no. Tell you what—Rose Wittington seems like a motherly soul. Let's take Lily to the lodge."

Ripinsky grinned. "Rose'll probably mother her to death. Gives me a kind of perverse pleasure. We ought to go over there anyway, brief Anne-Marie and Ned on what's happened." He started for the door, then paused. "One thing, though: you take Lily in your car. Half the time she hates my guts; no telling what she'd do to me if I drove her."

I agreed, and we went to Bob Zelda's office. The Tiger Lily's petals were badly wilted. She sat on a broken-down couch with the restaurant owner, clutching his plump hand. When she saw me, she drew back and tried to grin in her usual sardonic manner, but she merely looked pathetic. I thought of what Hy had said about Lily's toughness being mainly facade, and of how it had cracked earlier in the day when she spoke of the man who died and the children who were taken from her by county welfare. Since the tough appearance was clearly important to her, I greeted her without fussing and told her our plan.

"No way!" She shook her head vehemently. "I'm going home—on my own."

"You can't, Lily. Detective Gifford said he doesn't want you driving."

"Why the fuck not? I've driven in worse shape, and I'm not bad off anymore, anyway. Look—steady as a rock." She held out her right hand; it shook badly. "Well, almost," she added.

"It'll only be for the one night," I said.

"Might be a good idea, Lily," Bob Zelda told her.

She looked as if she would weaken, but then she glanced at the door and saw Ripinsky, who had been hanging back, trying to be inconspicuous. "What's that asshole doing here?"

Ripinsky said, "Now, Lily, don't start."

"Start? Shit, I finished with you years ago." She turned to me. "He's not coming with us, is he?"

"No. You can ride with me."

"And you'll bring me back for my Jeep first thing in the morning?"

"Yes."

She yawned elaborately. "Well, I *could* use some shut-eye."

Nickles collected her jacket from where she'd left it near the dance floor, and she and I went outside to my car. Ripinsky remained in the restaurant, signaling that he'd see me later. It was close to midnight now; the parking lot was deserted, and the sign on the roof had been turned off.

"Nothing like a good murder to clear a place out," Nickles said, sounding more cheerful now.

I chose not to respond, merely unlocked the passenger door of the MG for her. Apparently she sensed I'd found the remark in bad taste, because she didn't speak again until we pulled up at the lodge. Then she said, "Rose is gonna have a shit fit when she sees me."

"Why?"

"She caught her husband fooling around with me a couple

of years ago, right before he died. Probably blames his stroke on the excitement."

I wasn't terribly worried about how Rose Wittington would receive her; Nickles's sexual escapades had begun to sound like just so many locker-room tales to me.

We went into the public room of the lodge. Anne-Marie and Rose were watching Peter Lorre look nervous on the big screen. They seemed surprised to see Nickles with me, but when I explained the situation Rose got up, clucking and fussing, and gathered Lily to her comfortable bosom. She led her away, chattering about how the Willow Room was all made up, and wouldn't Lily like a hot bath or maybe a nice glass of warm milk before she turned in? Nickles looked over her shoulder at me, eyes alarmed and pleading, but I merely smiled a cheerful good night. If she had indeed fooled around with Rose's late husband, she was about to swallow a hearty dose of revenge-by-mothering.

Anne-Marie stood, about to speak, when Ripinsky put his head through the door. "All clear?"

"Yes." To Anne-Marie I added, "Let's go down to our cabin and talk. And we'd better wake Ned—I assume he's asleep."

"Oh, probably for hours now. Ned's the early-to-bed type."

"In that case, he ought not to mind being early-to-rise."

She went to fetch Sanderman, and Ripinsky and I walked silently downhill to the cabin. It was very dark under the trees; at the lake's edge I could see the outlines of the willows that trailed their long branches in the brackish water. Something rustled above us, and a bird gave a plaintive cry. I started and brushed against Ripinsky. He put his hand on my shoulder.

"Nutcracker, from the sound of him," he said.

"He's lonesome."

"Probably; nutcrackers like people."

We climbed onto the porch and stood for a moment, backs to the door, facing the dark lake. The moon was nearly down now; a red warning light at the end of the dock showed the water's gentle rippling.

"You love it here, don't you?" I said.

He shrugged. "It's home."

"It's more to you than that."

"What makes you an expert on me?" His voice held an edge of annoyance, but when I didn't reply he relented. "Yeah, it's a lot more than that, but it took me a long time to figure it out. When I was just a kid I read what Mark Twain wrote about Mono Lake and decided it went double for Tufa: 'A lifeless, hideous, treeless desert . . . wild, gloomy, foreboding . . . suggestive of sterility and death.'"

"Twain was wrong; he didn't see its beauty. And given the way he felt about Mono Lake, I doubt he ever ventured up here."

"No, but I couldn't get the words out of my head, and for years I dreamed of leaving Vernon. So I did."

"And?"

"And now I'm back for good." His tone was final; end of discussion.

I unlocked the cabin and we went inside. By the time Anne-Marie arrived I had the fire started.

"Ned took a bit of rousing," she said, "but he's on his way. Do either of you want coffee?"

Ripinsky shook his head. "I'll take a beer, if you've got one."

"Brandy for me," I said.

"And Ned wants seltzer, and I want herbal tea." She went to the kitchen, grumbling loudly about people who complicated matters.

Within five minutes Sanderman arrived, clad in freshly pressed cords and a pullover, his hair slicked back over his incipient bald spot. He'd taken time to shower—and probably time to shave—but his ablutions hadn't done much for his mood. His face had the look of an infant who had been rudely awakened from his nap; judging from the way his lower lip protruded, I wouldn't have been surprised if he'd started bawling. He sat stiffly on one of the chairs from the dinette set and accepted the glass of seltzer Anne-Marie offered, glancing disapprovingly when she handed Hy his beer and me my brandy.

Ripinsky said we should start at the beginning and motioned to me. I told them about my day's activities in Stone Valley, my visit to Hy, and our trip to Zelda's. When I got to the part about seeing Nickles across the dance floor, Anne-Marie's expression grew speculative; I knew I would have to field some questions about Hy after he and Ned left. Her face became grave when I told about the body in the lake, however. Sanderman's gaze turned inward; he was probably trying to visualize the scene.

After I finished, Ripinsky said, "You can see that it's a damned strange set of circumstances. First no one's ever heard of or seen this Franklin Tarbeaux. Then a man turns up in the lake, shot sometime today or tonight, and he's got Tarbeaux's I.D. in his wallet. And the I.D. looks fake. What I think we ought to—"

Sanderman interrupted, his voice sharply edged. "What did you say his real name was?"

"Erickson. Michael M. Address in Barbary Park in San Francisco. As I was saying—"

"How can you be sure that Tarbeaux wasn't actually his name? Maybe the Erickson I.D. is the false one."

Hy sighed. "I've seen enough fake I.D. to know the difference."

When he didn't continue with whatever he'd been trying to say before Sanderman's interruptions, Anne-Marie turned to me. "Do you think this Erickson was killed because of the land deal?"

"It would seem that way." I considered for a moment. "The fact that Erickson may have used a false identity sheds a fairly bad light on that deal. Maybe someone connected with

Transpacific silenced Erickson to ensure the fact that Tarbeaux didn't exist would never come out."

"But he had the I.D.," she reminded me.

"In a hidden pocket in his wallet," Ripinsky reminded her. "The killer wouldn't necessarily have known that."

Sanderman stood up and began pacing around the room, hands clasped behind his back, head down. "If that's the case," he said, "the killer must have been one of those armed guards at the mine site."

"Maybe, maybe not. We can't jump to that kind of conclusion at this point," I said.

"Well, what *can* we conclude?" he asked.

"Nothing, yet," I said.

"Great, just great!"

"Take it easy, Ned," Anne-Marie cautioned.

Sanderman stopped by the window and stood with his back to us, one fist rapping on its frame. Anne-Marie looked concerned; Ripinsky regarded him with hooded eyes.

I said, "Let me propose a plan of action. I want to talk with the people I couldn't locate today in Stone Valley, as well as the one who waved the shotgun at me. I'll take Nickles along to ease matters. If any of them knew Erickson or even saw him in the valley, I'll find out."

"What about here in town?" Anne-Marie asked. "He's got to have stayed someplace, talked with someone. You could ask—"

"The sheriff's people will do that, and I don't want to get in their way. Kristen Lark was relatively agreeable about allowing me to continue my investigation; I don't want to do anything to antagonize her or anyone else in the department. You, on the other hand . . ." I looked at Ripinsky.

He was still staring at Sanderman's back. He moved his focus to me and said, "I, on the other hand, am a concerned local citizen who happened to be there when the body was discovered. It's natural that I talk about it—and to anybody I damned well please."

"Right."

"And after that?" Anne-Marie asked me.

"Transpacific seems to be a big unknown in all this. I need to get back to the city and look into them. I'll leave Monday morning, stop by the sheriff's department in Bridgeport and find out what they've got on the murder. Then I'll drive home by way of Carson City and Reno, ask around the casinos for Earl Hopwood." I turned to Ripinsky. "Is there anyplace I can get a picture of him?"

"I can probably find one at home if I dig deep enough. Julie was fond of him, used to have him to our 'strays' dinners at the holidays."

"Good. If Hopwood's in Nevada, he's likely to frequent one of the seedier casinos. Their security people may recognize him from a photograph."

Sanderman turned from the window. "I don't know why you're so interested in Hopwood," he said peevishly.

"I'm interested in anyone who had anything to do with that land deal."

"Sounds like a waste of energy to me."

"Ninety percent of what an investigator does could be classified as a waste of energy."

His mouth pulled down. To a man whose computer went everywhere with him, my methods must have seemed quite inexplicable, to say nothing of irritating. After a few seconds he moved toward the door. "I trust no one minds if I try to get a few more hours' sleep?"

Ever the peacemaker, Anne-Marie said, "Of course not. Thanks for sitting in, Ned."

He nodded curtly and left the cabin. The three of us were silent until his footfalls died away in the grove. Then Anne-Marie said, "Behold the new breed of environmentalist."

Ripinsky didn't speak. His eyes were on the door—cold, contemplative.

After a moment I said, "Enough about him. What I want to know is this: is anyone else starving?"

Anne-Marie's eyes lit up. "Now that you mention it, I'm ravenous!"

"I haven't eaten since lunch, except for a few pretzels."

"Scrambled eggs? With toast? And I think there's some sausage."

"Chop up some onion and green pepper and mix it with the eggs."

"What about mushrooms?"

"And cheese—I saw some Parmesan in there this morning."

"Black olives. And strawberry preserves on the toast." She got up and started for the kitchen. "Hy?" she called over her shoulder.

"Just another beer. Well, maybe some toast. Oh, what the hell—everything." He looked at me, and I knew we were both thinking that this was a pretty perverse but not uncommon reaction to finding a corpse. After a few seconds he asked, "You folks get the late-night munchies often?"

"We used to." I thought of the old days, before Anne-Marie had bought her building in the Noe Valley district and married Hank. Back then she'd lived in a tiny room on the second story of All Souls, and if I'd been working late, I could always count on her to join me in whipping up some peculiar, delicious concoction in the big kitchen at the rear of the Victorian.

Anne-Marie called out for help. Hy and I crowded into the tiny kitchen and pitched in as best we could, an effort that produced much confusion, stepping on of feet, and laughter. Finally we heaped plates—hideous yellow crockery that clashed with the unfortunate orange tile countertops—and carried them to the dinette set. And ate like hungry wolves.

At one point I looked up and found Ripinsky staring at me. "You always stuff yourself like this, woman?"

"Pretty much."

"How do you stay so skinny?"

"Good genes."

He nodded and went back to his eggs.

When we'd finished we dumped the dishes into a sinkful of sudsy water. Ripinsky said, "I'd better get going before I get so sleepy I have to beg the use of your couch." Then he looked at me. "Walk me up the hill?"

"Sure." I grabbed my jacket and left with him.

It was well after two. The early-morning hours in the high desert were frigid; our breath billowed white as we walked to his car.

"McCone," Hy said, "are you firearms-qualified?"

"Yes."

"Good shot?"

"I'm good. A woman in my profession has to be." Now I was holding back, as he had earlier when he'd refused to elaborate on the years he'd spent away from Tufa Lake. Holding back not so much facts as emotional shadings, about things I'd been forced to do and sometimes wished undone.

He asked, "Got a piece with you?"

"No, it's at home. I used to keep one in the glovebox of my car, but when it was broken into and the gun stolen, I decided that was too risky."

We reached the Morgan. Hy leaned against it, arms folded, face concerned in the glow from the lodge's security lights. "I'd loan you one of mine, but by the time I got it and brought it back—"

"Don't bother. I'm also a mean hand with a fireplace poker."

His lips twitched, but he sobered quickly. "I don't know, maybe I'm overreacting. But old habits die hard. You do me a favor—keep that poker next to your bed tonight."

"I will."

He made no move to get into the car. I shifted from foot to foot—not really cold or impatient, but suddenly ill at ease.

Hy said, "Come here, McCone. Give me a hug."

Without hesitating, I went to him. He held me tightly, his breath warm against my forehead. The closeness seemed as natural as when we'd danced at Zelda's. After a few seconds he released me, a melancholy smile on his lips.

"See you later on today," he said, and folded his long body into the Morgan.

Seven

▲ ▲ ▲

I didn't sleep restfully or long, and by seven I was up and dressed. A quick glance into Anne-Marie's room showed that she'd burrowed deep and pulled the pillows over her head as defense against the sound of the shower. The fact that she'd already been in bed when I'd returned to the cabin after walking Hy up the hill told me how tired she must have been; I'd seldom known her to restrain her curiosity about anything so provocative as why I'd allowed Ripinsky to talk me into dancing at Zelda's.

I made myself a mug of instant coffee, pulled on my jacket, and stepped onto the porch. The gray outlines of the willows framed the pink-streaked lake. Waterfowl glided across its surface, pausing occasionally to turn tails-up to feed; gulls and plovers made touch-and-go landings on the gnarled tufa islands.

My gaze rested on the nearby dock, where a figure sat facing lakeward, one knee drawn up. Apparently Ned Sanderman couldn't sleep either. At first I almost went back inside, but finally I descended the steps and carried my

75

coffee over there. He glanced back as my footsteps set the boards vibrating.

"Good morning," I said. "It looks as if it'll be a pretty day."

He nodded curtly.

"Mind if I join you?"

"If you like."

Good Lord, I thought, he can't still be pouting! I asked, "Were you able to get more sleep?"

"No. I kept thinking about . . . Actually, I'm glad you're up early so we can talk privately. There's something I have to tell you."

I sat next to him and offered him a sip of coffee.

He shook his head. "I never touch the stuff, or tea, either. Caffeine's a killer."

I ignored the implied criticism. "So what is it you want to talk about?"

"The murdered man. I think I know him."

"How?"

"Well . . . I don't know that he's the same Michael Erickson. The name's a common one, but the address at Barbary Park . . . Can you describe him?"

I told him what I'd observed of the dead man's appearance. As I spoke, Sanderman's already pale skin went pasty and his eyes—red from lack of sleep—clouded.

After a moment he said, "That's the man. And Michael Erickson is his real name. Mick, for short."

"How do you know him?"

"From my former firm in Silicon Valley. Techworks, it's called. I was a computer engineer developing . . . well, that's irrelevant. Mick was on the marketing side, mainly servicing our Pacific Rim accounts, but he had a technical background, too—a degree from Colorado School of Mines."

"Did you know him well?"

"Not really. The technical and marketing staffs didn't mix all that much, although it was a small company, friendly. After I left, I didn't see him for a few years, never even thought of him. But two years ago I ran into him at Union Square in San Francisco. It was Christmastime. We were both trying to finish our shopping and pretty tired, so we went and had a couple of drinks."

Sanderman seemed to have run out of steam, so I prodded him. "What did you talk about?"

"The old company, people we knew there, what they were doing. Mick had left a couple of years after I did and formed his own consulting firm. But he didn't talk much about that; what he was interested in was my work with the Coalition. I told him about how we'd cooperated with the Friends in their efforts to stop the water diversions from Tufa Lake, and of our concern about the gold-mining potential in the Tufa area. He seemed fascinated."

"Did you see him after that?"

"Twice. A few months later he turned up in Sacramento at the Coalition headquarters. Said he'd had business in the area and just dropped in on impulse. He invited me to have drinks again after work, asked me to bring along some of the Coalition literature and position papers on the situation here in Mono County. I was happy to; we're always short on funds, and Mick seemed well off. I was hoping for a donation."

"Did you get one?"

"Yes. Two or three weeks later he showed up again. This time he took me to dinner. He asked a lot of questions about Tufa Lake and Stone Valley. Before he left he gave me a thousand dollars for the Coalition."

"And then?"

"That's the last I saw of him."

I thought for a moment about what he'd told me. "Tell me more about Mick Erickson. What was he like?"

"Like?" Sanderman stared off at the lake, where the tufa islands were taking on sharper definition as the rising sun gilded them. "An attractive guy. Well dressed, drove a Jaguar. Not handsome in the classical sense, but there was something about him that made women sit up and take notice. Very smooth, with a good sense of humor. He wasn't the sort to tell jokes, though; they were more like amusing stories, anecdotes. Not your stereotypical marketing type—much more sophisticated."

"You know anything about his personal life?"

"I think he was married. At least, when I ran into him that Christmastime, he complained about how difficult it was to choose perfume for his wife."

"Anything else?"

He shook his head.

"What about the consulting firm he'd set up?"

"I can't even recall its name."

"Okay, now let me ask you this: You must have suspected the dead man and Mick Erickson were the same person when we all talked last night. Why didn't you mention it then?"

He wet his lips, compressed them.

"Ned?"

"I just . . . I didn't want to say anything in front of Ripinsky, not until I'd thought it over."

"Why not?"

"Well, the way it looks to me—and I'm sure it will to him—is that I inadvertently gave Mick an idea that he later exploited."

"About the gold-mining potential here."

"Yes."

"Hy could scarcely blame you for that. As far as you knew, Erickson was interested in the Coalition's work. He *did* give you a sizable donation."

"You and I see it that way, but Ripinsky will manage to turn it around. He's like a lot of the old-style environmentalists—a zealot who resents the new breed."

"I'm not sure I understand."

"Ripinsky's in love with Mother Nature. Every tree, every rock, every bird, must be preserved at whatever the cost."

Sanderman's lips twisted scornfully. "He doesn't see the realities of what we're up against. Doesn't see the need to compromise, make accommodation. And he doesn't understand just how bad our need for money is. We can't exist on the dribs and drabs that trickle in from our members and private foundations. We need big money, and we have to learn how to tap into the sources for it."

"Did you think you could do that through Mick Erickson?"

". . . Well, he certainly seemed like a man who could provide a good entrée to the big-money interests. But try telling that to Ripinsky. He'd accuse me of selling out the entire Tufa Lake area. And the devil of it is that if anyone else—Anne-Marie or one of the Friends, for instance—had made the same error in judgment, he'd have understood how it could happen. But because it was me . . . Ripinsky's out to get me."

"Why?"

He shrugged and looked away.

"I don't think he's out to get you, Ned. The two of you just don't get along because of the difference in your personal styles."

Sanderman still did not meet my eyes. He seemed to want to tell me something, but was unable to broach the subject. Finally he said, "Maybe you're right. This kind of conflict isn't new to me. All my life . . . I don't relate well, and people don't relate to me."

I hadn't suspected he possessed such self-knowledge. "In what way don't you relate?"

"Basically I find other people uninteresting. Compared to ideas, they seem pretty trivial. Their concerns, their lives—when you examine them, you've got to admit they're frivolous. I'm happiest when I'm alone: working out theoretical problems, catching up on my technical reading, creating crossword puzzles or acrostics. But I'm socially aware enough that I realize I *should* relate, so I compensate by talking too much. People find me boring." He fell silent, putting a hand to his lips as if trying to force back the pain that underlay his words. I sensed that this was the first real confidence he'd shared with anyone in a good long time.

It struck me that I had the reverse of Sanderman's problem: all my life I've related—perhaps too well. People tell me things, frequently things they've never told another living soul. Maybe it's because I have an open manner; maybe it's because I ask the right questions; maybe I simply behave like someone who will respect and guard a confidence. Often it's gotten me into trouble when someone later regrets having been too frank, but occasionally it's formed the basis for solid friendships—to say nothing of having been extremely useful in my work.

I asked, "Do you care that people find you boring?"

"Of course I do! I have feelings, you know. Just because I don't spread them out for everyone to see . . . You remember the other night when I said I had my mid-life crisis at thirty-nine?"

I nodded.

"Well, what brought it on was my wife leaving me. I know that doesn't sound particularly unusual. In Silicon Valley, people are always divorcing. Men leave their wives for their secretaries; women leave their husbands for their co-workers or bosses. Hell, two of my wife's women friends left their husbands for each other. But you know one of the reasons why my wife claimed she left me?"

"Why?"

"Because I was so boring that every morning she had to remind herself that I existed." His pain was clearly apparent now. "How do you like that? To my own wife I was a nonentity!"

Had I heard his story secondhand—had he, for instance, been one of Hank's clients, who as a group have endured some of the most hilarious divorces on record—I would have been amused. But his outrage was such a transparent mask for hurt that I found no humor in the tale I said, "Your wife doesn't have much depth or compassion, does she?"

It was the right response; Sanderman's tense face relaxed. "No, she doesn't. But she's right about one thing—I *am* boring."

I smiled. "Boring and proud of it—that's the spirit. But, Ned, to get back to Erickson, you should call the sheriff's department and tell either Kristen Lark or Dwight Gifford what you know."

"I plan to. What about . . ."

"Don't worry about Anne-Marie and Hy. We'll just say that you didn't make the connection between the dead man and your Mick Erickson until we spoke this morning."

"Thanks."

I stood up. "No problem."

"And thanks for listening. I've talked *at* you a lot since you've been here, but it was better talking *with* you."

"Any time you want to talk some more, I'm here. And, Ned, if I ever take up needlepoint, my first project will be a pillow for you saying—"

"I know: 'Boring and Proud of It.'"

Two hours later, just as I returned from a long walk along the shoreline, Nickles tottered down the hill looking like death warmed over. She cringed at my offer of breakfast, but agreed to help me locate the other prospectors in the valley. On the way into town to retrieve her Jeep, I asked her how it had gone with Rose Wittington, but she didn't want to talk about that. All she would say was, "The woman's fuckin' crazy."

Because of the early hour, Stone Valley still held the chill of night, but by the time Nickles, with the unerring sense of a born tracker, ferreted out the two prospectors I hadn't been able to find, the temperature was on the rise. Neither man was able to tell me anything about Michael Erickson, under either his own or the Tarbeaux name; neither had seen Earl Hopwood in at least two weeks. As we approached the hillside encampment of the man with the shotgun, I began to wonder if all this running around in the heat was really worth it.

The man's abode was merely a shack of wood, tar paper, and sheet metal, with a battered and faded psychedelically painted VW van parked next to it. Nickles stopped several yards away and called out. He emerged, shotgun cradled in his arms. He was big but running to flab, clad only in shabby jeans and an open leather vest; his full beard hung nearly to his belt, and his matted curls were restrained by a blue bandanna. A cross between a desert rat and one of the area's leftover hippies, I thought. When he saw us, he planted his feet wide but didn't raise the gun.

"Hey, Bayard," Nickles said, "I got a friend here, needs to ask you some questions."

Bayard just stood there.

Nickles motioned to me, and we went closer. Now I saw that his eyes were dull and burned out. I also could smell him, the shock waves of body odor almost palpable in the hot, still air. Definitely leftover hippie.

"My friend tells me you were kind of inhospitable yesterday," Nickles said. "You better watch what you do with that shotgun, Bayard. Could get you in a lot of trouble."

The man shrugged and spat to one side. "Thought she might be from the welfare, wondering why the kids ain't in school."

Kids? I glanced at the shack and caught sight of a pale, rabbity little face peering around the doorjamb. It withdrew as soon as its washed-out eyes met mine.

Nickles laughed. "Nobody's gonna bother about those kids goin' to school—they're too damn dumb."

Her remark didn't faze Bayard; he merely nodded. "Dumb as posts, so why bother? What's your friend want to know?"

I started to speak, but Nickles answered for me. "Same

kind of stuff those tree huggers came asking about. You ever hear of a Franklin Tarbeaux?"

"I told them no."

"What about Michael Erickson—Mick, for short?"

". . . Him neither."

"When's the last time you saw Earl Hopwood?"

Bayard scratched his head. "Hopwood?"

"Yeah, you know—the old guy from up the stream." She looked at me and without lowering her voice said, "You gotta be patient with Bay. He did too many drugs back in the sixties."

That remark seemed to slide right by him, too. I was beginning to feel as if we were speaking two languages here, with Nickles as interpreter. After a moment some rusty mental mechanism seemed to kick in, because Bayard said, "Old Earl. Saw him just last week driving by on his way to his claim. Driving too damn fast for that van of his—must be older'n mine."

Nickles glanced at me and frowned. "You sure it was last week, Bay?"

The man looked mildly irritated. "Sure I'm sure. This past Wednesday it was. I know because my check just come."

"You talk with Earl?"

"Yelled at him to slow down."

"See him after that?"

"Nope."

"Well, thanks, Bay. Say hello to the missus for me."

Without a word he turned and went back into the shack.

"He's got an entire family living in there?" I asked in amazement.

Nickles grinned slyly. "Well, sure. Kind of ruffles your middle-class sensibilities, don't it?"

I ignored the comment—probably because it hit too close to home. "Listen, is it likely what he says is true?"

"Pretty likely. The check he's talking about is from state

disability. It's the big moment in Bay's life; everything dates from before or after that check comes."

"He could have seen Hopwood some other week, though."

"No, Bay's memory ain't that good. If he says it was last week, that's when it was. Now how about you and me going to my place so we can get out of this sun?"

I agreed and we walked back there in silence. Nickles asked me if I wanted to come in for a glass of water. "I'd offer you a beer," she added, "but I'm fresh out. Couldn't stomach looking at one today, anyway."

I was anxious to get away, but her wistful expression made it so plain she didn't want me to leave that I said, "Water sounds great."

"Come on in, then."

The interior of the house was surprisingly cool. I followed Nickles along a narrow hallway with peeling floral wallpaper and past a parlor full of mining gear; the hydraulic concentrator occupied the place of honor on a rag rug in the center of the floor. Another room had a mattress and box springs with a sleeping bag spread on top and clothing hanging from pegs on the wall. All the others were empty except for what little the original owners had abandoned. The kitchen was at the rear: iron cookstove, chipped enamel–topped table, dry sink, shelves of dishes and utensils. Several big bottles of water stood in the sink.

"Stream water," Nickles explained, taking down a pair of plastic glasses and inspecting them for cleanliness. "I collect it, let the sediment filter out. Pure as any bottled stuff I could buy." She poured and added, "Sorry I can't give you ice. What was in the chest over there is bound to be melted—I was after more when I got sidetracked to Zelda's last night by that little weasel. Let's go out on the porch."

In the midday sun the valley looked as washed out as an old color photo; heat waves danced off the iron roofs of the ruins below. Nickles and I sat on the steps, looking out.

I said, "You've really got to be tough to survive here."

"Yeah, you do. Summers you roast, winters you freeze, all year long you don't see another living soul for days—hell, weeks—at a stretch. You know, McCone, last night after Rose tucked me in—God, she scared me; hinted she might've poisoned my hot milk—I got to thinking. I'm gonna give it another season here, but if I don't score pretty damn good, I'm going back to Nevada."

"And do what?"

"Get myself into a decent house, if I can. Make some real money."

I raised my eyebrows inquiringly.

"Yeah, that's what I mean. A cathouse. That bother you?"

I shrugged.

"In this world you use what skill you got. Except for looking for gold, that's all I know. Besides, it pays a damn sight better than the casinos. At least I won't die poor, like my mama did."

I thought about that for a moment. "What you said before about my middle-class sensibilities—it's good for me to have them ruffled now and then."

"Oh, McCone!" She punched me on the shoulder. "Any time those sensibilities need ruffling, you just come see me."

I stopped by Ripinsky's place half an hour later to see if he'd unearthed any pictures of Earl Hopwood. When he came to the door he was barefoot, in cutoffs and a tank top, dark-framed reading glasses pushed up on top of his curly head. A silver-and-gold holiday gift box full of photographs sat on the coffee table, and beside it lay several snapshots. One showed a smiling woman in a wheelchair and an unsmiling older man standing behind her; it had been taken in this room in front of the stone fireplace.

"Earl Hopwood and Julie," Ripinsky said, handing it to me.

Hy's late wife had been gaunt, with long gray-brown hair combed back from a widow's peak. Her smile lit up her face;

her eyes, sunk in a web of lines that betrayed chronic weariness and pain, contradicted her physical debilitation, spoke of an iron will and mental vigor.

I said, "From what people tell me, Julie was a pretty amazing woman."

"She was. Went all out in everything she did. Tufa Lake would have been doomed without her, and she damned near saved me from hell."

I glanced up at him, hoping he'd elaborate, but he merely took the reading glasses off his head and went to put them on a table.

I turned my attention back to the photograph, studying Hopwood. The old man was lean and sinewy, with sharp features, thin colorless lips, and weathered skin whose grayish cast matched his hair. But as with Julie Spaulding, what struck me was the eyes. Black and burning, even in this faded photo, they dominated his otherwise passive face. Zealot's eyes, I thought, maybe even a little mad. Perhaps that was what living alone in the desert had done to him; perhaps what others described as laziness was a sapping of outward energy by his internal fires—whatever might fuel them. I looked at the photo a bit longer, then asked, "May I take this?"

"Just so you return it. You find out anything in the valley?"

"Only that Hopwood may have been there as recently as last week." I repeated Bayard's story. "You know," I added, "it fits in with something I should have picked up on right off. That piece of dynamite crate I found at his place wasn't weathered the way it would have been if it had been tossed on the dump weeks ago."

"What of it, though? Other people probably know about the dump and use it. They don't have garbage-collection service out there, you know. And you say his cabin has an unlived-in feel."

"Unlived in and slightly . . . wrong is the only way I can

describe it. Did you have a chance to ask around town about Erickson?"

"I did, and nobody remembers seeing him. Distinctive looking as he was, you'd think somebody would." Then he grimaced ruefully. "I *did* find out why the Tarbeaux name is so familiar."

"Oh?"

"Yeah, it came to me after worrying on it half the night." He went to the side of the fireplace where the nonfiction books on the Old West were shelved and pulled down a volume. It was titled *Knights of the Green Cloth: The Saga of the Frontier Gamblers*.

"I bought this years ago and glanced through it but never got around to reading it all." He opened it to a bookmarked section and then extended it to me.

The chapter he'd opened to was headed by a quotation: "Gyps and cons are all cases of the biter being bitten. I got into my three-card monte gyp because I loved to kid, and because I loved to trim suckers."

The quotation was attributed to one Frank Tarbeaux.

I looked up at Ripinsky. "Frank Tarbeaux . . . Franklin Tarbeaux. A frontier con man?"

"One of the greatest con men of all," Hy said. "And a kidder. A goddam kidder."

Eight

▲ ▲ ▲

Ripinsky and I went looking for Anne-Marie and Sanderman. The Coalition trailer was locked, as was Sanderman's cabin at the lodge. There was no sign of Anne-Marie, and Rose Wittington had no idea where she'd gone. I tried to phone Kristen Lark or Dwight Gifford at the sheriff's department in Bridgeport to tell them what Ripinsky had realized about the Tarbeaux alias, but both detectives were out of the office. While I waited for a return call, Hy and I passed the time by watching a colorized version of *D.O.A.* on the lodge's big-screen TV—I tipped him to turning off the set's color so it was at least palatable. We didn't discuss the latest turn of events because of Rose's nearby presence as she went about various housekeeping chores.

Lark finally called around six. She found the information about the alias interesting, but didn't attach much importance to it. Since I wasn't sure what, if any, relationship the choice of name might have to the as-yet-undetermined events surrounding Erickson's death, her lack of enthusiasm didn't particularly trouble me. I asked if she'd gotten

88

anything back from the medical examiner, and when she said not yet, I told her I'd see her the next morning.

Anne-Marie finally rolled in around seven, with two Friends of Tufa Lake in tow. They'd taken a long hike up one of the feeder streams, then stopped at the home of another member to look at his collection of historical photographs of the area. The two knew Ripinsky well, so they settled in and chatted for more than an hour. By the time they left, I was ravenous.

Ripinsky waited impatiently for Anne-Marie to return from seeing them to their car, then asked, "Where the hell is Ned?"

"Sacramento. He packed up his computer and drove back for a couple of days, said there were some files he needed to access."

"He couldn't do that from here?"

"Apparently not."

"Terrific." Ripinsky's fist slammed onto the coffee table; his face congested with anger.

I thought of Sanderman's somewhat paranoid claim that Hy was out to get him. While I was sure it didn't amount to that, Ripinsky certainly did have some problem with Ned, and I had no clue as to what was at the root of it. I did understand Sanderman's sudden trip to Sacramento, however: he was fleeing the explosion that was sure to come when Ripinsky found out about his dealings with Mick Erickson.

Hoping that the explosion would be less violent in a public place, I suggested we go to Zelda's for dinner.

Over the meal Ripinsky explained to Anne-Marie about the Tarbeaux alias. When he finished, I related what Sanderman had told me about Mick Erickson. To my surprise, Hy absorbed this new information as calmly as Anne-Marie, his face intense but thoughtful.

Again our conversation was inhibited by Rose Wittington, who had arrived shortly after us with a woman friend. When her companion left, Rose brought her coffee to our table unbidden and began questioning Hy and me about finding the body the night before. I let him do the talking—a scaled-down version that would only minimally satisfy the local gossip mills—then asked, "You have any trouble with Lily last night?"

Rose shook her head. "I can handle her kind."

I couldn't think of any tactful way to ask if she'd really hinted to the Tiger Lily that she'd poisoned her hot milk or if she'd actually caught her in flagrante with her late husband, but Rose's gentle amusement when I mentioned how Nickles had reacted to the presence of Chinese guards at the mine site convinced me it was yet another of the prospector's tall tales.

"Lily's always been a little cracked on the subject of Orientals," Rose said. "Reminds me of a character in a Fu Manchu movie."

"She told me there hadn't been any of 'that kind' around here since they hanged the Chinaman back in the eighteen fifties. What was that about?"

"Dark chapter in Promiseville history. You know a lot of Chinese escaped the famines and wars at home by coming over to work in the goldfields?"

I nodded.

"Well, at first folks tolerated them, but by the mid-fifties things had turned around. Got pretty grim; there was a lot of anti-foreign feeling, color prejudice. In fifty-two the governor actually declared them a menace to the state. Some gold camps a Chinese didn't dare set foot in for fear of being murdered."

Hy said, "The Promiseville Chinese owned the store, didn't he?"

"Yeah—good merchant, charged reasonable, was free with credit. Only reason they let him stay. But then he got into a fight with a southerner—they were the ones who really whipped up the race prejudice—and killed him. It was self-defense, but they hung the Chinaman just the same."

"You're quite a historian," Anne-Marie told her.

"Not half as much of one as old Earl Hopwood, that turncoat who sold his land to this mining company."

"Speaking of him," I said, "he seems to have disappeared. And do you have any idea where his daughter Peggy is living or what her current married name is?"

"No, I haven't heard from Peggy in years, close to ten now. At one time I think Earl said she was living in Marin County, but she's moved since then."

"I hoped she'd know where her father is."

"Not likely; they seem to have had some sort of falling-out. But why do you say Earl's disappeared? I saw him middle of last week, at the filling station."

Ripinsky and I exchanged glances. That made two sightings of the old man during the past week. While Bayard's memory might have been skewed by drug abuse, I was reasonably sure I could trust Rose's recollections. "Did he say anything about having been away? Or that he was planning to take a trip?"

"Well, he did mention he wouldn't be coming to our Bible study group last night. He's missed for a month or more now."

"And you have absolutely no idea where Peggy might be?"

"Well, she's always lived in the Bay Area, but it wouldn't surprise me if she'd put even more distance between herself and her father by now."

"Why?"

"Peggy needed to escape his clutches so she could have a life. After her mother died, Earl clung to that girl the way a parent does when he's got nothing else left. No one was ever good enough for her; he ran off every boy that ever showed an interest in Peggy—including somebody seated at this very table." She glanced pointedly at Hy, but his eyes were focused on the red-checkered tablecloth.

I asked, "She left Vernon as soon as she graduated from high school?"

"Right. She'd been accepted at Berkeley on a partial scholarship, but Earl didn't want her to go. They had terrific battles over it, and eventually she just packed up and took off, went down there and got some sort of job and put herself through college. It was years before she and her father mended fences, but even then it was push-pull, push-pull. No sooner would they start getting along than he'd start interfering. She blamed his butting in for the collapse of her first marriage. I don't suppose things will ever be right between them."

"And when she left for Berkeley, that's when Earl lost interest in everything and moved out to Stone Valley?"

Rose looked puzzled. "He moved to the valley, yes, but I wouldn't say he lost interest in things. What he did was become a fanatic."

"About what?"

"Like I said, he's a historian, at least when it comes to Promiseville and the mine his family used to operate." She looked at Hy. "Didn't you ever see his little museum?"

Ripinsky shook his head.

"That's right," Rose went on, "by the time he set it up, you'd left here yourself. But I'm surprised he never dragged you and Julie there; I thought the three of you were close."

"Julie was always fonder of Earl than I was." Hy shut his eyes, trying to call up a memory. "Now that you mention it, though, I think he may have taken her there back when I first knew her. I've got a vague recollection of something to that effect."

"Well, as far as I know, not many of us have seen it. Earl's gotten hermitlike in his old age."

Anne-Marie asked, "Where is this museum—in his cabin?"

"As a matter of fact, it's in what's left of the Chinaman's store out the end of Main Street. Earl collected old stuff that was left after the big fire—everything from mining equipment to household goods—and brought it all together there. He let me have a look around just once; it struck me as . . . well, kind of pathetic."

I recalled seeing a store near where I'd parked my car the day before, rusted cans and dusty bottles barely visible through its grime-caked windows. "How long ago was that?"

"Ages, it seems. He may have given up on it by now, but I kind of doubt that. That town and the old mine are Earl's obsession."

"If so, it's odd he would sell his land. Did he ever tell you how that came about?"

Rose's jaw pushed out pugnaciously. "He knows better than to talk to me about commercial mining in Stone Valley."

"Do you know that he got under fair market value for it?"

"No, but it doesn't surprise me. Earl doesn't give a hoot about money. What he does care about is seeing that mine operate again. It's part of his fixation, that Promiseville will rise out of its ashes." She snorted. "We all tried to get it across to him that a big modern mining operation will just spoil the place, but what can I tell you? Earl's not all that bright."

"Maybe he just wants you to think he's not bright," Hy suggested.

"I've known Earl pretty much all my life, and I can guarantee he's at least medium stupid." Rose glanced at her watch. "Will you look at that! It's after eleven already, and there's a Clint Eastwood movie on at half past. You're all welcome to watch it with me."

We declined politely, and Rose departed. Once she was gone, a listlessness settled upon us. I kept glancing at the door to the balcony, reliving what had happened on the dock the night before. When Anne-Marie signaled for the check, I expelled a sigh of relief.

The temperature had remained surprisingly warm, almost muggy, and there was a heavy cloud cover. We stood chatting in the parking lot for a few minutes. Anne-Marie looked

weary from her long hike, but now that we'd left the
restaurant I'd regained my energy and I sensed Hy felt
the same. He suggested he pick up a couple of six-packs at
the Swifty Mart and meet us back at the cabin so we could
brainstorm uninterrupted by Rose. I was agreeable, and
Anne-Marie didn't seem to care one way or the other, so we
reconvened and rehashed everything we knew about the
goings-on in Stone Valley—to the extent of several Buds and
no useful conclusions. Sometime during the last half hour
Anne-Marie fell asleep in her chair; it was close to two
before she roused herself, mumbled apologies, and stumbled off to bed.

Hy was still going strong. He stood up and said, "Let's
take a ride, McCone."

The idea appealed to me; I was too primed by the futile
brainstorming to sleep. "Okay," I agreed, getting up and
grabbing my jacket.

Hy picked up the remains of the second six-pack and went
toward the door, beer cans dangling by their plastic straps.
I followed, about to protest against drinking while driving,
but once outside he turned toward the lake.

"What . . . ?"

"A *boat* ride, McCone. I'm not about to get behind the
wheel."

"But where—"

"Quiet—you'll wake up the whole north shore." He waited
for me to lock the cabin door, then led me down the slope to
the dock where the lone warning light spread bloody stains
on the water. A rowboat was tied up beside it. Hy handed
me the beer and motioned for me to get in; then he untied the
lines, climbed aboard, and pushed off from the dock.

"Where are we going?" I asked, sitting down on the center
seat.

"No place. We'll just drift." Hy took the front seat, angling
his lean body so his knees were draped over one side. "Give
me a beer, will you?"

I did, and took one for myself. The popping of the tabs was loud in the still night; all I could hear was a faint rustling in the trees and the gentle lapping of the water.

"Awfully quiet, isn't it?" I said.

"You don't like quiet?"

I thought of another dark night not so long ago, remembered water lapping and trees soughing, and the terrible, final sound of a gunshot. "Sometimes it gets to me."

If he noticed any excess of emotion in my voice, he didn't comment, merely tipped his beer can and drank. I did the same, then set the can on the seat beside me and huddled inside my suede jacket.

"So," Hy finally said, "what do you really think?"

"About the situation here?"

"Uh-huh. I sensed you were holding back some while we were talking in the cabin, afraid of worrying Anne-Marie, maybe."

"I'm not really holding back, at least nothing concrete. It's more a feeling, the kind you get when something's wrong but you can't put your finger on it."

"Yeah, I feel it, too."

"This Tarbeaux alias that Erickson used—from what Ned told me about him, it strikes me as just the sort of joke he would play. Ned said he had a good sense of humor, but of a subtle, sophisticated sort. He must have enjoyed putting something over on the Bureau of Land Management."

"But why? Why not just patent the land in his own name?"

"Because of who or what he was, I suppose. His connection to Transpacific, maybe. We won't know until we know more about him. What about the real Tarbeaux, Hy? Did you do any reading on him after you realized where you'd heard the name?"

"Just what there was in the book I showed you. He played cards strictly for the money. Lulled the suckers into a false sense of security, then milked them for all they were worth. Bloodless bastard; a writer once described him as showing no emotion—only vigilance. Ice-cold and totally focused, that was old Frank."

Totally focused, perhaps obsessed. The way Rose Wittington had described Earl Hopwood. A zealot, as Sanderman had called Ripinsky. But wasn't Sanderman merely another type of zealot?

What made people that way? Well, the events of Earl Hopwood's life provided one answer: first he'd lost a young wife; then his possessiveness had driven his only daughter away. And Sanderman had plunged into his environmental work in the aftermath of a painful divorce. Hy had also lost his wife, and there had been things before that had turned him bitter and withdrawn—things I couldn't begin to guess at.

I said, "People whose dreams all died."

"What?"

"It's how the Tiger Lily described the people in the Promiseville cemetery. Your dreams die, and life narrows. You can turn inward, become obsessed, like Hopwood."

"You really talking about Earl, McCone? Or are you maybe talking about me?"

There was a rough undercurrent in Hy's voice, a hint of paranoia. I thought of Anne-Marie's assessment of him: "He's still dangerous."

I felt a tension in the boat now. Hy crushed his beer can and tossed it under the seat. When he reached for another, I shifted so his hand wouldn't brush my knees.

"Well?" he asked.

"I'm not sure," I said. "I could also be talking about myself."

He grunted disbelievingly.

But it was true—although up to now I wouldn't have admitted it. Lately I gave a good deal of lip service to how on-track my life was now that George and I were together; it had taken some probing on Anne-Marie's part to make me voice my reservations about where the relationship was leading. But events that I hadn't sought had changed me since George and I first became lovers, and the changes, while subtle, went deep.

I picked up my beer, drank, then cradled the can between my hands. From the grove came an animal's cry—swift, shrill, as if the creature had been seized as prey. The sound echoed and sent chills across my shoulder blades.

I shivered and closed my eyes against the bloody glow on the water. Remembered my impression upon arriving here that Tufa Lake was a place where echoes lived. There was also a place like that in the mind, where the past played and replayed. . . .

Hy said, "Go ahead and talk about it, McCone."

"About what?"

"Whatever it is that's eating at you."

I shook my head, even though I knew he could barely see me. Opened my eyes because even the bloody sheen on the water was preferable to the scenes that played in that place inside me. The silence lengthened, grew oppressive. And then I heard myself speaking swiftly in a little more than a whisper.

"This past year I almost blew two people away."

Hy waited.

"One of them was the most evil person I'd ever known. The other had just shot one of my closest friends. It's not as if I were a stranger to that kind of thing; I killed a man years ago, because I had no other choice. But this was . . . different."

"How?"

"Each time I really wanted to do it. I was completely in control. All I felt was this ice-cold rage. I wanted to . . . act as an executioner."

"But you didn't."

"No, but I came damned close, and there were repercussions. The first time . . . I still have nightmares in which I pull the trigger. The second . . . people were there, people

I care about. They saw the side of me that I try to keep hidden. And it changed things."

"You're an outsider to them now."

"It's as if I've stepped over some line, and they can't follow. No one's ever said anything to me, but they don't have to. Now there's . . ."

"A distance."

"Yes. And I can't do anything about it."

"No, you can't."

"But I keep wishing. I'm one of those people who think that if there's a problem, there's some way to push things around and solve it."

"You mean you *used* to be one of those people."

I'd suspected that, but it jolted me to hear it. After a moment I said, "Yes, I used to be. Now . . . I don't know. How can I go on doing what I do when I don't believe that anything can really be fixed?"

Hy was silent.

"I guess you just go on," I added. "At least that's what I've been doing. Going through the motions. Because maybe *some* things can be fixed. Because maybe there's . . ."

"Maybe there's what?" His voice was deeper now, enriched by some indefinable emotion.

"Maybe there's . . . something."

He slipped off the seat into the bottom of the boat and grasped my hand. "Come here, McCone."

I hesitated only a beat before I moved to sit beside him. He put his arm around my shoulders, and I tipped my head back against it. After a while he felt around and located the last beer. We shared it as we drifted in the silent darkness.

Part Two

▲ ▲ ▲

San Francisco

Nine

▲▲▲

Rae said, "So that's where
things stand with me. After I draft those two client reports
I mentioned, which won't take long, I can get started on the
skip trace on Earl Hopwood."

It was nine-thirty on Tuesday morning. My assistant
perched cross-legged on the end of the chaise longue in my
office at All Souls, clad in jeans and a russet sweater that
was a near perfect match for her freckles and curly auburn
hair. Although Rae's wardrobe had steadily improved as
Willie Whelan introduced her to the joys of deficit spending,
she still tended to choose shades that blended with her
natural coloring, thus conveying the totally false impression
that she was a bland little person. Was this a last vestige of
insecurity stemming from her early, emotionally abusive
marriage? I wondered. Or did it have to do with the fact that
she'd soon be a fully licensed private investigator and for
some misguided reason thought she had to appear inconspicuous at all times?

"Shar? Are you still in there?"

"I'm here. My mind was wandering. Listen, if Tracy Miller

101

at the DMV doesn't want to pull Hopwood's records so soon after the last time we used her, just let it go. This new privacy law has put her in a difficult position." The law on confidentiality of Department of Motor Vehicles information had been sparked by the murder of an actress by a deranged fan who had hired a detective to find out her address. Now the DMV, long one of an investigator's most valuable resources, would reveal nothing except to law enforcement agencies and such automobile-related businesses as insurance companies. My friend Tracy was still willing to run the occasional check for me, but I hated to ask her unless it was very important.

Rae asked, "If she doesn't want to, where should I go next?"

"Concentrate on getting a current married name for Hopwood's daughter and locating her. All I'm really hoping for from the DMV is a recent traffic citation on Hopwood that might tell us where he's been keeping himself—and that's a long shot."

She nodded and made a note on the pad she held. "How about telling me more about the case?"

"Tomorrow I will. I'll even spring for lunch. But today I don't have a minute to spare before I have to pick up my mother at the bus station at five-thirty."

Rae's blue eyes flickered and she quickly looked away. She was one of the All Souls people who had seen the coldly murderous side of me the summer before, and it was with her that I most noticed the seemingly unbridgeable distance. Before that she would have wheedled and badgered until I gave her the details of the case; now she merely arranged her face into coolly professional lines and awaited a dismissal.

I said, too heartily, "I meant to ask—how was your weekend?"

She shrugged.

"You and Willie do anything special?"

"Not really. Rented some videos, ordered in a pizza. Spent most of Sunday doing the wild thing."

". . . The what?"

"Wild thing. You know."

"You mean . . ."

"Yeah, that." She frowned, cocking her head, her earlier hurt forgotten. "You never heard it called that?"

"Uh, no."

"Well, what do *you* call it?"

"Making love."

"No, I mean informally. What does your generation call it?"

My generation. Quickly I reminded myself that Rae was over a decade younger than I; in many senses we *were* products of different eras. "Well, when I was in high school, we just said 'doing it' at first. But that was in the sixties and everybody wanted to be shocking, so before long it was 'fucking.'"

"And after that?"

". . . I don't know. I guess we fucked pretty much through the seventies, and in the eighties we 'significantly related' or some such godawful phrase. And now . . . I can't believe I'm having this conversation!"

"Why? This is historically significant stuff."

"Sure it is." But I had to admit it was far more absorbing than any other subject we might have been discussing. "In my older brothers' day, I think they said 'going all the way.' My parents called it 'taking a nap' and sent us all to my aunt's house."

"When I was in school, it was 'getting it on.' The grandmother who raised me called it 'having carnal knowledge' and forbade it."

"What a long way we've come—doing the wild thing. Can you also call it wild thinging?"

"Sure. You can even conjugate it: I wild thing, you wild thing, he wild things—"

"*Conjugate* it!" I clapped my hand over my mouth and snorted.

Rae looked puzzled for a few seconds. Then her lips formed a little O and she started to giggle.

I laughed harder. Rae let out a whoop and doubled over. As I pounded the desk with my fist, she slid from the chaise to the floor. And Hank stuck his head through the door.

"Am I interrupting an important conference?" he asked.

I wiped tears from my eyes and waved him in. Apparently he had a court appearance later that day, because he wore a gray suit and one of what he calls his "serious" ties. As he surveyed us he scratched his head, which every year resembles more closely a pad of steel wool, and behind his horn-rimmed glasses his eyes were bemused and begging to be let in on the joke.

Rae looked up from where she sprawled on my Oriental rug. "We were discussing conjugating," she said and burst into another fit of giggles.

Hank blinked. "You mean like 'I am, you are, he is'?"

"More like . . . never mind!" She stood up, grabbed her notepad from where she'd dropped it, and pushed past him. Her cackling was audible until her office door slammed downstairs.

I swiped at my eyes again, wondering if our mirth hadn't been exaggerated by mutual relief at finding we could still laugh together. Maybe such small shared moments would eventually bridge the distance, make it unnecessary for me to confront the issue. . . .

Hank took the place Rae had vacated on the chaise. "What was that all about?"

"We were discussing sex, more or less."

"So that's the significance of the leer she gave me when she left. God, the woman has a smutty laugh."

Briefly a silence fell between us—but a companionable one rather than the emotionally charged ones I experienced with Rae. If anyone should have changed in his feelings toward me, it was Hank: because I'd failed to adequately protect him, he had been near-fatally shot last summer, and in the aftermath I'd come close to killing the sniper in cold blood. But unlike those who witnessed my rage, Hank—one of my oldest friends and, in some ways, my dearest friend—had grown even closer. He is a man with that rare gift of viewing events on the positive side; in his opinion, I hadn't failed to protect him, but had saved his life by pushing him out of the path of a bullet. And my violence toward the sniper had only served to make him realize how deep my very platonic love for him runs.

After a moment he said, "Sex isn't a topic I care to dwell on just now, seeing as my wife has been away a total of twenty-three days. How does she seem to you?"

"She looks terrific, sounds terrific, too. Hank, it's as if she's come alive again."

"That's the impression I get from our phone conversations. To be happy, Anne-Marie needs a cause she can fight for; this job with the Coalition's given her that."

I hesitated, then asked a question I hadn't posed to Anne-Marie for fear she'd feel I was pressuring her. "Do you think she'll ever come back to All Souls?"

"No. And I wouldn't want her to. When we were fresh out of law school and just establishing the co-op, this was a stimulating atmosphere for her. But now . . . hell, we *are* establishment."

"What's wrong with that? We've gotten across the idea that people with low incomes are entitled to quality legal representation. Gotten it into the mainstream."

Hank took off his glasses and began polishing them on his handkerchief. "Nothing's wrong with that at all. I like being mainstream. I like having one of the deputy mayors call me up to pick my brains. Hell, I even like lunching with the crowd from City Hall. But Anne-Marie—she needs to be on the cutting edge of change."

"Even if it means spending so much time away from you and her friends?"

"Even if. And I wouldn't have it any other way." He put his glasses back on and stood. "I'd better let you get back to work. If you need extra time on this case of Anne-Marie's, take it. She promised me last night that the Coalition will reimburse us handsomely for your time."

"Handsomely?"

"Maybe she said adequately."

"Sounds more like it."

He winked at me and left the office.

I smiled as the door closed behind him. Our brief talk had reassured me that Hank and Anne-Marie's marriage was firmly on track. After their initial difficulties they'd settled into a relationship that was both close and free, supportive and hands-off. Maybe marriage didn't have to be such a confining institution after all. . . .

My eyes rested on the long-stemmed yellow rose in the vase on my desk. It had been delivered shortly after nine, wrapped in waxy green paper and tied with a yellow ribbon. No card, just a single perfect rose. On impulse I dialed the number of George's condominium on Russian Hill, even though I knew he'd be teaching a class at Stanford by now.

After the beep that his recorded voice warned me to wait for, I said, "Hi, I'm back—but I see you know that. Ma gets in at five-thirty. We'll be at your place with bells on at seven. Well, skip the bells. We'll just wear normal clothes and bring the wine and dessert as planned. See you then."

It had been too late to call him when I'd returned home, to an ecstatic Ralphie and Allie, the night before. En route to the city that morning I'd stopped in Bridgeport, a town of some five hundred people that sprawled on a high plain fifteen miles north of Vernon. Most of its business appeared to be tourist-oriented, and their glossiness contrasted sharply with the 1880s charm of the white Victorian courthouse that sat on a wide lawn on the main street. In the modern sheriff's department building on the street behind it—oddly enough called Bryant, the same as the one where San Francisco's Hall of Justice is located—I spoke with Kristen Lark about the Erickson homicide. The medical examiner, Lark told me, estimated the time of death at no more than two hours before Nickles and her dancing partner had spotted the body in the lake; the murder weapon had been a .22 caliber automatic. The investigating team had turned up no leads to where Erickson had been shot, where he'd gone into the water, or where he'd stayed in the area. His fingerprints had not matched any lifted after the break-ins at Ripinsky's home, the trailers, or the cabins at the lodge. Lark had contacted the SFPD, who in turn had notified Erickson's wife of his death.

"I requested background information on the victim," she said, "but I don't suppose I'll get much. They're backlogged there, and frankly, a killing in Mono County isn't a priority for them. Other than that he has a wife living at a fancy address and an office in a downtown high-rise, we don't know a thing about him."

Ned Sanderman hadn't bothered to contact her or Gifford, then. Briefly I related what he'd told me, then asked, "Where is Erickson's office?"

"Embarcadero Center." She took a business card from the file in front of her and pushed it toward me. "He had a little case full of these in the glovebox of that rented Bronco."

I examined the card. It was of good quality, the blue letters embossed on a pearl gray background: Cross-Cultural Concepts, Inc. In smaller type it said, "International Marketing Practices" and gave Erickson's title as president.

When I looked up, Lark was eyeing me hopefully. "We'll probably have to send somebody down to talk with the wife and his employees," she said. "That'll put a strain on our budget, and with upcoming vacation schedules, we really don't have anybody we can easily spare right now."

I seized the opportunity she offered. "How do you feel about private investigators cooperating in your investigations?"

"We're much looser here than in a lot of other jurisdictions, mainly because our tax base doesn't support us the way theirs do."

"I'd be glad to help by seeing what I can dig up on Erickson."

Lark grinned. "You know, I kind of thought you would."

I promised to stay in touch and took down the name of her contact on the SFPD Homicide detail—Bart Wallace, a man I knew and liked. Then I continued my trip over the Nevada border to Carson City.

There I avoided the reasonably expensive Ormsby House and concentrated on those casinos that looked to be the sort a backcountry prospector like Earl Hopwood would patronize. I drew blanks, however, when I showed his photograph around to their security personnel. In Reno I got similar results until, at the end of the Strip, I came upon a shabby casino advertising senior citizens' discounts, RV parking, and early-bird dinner specials. The head of security there recognized Hopwood's photo immediately.

"He's been a regular for ten, maybe twelve years," he told me. "When he's flush, blackjack's his game—the two-dollar tables. Otherwise he plays the slots—quarters, mostly."

"Have you seen him during the past two weeks?"

The man thought for a moment. "Not since last summer, come to think of it."

"Are you certain of that? Could he have escaped your notice or perhaps come in while you were on vacation?"

"No. Hopwood's a nice guy, the staff like him. Even if I didn't see him myself, somebody would have mentioned him being back. And I haven't had a vacation in over a year."

And that put a sizable hole in the theory that Hopwood was in Nevada blowing the proceeds of his land deal.

By then it was well after five. I took the free-drink coupon the security man offered and had a glass of wine and played a couple of games of keno in the casino lounge. For a while I contemplated going back down the Strip and taking a room at Harrah's or the Sundowner. I could have dinner, do a little gambling, and drive home fresh in the morning. But I found that Reno depressed me; on each of my infrequent trips it seemed increasingly tacky, a decaying small city full of hard-eyed hustlers and losers whose only hope was the elusive big score. It has none of the natural beauty of Lake Tahoe, nor the upscale glitz of Las Vegas, and the friendliness on which it used to pride itself has stretched to a phony smile that barely conceals the malignant pursuit of tourist bucks.

So in the end I grabbed a burger and coffee and headed back to the Bay Area. After fighting my way along a freeway snarled by nighttime construction in Sacramento and past an accident that closed two lanes on the San Francisco—Oakland Bay Bridge, I had arrived home at one-thirty, grumpy and exhausted.

But this morning Ralphie and Allie had awakened me with much purring and affectionate pawing, and I'd realized that tonight I'd see both George and my mother. In spite of my fears that the evening might turn out badly, I found myself looking forward to it. But first I had things to accomplish. . . .

I picked up the phone receiver again and dialed Homicide at the SFPD. Bart Wallace was at his desk and said Kristen Lark had already called him to explain that I would be cooperating with her on the Erickson investigation. Wallace had no problem with that and offered to assist in whatever way he could.

"All I need right now is the answers to a few questions," I told him. "Is the address for Erickson at Barbary Park current?"

"Yes. I went there myself and broke the news to his wife early Sunday morning."

"And the wife's name is . . . ?"

"Margot. With a *t.*"

"How did she take it?"

"Badly. She thought her husband was on a business trip to Japan. Finding out he wasn't where he'd said he'd be made it even worse."

"Were you able to question her?"

"Not in any detail. I'd planned to go back, since Mono County requested further info, but now they've got you to take up the slack."

Wallace sounded pleased; from my knowledge of the typical homicide inspector's caseload, I could understand why. I thanked him and hung up.

Next I went down the hall and knocked on the door of Larry Koslowski's combined office and living quarters. Our senior corporate specialist and resident health nut was busy at his computer but welcomed me cheerfully. I sat down and waited for him to finish the entries he was making.

Larry's room has a pleasant jungly feel, with verdant moire walls and a greenhouse window where he grows the weeds and seeds that natural-foods enthusiasts deem essential to their well-being. A rack next to the marble sink holds a blender, measuring implements, and dozens of bottles and jars filled with strange leaves and pills and powders. I often wonder if his new clients don't think they've mistakenly wandered into the laboratory of a mad scientist.

A couple of years before, Larry had been my Santa for the annual All Souls Christmas present drawing. What I received was a big plastic bag of a substance resembling sawdust—an instant version of his breakfast protein drink. The bag is still tucked away in a corner of my pantry, but Larry, who has no way of knowing that, takes credit for setting me on the path to renewed health and vigor. Periodically, around New Year's or Lent, he conducts a purge of the co-op's kitchen, hurling out refined sugar, Spam, Oreo cookies, bleached flour, and Hamburger Helper. We would all hate him for such excess, save for the fact that he can occasionally be found guiltily indulging in a pizza (with both anchovies and pepperoni) or sucking up as much beer as any of us down at the Remedy Lounge on Mission Street.

After a minute or two he swiveled back from his desk and faced me, smoothing his waxed handlebar mustache. "Where were you yesterday?" he demanded. "Ted and I wanted to order from Mama Mia's, but without you we couldn't get enough takers."

So Larry had fallen off the wagon again; Mama Mia's was the co-op's pizzeria of choice. "I went up to Tufa Lake to help Anne-Marie out, took an extra day on the weekend."

"Right—Hank mentioned that. A case?"

"A murder case now. I'm assisting the Mono County Sheriff's Department."

Something stirred in Larry's soft brown eyes—a mere shadow that told me the word "murder" had called up memories of that night last July. But unlike Rae's reaction, it was gone quickly; Larry is older than she, has seen more of the world's unpleasant side, and is not a man who dwells on past events.

I added, "I think you may be able to help me."

"Sure. How?"

"Have you heard of a consulting firm called Cross-Cultural Concepts? They have offices in the Embarcadero Center, and their business card claims they're into something called international marketing practices."

Larry's eyes narrowed thoughtfully. "I don't recognize the name, but I can tell you what they probably do. It's a fairly new area of specialization that's sprung up to cope with the problems associated with the growth in international trading, particularly with Pacific Rim countries. Firms like the one you're asking about educate business people on how to deal with customers and clients of other cultures, whose practices and expectations may be different from their own."

"Sort of like business etiquette?"

"In a way. For instance, if you're going to be trading in Japan, they teach you how to select the proper gifts to present to the customer. They might take you to Japanese restaurants and educate you about the foods and the use of chopsticks. Overseas clients are trained in similar ways, so they can operate smoothly in America."

"I see. It sounds like a scam to me."

Larry shrugged. "It's a legitimate service, but a lot of the less reputable consultants take advantage of the fact that its parameters aren't terribly well drawn."

"Okay, another question: What do you know about the Hong Kong—controlled business community here? In particular, Transpacific Corporation."

"Transpacific. Very little, other than that their CEO is Lionel Ong. Ong's reputed to be one of the most flamboyant and brightest of the Hong Kong money elite. But that's all I know; the person you want to talk with is Marcy Cheung at the Sino-American Alliance."

"What's that?"

"Trade organization for overseas Chinese doing business in the U.S. Marcy's their publicity director and a good friend of mine. Let me see if I can reach her." He swiveled back to the desk, looked up a number, and dialed.

After asking for Cheung three times, he said, "Marcy, Larry Koslowski. How you doing? . . . Not bad. Have you tried that recipe for kasha varnishkas yet? . . . Like varnish, huh? . . . No, that's not what 'varnishkas' means, but I guess buckwheat groat's an acquired taste . . . You don't want to acquire it? Well, that's your problem. Listen, will you do me a favor? Our head investigator needs to talk with somebody about Transpacific Corporation. You have any free time?" He listened for a moment, then asked me, "Can you be at her office in the financial district around two?"

"Yes."

"She'll be there," he said into the phone. "Her name's Sharon McCone . . . No, she's not undernourished. As a matter of fact, she resists my dietary suggestions. But I'll convert her yet. This woman adores my instant protein drink, and from there it's only a short step. . . ."

Ten

▲ ▲ ▲

The red brick town houses of Barbary Park were scattered throughout an urban oasis four stories above the sidewalks of the financial district. Beneath the landscaped grounds were offices and shops, an underground garage, and a health club, but they seemed far removed from the park's container-grown conifers and hawthorns and Japanese maples. Even the traffic sounds that filtered up were muted, as if in deference to the residents' desire for tranquillity.

I'd called Margot Erickson to arrange an eleven o'clock appointment, and she'd sent my name down to the reception desk in the building's lobby. A rosewood-paneled elevator took me to the park level; from it I followed a pebbled path past a koi pond spanned by a humpbacked stone footbridge to number 551. Like the other buildings, it was two-storied and ivied, with arched windows and an abundance of skylights; each of its four units had a private glass-roofed entry court.

The uniformed maid who came to the door was Filipino. She showed me into a large living room, then disappeared up a flight of stairs. The room's windows faced the bay, and through them I could see Alcatraz, that rocky, precipitous island topped by empty cellblocks and unmanned guard towers, no longer a prison but nonetheless a subtle reminder to us all.

I remained standing in the center of the room and looked around. A flagstone terrace to the left of the windows was full of white wrought-iron furniture and plants in ceramic tubs. The living room itself was a confection of cream and peach and pink, too artfully arranged to be comfortable. Except for a few Asian artifacts such as a verdigrised bronze lion and an Imari bowl on a lacquered stand, nothing marred the bleached-teak tables; there wasn't a book or magazine in sight, and I couldn't even detect vacuum-cleaner tracks on the pristine cream carpet.

A photograph on the mantel of the marble fireplace caught my attention, and I crossed to take a closer look. It showed a man and a woman seated close together on a stone wall, a rocky seacoast in the background. As Ned Sanderman had told me, Mick Erickson had been handsome. His prematurely white hair curled bushily about his head, catching the sun's rays; his youthful face was deeply tanned, fine lines crinkling at the corners of his eyes as he smiled at the woman. She wore a lacy pink sun hat that covered her hair except for a fringe of blond bangs; her face was on the round side, dimpled, with a rosy glow. Both looked to be in their mid-thirties, at ease with each other, and—then, at least—happy with their lot in life. I spied evidence that difficult times might have followed, however: the glass over the photograph was cracked, and one side of its silver frame was dented, as if it had been thrown at something—or someone.

The sound of feet padding lightly on the carpet was all that alerted me to Margot Erickson's presence. As I turned, she came toward me, graciously holding out her hand. She was shorter and more fine-boned than she looked in the photo, and beneath her beige silk jumpsuit her body seemed too thin. I found myself clasping her extended hand gently, as if it might break.

If she had noticed me studying the picture she gave no sign, merely motioned for me to sit and dropped into a chair herself, crossing her slim legs and running a hand through her close-cropped sun streaked hair. Her face was pale under its tan, her gray eyes shadowed and reddened by grief. Prominent lines that hadn't been noticeable in the photo were etched on either side of her mouth.

I sat on the sofa and placed my briefcase on the coffee table in front of it. "I'm sorry to bother you at a time like this," I told her.

"I understand that it's necessary." Her voice had the harshness of the habitual smoker's; she reached for a porcelain box, extracted a cigarette, and lit it with an unsteady hand. As soon as she exhaled, she made a face and stubbed it out. "During the past three months I've cut down to only five a day," she said. "But in the past forty-eight hours I've smoked enough to make myself ill."

"That's natural."

"Yes, but it's also weak, and I don't like myself for it. I've always thought I was strong and could face anything that came along. What I've realized since Sunday morning is that I'd never had anything major *to* face."

"Do you feel up to talking about your husband, Mrs. Erickson?"

"It would be in my best interests, wouldn't it?"

That struck me as an odd way of phrasing it. "Of course," I said as I took my tape recorder from my briefcase. Margot Erickson glanced apprehensively at it, and at first I thought she might object, but when I asked if it was all right to record our conversation, she merely shrugged her assent.

Once I had the tape going, I said, "I understand that it may be painful to answer some of the questions I have to ask, so I'll try to be brief. Inspector Wallace tells me that you were unaware your husband was in the Tufa Lake area—had, in fact, thought him to be in Japan."

The expression that passed over her face surprised me; although it was there and gone in an instant, I was certain I'd glimpsed relief. "As far as I knew," she said, "Mick was in Tokyo conducting a series of seminars for one of his Japanese clients."

"What sort of seminars?"

"Teaching executives how to interact with the American business community. Mick's firm specializes in cross-cultural education for the Asian sector."

"And he had been away for . . . ?"

"Four days."

"Had you heard from him in the interim?"

". . . No."

"Not at all?"

"No."

"Did you find that odd?"

"Not really. He was in touch with his secretary. Connie was to relay any necessary messages to me."

"Such as?"

"Well . . . changes in Mick's travel plans. Things he wanted me to take care of." Her hand strayed toward the cigarette box; she pulled it back into her lap. "Actually, Ms. McCone, there wouldn't have been any messages. Mick and I . . . we hadn't been getting along. We both viewed the trip to Japan as a trial separation."

"I see. May I ask—"

"No." She shook her head, clearly wanting to be off the subject. "It was purely a family matter and had no bearing on . . . what happened to him."

"Let's talk about Tufa Lake, then. Do you know of any reason your husband would have gone there?"

"No."

"Did he have friends there or some other connection with the area?"

"No."

"You seem quite definite about that."

"Of course. Mick was my husband; I would have known."

"But during the past four days, Mr. Erickson kept his whereabouts from you. Even given the separation, that's unusual. Isn't it possible he might also have withheld information about a connection in Mono County?"

". . . It's possible."

The admission should have disturbed her, but again relief flickered in her eyes. Margot Erickson struck me as a woman who normally told the truth, would lie only out of extreme necessity, and then with difficulty. Her alternating apprehension and relief probably had to do with some line of questioning she was afraid I'd start on—but I was damned if I knew what it might be.

I asked, "How long have you and Mr. Erickson been married?"

"Seven years."

"Had you known him long beforehand?"

"I . . . What does this have to do with his death?"

"Seven years is a relatively short time span. People can be married dozens of years and not know all that much about each other's past."

"I see what you mean, but I'd known Mick for quite a while before we married. He and his former wife lived next door to my former husband and me in Mill Valley; our divorces and remarriage caused one of those little neighborhood scandals." She laughed nervously. "I'd say I know him as well as it's possible to know another person. Or I thought I did."

"About the second set of identification Mr. Erickson was carrying—Franklin Tarbeaux's—had you ever heard the name before?"

"Never." But her face tensed and she looked away. Lying, and as I'd suspected, with difficulty.

"Are you sure?"

"Of course I'm sure!"

"Did your husband have an interest in history—the Old West, perhaps?"

"I don't see what—"

"Frank Tarbeaux was a frontier gambler and con man. Apparently your husband adopted a slightly altered version of his name as a sort of joke."

Now she looked surprised. After a moment she said, "Well, Mick likes to gamble. We go to Tahoe several times a year, and in his den he has a collection of books on the history of gambling. I suppose that's where he got the name." She paused, reflecting on what she'd just said. "It's so hard to speak of him in the past tense. I keep expecting him to walk through the door and put our lives back together the way they were before. . . ."

"I understand. And I'll try to finish as quickly as I can. What I'd like to do is run some names by you—people and places your husband might have mentioned."

"Go ahead."

"Ned Sanderman."

"No."

"Transpacific Corporation."

"That's one of Mick's biggest clients."

"Lionel Ong."

"Of course. Lionel *is* Transpacific."

"Were Mr. Ong and your husband friends or merely business associates?"

"More business associates. In the past five years I think we've attended at most three dinner parties at Lionel's house."

"Did your husband ever mention Stone Valley or Promiseville?"

". . . Not that I recall."

"You're not aware that Transpacific has recently bought land in Stone Valley and plans to reopen an old gold mine there?"

"I . . . may have heard something to that effect."

"What about Earl Hopwood? Is that name familiar?"

She closed her eyes. After a moment she shook her head wearily. She was even paler now, and the shadows under her eyes had taken on darker definition. I felt sorry for the woman and would have backed off, had it not been for the undercurrent of falseness I sensed in some of her responses.

I said, "Just a few more questions, Mrs. Erickson. Have you ever heard of the California Coalition for Environmental Preservation?"

She opened her eyes, nodded. "I'm a member of the Sierra Club, so I receive their solicitations."

"What about the Friends of Tufa Lake?"

"I've seen the name."

"Heino Ripinsky?"

"What on earth is . . . What does ecology have to do with this?"

"The environmentalists want to stop the Transpacific mining project. Did your husband have any technical knowledge of gold mining?"

"I . . . I suppose he did. He had a degree from Colorado School of Mines."

"But he never discussed the Transpacific project—at least in any way that indicated he might be connected with it?"

She leaned forward, elbows on her knees, hands over her face. Through her fingers she said, "I don't recall. I . . . just don't recall."

I switched off my tape recorder. Enough was enough, I thought. "Mrs. Erickson, I'm sorry for putting you through this."

She shook her head and made a gesture that said no apology was necessary. Then she stood, glancing jumpily around the spun-sugar room as if its walls were closing in on her. Without a word she turned and ran toward the stairway.

Feeling like what my niece Kelley calls a "horrible sadistic monster," I packed the recorder in my briefcase and prepared to leave. The Filipino maid appeared in the doorway, her face impassive, waiting to see me out.

Before I crossed toward her, I let my gaze wander around Margot Erickson's unlivable living room. There was emptiness here, and sterility, and something else. . . . Fear? Yes, fear. Its pervasive presence made the pretty room as formidable a prison as the one visible in the distance through the windows.

Eleven

▲ ▲ ▲

Cross-Cultural Concepts occupied a handsome suite on the ninth floor of Embarcadero Two. Like the Erickson town house, its decor was sterile and expensive, but the reception area and those offices that I glimpsed exuded masculinity in what had to be a calculated effort to reassure clients from male-dominated Pacific Rim countries. The forest green carpeting, dark paneling, and leather furnishings seemed to say that in spite of being an American firm, and therefore subject to all sorts of foolish notions about equal opportunity, Cross-Cultural Concepts knew who *really* held the reins of world commerce.

Connie Grobe, Mick Erickson's secretary, complemented the offices perfectly. While she didn't look masculine, her severely styled dark hair and tailored clothing would have better suited a clerical robot than a woman. The fashion magazines say that the "power suit" of the eighties has given way to a new softness and femininity in clothing now that we women—so they claim—no longer need to prove ourselves. Connie Grobe apparently didn't pay attention to their opinions, and as I followed her down the corridor to her office, I reflected that her thinking might be justified. What with the recent court reversals on abortion rights and comparable pay for comparable work, I was beginning to suspect that soon we'd have to start proving a few things all over again. . . .

Grobe's office was a small cubicle on an inside wall: a bank of file cabinets, a desk, and two chairs. No window; maybe the powers that be at Cross-Cultural thought secretaries really were robots with no need for light or fresh air. As I sat in her visitor's chair I experienced a residue of the anger I'd felt when I worked part-time as a guard for one of the city's large security firms while putting myself through college. Every Friday I'd go in to pick up my meager paycheck and see the clerical staff stuffed into tiny, airless cubicles, while the spacious windowed offices of the bosses—who were usually out in the field or wining and dining prospective clients—stood empty. It was back then that I'd vowed I'd never become the victim of a system that abused its clerical workers and then tossed them out the same way it did pencil stubs and bent paper clips.

When she'd settled herself on the other side of the desk, Grobe folded her hands and asked, "May I see some identification, Ms. McCone?"

I slid my leather I.D. folder across to her. She studied its contents for a moment before handing it back. "And is there someone on the police force whom I may contact to verify that you are working with them on the investigation of Mr. Erickson's death?"

Swallowing my annoyance—after all, the woman had a right to be cautious—I said, "You can contact Inspector Bart Wallace on the Homicide Squad of the SFPD. Or Detective Kristen Lark at the Mono County Sheriff's Department."

She made notations on a scratch pad but didn't ask for phone numbers. After staring at the sheet for a moment, she sighed and ripped it off, balling it up before tossing it into the wastebasket. At my surprised looked she said, "Excessive caution was something required by Mick Erickson, Ms. McCone. But Mick is dead, so it doesn't matter anymore, does it?"

"I guess not. Why was he excessively cautious?"

"Many of our clients are major Pacific Rim corporations. The political ramifications of their business dealings in the United States can be extremely widespread and serious. Others are in sensitive positions, such as a number of our Hong Kong firms who wish to move their assets here before the territory reverts to the People's Republic in nineteen ninety-seven."

"Transpacific Corporation is one of those?"

"Not precisely. Transpacific is an American corporation. Their CEO, Mr. Lionel Ong, is a naturalized citizen and a graduate of Harvard Business School."

"But they *are* funded by Hong Kong interests?"

She hesitated. "When I said that excessive caution doesn't matter anymore, I meant as it applies to Mick Erickson, not our clients. As long as Cross-Cultural is a legal entity, I'm bound to protect them."

"That's fair. Can we talk about Mr. Erickson's supposed trip to Japan, then? His wife tells me he was presumed to be conducting a series of seminars for an important client."

Connie Grobe's mouth tightened, for exactly what reason I wasn't sure. "The client was Sumeri International, in Osaka."

"And Mr. Erickson's travel arrangements were made through this office?"

"Travel arrangements, shipment of materials for the seminars, all the attendant details."

"Did Mr. Erickson contact you after his departure?"

"Yes, by telephone upon his arrival in Japan. At least that's where he claimed he was."

"And after that?"

"He told me when he called that his plans had changed, that he would be out in the field at their various locations. If I needed to get in touch with him I was to contact the Sumeri office here in the city."

"Not their offices in Osaka?"

"No."

"Did that strike you as odd?"

"A little, but Mick often conducted his business in unorthodox ways."

"Did you have need to contact him through Sumeri's local office?"

"No. Mick travels frequently; the office is set up to run well without him. I would have needed to get in touch only in case of an emergency."

And he'd counted on that, I thought. "May I have the name of the person you were to contact here?"

She hesitated, then shrugged. "I suppose it would do no harm. His name is Mr. Hiroshi Kamada."

I made a note of it. "When Mr. Erickson called in while traveling, did he typically use a credit card?"

"If he was in an airport or some other public place, yes. Otherwise the calls were billed to his hotel room, or he called at the client's expense."

"So unless he was in transit and used his credit card, you would have no immediate way of knowing the origin of the call?"

"That's correct."

"This trip to Japan—had it been planned for a long time?"

"Actually it came up rather suddenly." She bit her lower lip, pain evident in her eyes. "Our staff worked very hard in overtime to prepare the materials for the seminars. Mr. Erickson canceled two lectures for important clients here in order to make the trip. Finding out he was merely covering up some deception makes me angry. Angry and terribly sad."

His wife wasn't the only one Erickson had betrayed, I

thought. Somehow Connie Grobe's self-proclaimed anger and sorrow were more poignant than the leashed grief and latent fear I'd sensed in Margot Erickson.

"Ms. Grobe," I said, "in a homicide investigation it's often necessary to focus on very personal aspects of the victim's life. Do you have any problem with discussing what you know of Mr. Erickson's private affairs?"

She considered. "No, I don't," she replied after a moment. "Mick's dead, and the important thing is to find out who killed him. What do you want to know?"

"Margot Erickson told me she and her husband viewed the trip to Japan as a trial separation. Were you aware of that?"

Again her mouth tightened; this time I realized that it was a reflexive reaction to the mention of Margot. "I could hardly help but be aware of it. Mick had been sleeping on the couch in his office for a month. I'd say that was the trial separation."

"He slept here for an entire month? Why didn't he go to a hotel or rent an apartment?"

"I suppose he was hoping they would work things out. And, of course, there was the problem of finances. That town house in Barbary Park is outrageously expensive; when Mick and Margot bought it, mortgage interest rates were very high. They planned to refinance when the rates dropped, but in the meantime it was costing more than he could afford."

"Are you saying that Mick Erickson was in financial trouble?"

"Not really. If anything, his finances were about to improve. You see, this firm was originally a joint partnership between Mick and his former wife. When they divorced, she moved back east to establish a similar company, and he had to buy out her interest in this one. He made his final payment to her a few months ago, and without that expense, his financial position was bound to get better."

"I see. Let's get back to the Erickson marriage for a moment. All Mrs. Erickson would say about the separation is that it was strictly a family matter."

Grobe nodded. "That's all Mick would say, too."

"In your opinion, what did they mean?"

"Perhaps something to do with having or not having children."

"Why do you think that?"

"Mick and Margot were a couple, not a family in the sense the word is normally used. They'd both been married before, but neither had children."

"Did either want them?"

Grobe's gaze grew introspective. "I think Mick did," she said. "I'm a single mother; my son Jon is ten. Mick had season tickets for the Giants games, and he took Jon along a few times. Both of them really seemed to enjoy the time they spent together."

"Did Margot go with them?"

"No. Jon used her ticket; she seldom went, because she hates baseball."

"How do you think she feels about having children?"

"I don't know, but I can't imagine Margot as a mother." Grobe allowed herself a small but malicious smile. "After all, she might lose her size-four figure."

I was silent for a bit, thinking over her theory about the breakup of the Erickson marriage. They were in their mid-thirties—a now-or-never age for starting a family. If one partner was intent on doing so and the other not (here I felt a twinge about my own lover's intentions), it could cause serious difficulties. But I wondered about Grobe's evaluation of Mick's feelings on that issue; a few pleasant outings to baseball games with an employee's son did not constitute an overwhelming desire for children of his own.

When I probed for more details about the couple, the only thing I really learned was how much Connie Grobe disliked Margot. She didn't know the woman well, had never seen her socially, and had been to the town house only a few times to drop off some papers. Her feelings, I decided, were merely the not uncommon reaction of the employee who works side by side with her boss while his wife stays home and, to the secretary's way of thinking, idly reaps the fruits of their labors.

Grobe expressed considerable surprise that Mick's body had been found at Tufa Lake; she knew of no personal or business connection he might have had in the area, could think of no reason for him to have gone there. She had never heard the Tarbeaux name, and she claimed she knew nothing of Transpacific Corporation's plans to began working the old Promiseville mine. Finally I thanked her and departed with only twenty minutes to spare before my two o'clock appointment at the Sino-American Alliance.

I used a few of them to call Hiroshi Kamada at Sumeri International's local office. He was a good deal less cautious than Connie Grobe about giving out information—a fact I took to mean that borderline paranoia did not permeate the entire Pacific Rim business sector. Kamada said that he'd been asked by Mick Erickson to act as a message taker for him for a few days. Kamada was merely to hold any messages until Erickson called in for them.

Had he called in? I asked.

No, Mr. Kamada said, he hadn't. But there had been no messages to pass on, anyway.

What about the materials for the seminars that Erickson's office had shipped to Sumeri's headquarters in Osaka? I asked. Hadn't their arrival seemed strange to the staff there, seeing as there was no program scheduled?

Oh, no, Mr. Kamada told me. I did not understand. The materials were for *next* month's seminars.

So that was how Mick Erickson had engineered his excuse to drop out of sight: the contract for the Sumeri seminars was legitimate; he'd merely misrepresented the date. I wondered how he'd planned to explain that when the actual date for the presentation arrived.

As I hung up the receiver of the pay phone, I thought about Erickson's motivation. The reason for his trip to Mono County must have been very sensitive and secret in order for him to concoct such an intricate scheme to permit only a few days' unexplained absence. A few days—to do what?

The one thing of which I was certain was that it had to do with Transpacific's plans to reopen that mine. Perhaps Marcy Cheung at the Sino-American Alliance could shed some light on both the company and its CEO, Lionel Ong.

Walking along the easternmost blocks of Jackson Street near the Embarcadero and the U.S. Custom House is like stepping back into old San Francisco. Although they are virtually in the shadow of the Transamerica Pyramid—our prime example of the architectural excesses of the late twentieth century—and only a brief stroll from the noisy steel-and-glass canyons of the central financial district, these few blocks are quiet, narrow, and tree-lined. Their renovated brick buildings, many of which date from before the 1906 earthquake, house small businesses, antique shops, and furniture-and-fabric showrooms. The Sino-American Alliance had the whole ground floor of one, on the corner of an alley with a Parisian-style sidewalk café tucked away at its end.

The tranquil feel of the street permeated the reception area. Its decor was typical Chinese—black lacquered furnishings, melon-jar lamps, scroll paintings—and even the sleek-haired woman who presided over the desk wore jade green watered silk with a mandarin collar. As she buzzed Marcy Cheung's office and announced me, her movements were unhurried, her voice as soft as my footfalls on the apricot-and-blue floral rug.

After I passed the tri-paneled silk screen behind the desk, however, I realized that the calm had broken; on its other side a storm of ringing phones, clacking typewriters, and raised voices raged. And when I entered the room labeled Publicity Department, I was abruptly thrust into the whirling eye of chaos.

Two desks overflowed with heaps of photographs and papers; file drawers gaped open, their contents protruding at odd angles; color slides were scattered on a light table; a sketch hung three-quarters off a drawing board. The walls were a layered mass of posters, fliers, and schedules. One of the latter, headed "December Issue," had a big red X drawn through it, with a dart stuck in its center. And on the floor, surrounded by more stacks of papers and photographs plus the remains of a lunch, sat a young woman with waist-length hair that was fastened at the nape of her neck with a rubber band. Her blue-jeaned legs were folded Indian-style, her feet were bare, and she hunched forward, reaching for half of a deli sandwich as she spoke into the phone. She didn't bite into the sandwich, merely waved it to punctuate her words.

"*You* got problems? Well, so do I. My idiot assistant quit. And I need those proofs today, dammit!"

I stepped around a blown-up plastic dragon that breathed a fiery banner: "The Sino-American Alliance Wishes You a Happy Chinese New Year!"

"I don't *care* how much it'll cost you to messenger them over here—just do it!" She slammed the receiver down just as a slice of tomato fell out of her sandwich and bounced off her knee, leaving a streak of mayo. "Shit," she said miserably and looked up at me.

Marcy Cheung had a round, slightly pockmarked face and a chipped front tooth. As soon as she smiled at me, she clapped an ink-stained hand over her mouth and mumbled around it, "I busted it white-water rafting two months ago and still can't afford to get it fixed. You'd think I'd have gotten over being self-conscious by now. Are you Sharon?"

"Yes. You're Marcy?"

"Uh-huh. I'd offer you a chair, but . . ." She motioned around; all of them were stacked with boxes, papers, and magazines.

Fortunately, I was wearing dark-colored slacks. I sat down on the floor near her, avoiding the slice of tomato, which she seemed to have forgotten. "No problem."

She dumped what was left of the sandwich into a wastebasket. "So," she said, "Lar tells me you hate health food."

"Yes. I can't believe you actually tried his recipe for buckwheat groats."

"I didn't—I lied to him."

"I never tried his instant protein drink, either."

She smiled, unconcerned about the chipped tooth this time, and held out her hand. We shook, our rapport firmly established.

The phone beside Cheung buzzed stridently. She glared at it, snatched up the receiver, and said, "I can't talk—I'm busy." The she depressed the disconnect button and left the receiver off the hook. "It's the only way I can get any peace around here."

"Your office is . . ."

As I was searching for a word that wouldn't offend, she finished for me. "A hellhole."

"And on top of that your assistant quit."

"Yeah." She looked around glumly. "He was an absolute idiot; it may have been the only smart move of his life."

"I feel bad about taking up your time."

"Don't. If you hadn't come in I'd still be arguing with the printer—another idiot. Lar said you want to know about Transpacific Corporation."

"And Lionel Ong, if you know anything about him."

"Why?"

"I'm investigating a homicide in cooperation with the SFPD and the Mono County Sheriff's Department. One of Ong's associates was shot."

"Do they suspect Lionel?"

It was not the question so much as the matter-of-fact way she asked it that surprised me. "So far, no. I'm after background information."

"My boss probably wouldn't want me talking about one of the members. But if it's police business, I guess I should. And you asked at the right time." She stretched out a bare foot and pulled a cardboard file box toward her with her toes. Felt-tip markings on its side said, "Feb. Interviews."

"These," she said as she rummaged in the box, "are materials for our February magazine. We send it out to the business community at large, plus politicians, trade associations, anybody else who might be interested. This one's to showcase our Hong Kong members—or it will if I ever get it out. My assistant was supposed to tape the interviews, but he only did two. Somehow I've got to do three more, including Ong.

"Anyway," she went on, extracting a file and extending it to me, "this is the research I did on him in preparation. You're welcome to look at it, make copies if you like."

"Thanks. But first, would you mind telling me about him in your own words?"

Cheung crossed her outstretched ankles, put her arms back for support, and promptly set one hand down on the forgotten slice of tomato. Her nose wrinkled violently. "Oh, *gross!* I can't believe—"

I reached into my jacket pocket and brought out a reasonably clean tissue.

"Oh, thanks. I'm such a slob. You know, I went to J-school—journalism—at Northwestern, and the whole time I pictured myself all dressed up in a terrific suit shouting terribly penetrating questions at a White House press conference. So instead I end up in jeans on the floor of my crummy office, up to my wrists in slimy tomato pulp."

"Don't feel bad: I studied sociology at Berkeley and dreamed of doing Important Research that would Help

People. Instead I ended up running skip traces. And once getting shot in the ass."

Cheung stopped scrubbing at her hand and stared at me, clearly fascinated. "Really? That must have hurt like hell."

"Plus you can imagine how embarrassing it was."

"Still, there must be a lot of satisfaction in your job. I mean, in a way you *are* doing that important research."

I shrugged. In my up moments I tend to romanticize what I do—the memory of which is always vaguely humiliating in my down moments. During those, I often bleakly reflect that I'm fighting, and mainly losing, a minor skirmish in a global war.

Cheung said, "Well, to get back to the subject—in order to understand Lionel Ong, you've got to understand the Hong Kong money elite. You know much about them?"

I shook my head.

"First of all, except for a few patriarchs, they're relatively young—forty-five, tops. And they control billions. They're also extremely well educated; the rich Hong Kong families send their sons and daughters to the best U.S. colleges and business schools—Harvard, Wharton, M.I.T., Stanford, Michigan—and then turn over their U.S. operations to them."

"What kind of operations are we talking about?"

"Real-estate development is the big one; they own about a tenth of the downtown here. They're also into parking garages, hotels, apparel companies. Lately there's been an increase in the number of Chinese-owned banks. Not many restaurants." Cheung smiled. "Too risky, and you can't move enough money that way. Besides, these people shy away from stereotypes.

"They're the real movers and shakers in San Francisco finance these days," she went on. "Very well connected politically, with a lot of clout with City Hall and the state legislature. Family ties are important; that's the Chinese way. And they can be tough adversaries."

"How so?"

"Have you ever heard of Sun Tzu's *The Art of War?*"

"No."

"Well, it's a twenty-five-hundred-year-old classic work on military philosophy. There's an in joke that the Hong Kong business community patterns its strategies on it. But nobody really laughs at that. Let's just say they're people who don't enjoy losing—at *any* game."

I thought of the bullet holes in Mick Erickson's chest and the armed Chinese guards on the mesa above Stone Valley. "How far would they go to avoid losing?"

"That would depend on the individual."

"And if the individual were Lionel Ong?"

She considered. "I'd say he'd go very far indeed."

"Tell me more about him. I know the facts are in the file, but I'm also after subjective impressions."

"Just as you've got to understand the Hong Kong money elite to understand him, you've also got to understand the Ong family. They're hard-driving and ruthless. A lot of deprivation and tragedy in their past. According to my research"—she motioned at the file—"they came out of Guangdong province in south China in the thirties, during the Japanese occupation. I'm not clear on the details, but a couple of the children died, and the mother—Lionel's grandmother—was shot to death during the border crossing. Once they got to Hong Kong, the grandfather became relentless; in less than a generation the family went from virtually nothing to billions."

"In what industry?"

"Primarily shipping."

"Lionel was born in Hong Kong?"

"Yes. Attended Saint Stephen's Prep School—a lot of the elite did. The grandfather chose him over his older brother as the one to guide the family enterprises. Lionel was sent to Stanford and later to Harvard Business School with only two instructions—to earn top marks and become an American citizen. And those were all the instructions he needed."

"The entire family is in the U.S. now?"

"Just Lionel. The rest will probably remain in Hong Kong until all their assets are moved out of there and the territory reverts."

"Where does Ong live?"

"Here in the city. Most of his peers favor the upscale suburbs—Hillsborough is most popular—but Lionel prefers to be close to the action. He's got a huge house just below Sutro Tower—needs it, too, since he and his wife have done their duty to the family by having five kids. Not that it slows him down any; most of the Hong Kong families like to keep a low profile, but Lionel's all flash. Sharp dresser, drives a red Mercedes convertible with vanity plates, lunches in all the right places with all the right people. There's a girl-friend—Caucasian—living in a Transpacific-owned condo in Telegraph Hill, and another for weekend getaways in Sausalito."

"So he's smart, shrewd, and self-indulgent."

"He's a moneymaking machine that's fueled by greed and instant gratification. That's all he's supposed to be; the grandfather didn't see the need to instruct him to be hu-man."

Cheung's voice had taken on a bitter tone. I could under-stand how a man like Ong would be an affront to a modern and thoroughly American young woman of Chinese descent.

I wanted to ask more, but the receptionist appeared at the door, her brow creased in annoyance. "Marcy," she said, "will you *please* put your phone back on the hook? The printer's called three times now."

"The idiot! I told him—" She broke off and took the file from my hands. "Listen, if I promise to put it back on the hook, will you make copies of these for me?"

"It's a deal." The woman took the file and disappeared down the corridor.

Cheung made no move toward the receiver. To my questioning look she said, "Not until she brings your copies back."

"I'm really sorry to have taken so much of your time when you're swamped with work." And then I thought of a favor I could do her—which would also help me. "Marcy," I said, "how about if I conduct the interview with Lionel Ong? I interview people every day, and I'm good at it. You have a prepared list of questions, don't you?"

She was looking surprised but somewhat receptive. "Uh-huh. And as I said, it's to be taped, so you wouldn't even have to transcribe it. Besides, you could be the worst interviewer in the world and still do better than my former assistant."

"Have you scheduled an appointment with Ong?"

"For four o'clock tomorrow afternoon at his home."

"Well, how about it?"

"Why not? It would sure free up my schedule."

"Do you mind if I add some questions of my own?"

"Not at all. If it's material I can use, I will; otherwise I'll edit it out." She hesitated. "A couple of things, though: I don't ever want it to get back to my boss that I talked this candidly about Ong. Or that you're anything other than a professional interviewer who's doing me a favor."

"Fair enough."

"Just remember to watch yourself. Lionel Ong would make one hell of an enemy."

Twelve

▲▲▲

After I left the Sino-American Alliance, I walked down the alley next to the building and took a seat at an umbrellaed table outside the little café. I wanted a Pernod with my steamed mussels—in memory of my one trip to France—but in the interests of clear thinking I ordered mineral water instead. As I ate I read through the file Marcy Cheung had given me. The background on Lionel Ong was a bare-bones sketch of what she had told me, but the information on Transpacific Corporation held my attention.

For one thing, their recent divestments and acquisitions struck me as inconsistent with their intention to go into large-scale commercial mining. There was no history of involvement in heavy industry, unless you counted shipping in that category—which I didn't—and most of those assets had been liquidated as the company moved its operations to the U.S. Here Transpacific had acquired commercial real estate, including office buildings, parking garages, and hotels. It held a minor interest in the city's newest Chinese-owned bank. But many of its downtown properties had been sold several years ago in order to finance a large resort complex in Carmel Valley, and plans were under way for a second in Palm Desert.

I wondered why Ong and his associates had decided to plunge into such a different field of endeavor. And how had they learned of the gold-mining potential in Stone Valley in the first place? Through Mick Erickson, most likely. But where had they acquired the expertise to evaluate the feasibility of the project? Geologists had been hired, of course, but they could only make recommendations; it was the management team's responsibility to make the final decisions. And why diversify now, when to all appearances the company's focus had been narrowing? I'd have to talk to Larry about this, see what he thought. If I needed information on exploration and development of natural resources, I could ask George to refer me to someone in his family's former company; the Kostakos money had been made in oil and natural gas.

Finally I turned to Cheung's list of questions for the Ong interview. They were straightforward, designed to place him and Transpacific in the best possible light. I read through them twice, marked a few places where I could insert questions of my own without interrupting the flow or alerting him to the fact that I was after anything more than a flattering puff piece. Then I stuffed the file in my briefcase, paid the lunch tab, and went to hand over an amount that I was sure would be only slightly less than the value of my car to the Embarcadero Center parking garage.

It was after four when I got back to All Souls. Ted and the Xerox repairman were in conference over the corpse of our oft-dead copy machine, so I grabbed my waiting messages and took them upstairs. The only one requiring immediate attention was from Kristen Lark. I dialed Bridgeport and spoke with three people before she came on the line.

"I was just checking to see if you'd come up with anything on Michael Erickson," she said.

I explained what I'd learned so far, summing up, "I'm fairly certain his wife is afraid of something, but I can't pin down what."

"Well, her husband was just murdered. I don't know about you, but that would throw me some."

"Of course, but this is different."

"Maybe she's got reason to suspect they'll come after her next."

"Maybe, but I don't think that's it. I had the impression it was more a fear of something I might ask, something that might come out during the investigation."

"Why did she agree to talk with you, then?"

"It probably never occurred to her not to. I said I was working with the police; I have the feeling Margot Erickson is one of those people who wouldn't dream of not cooperating with the authorities. On the other hand, she could have agreed because she wanted to find out how much I know."

"You think she knew what her husband was doing here?"

"I doubt it. He covered his tracks so well even his secretary thought he was really in Japan."

"They both could have been lying."

"Anything's possible. I'm just going on my gut-level reaction here."

Lark sighed. "Sometimes that's all you *can* go on. You say he was out of contact with his office after the first phone call?"

"Yes."

She was silent for a moment. Finally I said, "Kristen?"

"Just thinking. There are a few things I didn't tell you when you stopped by yesterday morning. Didn't think you needed to know, just to gather background material on the victim for us. But given the kind of things you're finding out . . . well, I'm telling you now. First, there were bruises on Erickson's body, looked like he'd been in a fight. They weren't inflicted at the time he died—too well developed for that—but the fight could have taken place earlier that day."

"Okay. What else?"

"That rented Bronco—it had been wiped."

"Completely?"

"No, just the steering wheel, shift, door handle on the driver's side."

"Keys in it?"

"Yes."

"So someone moved it after he disposed of the body."

"Looks like. We checked for hair and fiber samples, anything that might identify whoever drove it, but all we came up with was dirt and leaves—could have come from anywhere in the area."

"Any evidence it was used to transport the body?"

"None."

"So it was moved only to cover up where he was killed."

"Probably. What we found and didn't find in the vehicle is interesting, too. We didn't find any clothes, suitcase, shaving gear; since he'd shaved that day, he must have had stuff with him, left it wherever he was staying. But we haven't been able to get a line on where that was. And what we did find was a gun—forty-four Magnum—in the glovebox. It had been fired three times and fairly recently."

"You trace the gun's ownership?"

"We're still working on that, but it wasn't registered to Erickson."

"Any fingerprints on it?"

"A few partials, not enough to identify them. And the deceased's."

"And no shootings reported?"

"None."

I thought for a moment. "He could have been using it for target practice."

"Maybe." But Lark sounded doubtful.

I thought a bit more, but came up with nothing that made sense of her mixed bag of findings. "So where are we?"

"Things are even less straightforward than before."

"Well, maybe my interview with Lionel Ong will produce something useful. I'll keep you posted."

"You do that, McCone. And send me the tape of your interview with Erickson's wife." With characteristic abruptness, Lark hung up.

I stuffed the tape into a mailer, addressed it to Lark, and put it in my out-box. There was a note from Rae on my desk, saying she wanted to talk with me. I went down to the converted closet under the stairs, smiling as I recalled my earlier thoughts about the bosses' offices standing empty while the staff toiled in cubicles. But I myself had occupied Rae's closet until Hank bequeathed me the room upstairs after he married Anne-Marie and moved out of the co-op, and Rae's name wasn't far down on the waiting list for larger space once it became available. In the meantime she had made the most of her cramped quarters. The walls, once faded yellow, were now pale blue, covered with a collage of posters from art exhibits at the de Young Museum. She'd refinished the battered desk, installed a good light fixture, even imported a ficus plant that thrived on the rays from an ultraviolet bulb and frequent airings on the service porch. It embarrassed me that in a short time she'd managed something I hadn't gotten around to in years.

She was at her desk, making notes on a legal pad, the tip of her tongue caught between her teeth as she struggled to write legibly. When she saw me she put down her pencil, sighing with relief. "I didn't think you'd get back this afternoon, so I was just drafting a report," she said, "but now we can talk in person."

I started to sit in the ratty armchair she'd inherited from me (even that was spiffed up with a blue-and-white slipcover), but she stopped me. "Don't—I'm feeling claustrophobic. Besides, you could probably use a glass of wine before you pick up your mother."

I looked at my watch. "My mother and the dessert to take to George's. But I've got a little time, so let's."

We went back to the big old-fashioned kitchen at the rear of the house, and Rae dug out glasses while I located a jug of Chablis in the overcrowded fridge. After we sat down at the round oak table by the windows, I propped my feet on a chair and asked, "So what were you putting in your report?"

Rae's round face lit up in triumph, as it always does when she scores an investigatory coup. "The DMV had a recent traffic citation on Earl Hopwood."

"Great! Where and when?"

"Here in the city—corner of Clay and Sansome. A month ago yesterday—illegal left-hand turn."

The intersection of Clay and Sansome is in the financial district, in reasonable proximity to where I'd been earlier.

"What do you think?" Rae asked.

"I think you did good work. Keep trying to trace the daughter. Check Vital Statistics for marriages and divorces— she's rumored to have had three. Maybe Cal has a current address for her—or the alumni association."

Rae looked vaguely disappointed. I supposed she'd thought the information about Hopwood's traffic citation more important than it was. But the financial district encompasses many people and places; he could have been visiting any one of its numerous offices or just passing through.

After taking a sip of her wine Rae asked, "Do you have time to tell me about the case?"

"Briefly, I can."

As I spoke she nodded periodically, then scrunched up her face in concentration. "Nothing fits," she said.

"Not at this point." I looked at my watch again, saw it was close to five. "I'd better get going if I'm to pick up the cake before I fetch Ma."

"You getting it from Elena's?"

"Yes. Her Double-to-die-for Chocolate Fudge Cake."

Rae rolled her eyes. "She'll love it!"

"She'd better," I said—a shade grimly.

"This morning you told me you were looking forward to the dinner."

"It's one of those events that pales as it approaches. Just as Ma's visit was a more pleasant prospect in the anticipatory stages than in the countdown. I'm looking to survive it, that's all."

Thirteen

▲ ▲ ▲

Your friend must be a mountain goat to live in a place with so many steps," Ma grumbled.

I set my teeth and climbed doggedly, ignoring her and clutching the bag containing the wine and Elena's Double-to-die-for.

"How do old people like me get to their apartments? Or don't they let seniors in here?"

"Old people who live on Russian Hill stay in shape because of all the climbing they have to do."

"Humpfh" was Ma's only comment.

Actually, her complaints about the steps leading to George's building—thirty-six in all; I'd counted them one day while we were hauling up a heavy load of groceries— were the first she'd uttered since I'd picked her up in front of the Greyhound station. She'd been unusually quiet as I drove her to my house, got her settled in the guest room, and introduced her to Ralphie and Allie—behavior that put me more on my guard than if she'd carped about the fact I was five minutes late fetching her.

We reached the top of the wide stairway, and Ma stopped, surveying the courtyard. Set atop a reinforced concrete wall high above Green Street, the white Mediterranean-style building had an elegant and faintly decadent atmosphere that was straight out of the 1920s. Its fountain was vintage mosaic tile; the planters looked like marble funerary urns; the balconies and Moorish arches were overhung with gnarled wisteria vines. Late at night when the foghorns bellowed outside the Gate and the courtyard was shrouded in mist, one expected to see sinister figures gliding through the faint light from the wrought-iron lanterns, or lovers entwined in the hurried embraces of assignations.

Ma was seeing nothing so romantic, though. She said, "I hope he lives on the first floor."

"Second." I nudged her toward the private staircase to George's flat.

My mother gave a martyred sigh as she began climbing again.

Her complaints, I knew, were mere ritual, totally lacking in substance. At sixty-two, Ma is as spry as I am and equally healthy. We have the same body type—medium height and slender—and except for the gray streaks in her red hair, anyone following us upstairs could have taken us for sisters. But Ma considers it her God-given right to complain about any number of things at any time, and in a way I suppose she's entitled. After all, she's raised five troublesome Mc-Cones, tended to numerous grandchildren, and put up with my father's many idiosyncrasies for more than forty years.

George came to the door wearing a blue-and-white-striped apron that I'd given him as a joke present for his birthday last August. As always, I felt a rush of pleasure at the sight of his tall, trim body and handsome rough-hewn face, which was now flushed from the heat of the kitchen. An unruly lock of gray-frosted hair hung over his forehead. He hugged me clumsily because of the asbestos mitt he wore, removing it before shaking hands with my mother. Wonderful smells came from inside.

"What's that?" I asked as we stepped into the hallway.

"That stew—you know, with all the spices and the biscuits baked on top."

Ma looked impressed. I smiled knowingly. George's harried domestic appearance was all show to get Ma on his side; the stew came frozen from a little bistro down on Hyde Street; you heated it, then opened a roll of refrigerated buttermilk biscuits and browned them on top. I hoped George had thought to throw the wrappings down the garbage chute, in case Ma decided to snoop through his kitchen.

He added, "Why don't you take your mother into the living room? I'll be along with champagne."

"Champagne," Ma said. "Huh."

I wasn't sure what that meant, but decided to not ask and led her down the hall to the front of the flat, where the windows looked toward the bay over the roofs of the facing buildings. Ma set her purse on a side table and gave the room a good once-over. George's taste in furnishings ran to modern, but conservative modern; apparently she couldn't find fault with the sand-colored walls and deeply cushioned brown sofa and chairs, but she did look askance at a chaotic abstract painting over the fireplace and a bent-wire sculpture on the coffee table. There was a plate of pâté and crackers next to the sculpture; Ma, who hates liver and never even made us eat it as kids, sat down as far as she could get from it.

George came in with a cheese platter, set it down, and went back for the champagne. Ma moved a little closer to the cheese. When he returned, he made a big production of opening the champagne, pouring, and toasting "the two lovely McCone ladies." I winced inwardly, afraid he was laying it on too thick, but to my surprise, Ma actually blushed.

Maybe the evening was off to a good start after all.

"What time did your plane get in?" George asked her.

"I came by bus. I don't go up in the air or cross water, if I can help it."

"Makes sense to me, given the airlines' safety records these days."

"It's also less expensive." She gave him a severe look. "I don't suppose that matters to you, though. Sharon tells me you're quite wealthy."

My champagne went down the wrong way and I started to cough. George came over and patted me on the back, his hazel eyes dancing in amusement.

"Yes," he said over my head, "that's true. I wish I could say I'd earned it, but it's only inherited."

"Money," Ma told him, "is fine, so long as you don't let it rule you. I myself have a high respect for the value of a dollar, and I've tried to pass that along to my children."

I stared at her in amazement. The importance of money had been de-emphasized in our household, largely because no one remotely connected with the McCones ever had the ability to attract it.

"I wouldn't feel uncomfortable about your inheritance if I were you," Ma added. "After all, you work. Stanford is a very good university."

George went back to his chair. "My father raised me to believe that regardless of how well off they are, adults should do some sort of useful work."

Ma nodded and relented so much as to smear a dab of pâté on a cracker. "Your father was right. Andy—that's Sharon's father—and I tried to instill that attitude in our children. Unfortunately, they all resisted it except Sharon. But they are very independent, very much their own persons."

Now my mouth fell open. My older brothers, John and Joey, have spent most of their adult lives moving in and out of my parents' big rambling house in San Diego. Charlene lived there during each of her six pregnancies. Patsy never goes home, but she's managed to cadge a substantial amount of money from our folks over the years. And Ma has always viewed my independent ways as evidence of some major character flaw.

George refilled my mother's empty champagne glass. I frowned. Ma had never been much of a drinker. She smeared another dab of pâté on a cracker, wolfed it down with apparent enjoyment, and leaned forward confidingly.

"Are you Catholic, George?"

"No, I'm afraid not."

She waited.

"I was raised Methodist."

"Well, then you believe in something." Ma took a swig of champagne and proceeded to rewrite family history.

Misrepresentation: She and Andy were very devout.

Fact: Ma hasn't been to mass in at least ten years, and my father spends his Sunday mornings puttering in the garage while singing dirty folk songs.

Misrepresentation: We children were raised in the church and had good Catholic educations.

Fact: John and Joey attended Catholic school, but were expelled for too-frequent fighting and other disgraceful episodes that to this day nobody will talk about. Being the family's only white sheep, I made it through catechism, but Charlene was dismissed as incorrigible, and Patsy flatly refused to go at all.

Misrepresentation: Our solid Catholic values had continued to stand us in good stead and guide us once we were out in the world.

Fact: John is divorced. Joey lives in sin off and on. I gave up going to both confession and mass the summer I was sixteen and had sex for the first time. The size of Charlene's family has nothing to do with papal dictate and everything to do with the fact that until she got her tubes tied she never quite got the hang of any form of birth control. And Patsy's three children were born out of wedlock, each to a different father.

History revised, Ma now got around to raising the issue I'd been dreading. I refilled my glass and braced myself.

"You're recently divorced, George?"

"Yes, ma'am."

"Not because of my daughter here, I hope."

"Uh, no. My marriage was over long before I met Sharon."

"You'd grown apart?"

"Yes."

"Felt stifled?"

"That, too."

"Decided to cut your losses while both of you were still young?"

"That's right."

"Well, in spite of being Catholic, I've always felt that was the sensible approach. Life is too short to be ruined by vows made when you were too young to know what was what. Even if they were made in the sight of God."

Suddenly I knew what people meant when they said, "You could have knocked me over with a feather." In our household, divorce was lamented as if there had been a death in the family. It was the "d" word—as unspeakable as the one that began with "f."

"I appreciate your understanding," George said. Then he flashed me a bemused look and went to toss the salad.

"A very nice man," Ma said when he was out of earshot. "Sensible. Mature. Of course, the good looks and money are pluses, too." She waved a hand at the archway to the dining room, through which a well-set table, including candles and cut flowers, could be seen. "I like a man who works at making a nice home for himself."

All day I'd been praying that she'd approve of George, but now I had to bite my tongue to keep from revealing that the table-setting and last-minute straightening-up had been done by his cleaning woman.

Dinner went splendidly. The stew was perfect, and George had even remembered to transfer it from the telltale oven and microwave-safe container to a casserole. While we ate I chatted about my trip to Tufa Lake, omitting the part about the murder, which would only have unsettled both of them and wasn't proper dinner-table conversation, anyway. Then George explained to Ma about his forthcoming book: a self-help manual utilizing a behavioral model derived from various classical and modern schools of thought. Ma seemed fascinated; she kept asking which of "those little circles that you fit people into" she was. When George told her he suspected she belonged to a group he labeled as leaders, she seemed gratified. I had to stuff a piece of biscuit into my mouth to keep from blurting out that some of the category's less desirable attributes were ruthlessness, tyranny, and megalomania.

After dinner we took coffee and dessert into the living room. Ma had grown a little quiet again, but I assumed it was because she'd gotten the answers she wanted to the questions she'd come prepared to ask. She excused herself and went down the hall to the powder room, but was back so fast I knew she hadn't even troubled to snoop through the master bedroom and bath for the toothbrush and robe I kept there. And as we wound down the evening, she posed no embarrassing questions about George's intentions toward me. At the door she kissed him on the cheek, told him he could call her Katie from now on, and took the lead down the staircase—never once complaining about her poor old joints. It wasn't until we were halfway to my house that I remembered I'd forgotten to thank George for the yellow rose he'd had delivered to my office that morning.

When we arrived home, Ma seemed disinclined to go to bed, so I lit a fire and asked her if she'd like some tea or more coffee.

"Do you have brandy?" she asked.

I wasn't sure she should have any more alcohol, but

somehow it's difficult to eighty-six one's own mother, so I brought her a snifter and a small glass of wine for myself. Ma sat in the rocker near the fireplace with Allie curled into a calico ball on her lap.

"So," I said, feeling an unreasonable desire to needle her, "do you think I should move in with George?"

"You could do worse. He's a good man, and that's a very nice condominium." She looked around my seldom-used front parlor. "But I wouldn't sell this house if I were you. It must be worth quite a bit by now. You've done well for yourself, Sharon."

This was not—*could* not be—my mother speaking. In her canon of wicked institutions, live-in relationships ranked right up there with divorce.

"I suppose your approval is a ploy to get me to marry him," I said.

Ma sighed, stroking the cat. "Sharon, you sound like a ten-year-old. It's no ploy. I just want you to be aware that when it comes to marriage, you should be very, very careful."

Now I *knew* an alien had taken up residence in my mother's body. For years she'd deplored my single state, practically begged me to marry every reasonably presentable man who had come along. If arranged marriages had still been the thing, she'd have visited a matchmaker as soon as she brought me home from the hospital.

I asked, "What do you mean—be careful?"

"Just that." She took a sip of brandy and set the glass on the table next to her. "And now that we're on the subject, I'd better tell you why I'm making this pilgrimage to see all my children. It's to break the news in person. Sharon, I have left your father."

It was one of those pronouncements that rendered a person speechless. Senseless, too: my mind went blank; I simply couldn't think.

After what seemed like a long time, Ma added, "I've already spoken with John and Charlene and made them promise not to discuss it with anyone until all of you children know. I expect you to do the same, until after I've seen Patsy and Joey."

Words finally came. "Ma—why?"

She was silent.

"What did he do to you?"

Now she looked amused. "Andy? *Do* something to me?"

"Well, he must have. You don't leave a man you've been married to for over forty years for no reason."

Again she was silent, reaching down to pet Ralphie, who was brushing jealously against her legs and leaving yellow hairs on her black pantsuit. Finally she said, "Sharon, for those forty-some years I haven't had a life. I've been a wife to Andy, a mother to you children, a mother-in-law, and a grandmother."

"That wasn't enough?"

"Would it be enough for you?"

"No, but you're . . . different."

"You mean I'm your mother and I'm not supposed to want anything more. But I do. I have—for a long time."

"And you think you'll find it by leaving Pa?"

"I don't know, but I need to try. Whatever comes of leaving him will at least be different from the way it would have been if I'd stayed. I am sixty-two years old. I want something for myself before I die."

"What does Pa think about all this?"

"Naturally he's not too thrilled about the idea. But you can't expect a man who's hidden out in the garage for fifteen years to be terribly upset."

She had a point there, although surely she exaggerated how long it had been going on. In recent years Pa had seemed more absent than present. Often he slept all night in his workshop on a cot that he claimed was only for naps. I thought of what my mother's days must be like now that her children were scattered along the West Coast from San Diego to Portland: she had less to do, but few outside interests because she'd never had time to develop any. What friends she had came in couples, but my father had grown less and less inclined to socialize, so she went through the motions—cleaning and shopping and washing, making largely unappreciated meals and caring for the occasional grandchild.

But didn't that happen to other women of her age? What did they do? They took up hobbies, went to classes, joined clubs. Instead of leaving my father, why for god's sake couldn't my mother take up quilting?

And then I realized that there was more to this than she was telling.

"Ma," I said, "is there . . . ?"

She watched me, expression unreadable in the firelight.

"I mean, do you . . . ?"

She smiled. Dammit, she was *enjoying* watching me struggle to ask if she had a lover!

Finally she relented. "There is a gentleman, yes. He takes me places and talks to me and treats me like a lady. He gives me champagne and cooks me dinner like your friend George does for you. And of course we also enjoy other things—"

I held up my hand in an "I don't want to know about those things" gesture. "Ma," I said, "who is this man? Where did you meet him?"

"His name is Melvin Hunt. He's fifty-seven." She grinned wickedly. "A younger man, and quite well off. I met him at the Laundromat where I have been going every week for three years because your father can't be bothered to fix my washer and won't pay for a repairman."

"He can't be that well off if he hangs out at the Laundromat."

Ma gave me a withering look. "Melvin *owns* the entire chain."

"Oh. Well, do you plan to marry this man?"

"No, I don't. But as soon as I get back to San Diego, I'm moving in with him."

Now I understood her tolerance of me moving in with George; it *had* been a ploy, to get me to accept her live-in relationship with . . . what's-his-name. And I also understood the other things that had puzzled me during the evening. Her rewriting of family history was an attempt to reassure herself that she had done well by her children and now deserved to enjoy a new life. Her sudden approval of money and tolerance of divorce were mental adjustments made to justify her future plans.

"Ma," I said, "how long have you been seeing this man?"

"He has a name, Sharon. And I've been seeing Melvin for a year now."

An entire year. Through all those phone calls and last Thanksgiving dinner and my brief visit in May she'd been hiding the existence of this . . . person from me. From all of us. Stunned, I stood up.

"Where are you going?"

"Bathroom. If you like, help yourself to some more brandy." She would, too. She'd developed some pretty fancy tastes since being with . . . him.

I hurried down the hall and through my informal living room and kitchen to the bathroom. Shut the door and leaned against it.

This can't be happening, I thought. Mothers aren't supposed to up and run off with men they meet in Laundromats. Not even if the man owns the whole goddamn chain.

How could she do this to me?

Tears flooded my eyes. I tried to blink them back, but they came anyway.

Now look what she'd made me do!

This whole thing was ludicrous, unseemly. Having an affair with this man. She just wasn't acting her age!

Damned if I was going to let her make me cry, though.

I switched on the light, put my hands on either side of the

washbasin, and leaned in toward the mirror. It was a trick Ma had taught each of us at an early age: seeing how ridiculous you look when crying always makes you stop.

The face that looked back at me could have been that of a squally little baby. Except its hair had a long gray streak that had been there since its teens. And there were laugh lines around its eyes. And there was a wrinkle that I'd never noticed till now. . . .

How could she do this to me?

Now look what she'd made me do!

She just wasn't acting her age!

She wasn't acting her age?

My pout vanished as laughter bubbled up. The heretofore unnoticed wrinkle on my brow smoothed. The tears stopped.

I chuckled. Put my head back and howled with laughter.

The door opened. Ma said, "I thought I'd find you in front of the mirror. It works every time, doesn't it?"

Fourteen

▲▲▲

I was at my desk by eight-thirty the next morning. At home in my guest room my mother slept the sleep of the righteous—something I wasn't at all certain she was entitled to. My first act was to try to reach my father in San Diego; the phone rang a dozen times before I realized he was probably out in the garage where there wasn't an extension. Next I called my brother John's number in Chula Vista, but got only the machine for the housepainting company he runs out of his apartment. No one was home at Charlene's, either, and Ma had forbidden me to speak with my other siblings.

This is ridiculous, I thought. In the midst of the biggest family crisis ever, there isn't a McCone available to discuss the problem.

Still glowering, I sipped coffee and paged through my desk calendar. I had nothing on tap until one, when I was to meet with an assistant D.A. to go over my testimony for an upcoming murder trial. As I scanned my file on the case, my somber mood deepened; it was the one I'd been working when I met George, and the facts seemed as sordid and depressing today as they had many months before. I needed no real preparation for the conference, so I quickly turned my attention to more pressing business and dialed the number of the Coalition's trailer in Vernon. There was no answer, so I called the one next door that housed the Friends of Tufa Lake.

Ripinsky answered. He sounded sluggish and grouchy—he was clearly not a morning person—but brightened when I identified myself. "Hope you're calling to report something positive."

"Actually, only to ask a question."

"Go ahead."

"The first night I was there you mentioned you'd taken a public relations tour of the mine site and spoken with Transpacific's supervising geologist. Was he on their staff or a consultant?"

"Consultant. I've got his card here someplace. Hold on." There was a clunk as he set the receiver down. He came back on the line about half a minute later. "Got it. His name's Alvin K. Knight. Address on Los Palmos Drive there in San Francisco." He read it and the phone number off.

"Is there a company name?"

"No, the card just says 'mining geologist.' Probably a one-man operation."

"Odd—I'd have thought Transpacific would use a large firm for a project of this size."

"Maybe the guy's good, McCone."

"Maybe." I hesitated. "Hy, is everything okay there?"

"Except for the fact that Ned's still in Sacramento and Anne-Marie is mightily pissed at him, yes."

"No more break-ins or . . . anything?"

"Everything's copacetic. In fact, I've got so little to do that I'm thinking of closing the office and taking the day off."

"Where's Anne-Marie? I tried the Coalition's trailer, but there wasn't any answer."

"At her cabin, working on the project that was interrupted when she came down here."

"So what you're both doing is waiting for me."

"That's about it."

"Well, I'll try to come up with something soon."

"Do that. And keep in touch."

I hung up, then dialed the number of Alvin K. Knight, mining geologist. Another machine answered and took my message; sometimes I hate the cheerful efficiency of answering machines.

There were routine tasks that had to be done—the record keeping and correspondence that are the downside of a private investigator's job. By eleven-thirty I'd fielded five phone calls and waded through most of the paperwork. Since the calls had all been vaguely annoying, I glanced irritably at the flashing light when the sixth came through, and hit the intercom button rather than just picking up.

"What?" I demanded.

"And top o' the morning to you," Ted said.

"Sorry. I wasn't here for the usual Monday hassles, and Tuesday went all right, so I guess Wednesday's out to get me."

"Apology accepted. It's George—that should perk you up."

"Thanks." I punched the flashing button. "Hi. Have you recovered from Ma's visit yet?"

"What's to recover from? She was charming. In fact, she just called and suggested we have lunch so we can get to know each other better."

"*What?* Are you going?"

"Sure. I don't teach today, and I was at loose ends."

"Well, good. Maybe you can talk some sense into her. You know what she sprang on me last night after we got home?" I went on to tell him in considerable detail about Ma's plans.

When I finished he was silent for a moment. "Well, I can see where that comes as a shock."

"A shock? It rivaled the big quake! She's making an awful mistake."

"Are you sure? From what you've told me about your parents, they haven't had much of a marriage for some time now. And if she's been seeing this Melvin for a year, it's not a snap decision."

"That's not the point, George."

"What is, then?"

". . . I don't know. It's just . . . Oh, hell, I don't want to discuss it now. Where are you taking her?"

"She hinted that she's never been to Top of the Mark."

"God! I never should have told her you've got money."

"I've got nothing better to do with it than spend it."

Was that his way of telling me he had no child to leave his considerable fortune to? Or was I merely being paranoid? Quickly I said, "Well, I'll let you go now so you won't be late for your big date."

"Wish me luck."

"I think you'll need it."

I hung up and swiveled around to stare out the bay window behind me. In spite of the sunlight and the fall color on the trees, the triangular park in front of All Souls looked drab and uninviting. Across it, the facing houses looked shabbier than usual and abandoned. Sometimes when I contemplated the view from my office window I had the eerie feeling that I was the only person left on Bernal Heights, everyone else having fled some imminent danger whose warning signs I'd failed to notice.

Although I knew the delusion was only the product of a momentary mood, it wasn't an isolated instance, and it seemed to come more frequently of late. Was I still suffering from posttraumatic shock induced by the events of last summer? Or by the big earthquake? Neither seemed likely, but if one or the other wasn't the cause, I didn't want to speculate. . . .

I turned back to the desk and buzzed Rae to remind her I

was buying lunch today. Her reaction to my mother's bomb-shell was certain to be more satisfying than George's, and perhaps my family crisis would further help us to bridge the chasm between us, just as laughter had the day before.

Much of San Francisco is laid out in a grid pattern—the Avenues in the western part of the city are a good example of this—but when one ascends to the hills, all semblance of orderliness vanishes. Here the prime objective is to gain as much of a view as possible; the streets meander precipitously close to sheer drop-offs, and the precarious position-ing of the houses is testimony to the marvels of modern engineering, or to man's foolishness. It's easy to get lost in the tangles of lanes and cul-de-sacs that crown our hills—which is exactly what I did when I went looking for Lionel Ong's home late that afternoon.

When I reached the street that borders Sutro Forest, an urban wilderness at the base of the rust-red futuristic communications tower, I realized I'd gone wrong, so I retraced my route and found I'd overshot Saint Germain Avenue a block below. It was narrow and short, ending in a brick retaining wall beyond which tall conifers and cy-presses framed a panoramic view. The houses to the right were built high on the slope so their windows could look out over the roofs of their neighbors; those on the left—Ong's side—were low and sprawled down the hillside.

The Ong house was light gray, surrounded by a high wall that was actually an extension of the three-car garage. Above it I could see the spiky leaves of yucca trees and part of the house itself: a series of angular protrusions containing skylights and small windows that glinted in the late-afternoon sun. The gate was of heavy crosshatched timbers; an intercom was set into the wall next to it.

I pressed the buzzer and identified myself to the male voice that answered. Within a few seconds the gate swung open, and I stepped into a stylized courtyard full of yucca and citrus trees; the entrance to the house was directly across it. As I approached, a man appeared, stood framed in the doorway.

He was of medium height and slender, with thick black hair and cool appraising eyes. They sized me up as I moved toward him, then became properly welcoming and polite, as if some internal switch had kicked on, storing whatever information he'd gleaned from observing me and shifting him into a more sociable demeanor.

"Ms. McCone." He came forward, hand extended. "I'm Lionel Ong."

I shook the offered hand and followed him into a stark black marble–floored foyer. Its walls were winter white and devoid of ornamentation; the rays that fell from the central skylight did nothing to warm them. Wide sliding doors bisected the wall directly ahead of us, but they were shut.

In attire, Ong matched the room: he wore black suit trousers; his black silk tie was loosened; the sleeves of his white shirt were rolled up a couple of turns to expose a watch with a heavy gold-link band that seemed too massive for his fine-boned wrist. The look was casual—and calculated. I sensed Ong did nothing, not even roll up his shirtsleeves, without considering what the visual effect would be.

"You had no difficulty finding me?" he asked.

"Some," I admitted. "I'm not overly familiar with this area."

"Not many people are—that's one of the reasons I chose it. It's quiet, and a good place to raise my family."

It certainly was quiet; I couldn't hear a sound, and none that would indicate the household contained five children.

Ong seemed to realize what I was thinking; he smiled. "My family is in Hong Kong visiting relatives, and I've given my help the time off. We'll talk in my den." He gestured toward a wrought-iron spiral staircase that descended to the lower level.

The room down there had a wall of plate glass opening onto a terrace that overlooked the northern sprawl of the city and the distant bay. Two other walls were covered with built-in bookcases that appeared to be constructed of white pipe trusses; more trusses with an ornamental zigzag motif supported the ceiling and railed off a balcony that looked down from the room above. The den was sparsely furnished with glass-and-chromium tables and low-slung chairs upholstered in black-and-white stripes. What struck me immediately was the absence of anything reflecting Ong's Chinese heritage.

He motioned for me to be seated and went to a wet bar opposite the glass wall. "Cognac?" he asked.

I'd heard that the affluent Chinese were partial to cognac; one of the big liquor distributors had recently begun pitching a super-premium French brand especially to the Asian market. But it was something I couldn't drink on a near-empty stomach. "Do you have anything lighter?"

Ong nodded and produced an iced Napa Valley chardonnay from the small refrigerator. I gave it the nod and began removing my tape recorder and Cheung's file from my briefcase. After toasting the success of our interview, Ong and I got down to business.

Cheung's first questions were commonplace, and Ong answered them smoothly, as if they'd been put to him many a time before. On his boyhood in Hong Kong: "I'm ashamed to admit how fortunate I was; we had servants, went to private school. My brothers and I were spoiled rotten." On his arrival in the U.S.: "As soon as I saw San Francisco, I knew this was where I wanted to settle. It's a lot like Hong Kong, you know—a port city built on hills. But the freedoms we enjoy here, those were the real appeal." On his schooling at Stanford and Harvard: "Top drawer all the way. Chinese families view their offspring's education as an investment in everyone's future, and they invest wisely." On the family moving the major portion of its assets out of Hong Kong:

"The nineteen ninety-seven deadline hung over us like a sword. Tiananmen Square proved our fears were justified."

Only one of Cheung's initial questions elicited any strong response from Ong, and its intensity startled me. I asked, "Do you attribute your family's success to the hardships your people endured before you left China?"

His face tensed, eyes becoming shiny black stones. He said, "I would say that the adversities my family encountered in China and elsewhere are the driving force behind our successes. They have certainly caused me to strive for greater heights." And then he smiled ironically, as if mocking the emotion he'd allowed to crack his well-constructed facade.

As the interview proceeded, Ong explained how Transpacific Corporation had come to diversify. "The Port of Oakland did not seem receptive to another major home-based ocean carrier at the time we looked into moving our shipping line there. San Francisco was hopeless: the port's declined and never was suited to container cargo, since its geography prohibits a major rail network. We had to get out of shipping."

"So you liquidated the shipping line and moved your assets into real estate?"

"Yes, and that was extremely lucrative for a time. But San Francisco has a problem in the commercial sector: because of rising costs we've had to price ourselves out of the market; companies are moving out of the city, to areas like north Marin or Contra Costa County. Again, we've had to diversify—to hotels and, ultimately, to resort development."

"The hotels came first, then."

"Yes. They're still profitable, but again San Francisco has a problem: a lot of hotel rooms are sitting vacant."

"Why?"

"We—local hoteliers—overbuilt in the eighties. Then there was bad press that caused tourism to decline: the

AIDS epidemic, the eighty-nine quake, the severity of the homeless problem."

"So now you're into resorts. Carmel Valley, and soon Palm Desert?"

Ong nodded and went into an enthusiastic description of the resorts and their amenities. The golf courses and discos and world-class restaurants and group activities might have thrilled a habitué of Club Med, but they left me cold. A good book and a largely uninhabited beach—or even my backyard deck, if finances didn't permit—were greatly preferable to me.

"And now," I said when he finished, "you've diversified further—into gold mining."

Ong's brow furrowed at this question that I'd slipped into Cheung's prepared list. Reaching for his glass of cognac, he asked, "How did you come upon that information?"

"I thought it was common knowledge."

"It's not. We haven't made an announcement yet about the Golden Hills project because our sampling process isn't complete. How did you hear about it?"

I improvised. "A relative of mine lives in Mono County; the prospect of the Promiseville mine being worked again is big news there."

He nodded, seeming satisfied with the explanation. "I prefer not to go into the subject for purposes of this article. As I said, the sampling process has barely begun. We're not sure how much gold is left in the mesa—if it's enough to justify a full mining operation."

But according to what Lily Nickles had observed, the sampling process had begun and abruptly been aborted. And Transpacific's consulting geologist, Alvin K. Knight, had told Ripinsky that the company expected to take a minimum of half a million ounces of gold out of the mine. I said, "Off the record, then: how did Transpacific learn of the gold-mining potential in Stone Valley?"

Ong smiled thinly. "We have our fingers on the pulse of

opportunity, Ms. McCone. If profit potential exists, Transpacific is aware of it."

"Even if it's in an area of investment that's so far removed from your typical ventures?"

"Even then."

"How do you go about assessing the feasibility of such a project?"

He got up, took both glasses, and went to the wet bar. In the mirror that backed it I could see his face; it was tensed, eyes vigilant. I was reminded of Ripinsky's description of Frank Tarbeaux, the gambler: "Ice cold and totally focused."

Ong played for time, rinsing the glasses before refilling them. When he carried them back to where we were sitting, he asked, "Would you repeat your last question?"

I did.

He shrugged, as if he found the inquiry naive or stupid, then sat again. "As any company does, we rely on the opinions of experts."

"That would include geologists, of course. What about the parties you purchased the land from?"

"What about them?"

"When you made your initial contact with them, did they voice any opinions as to the mine's potential?"

A fleeting expression of annoyance crossed Ong's face. "Of course," he said with exaggerated patience. "After all, they were trying to sell the land to us. If anything, they overrated its value."

"Did either Franklin Tarbeaux or Earl Hopwood seem qualified to evaluate that potential?"

Annoyance again, tinged with surprise this time. "How did you learn those names?"

"Through my relative in Mono County."

"I see." But it was clear he didn't believe me. He took a long drink of cognac—I'd noticed that, instead of sipping, he drank it as he might beer. In the silence that followed, he appeared to be trying to frame a reply.

I added, "Were you aware of Franklin Tarbeaux's real identity? And that Mick Erickson was shot to death in the Tufa Lake area Saturday night?"

Slowly he turned his head to look at me, eyes narrowed and hard. He set his glass down carefully and seemed about to speak when the phone next to his chair rang. Quickly he picked up the receiver.

"Ong here. . . . Who? . . . You're where? . . . All right, take Seventeenth Street and— Yes, left off Glenbrook onto Saint Germain." When he hung up, he'd composed his face into its former pleasant lines.

"You must excuse me," he said. "My office is messengering over some contracts; it seems to be a different service than the usual, and the driver is lost. I need to go outside and make sure he finds the house." He took another gulp of cognac and clattered up the spiral staircase.

Irritated at the untimely interruption, I turned off the tape recorder and went to the glass door that opened onto the terrace. It was unlocked, so I stepped outside. The wind— strong up here even on the warm October days that are jokingly referred to as San Francisco's summer—whipped my hair about and molded my skirt to my thighs. The city spread below, edges softened by a faint haze.

I stood for a moment contemplating the minuscule cityscape, the smallest of the houses barely distinguishable, the largest no more imposing than Tinkertoys. For those who craved power, there must be inspiration in a view that made it seem possible to scoop up the Bank of America building in the palm of one's hand. For an already powerful man like Ong, the vista would be an affirmation.

After a bit I moved to the terrace wall and peered down the overgrown slope. Through a tangle of conifer branches the red-tiled roof of another house was visible. The road I'd ascended on curved in the distance, an old yellow van—the awaited messenger?—toiling up it. I watched until it passed from my view, then went back into the house.

Ong was still absent. At first I could hear nothing from upstairs; then a car door slammed and faint voices drifted down from the courtyard.

I crossed the room and began looking at Ong's bookshelves. Their contents gave evidence of fairly eclectic tastes: besides the expected volumes on finance, real estate, and management, there was an impressive collection of works on world history and philosophy, as well as mainstream fiction and poetry. I reached for a slim volume by Robinson Jeffers, one of our own California poets, and was about to open it when I noticed that the voices in the courtyard were now raised. I set the book back in its place and moved toward the staircase.

Ong said, "This is absurd!" The outrage in his voice thinly masked an undercurrent of panic.

The other person spoke—the voice higher pitched and not so loud. I couldn't make out the words or if the speaker was a man or a woman.

By the time I reached the bottom of the steps the voices had fallen silent. While I was debating whether to venture up there, I heard a car door slam. Then another, and an engine starting up. The messenger leaving?

But Ong still didn't return to the house. I put one foot on the bottom step, then withdrew it. Ong was a man who would not appreciate prying; I didn't want to destroy what fragile rapport remained between us after my questions about the gold-mining venture.

But where was he?

I glanced up the staircase, saw only the sterile wintry light of the foyer. Listened, but heard nothing save the wind rattling the fronds of the yucca trees in the courtyard.

Quickly I moved up the spiral staircase. The foyer was empty, the front door standing open. I hurried across the black marble floor and peered outside. No one was in the courtyard, and the gate was also ajar.

As I started along the path, an object on the ground near the gate caught my attention. A thick nine-by-twelve envelope. I went over and picked it up. There was no address label, no markings of any kind. Its flap had been undone, but its contents were undisturbed. I pulled them out, turned them over. Blank sheets of paper, about half a package of cheap lined notebook filler.

Nearby a terra-cotta pot containing a succulent plant had been knocked on its side. Pebbles littered the stone pathway, and the ground next to it was scuffed. I rushed to the gate and looked out.

The street was deserted. No delivery person or van. No Lionel Ong, either.

I glanced back at the house. No, I would have heard him if he'd returned.

This is absurd!

My mind replayed the panicky note in Ong's voice. Reviewed the signs of an apparent struggle in the courtyard. And I remembered that I'd heard two car doors slam.

Had Ong simply taken off without telling me? Or had he been abducted while I waited downstairs in his study?

Fifteen

▲▲▲

Cautioning myself against jumping to conclusions, I went back to the courtyard and looked around some more. The signs that indicated a struggle, I decided, could also be the residue of haste and/or clumsiness. The envelope full of blank paper that I held didn't necessarily have to relate to Ong, might even have been slipped through the gate for one of his absent children. And the panic in his voice? Could I have been mistaken about that?

No, I thought, I couldn't.

I crossed the courtyard and went back into the house. It held that heavy silence that only an empty dwelling does. Even though I was certain Ong wasn't there, I called out to him. My voice bounced back at me off the walls of the foyer.

And now what should I do? I wondered. Call 911? Tell them what? It wasn't a police matter if Ong had simply driven away with his visitor. And if I said I thought he'd been kidnapped, they'd ask what evidence I based that on.

Some scuffed-up ground, an overturned flowerpot, the envelope, the panic in Ong's voice that only I had heard: it

169

wasn't much. The police would tell me to wait twenty-four hours and if he didn't return have someone related to him file a missing persons report.

Besides, once they knew the whole story, the police were more likely to think that Ong had vanished of his own volition, perhaps because he'd gotten fed up with answering my questions or become uncomfortable with the direction the interview had taken. Illogical as it seemed that he'd leave a stranger in his unlocked house, that could conceivably be the case. And if so, once he returned and found I'd called the police, I'd be in trouble. He was the sort of man who shunned attention of the official sort. It would cause him embarrassment, constitute an invasion of his privacy—conditions that made people like Ong turn to their attorneys. . . .

I crossed the foyer and slid open the double doors. A living room—the one whose balcony I'd glimpsed from the study—lay directly ahead. There was a phone on a credenza just inside the doors; I picked up its receiver and called All Souls.

Hank was on another line, Ted told me. I read the number off the plate below the push buttons, asked that my boss call me back. Then I hung up and, with a haste born of nervousness, began to explore.

The first floor was all living and entertaining area, expensively furnished but again containing nothing that would suggest the family was Chinese. A second spiral staircase led down to a hallway on the next level; off that were three bath- and bedrooms and a master suite. I passed quickly along it to yet another stairway, which took me to a lower level that hadn't been observable from the terrace above it; the rooms there clearly belonged to young children, and a recreation area was stocked with toys, games, and electronic equipment. Still edgy about Ong returning and finding me where I shouldn't be, I wasted only a cursory glance through these rooms before going back to the study.

Set into the far end of one wall in the shadow of the

upstairs balcony was a door that I hadn't noticed before. Keeping an ear out for the sound of footsteps or a car, I opened it and found an office with a computer setup and a bank of steel file cabinets. The desk was clear of papers, but a leather briefcase lay on it; when I tried the catch I found it was secured with a good-quality lock; the same was true of the files. If there was a safe, I felt fairly sure I could locate it, but safecracking is not one of my collection of more dubious skills.

I sighed, listened some more, then sat down in the desk chair and contemplated the computer. My computer skills are only a small cut above my safecracking abilities, and Ong wouldn't have stored interesting material where it could easily be accessed, anyway.

The phone rang. I started and automatically reached for the receiver. Then I hesitated; probably it was Hank, but . . .

"Ong residence," I answered.

"Sharon?"

"Hank. Thanks for calling back. I need a legal opinion."

"Go ahead."

I explained what had happened there, finishing, "Am I right in protecting myself and All Souls by not notifying the police?"

Hank was silent; he'd never been one for making unconsidered judgments. In a moment he asked, "Ong gave no indication that he might be about to terminate the interview?"

"Well, he didn't like the direction my questions were taking. But if I read him right, I'd say he was interested in finding out why I kept asking them and how much I knew. I don't think he'd have voluntarily ended our discussion at that point."

"And you say this messenger called him?"

"Yes. Well, somebody called him."

More silence. "All right—two things. First, you're under

no obligation to call the police, because you have no real proof that Ong's met with misadventure; he could have left voluntarily, for whatever reason. You're treading in a gray area here, and if you do call them in, legally you're at high risk. But second, I think Ong may have set you up."

"In what way?"

"This disappearance—abduction, whatever—sounds staged to me. The absence of other people in the house, the timing of the call, the minor signs of struggle—they're all a tad too convenient."

I thought about that for a moment. "But why? Ong doesn't know I'm an investigator; he thinks I'm a free-lance journalist."

"I don't mean he was setting you up personally. You were a convenience. It looks to me as if he wanted to make it seem he'd been abducted and needed a witness."

Hank's scenario had a disturbingly familiar ring. First Mick Erickson had manufactured an elaborate ruse for dropping out of sight. Now Ong had probably done the same. And Erickson's contrived absence had ended fatally. . . .

"Well," I finally said, "we can speculate all day about this."

"Better you get out of there. We'll talk more later."

I thanked him and hung up, eager now to escape the overwhelming silence of Ong's deserted house. But as I started to leave the office something caught my eye— something that seemed not so much wrong as inappropriate. I stopped midway to the door and stared at it.

It was the only Chinese object I'd seen in the entire house: a landscape painting depicting a rugged mountain towering over a fir-dotted plain. In the foreground were small tentlike structures—pagodas?—and even smaller figures in coolie hats. Several lines of fine-brushed characters ran vertically down its right side, but on the bottom a superimposed English legend said, "Gum San, 1852."

What seemed inappropriate, of course, was the presence of such a work in a home where the family seemed determined to exclude all reminders of their ancestry. But the painting itself—prominently displayed on the wall opposite the desk—bothered me, too. It was not done on paper or silk like the Chinese scrolls I'd seen in museums, but on canvas, and a coarse-weave canvas at that. The workmanship looked amateurish even to my unschooled eye, and the English legend appeared to be a later addition lacking the limited skill of the calligraphy. Although the painting appeared to be quite old, I would have taken it for a cheap tourist item, had I not been unable to imagine Lionel Ong framing and placing on his office wall something from the sidewalk bins of Grant Avenue.

On impulse I took a piece of scratch paper from a pad on the desk and copied down the words "Gum San, 1852." Then I took Hank's advice and got out of there.

The address of Transpacific's consulting geologist, Alvin Knight, was relatively close to Ong's, in a quiet residential district between Mount Davidson Park and Monterey Boulevard, near the southern border of the city. I stopped at a pay phone in a small shopping center at the top of Portola and called Knight's number. When he answered I explained I'd just come from talking with Lionel Ong and asked if I might stop by. Knight sounded reluctant, but agreed to a meeting and gave me directions.

The streets in that part of town are as steep and winding as those in Ong's neighborhood, but the resemblance stops there. The small stucco row houses are built right up to the narrow sidewalks, there is little or no landscaping, and the views—where they exist at all—are of other hills tiered with similar homes. It is an area of middle-class families struggling to meet the high cost of living in San Francisco—a cost that seems excessive, given the sameness and drabness of the dwellings and their distance from the heart of the city.

Knight's home was distinguishable from its neighbors only because it was painted an odd shade of blue and had a fire hydrant out front. I parked uphill, curbing my wheels firmly, and walked back down. The geologist—a short, stocky man whose sun-toughened skin attested to a great deal of time spent outdoors—answered my ring promptly and led me to a small, cluttered office that had been created by converting a portion of the garage. Knight's manner, as he brushed aside my apology for asking to see him at what must have been his dinner hour, was cordial but guarded. I sat in the dilapidated director's chair that he indicated and glanced around.

The walls of the cramped space were layered with maps and charts; stacks of paper and bound reports covered the desk, the tops of the file cabinets, and part of the floor. Everything was filmed with dust. Knight dragged another chair from a corner and sat opposite me. "Excuse the mess," he said. "I've been out in the field for a month. You said you're with All Souls Legal Cooperative?"

"Yes." I'd decided to drop the constraining fiction of being a journalist.

"Attorney?"

"No, investigator." I gave him one of my cards.

"Ah." He studied it, a frown pulling his bushy gray eyebrows together.

"I was speaking with Mr. Ong about the Golden Hills project," I added. "He thought you could fill me in on the details."

"What's your interest in Golden Hills?"

"A man was killed up there over the weekend. I'm aiding the Mono County authorities in their investigation."

Knight's eyes narrowed, but otherwise he didn't react strongly. "Someone was killed? An accident at the site?"

I shook my head. "A murder—a shooting."

"Who?"

"Mick Erickson." When he didn't say anything, I added, "Or maybe you knew him as Franklin Tarbeaux."

"Who shot him?"

It wasn't the response I'd expected. I ignored the question, asked, "You do know both names, then?"

Knight also ignored my question. "Who shot him?" he repeated.

"It's unsolved as yet."

The sun-browned skin around his eyes furrowed; confusion and indecision showed in his eyes. He said, "I'd better call Mr. Ong to confirm that he sent you."

"Please do."

Knight stood. Instead of going to the phone on the desk, however, he moved toward the door. "Be back in a few minutes." Soon after, the risers of the stairway creaked under his weight, and then footsteps crossed the floor above me.

Interesting that he hadn't felt he could call Ong in my presence.

I got up and moved toward the desk, hoping the phone was an extension of the one upstairs. After I slipped the receiver off the hook, I eased up gradually on the disconnect button. Repeated ringing came to my ear; then Knight grunted in displeasure and broke the connection. I replaced the receiver and went back to my chair.

Knight's footsteps didn't recross the floor. I listened for a moment, then went back to the desk and lifted the receiver again. A voice other than the geologist's was speaking.

"I said I don't know where he is."

Who . . . ?

"He must have told you something."

"No. He should have, but he didn't."

I knew that voice!

"But she said she saw him—"

"Look, I'm sorry but I can't help you. I wish I knew when he'd get here, too."

Knight sighed heavily. "Okay, when he shows up there, just ask him to call me, would you?"

I put the receiver down and made a hasty retreat to the

director's chair, my mind fumbling with the possibilities. I would need to think this latest development through very carefully; it significantly altered my conceptions of what might be going on in the Tufa Lake area. And while I was at it, I'd better consider what had gone haywire with my ability as a good judge of others.

The person Knight had been speaking with was Hy Ripinsky.

Sixteen

▲▲▲

When he came back downstairs, Knight told me that he hadn't been able to reach Lionel Ong and couldn't talk about the Golden Hills project until he had Ong's okay. I asked him about the relationship between Ong, himself, and Ripinsky, but he became annoyed and claimed he didn't know who Hy was—a statement I found hard to believe, since he'd just finished speaking with him on the phone. When I began probing further about his knowledge of Mick Erickson and Erickson's use of the Tarbeaux name, he became even more irritated and insisted I leave. I told him I would call him the next day after he'd had time to contact Ong, although I was sure that by then—whether he spoke with Ong or not—he would have come up with an excuse for not dealing with me at all.

Actually I was glad to leave Knight; I needed to think about what I'd overheard. Now that my shock at hearing Ripinsky's voice on the phone had faded, I began to wonder what Hy had had in mind when he willingly gave me the geologist's name and number that morning. Had he assumed their connection was buried so deep I wouldn't unearth it?

Or had he alerted Knight to deny any association? Either way, he was treading on dangerous ground by putting me in touch with him, but I sensed Ripinsky was not a man to shy away from danger—not when it suited whatever his purposes might be.

The problem now was what action to take regarding Ripinsky. His involvement with Ong and his geologist was something Anne-Marie and Ned Sanderman needed to be made aware of. But on the other hand, I wasn't sure that I wouldn't be doing them a disservice by telling them without proof. Anne-Marie has never been one to conceal her emotions, and even if she tried, the rage she was bound to feel toward Ripinsky would be thinly veiled at best. Sanderman hadn't struck me as much of an actor, either; he also was likely to inadvertently reveal what he knew. Ripinsky, a man with a hazy and probably violent past, could pose a distinct threat to both of them if confronted. So in the end I decided to temporarily keep them ignorant of my suspicions.

Night had fallen by the time I neared the shopping center at the top of Portola. I checked my watch, was surprised to find it was after seven. Ma, I thought with a guilty pang. I pulled into the parking lot to call her and tell her I was on my way.

But I wanted to drive by Ong's house again to see if he'd returned. And to stake the place out in any case. I felt restless—far too edgy to spend the evening dealing with my mother and this latest McCone crisis.

There was no answer at my house. I tried George, thinking she might still be with him, but reached only his machine. Finally I called All Souls, hoping she'd left a message.

"A message from your mother?" Ted sounded amused. "No, but I'll buzz your office and you can talk to her."

"Wait a minute—Ma's in my office?"

"Uh-huh. She, George, Rae, and Hank. A few others, off

and on. She and your beloved spent the day together—
something was said about cable cars and ice-cream sodas at
Ghirardelli Square. When they couldn't locate you, she
ordered him to bring her here. She intended to see your new
office, she said, whether you were there to show it off or
not."

"God. Poor George."

"I wouldn't worry—looks to me like he's having a fine time.
They all are. The last I heard they were talking about
getting take-out from that Mexican place that does the
garlic-saturated chicken."

"How does she seem? Is she mad at me for disappearing
all day?"

"Doubt it. Everybody here loves her, and she's basking in
the attention. She showed family pictures—including the
naked one of you when you were a long, skinny baby—and
now the others are entertaining her with Sharon stories."

Sharon stories—just what Ma needed to hear. "My life has
been totally wrecked," I told Ted. "Buzz my office, will you?"

He obliged. A voice promptly said, "Ms. McCone's office,
her mother speaking," and laughter filled the background.

I closed my eyes, stifling a sigh. "Ma, it's me."

"Hello, Me."

"Ma, have you been drinking again?"

"We have had some wine, yes. When did you turn into such
a prude?"

Good question, I thought. I *was* acting prudish—but the
realization didn't make me feel any less stuffy. "Look, Ma," I
said, "I'm sorry I've been neglecting you—"

"There's no need to apologize. I'm having a very nice time
with your friends. We've decided to get some Pollo
Humungo—"

"Supremo."

"What?"

"It's El Pollo Supremo."

"Whatever. You may join us here at All Souls, if you wish."

But a solution to my problem had occurred to me. "I'd love to, Ma," I said insincerely, "but I'm on a case and I have to run a stakeout tonight."

My mother didn't reply. In the background I could hear assorted mumblings. "Ma?"

"Hank was asking how many chickens. Are you eating with us or not?"

"I just said I had to run a stakeout."

"Oh." Ma spoke away from the receiver. "She's not, but get an extra one anyway. I can make sandwiches to take on the bus tomorrow."

Oh, Lord, I'd forgotten she was leaving for my sister Patsy's in Ukiah at eight the next morning! "Ma—"

"Don't worry, Sharon. George has said he'll see me home. You just go have your steak."

"*Stakeout*, Ma."

"Right."

"Ma, does George want to talk—"

"I've got to go now, Sharon. I'll see you at home." And I was left holding a dead receiver.

Irked, I slammed it back onto the hook. The vehemence of my reaction startled me, and I said, "What's the matter with you, anyway?"

A woman on the sidewalk gave me an odd look. I glared at her. She glared back, and I retreated to my car, afraid of provoking one of those senseless incidents of violence that seem to be happening with greater and greater frequency of late. Maybe that was my problem—the craziness I'd been reading about in the papers had started to adversely affect me.

And maybe you're just slipping into grouchy middle age, my ever-vigilant inner voice suggested.

"Shut up," I told it and directed the MG toward Ong's neighborhood.

Saint Germain Avenue lay in darkness broken only by soft lights behind curtained windows. Beyond the brick retaining wall at the end of the pavement, wind-tossed cypress branches were backlit by the glow from the flatlands and East Bay hills. The Ong house was a black multi-angled silhouette against the night sky.

I drove all the way to the end of the street, pulled close to the wall, and turned off the MG's lights. For a few minutes I studied the surrounding houses for moving curtains or figures in the windows. There were none; the homes across from Ong's were built too high on the slope for their residents to pay much attention to passing or parked cars, and most of the others were walled on the street side, windows positioned to take advantage of the view in the opposite direction.

Satisfied that my arrival hadn't been observed, I slipped from the car and moved through the shadows to Ong's gate. On leaving earlier I'd shut it and placed a small piece of paper in the crack so I'd be able to tell if anyone had gone inside. The paper was still there. A red light below the lock indicated the alarm system was on—automatically activated at a preset time, I assumed—and security spots shone here and there throughout the property.

The night had turned cold; the wind blew strongly, rustling the fronds of the yucca trees in the courtyard. I hugged my suit jacket closer around me and retreated to my car. From there visibility was good; moonlight silvered the house's roof and glinted off the glass of the skylights. I settled down for a long wait. The large Styrofoam cup of coffee and squashed-down plastic-wrapped sandwich that I'd bought at a market in the small shopping center didn't exactly rate as creature comforts, but I was sure I'd appreciate them far more than they merited as the evening wore on. For a while I tried to listen to the radio, but static interfered—something to do with the proximity to Sutro Tower, I supposed. My legs cramped, but I couldn't get out and walk around in such a quiet neighborhood. I couldn't even drink as much of the coffee as I would have liked; if I did, odds were that I'd be squatting in the bushes at the exact moment something interesting happened.

For I while I tried to think over the facts of my case, but eventually my mind drifted, merely forming mental pictures: my first view of the glass-smooth surface of Tufa Lake, the alkali plain and craters of the fire mountains stretching to the south. The shattered basalt outcroppings of Stone Valley and the husks of a ruined civilization at Promiseville. The nightmarish terrain of the tufa forest.

And there were other pictures, more ordinary, yet somehow more evocative. The homespun ugliness of the cabin at Willow Grove Lodge. Zelda's beer sign and knotty-pine decor viewed through a haze of smoke. Hy Ripinsky's cozy living room, colorfully jacketed books flanking the native-stone fireplace. And Hy himself: hawk-nosed profile, shaggy dark blond hair curling over the collar of his shabby suede jacket, lanky body that always seemed primed for sudden action. . . .

God, I'd been wrong about him. I'd considered him my ally, a person caught up in the environmental cause who nonetheless had the perspective and toughness—call it cynicism—to maintain a realistic view of what was happening. And now I'd found he'd used that facade to mask his involvement in . . . in *what?*

But maybe I was getting ahead of myself, I thought. Maybe Hy wasn't involved in anything after all. Quickly I reviewed what I'd heard of his conversation with Knight, then shook my head. My desire to believe him innocent didn't stack up well against that evidence. And there were other things to support it: his shadowy past, his extreme reticence about himself, his unexplained antipathy toward Ned Sanderman. . . .

I went over the facts again, trying to figure out why Mick Erickson had gone to Tufa Lake, why both Ripinsky and Knight expected Ong to turn up there, too. And as I thought, I became aware of just how deep my pain over Ripinsky's betrayal was. Yet that made no sense: I'd known him a scant three days; we'd brainstormed and exchanged information, shared a few beers and dances. Why . . . ?

Because you trusted him. Besides the beers and dances, you shared a confidence. You told the man something about your-self that you've never told anyone—not even George.

That was the root of my pain, then. I'd thought I recognized a kindred spirit, had given him a piece of myself I never expected to part with. I should have noticed that in return Ripinsky had given me nothing of himself—

Motion up the street near Ong's gate.

I sat up straighter, leaning forward to peer through the windshield. A figure moved along the gray wall of the house, the wind billowing its dark garments. It stopped in front of the gate, probably ringing the bell, and waited. I strained to make out details, but all I could be sure of was that the person wore a loose coat and some sort of cap. The figure was not tall, but I couldn't guess its height with any accuracy, couldn't tell if it was male or female, Asian or Caucasian.

After a moment the person turned away from the gate, continued along the sidewalk to the double garage doors, and tried each with no success. Not a casual drop-in or solicitor, but someone who wanted very badly to enter the house. Possibly someone who knew the Ong family well.

I watched as the figure turned and walked down the street to where it intersected with Glenbrook. When it was out of sight, I started the MG and drove slowly without lights to the corner. A car was parked a little way downhill—one of those sleek Miatas I'd been noticing on the road lately. The figure was just climbing inside.

Why park all the way down there? I wondered. Why not drive directly to the house?

I stopped under the overhanging branches of an acacia tree and slouched as the Miata made a U-turn, its headlight beams washing over my car. When it vanished briefly at the first downhill curve on Glenbrook, I flicked on my own lights and followed.

The Miata moved briskly, negotiating the maze of winding streets without hesitation to Upper Market, where it turned toward downtown. At Castro it slipped through the stoplight on the tail end of the amber, but I caught up with it at Sixteenth Street. Sometimes in tandem, sometimes with a car or two between us, we continued almost to the foot of Market. I tried to get close enough to glimpse the driver, but kept having to fall back to avoid detection.

Finally the other car swung around a block and cut through the deserted financial district on Kearny. The street began to climb Telegraph Hill. At the access road that wound through the park at the base of Coit Tower, the Miata veered off.

Surprised, I slowed and pulled to the edge of the pavement. The road, I knew, ended in the scenic overlook and parking lot at the tower. While that area is clogged during the day with rental cars and tour buses, T-shirt and souvenir vendors, at night it is largely deserted. Owing to the clear weather, you would find people admiring the view, as well as the inevitable trysting couples, but I couldn't imagine why the driver of the Miata had gone there.

Unless, of course, he or she had spotted me and wanted to force a confrontation. I could wait here, since this road was the only outlet, then continue tailing the car when it came back down. Or I could go see who the driver was and find out what he or she wanted.

I shifted into first gear and pulled back onto the pavement.

At the summit of the hill the fluted white shaft of the tower gleamed brilliantly against the sky, a nozzlelike monument to San Francisco's brave fire fighters (or to Lillie Hitchcock Coit's lust for same, depending on one's interpretation of local history). The road ended in a semicircular parking area, where several dark cars sat, noses toward the shimmering expanse of the city.

None of them was the Miata.

"Impossible," I said aloud. The car hadn't passed me, and there was no other way off the hill. No place up here where it could be concealed, either.

And then I thought of the driveways that snaked downhill from the road below—narrow access lanes to the garages of the expensive homes and apartment buildings that nestled among the thick vegetation on the slope. The Miata could have turned into one, waited until I passed, then left the area. Or the driver could live close by.

I pulled into a parking space and got out of the MG. The wind gusted here as strongly as on Ong's hill, bringing with it a mixed bouquet of cypress, eucalyptus, and bay laurel. I locked my car, buttoned my suit jacket, and took a small flashlight from my bag. Training its beam downward, I crossed to where a narrow brick stairway descended into a thicket of conifers.

From previous visits—mostly with out-of-towners touring the city—I knew that the steps scaled the hill in a zigzag fashion, leading to paths and plank walks alongside the residences. Eventually the stairway came out at one of the streets below—Montgomery? Greenwich? I wasn't sure which.

I followed the beam of light down the steps, holding tight to the iron rail and wishing the low heels I had on were more suitable for this. The bay laurel scent was stronger here; a small animal skittered through the ivy on the upward slope. Through the trees and slightly below I could see a row of three multi-unit buildings. A party was going on on the brightly illuminated roof garden of the far one; laughter and music drifted down.

At the bottom of that section of steps a path branched; one arm continued toward another stairway that led past a rustic cottage, the other toward a boardwalk between the apartment buildings and the ivied slope. Their lighted entries faced the walk. I stopped, studying them.

As I stood there, the sound of footsteps came from the far end of the walk—a quick hollow tapping of high heels. I ducked behind a wind-warped cypress. The footsteps kept on, then stopped.

Cautiously I peered through the branches. A woman in an outfit similar to that of the figure I'd seen in front of Ong's house stood at the entry to the center building. Her back was to me, and she was punching at one of the buzzers: two, three, four angry rings.

The woman waited at the door for close to a minute, her fingers tapping impatiently on its frame. Then she stamped her foot and rummaged through her pockets and shoulder bag, as if searching for keys. When she came up empty-handed, she stepped farther back on the boardwalk, scanning the upper windows. They were all dark. Quickly she moved to the corner of the building and leaned out over the waist-high rail, checking the ones on the side. They were also dark, and in seconds she pulled back and turned my way, her face clearly revealed by the night-light.

Margot Erickson.

The surprise I felt at first turned to shock at the bruised and swollen condition of her face. Its right side was a mass of purply red contusions, the eye puffed nearly shut. I must have rustled the branches involuntarily, because she jerked her head toward my hiding place.

"Mrs. Erickson," I said, starting toward her.

Her hand flew to her cheek, vainly trying to conceal the damage. Her good eye widened, transforming her face into a grotesque mask. Even in the dim light I could see the full flowering of the fear I'd only sensed yesterday morning.

"It's okay," I said, holding out both hands. "I won't hurt you."

She flinched, flattened against the railing.

I went to her. Suddenly, before I could speak again, she lunged at me and almost knocked me down.

I righted myself, grabbed her elbow. She twisted, and her fingernails raked the back of my hand, made me let go of her arm. Her open palm smacked my left cheek so hard that I stumbled into the railing. When I came off of it she was running toward the stairway.

I went after her, calling out. She stopped, turned on me again, and kicked at my legs. One of her shoes struck my shinbone, and this time I did go down. Backwards, onto the steps that led past the cottage.

I grabbed the iron rail and turned around, but I couldn't recover my balance. Then I was falling forward, my hands thrust out and encountering nothing. My knees and shins scraped against the rough steps; my head slammed into the retaining wall beside them.

As I rolled and wedged sideways on the steps, I heard Margot running away on the boardwalk. Shock waves of pain racked my body. I bit down hard to keep from crying out. And tasted blood.

For a while I just lay there, canted downward on the steps. Oddly enough, nothing had changed around me: the party on the roof went on; a TV muttered in the cottage; a bird called high overhead. Then there was the squeal of tires on pavement—someone driving up a ramp from the garage under one of these buildings. Margot Erickson.

Why hadn't she gone up to the apartment through the inside entrance from the garage? Why go all the way down the boardwalk to the front door? The keys . . . it looked as if she'd misplaced her keys. She'd have had an automatic garage-door opener in the car, but without keys she couldn't gain entry to the building proper.

And whose keys were they? Hers? A friend's? Whose apartment was that?

I thought I knew.

After a while I eased into a sitting position. Began moving

my arms and legs slowly, feeling for broken bones. Everything seemed to be intact. I flexed my limbs again, then felt the more superficial injuries: bump on my forehead where I'd slammed it into the wall, swelling on the side of my face where she'd smacked me, a sore shinbone, and scrapes on my legs and knees where my panty hose hung in shreds. Palms lacerated. Teeth and jaw aching. Cut in mouth still leaking blood. Headache about to become full-blown.

Damn her, I thought angrily. Where does she get off, doing this to me when I was only trying to talk to her?

She's scared, scared crazy.

Of what?

You mean of whom. Who beat her up?

No answer to that one.

Finally I struggled to my feet. Dragged myself up the steps by clinging to the railing, and located my shoulder bag where I'd dropped it. Then I tottered down the boardwalk to the entry of the middle building.

The nameplates beside the three bell pushes were all blank. The windows on each floor were still unlighted. For a moment I contemplated ringing the bells anyway, then decided against it. No one home, no point in bothering. I could attempt to canvass the neighbors, but in my condition, I'd only scare them.

Besides, I'd had it for the night. I made a note of the building's address and hauled my aching body up the hill to my car.

Seventeen

▲▲▲

Ma was sitting in the rocking chair in my parlor when I arrived home, a fire going and both Ralphie and Allie on her lap. When she saw the condition I was in she half rose, dumping the cats on the floor. Allie let out an indignant mowl.

I said, "Ma, I'm okay."

"You don't look okay."

"Well, it's nothing that won't heal. I've got to clean up and make a phone call; then I'll tell you about it."

She nodded skeptically and sat back down. The cats immediately jumped onto her lap and huddled against her, instinctively aware something was wrong.

I went to my bedroom, stripping off my ruined clothing on the way. Thank God, I thought, that the suit was an old gray Pendleton—one that I was thoroughly sick of. After I'd dumped everything on the floor, I put on my white terry robe and sat down on the bed to call Rae at All Souls.

"Hey," she said, sounding somewhat high, "we had a great time with your mom—"

"Save it, Rae—I can't talk long. Will you do something for me right now?"

"Sure."

"Check the reverse directory and see who lives in the apartments at this address." I read off the street and unit numbers of the building on Telegraph Hill.

She went to the law library where the spare phone books were kept and returned a minute later. "Shar, there're no listings."

No phone service there, then. Strange—the building hadn't looked unoccupied. Perhaps the numbers were unlisted. "Okay," I said, "then you'll need to go to City Hall first thing in the morning and find out who owns the property."

"Will do. I planned to run by Vital Statistics anyway, to see if I can get a line on that Peggy Hopwood."

"Good. I have to deliver Ma to the bus station at eight. Then I'll probably be in my office. If I'm not, try me here as soon as you know."

Rae said she would, and I hung up and doctored my wounds as best I could. Then I filled an ice bag for my swollen cheek, poured myself a glass of heavy red wine, and went back to the parlor.

Ma looked me over carefully as I sat down in my favorite armchair. "Well?" she said.

I told her a half-truth. "Nobody did this to me. I fell."

"And?"

"And that's it."

"Sharon, you're not telling me anything."

I sighed, thought, What the hell, and went into a lengthy explanation of my investigation. When I finished, Ma remained silent for a minute.

Eventually she said, "I wonder why that poor woman was so afraid of you?"

"Well, somebody had beaten her up pretty badly."

"That's not enough. From what you tell me, she had no reason to think you meant to harm her. Maybe if you go see her tomorrow she'll have calmed down and be able to talk about it."

I waited. When she didn't go on, I said, "That's it? You're not going to lecture me about how I should get a nice, safe job?"

"No, I am not. I can't say I'm happy about the danger you're always getting into, but nothing I tell you is going to make a difference. You'll go on doing exactly what you want to, with or without my approval."

"This is a switch."

She shrugged. "I've decided to let you grow up." After a pause she added, "You know, someday you're going to have to do the same for me."

"What's that supposed to mean?"

"I know you're unhappy about the divorce—and Melvin. I'm sorry you feel that way, but it's my life and, like you, I intend to start leading it—with or without *your* approval."

She was right, of course; it was time I let go. Baby birds aren't the only ones who leave the nest. The mother bird does, too, and eventually the nest deteriorates and is borne away on the wind. But if that happened to my own family nest, it would mean that I would have to create a more permanent one of my own—or admit that I was incapable or unwilling to do so. . . .

"Ma," I said, "what do you really think of George?"

She didn't seem at all surprised by the non sequitur. "I've already told you I like him very much."

"But you also told me to be careful about marriage. That wasn't just because of your leaving Pa and your future plans with Melvin."

She sighed and adjusted the end of Ralphie's collar where it had slipped from the buckle loop. "Not entirely, no."

"What is it, then?"

"George is a simple man, Sharon. Maybe too simple for you."

"Simple? Ma, the man's a Stanford professor! He's written a ground-breaking book—"

"I didn't say he isn't intelligent. But think about that book: the man has classified personalities and stuffed them into little circles. Then he's divided them up according to whether they're healthy or sick, and tried to tell the sick ones how to get better."

It was a fairly basic description of the work George had told her about at dinner the night before, but hearing it in my mother's uncomplicated words made it sound somewhat silly. I hurried to defend it. "What's wrong with that? We could use a whole lot fewer pathological personalities."

"Sure, but the fact is the world just doesn't work the way George wants it to. People don't fit into little circles. Not everyone is going to be able to get healthy—or even want to."

". . . Well, I know that."

"George doesn't."

"So he's an optimist."

"Yes, he's an optimist. And he wants to be happy."

"And you don't think I can make him happy?"

"Sharon, don't get your feathers ruffled. I don't know if you can or not, but I think in the end he would make you miserable. You definitely will *not* fit into one of his circles."

"Are you trying to say I'm emotionally unstable?"

Ma shook her head, amused. "Other than the fact that you have your father's hair-trigger temper, you're perfectly healthy. But there's also another side to you, something . . . wild that can't be contained. That side of you will never permit you to live a comfortable life in one of those circles—not even with a good man you love. But it *will* make you feel guilty and unhappy because you can't."

I couldn't speak—shocked not only by what she'd said but also by the fact that for the first time in my life I was having a meaningful, adult conversation with my own mother.

After a moment I asked, "How do you know all that about me?"

"I haven't observed you your whole life for nothing. I wasn't just joking when I said you're like your father. What do you think he's been doing out there in that garage but giving in to his darker side?"

I nodded, thinking about Pa: his sudden shifts from his customary cheeriness to black depression; his compulsive need for solitude. And I thought of the confidence I'd unwisely imparted to Hy Ripinsky—that revelation of the side of myself that I'd only hinted at to George. And of how I took pains to protect my lover from all but the most routine or amusing aspects of my work.

"So," I said after a moment, "do you think I should stop seeing him?"

"Not necessarily. But you should go carefully and slowly."

Ralphie grunted and scrambled off Ma's lap, heading for the corner by the sofa that—this week, anyway—was his sleeping place. Allie sat up and shook her head in bewilderment, tags jingling. Ma looked at her watch and stood, bundle of calico fur in her arms. "I'd better get some sleep," she told me. "It's a long bus ride to Ukiah, and I expect I'm going to have trouble with Patsy. Although she's led a very disordered life, your sister is even more of a prude than you are." But she smiled to take the sting out of the comment and patted me on the cheek as she passed.

When she reached the door, I said, "Ma?"

"Yes?"

"I've decided to let you grow up."

"Thank you, Sharon. Thank you very much."

I set the ice bag down on the hearth and moved to the rocker, cradling my wineglass in both hands and staring into the guttering flames. While what Ma had said had surprised me, I now realized I'd known it all along, had refused to recognize it and pushed it deep beneath the surface of my awareness. I would heed her warning and go slowly—not because it was my mother who had cautioned me, but because in various ways I'd already begun cautioning myself.

But dammit—why were so many people telling me things lately that I didn't want to hear?

Eighteen

▲▲▲

I was in a foul mood the next morning, so after I saw Ma off on her bus, I went home to await the information I'd requested from Rae. The house seemed strangely empty. Ralphie and Allie noticed it, too; they prowled in and out through their cat door, periodically padding down the hall to stick their noses into the guest room. Finally I went to strip the bed, on the premise that brisk activity and returning one's surroundings to normal are the best way to get over missing somebody, but ended up staring at myself in the mirror over the bureau instead.

There was a bruise on my left cheekbone where Margot Erickson had hit me, and a purplish knot on my forehead. My lower lip was split and slightly swollen. Under my jeans was a further assortment of bruises, cuts, and scrapes. My muscles ached, particularly my lower back, and I had to hold myself stiff when I moved.

I sighed, envisioning a day of answering or evading unwelcome questions about what had happened to me.

And why had it happened, anyway? Ma thought that the beating Margot had received wasn't enough explanation for her violent attack on me, and in a way I agreed. She had reacted out of fear—a fear that had been present before she'd been beaten. But there had been anger in her attack on me, too, a deliberate and savage lashing-out, and some of my injuries duplicated hers; it was as if she'd set out to pay me back for what had been done to her.

By whom? And why?

I turned from the mirror, finished stripping the sheets, and tossed them down the chute to the laundry area in the garage. Then I went into the bathroom where the light was more direct and applied extra makeup, hoping to minimize the worst of my facial injuries. All it did was make them more lurid. Finally I washed my face and made up as usual.

Back in the kitchen, I shooed the cats outside, poured myself a cup of coffee, and took all three volumes of the city phone directory to the table. There was no listing for geologists under Professional Associations in the Yellow Pages, but in the State of California section of the White Pages I found a Sacramento number for the Board of Registration for Geologists and Geophysicists.

I called the number, explained that my firm was considering hiring Alvin K. Knight for a consulting job, and asked if they could supply any information about him. The man who had answered said the employee who could help me with that would not be in until afternoon; could she return my call? I left All Souls' number.

After that I dialed Lionel Ong's home; as I'd expected, the phone rang repeatedly. I called Transpacific Corporation and was put through to his secretary; she said Ong hadn't come in yet. When I explained I was a journalist working on a partially completed interview for the Sino-American Alliance's magazine and urgently needed to speak with Mr. Ong, she was vague about the time he would arrive in the office. I thought I heard an undertone of confusion and tension in the woman's voice.

Finally I called the Erickson condominium in Barbary

Park. A brief recorded message in a male voice told me that Mick and Margot were unavailable at the moment but would get back to me as soon as possible.

I hung up before the beep, certain Margot wouldn't return a call, but the voice—which had to be Mick's—haunted me. After a moment I took my coffee outside to the deck and wandered aimlessly, contemplating the tangle of rosebushes next to it. Their late bloom was nearly over; what blossoms remained were stunted and shriveled. Once again I heard Mick Erickson saying "unavailable" and "as soon as possible."

Permanently unavailable, I thought, and what had seemed possible when he'd made the recording was now and for all time beyond his grasp. Perhaps someday my own taped voice would outlive me, speak to my friends and relatives as if from the grave. . . .

It was unwise to dwell on such thoughts, even in the bright morning sunlight. I went back inside, glancing impatiently at the kitchen clock. Ten-seventeen. Why the hell hadn't Rae called yet? She'd said she'd go to City Hall and check the ownership of the Telegraph Hill building first thing.

My briefcase and the recorder containing the tape of the Ong interview were still in the car. I went down to the garage and fetched them, then replayed the tape. Nothing there that had any real bearing on my investigation; I'd only gotten to the questions I'd added to the prepared interview when Ong's phone rang. Next I went through my notes on the case, scribbled at random in the small loose-leaf notebook I keep in my purse. Facts, impressions, suppositions, theories. Some I starred or underlined; others I drew big Xs through. But this was just busywork. What I really wanted was to hear from Rae.

After fifteen more minutes I called All Souls, thinking she might have forgotten I'd said to call here if I wasn't in the office. No message from her, but there were two others: from

Marcy Cheung, asking how the interview had gone, and from Kristen Lark in Mono County, inquiring as to my progress with the case.

"Hank also wants to talk with you about . . ." Ted paused. I could hear him riffling through message slips. "About that business you discussed with him late yesterday afternoon. He's taking a deposition now, will be free around noon."

"Tell him I'll check in there later."

I broke the connection and called the Sino-American Alliance. Cheung's line was busy. The receptionist put me on hold, came back a few minutes later. "Still busy."

"Are you sure she hasn't just taken it off the hook?"

A sigh. "I *did* hear some cursing back there a while ago."

"Would you mind checking? I really need to speak with her."

"Hold, please."

About half a minute later Cheung's voice said, "Sharon—sorry. The idiot printer . . . but you don't want to hear about that. How did it go with Ong?"

"He cut the interview short, but I think I've got enough that you can run it."

"You get what you needed, too?"

"Not exactly. Look, are you going to be there over the noon hour? I'd like to drop the tape off and ask you a few additional questions."

"I'll probably be here the rest of my life, the way things are going. Why don't you pick up a couple of sandwiches and come by around twelve-thirty? There's some Tsing Tsao beer in the office fridge, left over from one of our receptions."

"Will do. See you then."

Now the question was what to do about Kristen Lark's call. I didn't really want to talk with the deputy until I had a firmer handle on what was going on. Meaning a better idea of what had happened to Lionel Ong . . . and why Alvin Knight was so nervous about talking with me without Ong's okay . . . and what Ripinsky's connection with both men was . . . and why he and Knight assumed Ong would eventually turn up in Mono County . . . and who had beaten up Margot Erickson. . . .

I decided to ignore Lark's message for now.

When Rae called, it was close to eleven-thirty, and I'd scoured the kitchen sink and accomplished the distasteful task of cleaning out the vegetable drawer. "What have you got for me?" I demanded before she could engage in any pleasantries.

"The building on Tel Hill belongs to Transpacific Corporation."

I'd suspected as much, and it dovetailed with something Marcy Cheung had told me—that Ong kept a Caucasian mistress in a company-owned condominium on Telegraph Hill. But Margot Erickson, the wife of his business associate? The woman I'd rated as a truth-teller, who had claimed she and her husband had not known Ong well, had seen him socially only a few times in the past five years? My abilities at sizing up people really seemed to be slipping.

"Shar?"

"Rae, thanks. Have you been able to get a line on Hopwood's daughter?"

"I'm on my way to Vital Statistics now."

"Now? Why were you so late getting down there?"

A silence. Then she said a trifle testily, "I overslept this morning. I was up late last night entertaining your mother while you were off God knows where, and she's not an easy lady to keep pace with. Holds her liquor far better than I do."

"Well, I didn't ask you to entertain her—or to drink yourself into a hangover. And the 'God knows where' that I was off to was a stakeout."

Another long pause. "I didn't mind entertaining her, Shar. We had fun. It's called having a life. Maybe you should try that sometime." And then she hung up on me.

I blinked in surprise and just sat there, the receiver still pressed to my ear. Throughout our worst times Rae had never spoken to me like that, much less hung up on me. Our relationship, both professional and personal, had broken down completely, and I wasn't sure what I should do about it.

The dial tone bored into my eardrum. I set the receiver down. A clearing of the air between my assistant and me had become necessary, and I knew it had better happen soon. But first I had to set out on my self-appointed rounds.

Said rounds began at Ong's house, still silent and deserted in the noonday sun. At Barbary Park I couldn't get past the security guard in the lobby. When I called up to the Erickson town house, the Filipino maid answered and said her employer had gone out of town, but I doubted that, since there had been a notice in the morning paper of a memorial service to be held for Mick tomorrow afternoon. I left a message for Margot to call me as soon as she returned, then drove over to Telegraph Hill. No one answered my ring at any of the three apartments in the Transpacific-owned building.

I arrived at the Sino-American Alliance half an hour late but bearing two pastrami-and-cheese sandwiches, two enormous garlic dills, and a small container of potato salad. Cheung was hunched over the light table examining a batch of color slides; her mouth dropped open when she saw the injuries to my face.

"Not Ong," I said quickly. "I had a run-in with a reluctant witness."

She picked up on the finality of my tone and tactfully didn't press me for details. After she'd enthusiastically pawed through the contents of the lunch sack, she went to fetch the promised beers, and as before, we settled down on the floor of the office. I'd felt so rotten that morning that I'd been certain I wouldn't eat all day; now my appetite had returned to its normal ravenous level.

I expected Cheung to play the cassette of the interview, but she merely tossed it on her desk and attacked her sandwich. When I asked if she didn't want to listen to the tape, she waved the suggestion aside. "Whatever you've got, I'll use it. It's the son of a bitch's own fault that he ducked out before you were finished."

I toyed with my pickle, wondering how far I could trust Cheung. She watched me with keen reporter's eyes, again picking up on a nuance but not prying. After a moment I opted for confiding in her; after all, she'd trusted me enough to allow me to do something that could have gotten her into serious trouble with her employer. I said, "Ong didn't exactly duck out, and I'm not sure he went voluntarily."

She raised her eyebrows, mouth full of pastrami.

After swearing her to secrecy, I recounted what had happened at Ong's house.

"Damnedest thing," she said when I finished. "What do you suppose happened to him?"

"I don't know what to think. My boss theorizes that I was set up—that Ong wanted a witness to a staged disappearance. But another person connected with the case—the murder victim—also arranged something along those lines, and I'm not sure I can buy two such incidents."

"So maybe he was kidnapped."

"Maybe. But then why no ransom demands?"

"You don't know but what they've already been made. It's not something the police or FBI would issue a press release on."

"True. I wish I could find out."

"Let's see if I can help you." Cheung reached for the phone cord and hauled the instrument toward her from where it sat under her desk. "I know Lionel's secretary fairly well. I'll call and say I need to check some facts with him for the interview piece. Even if she won't tell me anything, I can get a feel for the situation." She dialed, asked for Ong's office. And waited.

"Funny," she said, cupping her hand over the mouthpiece. "Lynn hardly ever goes out to lunch, but they're switching me to the message center."

"Leave one and see if she returns the call."

She did, then went back to her lunch. "So what do you plan to do?" she asked. "Go to the police?"

"If there is a ransom demand and the authorities are called in, I'll have to tell them what I know. But my boss has advised me to keep out of it otherwise. He's afraid of a suit against me and the co-op if I'm wrong about what happened."

"Lawyers. They all ought to be shot."

"Sometimes I agree with you—and yet most of my good friends are lawyers."

"Well, some of them have their human side, and the ones at All Souls are the best of the lot. Look at Koslowski—he's trying to save the world with his protein drink."

"Yes, and he'll probably end up poisoning us all." I finished my pickle and began to pick the sandwich apart, eating only the cheese and pastrami. "Marcy, I need to know more about Lionel Ong. The other day you mentioned a couple of mistresses, one in Sausalito and the other on Telegraph Hill. Do you know anything more about either of them?"

"Not much. The one in Sausalito I've only heard rumors of—something about the two of them liking to sail together and him buying her a boat. The other I could probably find out about; I've got a friend who's been to the condo and met her."

"Would you? I need an address, a name. A description of her, if nothing else."

"Sure." She checked her watch. "He won't be in the office now—he's one of these fellows who's either lunching with the mayor or sitting conspicuously at the next table to remind him he owes him a favor—but I'll catch him later on and get back to you."

"Thanks." I gave up on the sandwich and folded its wrappings around the ruins. "It amazes me how close-knit the Chinese community is; you seem to know everybody."

She shrugged. "We're very interdependent; it stems from our traditional reliance on the extended family. And we've had to be that way: our people have taken a lot of shit in this country. Remember the Exclusion Act of eighteen eighty-two? The 'heathen Chinee' are the only ethnic group in history to be specifically denied entry to the U.S."

"I remember. But in a way don't you think that all the discrimination helped sustain your ethnic identity? Look at me, for instance: I'm seven-eighths Scotch-Irish plus one-eighth Shoshone, and I don't identify with any group."

"So what? You want to be one of those idiot liberals that even the Indians can't stand, running around in a headdress and campaigning for Native American rights?"

I grimaced. "No."

"Good, because then you'd be just another phony jerk, and I wouldn't want to know you."

I smiled and sipped my beer.

Cheung finished her sandwich and collected the debris from the floor around us. I rummaged through my bag for my cards, thinking to write my home number on the back of one for her, and encountered the scrap of paper on which I'd copied the words from the bottom of the painting in Lionel Ong's office.

"By the way," I said, holding it out, "can you tell me what this means?"

She glanced at it. "Gum San. It's a colloquialism that roughly translates to 'Land of the Golden Hills.'"

Golden Hills. That was what both Ong and Alvin Knight had called the Stone Valley mining project. "Where is it?"

"California as a whole. It's what the Chinese who came here to work in the goldfields back in the eighteen forties named it. Where did you run across that?"

I described the painting on Ong's wall.

She nodded. "I've seen works like that. A couple of years ago we organized an exhibition of Chinese gold rush artifacts. The paintings were similar to our typical scrolls, except that the artists . . . well, most of them *weren't* artists. And they had to make do with whatever materials they had on hand—the one Ong has was probably done on canvas cut from a tent."

I remembered the tentlike structures in the foreground of the painting, which I'd taken for pagodas. "So that was actually a picture of one of the gold camps. Where would Ong have gotten it? Are they available in galleries or antique shops?"

"No, not too many survived. It's probably an heirloom. When we put on the exhibition I mentioned, Lionel underwrote it pretty substantially; he said he wanted to raise public awareness of the hardships and discrimination our people suffered in the goldfields, because his grandfather's brother died in a battle between rival tongs of Chinese miners near Weaverville in the eighteen fifties. The brother might have done the painting and sent it back to China like people send snapshots or postcards today."

"Then there's more to Ong than I assumed. From the way he acts and the appearance of his home, I could have sworn he'd done his best to distance himself from his heritage. On the other hand, he's passionate about the hardships his family has endured—attributes their success to them."

"I think, like most of us, Lionel has a confused sense of ethnic identity."

"It's strong, though, in its way. The fact that he's named this mining project Golden Hills—Gum San—indicates his feelings for his roots run deep. The project obviously means a lot to him—enough, perhaps, to make him go to any length to ensure it succeeds."

Cheung nodded, clearly disturbed by the idea, and finished gathering the remnants of her lunch. From the glance she threw at the slide-laden light table, I knew she was eager to get back to work, so I scribbled my home number on my card and told her she could call me there any time if I wasn't available at All Souls. She said she'd be in touch as soon as she spoke with either Ong's secretary or the friend who had been to the Transpacific condominium.

On my way through the reception area I paused before one of the highly stylized scroll paintings. It depicted a scene similar to the one on the canvas in Ong's office—a mountain towering over a conifer-dotted plain—but even I could tell it had been rendered by a more skilled hand. Somehow, though, the painting failed to stir me in the way Ong's had; despite its crude workmanship, that one possessed something this lacked.

Passion? Yes, passion. But something more. Anger?

Yes, anger.

Nineteen

▲▲▲

When I arrived at All Souls some forty minutes later, I found Ted at his desk in the once-grand foyer of the Victorian, long slender fingers skimming over his IBM keyboard. I smiled, thinking as I often did that with his fine features and neatly trimmed black goatee, he looked as if he should be composing a concerto at a grand piano rather than typing a legal document at a computer. Without glancing up or missing a beat he said, "One message in your box, and Hank asked me to tell you that he had to go out and will try to connect with you later."

I reached for the pink slip. A Ms. Ryder from the state Board of Registration for Geologists and Geophysicists had returned my call. "Is Rae in?"

Ted shook his head.

"And she hasn't called?"

"No."

"Dammit! What's wrong with her, anyway?"

Ted swiveled around and looked up at me. His face paled. "Jesus, what happened to you?"

Gingerly I touched my bruised forehead. "Bad fall. I was

tailing a witness on Telegraph Hill—where those steps lead down from the Coit Tower parking area, you know?—and I took a header." It was as much of the story as I was willing to tell him.

He looked vaguely disappointed; Ted is the co-op's chief gatherer and dispenser of gossip, and he likes his tales as dramatic as possible. In search of richer fodder, he asked, "What's Rae done now?"

"Hung up on me, for one thing."

"What'd you do to her?"

"Why do you always assume I'm the one at fault?"

He shrugged, the corners of his mouth twitching in amusement. "Rae's awfully easygoing. It would take a lot to make her hang up on anyone—particularly you. You're her idol, you know."

"You mean I *was* her idol, until everything fell apart last summer."

"After the shooting?"

"Yes, things are different between us now. She's never said anything, but I can see it in her eyes, hear it in the tone of voice she uses sometimes." *Yours, too.*

Ted nodded and studied me, stroking his goatee; it was as if he'd heard my unspoken words. After a moment he said, "Well, that was a bad time for all of us—for a variety of reasons." He'd lost his oldest and dearest friend to AIDS that week. "But the rest of us got over it eventually."

"Not Rae."

"No." His gaze turned inward for a moment, as if he was examining his true feelings to verify that he'd indeed put the incident behind him. "It's not that Rae thinks you're a bad person, Shar. She's just frightened."

"Of *me?*"

"That's not what I mean."

"What, then?"

"Why don't you ask her?"

"Would she tell me?"

"I doubt that she even realizes she's frightened. But if you talked about it, it might force her to confront what's really going on inside of her."

I shook my head in confusion. "Sometimes you can be so damned . . . *obfuscatory!*"

"Is that a word?"

"I don't know. Look it up and see." I headed upstairs to my office, message slip in hand.

The yellow rose in the vase on my desk had wilted and browning petals dusted the corner of the blotter. As I swept them into the wastebasket, I reminded myself to call George as soon as he was due home from Stanford. Then I sat down and dialed the Sacramento number on the slip.

Ms. Ryder was in charge of records for the Board of Registration, and she had already pulled Alvin K. Knight's file. Mr. Knight, she told me, had been a registered geologist since 1973. In the years since then, only one complaint had been lodged against him, and it was later withdrawn.

"What did it concern?" I asked.

"I'm sorry. Since it was withdrawn, I'm not allowed to go into the details."

So why go into it at all? I wondered. "Is there any other agency or professional association that can tell me more about Mr. Knight's credentials?"

"Try the American Society of Consulting Geologists and Mineralogists in Berkeley." She read me their number.

I called Berkeley and spoke with a Mr. Hay. Unbound by the restraints of state bureaucracy, he had a good deal to say about Alvin Knight.

"Mr. Knight dropped his membership with us five years ago," he said, "after he was requested to appear before our board for unethical conduct—falsifying the mineral survey on a mining claim that was in the process of being patented with the Bureau of Land Management."

I reached toward one of my stack trays, where I'd put the file Anne-Marie had prepared for me on gold mining. "Patenting a mining claim with the BLM actually amounts to buying the land, does it not? The title passes from the government to the applicant for a nominal sum per acre, with no strings attached?"

"That's essentially correct. The General Accounting Office has recommended that the mining law be changed to permit claim holders to purchase only the mineral rights on the land, rather than the land itself. That was in response to a number of incidents where people bought property cheaply and then didn't put it into mining use—a good way to acquire valuable land at very low prices. But so far nothing's come of the proposal."

"And what are the requirements for the patenting process?"

"The major one is that the applicant show the bureau that a valuable mineral has been discovered on the land and that the claim has been surveyed by a mineral surveyor selected from the BLM state roster."

"And Knight was qualified to do that?"

"Yes. Unfortunately there was some question about the validity of his survey. A complaint was lodged with a state agency by a concerned environmentalist group that feared Mr. Knight was cooperating in a scheme to gain ownership of the land for non-mining purposes. It was later withdrawn, but we still felt it necessary to call him before the board for explanation." Mr. Hay's voice had taken on a gleeful undertone. I gathered that he hadn't liked Knight—or maybe he was just the sort of person who enjoyed another's misfortune.

But what he had told me caused the germ of an idea to send out fragile tendrils. I asked, "So far as you know, is Mr. Knight still on the BLM surveyors' roster?"

"I see no reason that he would have been removed."

"But nevertheless he dropped his membership in your society rather than go before the board."

"Yes. Mr. Knight is not the sort of person who responds well to authority."

Since I didn't like Mr. Hay's smug tone, and because I also am unresponsive to authority, I found myself in sympathy with the geologist. But not in such great sympathy that I didn't begin to peruse my file carefully as soon as I finished the call. Of particular interest to me were copies of two newspaper articles entitled "Forest Service Warns of Non-mining Use of Former Federal Lands" and "Miner Got Land Dirt Cheap."

At close to three I called Knight's number and hung up as soon as the geologist answered. Then I set out to see him.

Alvin Knight was not pleased to find me on his doorstep, but my battered appearance caught him off guard, and before he could block me, I stepped into the house. He gaped and said, "Ms. McCone, what—"

"We need to talk. Shall we go to your office?"

"I'm very busy—"

I moved past him toward the room at the rear of the garage. "I doubt you're too busy to hear what I have to say."

Knight remained where he was, hand on the knob of the open door. I stopped at the far side of the foyer and looked at him, eyebrows raised in impatient inquiry. He frowned, lips pushing out and jowls bunching until he resembled a caricature of a bulldog. After a moment he half shrugged and shut the door. I went on to the office.

The dim little room looked the same as it had the night before; not a paper had been moved, not a speck of dust had been disturbed. Whatever Knight was busy with, it wasn't work. He entered behind me and after a brief hesitation motioned at the director's chairs before sitting down himself. I remained standing.

"Mr. Knight," I said, "you're on the Bureau of Land Management's roster of approved mineral surveyors, are you not?"

He nodded—warily, I thought.

"And five years ago a complaint was lodged against you by an environmental organization because they felt you might have falsified a survey on a gold-mining claim being patented with the BLM?"

"That complaint was totally invalid and later withdrawn—with a full apology."

"What group filed the complaint?"

"The California Coalition for Environmental Preservation."

"And where was the claim?"

"Lassen County."

"Not Mono County?"

He shook his head, wariness plainly apparent now.

"And was the claim eventually patented?"

"It was. As I said, the complaint was completely invalid."

"Yet when the American Society of Consulting Geologists and Mineralogists asked you to appear before their board to explain about the complaint, you opted instead to drop your membership."

"It was an insult! They're a do-nothing group, anyway."

"I see. And since then you've continued your surveying activities for applicants to the BLM?"

"Of course. Where is all this leading?"

I moved over and sat on a corner of his desk, placing my briefcase on a stack of papers beside me. "I'm interested in the patenting process. Is the applicant free to choose which surveyor to use from the BLM roster?"

"Yes."

"And what criteria does an individual or company go by when it makes the choice?"

"Sometimes it's as simple as proximity—is the surveyor located in the area? Or availability within the prescribed time frame. In other instances the person may know the surveyor or his work."

"Or he may know his reputation?"

"Well, of course."

I opened my briefcase and took out the file on gold mining. Knight watched suspiciously as I thumbed through it to the copies of the completed applications for patenting the 700 acres of land Mick Erickson—as Franklin Tarbeaux—had sold to Transpacific Corporation. I showed him the last page of the mineral survey and asked, "Is this your signature, Mr. Knight?"

He glanced at it and nodded.

"When Mick Erickson—or as he's known in these documents, Franklin Tarbeaux—chose you to survey this claim in Mono County, what criterion did he use?"

"I don't—"

"Did he use you because of your proximity? Availability? Had you worked for him previously?"

No reply.

"Or was it your reputation? Your reputation as someone who would misrepresent a claim's potential in order to facilitate the patenting process?"

Knight balled his stubby hands into fists. I tensed, but he merely placed one on either thigh and stared down at them. I relaxed, certain now that I was on the right track; an innocent man would have protested, ordered me to leave his house, but Knight was doing neither.

"Did you ask Erickson why he was using an assumed name on the applications?"

"Something . . . something to do with keeping the mining venture separate from his consulting business."

"And you believed that?"

Shrug.

"Or maybe you didn't care. Using an assumed name is nothing compared to falsifying the mineral survey. Did Erickson later get you the job as supervising geologist on the Golden Hills project?"

". . . Yes."

"And you conducted core sampling up there until a few weeks ago—or made out as if you were doing so?"

"Yes."

"Yes, you did, or yes, you made out as if you were?"

"All right—I made out as if I were."

"Because there's little—if any—gold on the claim Erickson sold to Transpacific. And the mine on the land that they bought from Earl Hopwood is pretty much played out, too."

Knight finally looked up. His face was flaccid with defeat, eyes dulled by fear.

I went on, "It was legal for Transpacific to do whatever they wanted with the Hopwood land, since it was purchased from a private party, but doing so posed a PR problem. And putting the seven hundred acres of former BLM land into non-mining use posed an even bigger one, because of the hassles with the government that were bound to ensue. But if that land was also purchased from an individual . . .

"The nonexistent middleman, Franklin Tarbeaux, was the perfect solution. He would sell Transpacific the land and then disappear. Later when core sampling supposedly showed that the company had been conned by Tarbeaux, sympathy would be on their side. Who could fault them for putting this tract of land that they had significant capital tied up in to a use that would recoup their investment?"

"What do you figure they could do with it in a godforsaken place like that?" Knight asked.

"Come on, Knight. You've been there. You've seen the lake, the volcanic craters, the ghost town. If they put a luxury resort with an airstrip on that mesa, they'll be in the black within a couple of seasons. And that's the area Transpacific has been moving into—luxury resorts."

Knight sighed heavily.

Taking his reaction to mean he'd given up his pretense of innocence, I pressed my advantage. "They must have paid you a great deal to aid in their plans," I said. "Unlike Mick Erickson, you had to put your true name on these documents. When the facts of the matter come out, you'll never work again. You could even be liable for criminal prosecution."

"You can't prove any of this. You can't do anything to me."

"I'm not interested in going after you. All I want is the truth, and then I'll leave you alone. Did they pay you enough to retire and disappear on?"

His nod was barely perceptible.

"Then why are you still here?"

"Because most of the money isn't to be paid until the first of the year. They promised me that nothing would be made public about their plans until I'm well away from here."

"And am I right about their plans?"

Silence.

"Well, for your sake I hope they're paying you plenty. Poor Earl Hopwood didn't do as well: he not only got screwed out of the fair market value of his family's land, but lost his dream of seeing the mine reopened. And the people in that part of Mono County aren't any better off: Promiseville will be ruined, and the ecosystem of Tufa Lake is sure to suffer.

"Of course," I added, "Lionel Ong and Transpacific got themselves a gold mine—of the tourist variety. And Mick Erickson: he probably got a fat finder's fee—before they killed him."

Knight shuddered.

"What did they give Hy Ripinsky?" I asked.

"I don't know—"

"And where's Ong? Has he arrived in Mono County yet? Have you heard from him?"

He shook his head.

"Why's he going to Mono County?"

No reply.

"Knight—"

He shook his head and stood, pushing heavily on the chair's arms. Before, his squarish frame had seemed powerful; now he looked weak and frail. He said, "You told me you wanted the truth and then you'd leave me alone. You've got it. Now go."

"You haven't told me everything—"

"I've told you what I know. You got one minute to get out of here, and then I'm calling the cops."

"That would put you in an awkward position."

"No more awkward than the one you'd be in."

He had a point, but I still took the entire minute to leave.

Twenty

▲▲▲

The phone booth at the top of Portola was occupied when I got there, and I was amused by the flash of proprietary annoyance I felt. When the user relinquished it, I quickly called Ted and picked up my messages: one from George and another from Marcy Cheung.

George's said he'd be at my house at seven. Try as I might, I couldn't remember what plans we'd made, so I called him and asked. His pained tone as he reminded me that we had tickets for that night's performance at A.C.T. made me realize how I'd neglected him of late; such forgetfulness, on top of his having to squire my mother about for an entire day, was far less than my lover deserved. I apologized—probably more than was necessary—and made a mental promise to do better in the future.

But as I dialed the Sino-American Alliance's number, I reflected that this was George's first taste of what I was like when working a complicated case. Although he'd already learned to put up with my long, irregular hours and occasional interrupted plans—as I'd learned to accommodate myself to the vagaries of his writing and teaching schedule—he might have difficulty dealing with the focused, compulsive woman I became while immersed in an investigation.

For once Cheung's phone wasn't off the hook. "I heard from Lionel Ong's secretary," she said as soon as I identified myself, "and she tells me they're starting to panic over at Transpacific."

"Has there been a ransom demand?"

"Nothing like that, but they can't reach Ong anywhere. He missed an important luncheon engagement, a couple of meetings, and now an emergency's come up with a stock issue on the Tokyo exchange that only he can make the final decision on."

"It doesn't sound as if he staged his disappearance, then."

"No. I also talked with my friend who met the woman Ong's supposedly keeping on Tel Hill. He doubts she's Ong's girlfriend. Says she didn't act like it, even though she used her own key to come into the condo and went through a stack of mail that was sitting there. But there was no spark between the two of them, nothing that gave him any sense of a real connection."

"What's her name?"

"Ong introduced her only as Margot. She's petite, blond, mid-thirties. Good-looking but not the type Ong's usually seen with. The condo is the penthouse at the address you mentioned. My friend has the impression the setup is a front."

"For what?"

"Well, Ong's one of the city's inner power circle; everybody knows the structure of our government rests more on a framework of interlocking handshakes than on the city charter. Since an awful lot of that shaking goes on in private, that building could be where Ong makes the deals that he can't make at the office or at home."

It was a reasonable analysis. "Anything else?"

"That's it."

"Thanks, Marcy. I owe you a dinner for this."
"Just as long as it's not health food."

The raw red color of the new brick town houses at Barbary Park was softened by the late-afternoon sun. A gentle breeze off the bay stirred the leaves of the containerized hawthorns and Japanese maples. I crossed the humpbacked stone bridge over the koi pond and followed the path to number 551.

When I'd called up there from the lobby, the Filipino maid again answered and said that Mrs. Erickson had gone out of town. I strongly suspected that Margot had cloistered herself within the spun-sugar confines of her home, so I retreated to the Embarcadero Center and loitered on the level where the pedestrian walkway linked it to the condominium complex. A man in business attire crossed it and inserted a plastic key card into a box next to the gate; it swung open and closed slowly behind him.

I sat on the edge of a large concrete container of marigolds and watched as two other people entered in similar fashion. When a third came along, I fell into a step a short way behind her, pretending to fumble in my bag for my own key card. The woman passed through the gate without taking more than perfunctory notice of me; I slipped through as it began its return swing.

Now I stepped into the private entry court of number 551. The sun slanted through its glass roof, creating a hothouse atmosphere; the containerized tropical plants that grew there had recently been watered, and a damp-earth smell rose to my nostrils. No one answered my repeated rings. Either the maid had gone home since I'd called from the lobby or she was ignoring me at her employer's instruction.

I went back outside, contemplating my options, then followed the path to the elevator. When it arrived, I pressed the button for the garage.

The garage was whitewashed and neon-lit, echoing with

the whine of tires as cars ascended from a lower level. I glanced at my watch as I passed the service bay; just about five, when the offices and parking spaces of the financial district begin to empty. At the office I waited while a man argued with the clerk about the increase in his monthly rent. The city's parking tax went up faster than his dick, he complained. The clerk—a dishwater blond youth who couldn't have been more than a year out of high school—frowned and pointedly glanced my way; so did the complainer, but seeing there was a woman present only made him repeat his comment. After he paid his bill he got into a Cadillac with a custom metallic green paint job, proving to my way of thinking that his bad taste extended to his choice of transportation.

I showed the young man my identification and asked if he knew Mrs. Margot Erickson. He nodded and said wasn't it a shame about her husband? She was a nice lady, and then to have an accident on top of him dying like that—

"What accident?"

"Oh, man, you should have seen her. Her face was all fu . . . messed up. When I asked what happened, she said she'd been riding in a taxi that got into a wreck." He paused, looking critically at me. "Something like that happen to you, too?"

"Something like that. When did you last see Mrs. Erickson?"

Now he looked unsure of himself. "I don't think I should talk about one of the residents."

"I'm investigating her husband's death in cooperation with the Mono County Sheriff's Department. If you'd like verification, you can call Inspector Bart Wallace at the SFPD."

"No, that's okay." He looked more uncomfortable about talking with a police officer than with me.

"Is Mrs. Erickson's car in the garage?"

"No."

"You last saw her when?"

"This morning when she paid for the servicing on the Miata. She called down first thing, asked that they get it ready for a long trip."

"Did she say where she was going?"

"Not to me. Maybe to Ken." He indicated a heavyset middle-aged man in mechanic's coveralls who was leaning against one of the gas pumps in the service bay.

I thanked him and went over to Ken, showing him my I.D. and giving him the same explanation I had the clerk. Ken was less wary of talking about the residents; from his lackadaisical speech and slouching posture I gathered that caution would simply have cost too much of an effort. Yeah, he said, he'd serviced the Miata that morning.

"Did Mrs. Erickson mention where she was going on this trip?"

"Yeah—home."

"Where's that?"

Shrug. "All she said was she needed to go home for a few days. And then she stiffed me out of a tip. You imagine that? I bust hump to get that car ready before I even have my coffee and doughnut, and she stiffs me."

"Are you sure she didn't mention—"

A car came up the ramp and pulled into the bay. Ken heaved a martyred sigh as it stopped at the full-service island. As he pushed away from the pump he said, "All she told me was home," and eyed me hopefully.

I turned and walked away, stiffing him out of both a tip and thanks.

When I got back to All Souls, Ted had already left his desk, but there was a message in my box to call Anne-Marie at the Coalition's trailer. I went down the hall to Rae's office but it was dark and untenanted. Upstairs I removed the folder containing the patenting applications for the Stone Valley land tract from my briefcase. There, in black and white, was what I'd failed to attach any significance to earlier: the address given for Franklin Tarbeaux was the same as that of the Transpacific-owned condominium on Tel Hill. That gave me a fair idea of what Margot Erickson's business there had been.

Next I dialed Mono County. Anne-Marie's voice answered on the first ring. "What's up?" I asked.

"That's what I called to ask you."

"Well, I've found out something that may help you stop Transpacific from developing the mesa, but I'd rather tell you about it in person."

"When are you coming back?"

I looked up as Ted entered the room and slipped a sheet of legal paper in front of me. "What's this?" I asked.

"What?" Anne-Marie said.

"I'm talking to Ted."

Ted said, "It's a message from Rae. You're to ask me if you can't make sense of it."

"Shar? Are you there?"

"Yes." I began scanning Ted's scribblings.

"I asked when you're coming back. If you have something significant, we need to move on it. Besides, things have gone to hell around here and I could use—"

"Hold on." I finished scanning the page, then read it more carefully.

> Peggy = nickname for Margaret Hopwood (got from
>   UC Berkeley records)
> Margaret H. m. James L. Hill, SF, 7/71
> MH div. JLH, SF, 10/74
> MH m. Robert Krause, SF, 12/75
> MH div. RK, Marin, 5/83
> MH m. Michael M. Erickson, Marin, 6/83

"Shar? This is costing you money."

"Just one more minute."

Margot—a fancy variation on Margaret. The sort of name

that would appeal to Earl Hopwood's upwardly mobile and much married daughter.

"Hy says he thinks you should fly up here tonight. He'll pick you up at the Reno airport."

Margot had told the service attendant at the Barbary Park garage that she was going home for a few days.

"You say fly to Reno tonight?" I asked.

"Yes, it's quicker. Hy'll let you borrow his Land Rover while you're here."

Ted turned and went out the door.

I hesitated, considering the proposed course of action. In light of my suspicions about him, I didn't relish the idea of driving the lonely mountainous stretch between Reno and Vernon with Hy Ripinsky. But there was no reason to believe he was aware of those suspicions, and it was possible his guard might be low enough so that I would learn something from him on the ride.

"Ted's checking the schedules now," I said to Anne-Marie. "What's wrong there?"

"Oh." Quick expulsion of breath, the closest to a whine I'd ever heard from her. "I'd better save it till you get here."

I wondered if her reluctance to talk about it was due to Ripinsky being in the office. Did she have her suspicions, too?

Ted reentered. "You're booked on the eight-ten AirCal flight out of SFO." He set a piece of paper with the flight number and arrival time in front of me.

I read off the information to Anne-Marie and told her I'd see her at the lodge.

"I take it I'm on cat duty until further notice?" Ted asked.

"If you don't mind."

"Mind? Hah! It means I can play a couple of rented tapes on your VCR without interruptions from the phone or our esteemed colleagues."

I watched him leave the office, reflecting on how much I—all of us—depended on Ted. It never occurred to us that he might actually want to be free of his duties when five o'clock rolled around. We thought nothing of burdening him with messages to pass on, plane reservations to book, references to look up, or lost objects to locate, no matter what the time of day or night. I seldom gave any thought to his private life, save to notice that he'd engaged in no intimate relationships since his friend Harry's death had brought the full reality of the AIDS threat home to him. Ted had never struck me as a lonely or overburdened man, but now I realized he was both, and it saddened me. I would have to think more of his needs in the future, just as I should of George's—

George! Quickly I dialed his number, apprehensive about how he'd react to my breaking our date on such short notice. The line was busy. "Dammit!" I slammed the receiver into its cradle, then immediately picked it up and called Bart Wallace at the SFPD.

Before he could ask about the progress of my investigation, I said, "I want to take you up on your offer to help out with this Erickson thing."

"Okay." Wallace sounded wary, but then, he had always been an extremely cautious man.

Quickly I gave him a list of names, including Ripinsky's, to run through the National Crime Information Center and the state Criminal Justice Information System. Wallace promised to get on it right away; I thanked him and said I'd check back tomorrow. As I hung up, Rae came through the door.

"Hey, good work on Peggy Hopwood," I told her, deciding to ignore the hanging-up incident for the moment. "You must have chased all over the place today."

She didn't reply. Her blue eyes were riveted on my bruised face, her freckles standing out against the sudden pallor of her skin.

She said, "Not again!"

"What?" I glanced around the desk and began gathering papers and folders to take with me.

"Just look at yourself!"

"I've looked, thank you, and once was enough."

"You're making a joke of this?" She came all the way into the room and stood in the center of my Oriental rug, hands on her hips, small chin thrust forward.

I was in no mood to deal with another lecture, so I kept my tone light as I replied, "If I didn't joke, I'd whimper, and what's the point in that?" I stood and began packing my briefcase.

Rae watched me for a few seconds, then asked, "What happened?"

I started to bring her up to date on the investigation, but when I got to the part about Margot Erickson attacking me, she became agitated. She began to pace the geometric pattern of the rug, then flung her arms out and exclaimed, "You can't keep doing things like that!"

"Like what? Running a stakeout? Tailing someone? Making like I've got two left feet at the top of a stairway?"

"See? You're joking again. This is not funny, Sharon."

I shut the briefcase and rested my hands on it. "Rae, if you can't see the humor—"

"Humor!" She stopped pacing and faced me, arms crossed over her breasts and gripping the opposite elbow with either hand. There was outrage in her eyes, but also another emotion, only half submerged beneath it. With surprise I realized Ted was right: Rae was frightened—and I knew of what.

I said, "This goes back to last summer, doesn't it? You saw a different side of me then, and it scared you."

"*Scared* me?" She made a dismissive sound with her lips, but her quick glance away told me I'd cut to the core of the problem.

"Yes, scared you. You're afraid that if you stay in this business you'll turn out like me."

She was silent, looking down at her folded arms.

"That's what all this lecturing and carping is really about," I said. "You can't deal with a very legitimate fear, so you've converted it to anger toward me."

I thought she'd deny it, but instead she looked up, relief stealing over her features. Quickly it was followed by fresh anxiety. "A legitimate fear?"

"Perfectly. When you spend years in a job where your basic function is to poke sticks into an absolute cesspool of human behavior, you're bound to become disillusioned and angry. How you handle those feelings depends on the kind of person you are."

"And you think you handle them well?"

"I didn't say that. I handle them the only way I can."

"Last summer you almost killed—"

"But I didn't." Hy Ripinsky might be a liar and a fraud, but he'd helped me to face one truth: the only thing that mattered was that, no matter how much I wanted to, I hadn't taken a life.

Rae said, "But up till then you'd always seemed so calm, so in control."

"Those are only my outer layers." I paused, thinking back to the things my mother had said the night before. "You know, I've always claimed that the undesirable changes in me—cynicism, anger, whatever—have come about as a result of the things I've seen and done in the course of my work. But now I'm not so sure that's wholly true. Maybe as we get older our experiences don't change us so much as make us more who and what we really are."

"So what does that mean—that deep down where it counts you're nothing but an enraged old cynic?"

"I hope not, but to tell you the truth, I don't know."

"Don't you think you should know who and what you are by now?"

"Oh, Rae." Suddenly I was struck by how very young she was. "None of us ever knows that. We just keep closing in on

it all our lives, and each time we think we've got it figured
out, everything changes."

"That's not very reassuring, you know."

"Sorry, kid—it's all I've got to offer."

Rae's face remained downcast as she thought the concept
over. It wasn't until I hefted my briefcase and moved around
the desk that she spoke again. "Um, Shar . . . I'm sorry I
hung up on you."

"That's okay—I understand."

"Where are you going in such a hurry, anyway? You didn't
finish filling me in about the case."

But there was no time left now. Besides, I was still feeling
a little put out by the hanging-up episode. Since Rae was
fond of bragging about her abilities as a detective, I decided
to give her something to work on.

"I am off," I told her, "to the fire mountains."

Part Three

▲ ▲ ▲

The Fire Mountain

Twenty-one

▲▲▲

It was cold in Reno. When the first blast of frigid air hit me, I felt thankful that I'd traded my suede for a wool pea jacket. As I descended the steps of the plane, I spotted Hy Ripinsky on the tarmac below, talking with one of the ground personnel. He had bundled up, too, in a leather bomber jacket with a sheepskin collar, and the hand he raised in greeting was gloved.

When I stepped out of the line of passengers and went up to him, the man he'd been chatting with slapped him on the back and moved away. Hy grabbed my weekend bag and looked closely at my face. "You get into a bar brawl, McCone?"

"I have only my own clumsiness to blame."

He looked disbelieving, but merely asked, "Have a good flight?"

"It was fine." Actually I'd spent most of it worrying: about George's reaction to my breaking our theater date for that evening, and about this initial encounter with Hy. Mainly I was afraid that something in my voice or manner would betray my suspicion of Ripinsky's involvement with Lionel

Ong and his geologist, but there was also the possibility that
Alvin Knight had alerted him. If so, I couldn't predict what
he might do.

But Ripinsky seemed at ease and plainly glad to see me.
He put a hand on my shoulder and began to steer me away
from the terminal building. "Hey," I said, "where are you
going?"

"Buddy of mine'll give us a lift over to General Aviation."
He motioned at the maintenance vehicle that waited several
yards away, amber lights flashing, exhaust billowing white
in the cold air.

"Why?"

He stopped and frowned down at me. "Didn't Anne-Marie
tell you we'd be flying back to the lake?"

"She said you'd pick me up, that's all."

"Well, I am—in my plane." Under his droopy mustache,
his lips curved in amusement.

When we'd first talked about him, Anne-Marie had mentioned something about Hy owning a plane, but it had
slipped my mind. Now it seemed I was supposed to fly over
the Sierra Nevada at night with a man whom I was leery of
trusting. I frowned, wondering if I could get out of it by
feigning a fear of small aircraft.

Hy said, "You can't be afraid. Anne-Marie told me you'd
taken a few flying lessons a while back."

That had been several years before, when I'd been enamored of an instructor at the Alameda Naval Air Station, who
had taught me for free. The lessons stopped when he
received orders to Pensacola and I realized how expensive
it would be to continue without his largess. Now I cursed
Anne-Marie's good memory. "I took enough to know how
dangerous mountain flying is," I told Hy. "Especially in the
dark."

"No need to worry—I'm an old hand at it." He nudged me
toward the waiting truck. "Been flying since I was old
enough to reach the controls. My daddy was a crop duster,

and he taught me well—at least until he got wrapped up in some high-tension wires south of Fresno."

"Thanks for sharing that encouraging information with me."

Hy shrugged. "Compared to crop dusting, mountain flying's a piece of cake."

We reached the truck and squeezed into the cab with his friend, whom he introduced as Dan. As we sped across the field toward a hangar where small aircraft were tied down, they discussed Dan's new girlfriend, a cashier at Bally's. I tuned them out and tried to assess how much danger the situation held.

By now Anne-Marie would have told Hy that I'd possibly found a way to stop Transpacific's Golden Hills project. Given his own apparent involvement, that might pose a personal threat to him. But now much of a threat, and to what lengths would he go to stop me?

Assume the worst, that he would go so far as to kill me. He couldn't just throw me bodily from the plane and claim I'd never shown up in Reno. The airline had my name on the passenger manifest; people like Dan had seen us together here. In order to make my death look accidental, he'd have to crash his plane, injure himself, too. That tipped the risk factor in my favor.

Of course, there was the possibility that once in the air he'd attempt to intimidate me. While I didn't relish the prospect, it wouldn't be the first time someone had used terror tactics on me, and I was sure I could make it through the ordeal unscathed. But somehow I doubted either of the scenarios would come to pass; nothing in Ripinsky's manner indicated that the ebb and flow of the relationship had altered—at least from his point of view. As the truck pulled to a stop aside a lighted office on one side of the hangar, I made my decision: don't blow your investigation; just sit back and try to enjoy the ride.

We got out of the truck and thanked Dan for the lift. He

gave us a quasi-military salute and drove away. Hy said, "Wait here," and went into the office. In a minute he returned. "All set—let's go."

All around the hangar small craft were tethered to the tarmac by chains. The cold wind blew strongly, and as Hy led me among them their wings bobbed and creaked. Ahead of us the lights of Reno glittered, spread across the flatlands and rising on the hills; behind us a jet's engines roared as it landed. I heard the shriek of rubber as its tires bit down, felt the shudder of its frame. We rounded a six-passenger Cessna, and then Hy stretched out his arm.

The sleek plane he indicated seemed like a toy next to the Cessna: white, with a high wing and a tail section that canted sharply toward the ground. A double blue stripe and identification number, 77289, ran along the side, and on the tail was a blue silhouette of an airborne gull—the symbol of the Friends of Tufa Lake.

"So what do you think of my baby?" Hy asked.

"What is it?"

"Citabria Decathlon." There was a thinly veiled note of pride in his voice.

I'd heard experienced pilots speak enviously of the Citabria, a fabric-covered special-purpose monoplane manufactured in limited numbers. "Aerobatic plane, right?"

"Uh-huh. The name's 'airbatic' spelled backwards."

"I'm impressed."

He ducked under the wing, opened the door, and tossed my weekend bag into the rear compartment. "Well, don't get too excited—we're not going to do any loops and rolls tonight. Plane's got a hundred and eighty horsepower—top of the line—but the altitude we need to fly at—twelve, thirteen thousand feet—is about the max it can safely handle."

I swallowed.

Hy turned, stripping off his gloves and peering intently at my face. "Oh, for Christ's sake, McCone," he said, "there'll still be plenty of power in reserve to handle the downdrafts. Just get in, will you?"

I stepped forward and he helped me up. The seats were in tandem, the cabin not much wider than my desk chair at All Souls. I said, "It's like a matchbox with wings."

"More streamlined, though." He fiddled with the seat belt, strapped it around me. The joystick protruded from behind the pilot's seat, directly between my bent knees. "Don't touch that," Hy told me.

"I know."

He unhooked a headset from the wall and fitted it over my ears. "You want to talk with me, you've got to put your lips right up against the mouthpiece."

"Hy—"

"Take it easy; I've made this trip more times than I can count." He drew back through the door and grinned at me. "Listen, McCone, this plane is such a class act that Bellanca, the manufacturer, wouldn't sell one to Lindbergh for his transatlantic flight. They were afraid it would detract from their prestige, since he was only an inexperienced mail pilot on the Saint Louis–Chicago run."

"What does Lindbergh have to do with—"

"Like I said, the Decathlon is top of the Citabria line. Besides the increased power, there's more of a camber on the bottom of the wings—allows it to fly inverted better."

"Inverted," I said miserably.

"I promise—not tonight." He winked and turned away.

I watched his long, lean figure as he bent to release the chain from the right-hand wing, made routine checks of the gas and oil, and passed in front of the plane, running practiced hands over the propeller. Ripinsky might not be on to what I'd discovered about him in San Francisco, but he had tipped to a basic fact about me personally—I like to pretend I'm braver than I really am. If I hadn't been hamstrung by the seat belt and earphone wires, I'd have climbed out of there and given him a good kick to get even for his obvious glee at needling me.

When he'd gotten into the pilot's seat and settled himself, he glanced at me while reaching for an instrument panel to my left. "Ready?"

"Yes," I said coolly, trying to look nonchalant as I stared up at the sky through the clear roof above him.

He flipped a couple of switches.

I jerked.

He grinned wickedly and turned his attention to the controls.

On the premise that sometimes it's best to ignore what's making you nervous, I concentrated harder on the black sky. Hy started the engine. It died. He tried again. It died again. A third try. Same result.

I gripped the back of his seat, staring straight ahead now.

"Relax, McCone," his voice said through the headset. "At this altitude the air's thin; it takes a bit to get her going."

I let go of the seat and clasped my hands between my knees, avoiding the joystick.

The engine caught and roared to life; the propeller spun, whirled faster—a silver blur against the night.

I looked up, trying to find something to concentrate on, something other than the mechanics of departure. George? Oh, God, George . . .

I'd tried to reach him from home but hadn't succeeded until minutes before I boarded my flight at SFO. Although he was disappointed at the sudden change of plans, he reacted with characteristic fair-mindedness.

"It's not as if you haven't warned me about how unpredictable the demands of your job can be," he had said.

Quite unreasonably I felt a prickle of irritation at his calm understanding. "I'd be furious if you did this to me."

"That's because you're an Unconventional." It was the little circle into which he—lately—felt I best fit. (*Damn* my mother for so dubbing George's personality classifications!

I'd never be able to think of them otherwise now.) Among my group's more unfortunate traits were extreme emotional sensitivity, a disregard for social mores, and a tendency to depression.

"No," I had said, trying to maintain a light tone, "you're being nice because you've got a touch of the Helpmate about you." The Helpmates were the wimps of his schema.

Normally George would have laughed, but he was adept at picking up on my vocal undertones. "Sharon, what's wrong?"

I had hesitated, one ear tuned to my flight's first boarding call. My annoyance was both illogical and ill defined; certainly it would fade before I next saw him. "I'm just upset about having to cancel," I finally told him.

But I must have sounded unconvincing. "We'll have to talk when you get back," he said.

"Yes, we'll talk," I agreed.

Now I found the memory of the conversation unsettling enough that I didn't care to dwell on it. While Hy spoke into the Citabria's radio, I turned my thoughts to my investigation.

Start with Mick Erickson. He found out about the gold-mining potential in Stone Valley from his old co-worker, Ned Sanderman. Since he had a degree from Colorado School of Mines, he might have been aware of the patenting process as a way to purchase federal land. Wait a minute here—wouldn't Erickson have already known about Stone Valley, since his father-in-law owned the defunct Promiseville Mine?

"Reno Ground, this is Citabria seven-seven-two-eight-niner. . . ."

All right, maybe Erickson's talk with Sanderman jogged his memory, got him to thinking about the land to be had in Stone Valley. Sanderman might even have unwittingly supplied Alvin Knight's name by telling Mick how the Coalition had filed a complaint against the geologist for allegedly falsifying a mineral survey.

"Two-eight-niner, squawk is oh-one-three-five. . . ."

Erickson probably knew that Ong was looking to buy large parcels of land in attractive locations for Transpacific resorts. So he went to Ong with the idea of developing Stone Valley, demanding a finder's fee, of course. He persuaded his father-in-law—or perhaps Margot did—to sell his property to Transpacific, and arranged with Alvin Knight to obtain the adjoining 700 acres.

"Clearance Delivery, this is two-eight-niner. I'm VFR southbound for Tufa Lake with Delta . . ."

Everything had gone as planned. Title to the BLM land passed to the fictitious Tarbeaux; Transpacific in turn bought it from him. Knight played his role as supervising geologist and made a pretense of taking core samples, then shut the site down. My guess was that Transpacific intended to wait through the winter before making the public announcement that they had been duped by the conveniently missing Tarbeaux. With their public relations people smoothing the way, they would then unveil plans for the Golden Hills project, no doubt making much of the new prosperity that the construction and, later, the service jobs would bring to Mono County.

"Ground Control, this is two-eight-niner. Request permission to taxi for takeoff."

"Two-eight-niner, taxi to runway thirty-four right."

The little plane eased into motion. I watched the other small aircraft slip by and, after we turned, saw a jet taxiing on the parallel runway. Even at this distance, its size made me feel vulnerable. I clasped my hands tighter, turned my attention back to the case.

Okay, I thought, everything went as planned. But then Erickson made a secret trip to Tufa Lake—so secret he went to great lengths to keep it from everyone, including his wife . . . estranged wife. A few days later he was shot and dumped in the lake. Hopwood had already more or less vanished, and now so had Lionel Ong. And yesterday someone had roughed up Margot Erickson; she'd also taken off for Tufa Lake.

Quite a gathering might occur there, should Ong turn up in the area, as Knight and Ripinsky seemed to believe he would. If Hopwood surfaced and Knight decided to make the trip, it would be a reunion of co-conspirators.

"Reno Tower, this is two-eight-niner. Ready on thirty-four right."

"Okay, two-eight-niner. Clear for takeoff. Right downwind departure."

Hy increased the engine power; the little plane strained and trembled. I dug my fingernails into the palms of my hands. The plane jerked forward, began rushing down the runway, wheels bumping and jarring my spine. I closed my eyes, felt the thump as the tires left the ground. The plane canted even more sharply; I was thrust back into the seat, planted my feet more securely on the floor. We climbed at a steep angle, kept climbing for what must have been a couple of miles, and then leveled out some. I opened my eyes.

Hy banked the plane, and I saw the neon glitter dusting the hills and flatlands to my right. "Hey, McCone," his voice said in my ear, "you still with me?"

I twisted sideways and pressed my nose to the window. "I'm here."

"Pretty, isn't it?"

"Sure is." Turbulence caught the plane, rocked it. My stomach lurched, but I kept my nose to the plastic, watching Reno grow smaller. The next updraft didn't bother me; instead I felt an excited flutter. It was the old half-remembered thrill of being cut loose from the earth. More than that: of having been cut loose from the bonds of the present, the past, even the future. . . .

God, I'd forgotten how much I loved to fly!

Hy said, "The way we're heading, you'll be able to make out Lake Tahoe if you look hard. That's Carson City dead ahead, and from there we'll just follow the road home."

"You mean three ninety-five?"

"Uh-huh. Not much between Carson City and Bridgeport except a few small towns. The highway's a good landmark, so why not use it?"

I settled back, enjoying the motion.

"So," Hy said, "you want to brief me on what you found out in San Francisco? Anne-Marie seems to think we've got the problem knocked."

". . . I'd just as soon go over it with both of you at the same time."

"Suit yourself."

We flew in silence for a while. I left off thinking about the case, watched the lights of Carson City appear and recede behind us. Then there was only blackness below, relieved occasionally by a few dim beacons. Now and then an updraft buffeted us. The first made me suck in my breath, and Hy said, "Hey, that's nothing." After that, as he would have said, they were a piece of cake. When a particularly strong one hit us just as the lights of Bridgeport appeared, I laughed. Hy's answering chuckle contained a note of pleased surprise.

"Getting into flying again, are you?"

"I'd better not be—it's expensive. That was why I stopped before."

"Hell, I got an instructor buddy owes me favors; I could get your lessons for free."

"But then what would I owe *you?*"

He laughed.

Wistfulness stole over me. The idle chatter was amusing, but I knew there would be no flying lessons. No future light conversations between Ripinsky and me, either. Once I'd finished with this investigation—

He said, "By the way, you like that rose I sent you?"

". . . *You* sent me?" I was stunned.

"Uh-huh. Bet you thought it was from your boyfriend."

It was lucky I'd kept forgetting to thank George for it,

especially in light of his present disappointment with me. "I did. How'd you know about him?"

"Anne-Marie told me. Sounds like a smart fellow."

"He is. Why'd you send me the flower?"

"Hell, McCone, why does any man send a woman a rose?"

I didn't respond, but after Bridgeport had vanished into the darkness I asked, "Why a yellow one?"

"You're not traditional enough for red, not sentimental enough for pink, and definitely not virginal, so white was out."

"Well, thank you for sending it. Yellow's my favorite."

"I think I kind of guessed that."

For a while after that we didn't speak. I stared at the back of his head, my thoughts and emotions in turmoil. Then he reached back and touched my knee, motioned at the left side of the aircraft.

Tufa Lake spread to the south, lights of the town strung along its near shore. Among them I could identify Zelda's sign at the tip of the point, its crimson bleeding into the water. The runway of the airstrip was outlined in a string of yellow lights to the west. And in the distance the alkali plain gleamed white in the moonlight, the black cones of the fire mountains looming over it.

The plane dipped and began its steep descent. Hy said, "Tufa Tower, this is double-luck-two-eight-niner, coming home."

Twenty-two

▲▲▲

When we got to Hy's ranch house, he pulled my bag from the carrying space of his Morgan and set it next to the Land Rover. "You sure you won't come in and get warm?" he asked.

I shook my head. "It's late; Anne-Marie will worry."

"Suit yourself." He fiddled with his key chain, then held one out to me. "There's a spare in one of those magnetic cases under the left rear bumper. Registration and insurance card in the glove compartment. Baby it a little when you start up in the morning—it's no more of an early riser than I am."

"Thanks. And thanks for the lift down here."

"Glad to be of help. Tomorrow we'll talk about what you found out."

Not replying, I tossed the bag onto the seat of the Land Rover and climbed in after it. The engine caught right away, and I eased the vehicle into gear and turned around. As I drove off, I glanced into the rearview mirror; Hy was standing where I'd left him, looking melancholy.

At the road I turned right toward Vernon, but after I

rounded the first bend I made a U-turn and parked on the verge near the sheep pen. The moon was a luminous disk suspended above the peaks; its chill glow frosted the barren countryside. The sheep huddled together, their wool resembling drifts of snow. The stick-and-barbed wire fences stood out against the pale meadow as if etched on ice.

The green numerals of the digital clock on the dash showed it was after eleven. I settled back and waited—five, ten, fifteen minutes. Then I restarted the engine and drove swiftly toward Stone Valley. As I passed Ripinsky's ranch house, I noted that its windows were dark, the Morgan where he'd parked it. Still, I kept a weather eye on the rearview mirror until I was certain he hadn't spotted the Land Rover and followed me.

As I topped the rise above the ruins of Promiseville I slowed, scanning the valley. No lights on the mesa or in the town. In the icy moonglow the fractured and shattered hills were reminders of the earth's violent self-destructive forces. The twisted skeleton of the old stamp mill sprawling down the side of the mesa and the sagging husks on the valley floor spoke of what those forces had done to the people who attempted to tame them.

The vast emptiness and silence threatened to overwhelm me. I gripped the steering wheel, pressed down on the accelerator. Drove into the valley, pushing aside intimations of futility and mortality. And kept my eyes on the road ahead as I passed the graveyard.

The Land Rover handled the rough trail next to the streambed effortlessly. I kept its speed down and switched to the parking lights as I neared the little box canyon. A short distance away I stopped and proceeded on foot.

Before I could see Hopwood's cabin, I heard the rush of the falls. Moonbeams played on the stream's eddying waters and lighted my way. The rocky walls narrowed on either side of me, and then I spotted the crude pine structure tucked under the cliff's overhang. No van or Miata stood in front of it, no light showed in its windows.

So where was Margot Erickson?

I stopped some twenty feet away, searching the shadows. The same sense of wrongness that I'd felt Saturday afternoon came to me—more strongly now. I went up to the cabin's door and pounded. As I expected, there was no response. Then I circled it, looking for something I might have missed the other day. Hesitated behind it, rationalizing what I was about to do.

The situation had changed since I'd come here the first time. Mick Erickson had been murdered, and there was a possibility the killer had gone after Hopwood, too. Margot had left San Francisco early this morning, should have arrived here by now; she had already been roughed up, might also be in danger. Technically I should have reported my suspicions to the sheriff's department, but it was a long way to a phone. Besides, I was working with them. . . .

I located a metal drum in the assortment of junk below the rocky overhang and dragged it beneath one of the windows. Upended it and climbed on top, attempting to look inside. Dirty white curtains blocked my view. I shoved upward on the sash, but the lock held.

I climbed down and scouted the junk pile until I found a pick with a broken handle. Carried it over, raised it in both hands, and shattered the glass. After pulling the more jagged shards from the frame, I pushed the curtain aside. The window let into a kitchen. I undid the lock, thrust the frame up, hoisted myself onto the sill, then dropped to the plank floor.

I'd locked my purse in the Land Rover, but had thought to bring along my small flashlight. Now I pulled it from my pocket and shone its thin beam around the room. The kitchen was even more primitive than the one at Lily Nickles's house and gave evidence of Hopwood's indifferent housekeeping: dirty plates and a pot full of a long-encrusted substance stood on a table near the propane burner; a loaf of bread had turned dark and fuzzy, its plastic wrapper nibbled by rodents.

A doorway led into a second room. Through it I could see an old-fashioned overstuffed sofa like the one at All Souls. I went in there, found a wood stove and a platform rocker. And saw that one of the end tables had been overturned, an oil lamp shattered on the floor. Beside it lay a crumpled rag rug covered with dark stains.

I squatted next to the rug, trained the flashlight beam on it. The stains were brown and dried; it looked as if the rug had been used to wipe the floor. I examined the planks more closely, saw smears on them and crusted brown matter down in the cracks. Part of the beige sofa was covered in a fine spatter pattern.

Blood, I thought, old blood. But how old?

I swiveled and trained the flashlight on the spatters on the sofa. The small size of the drops indicated they'd been produced by a high- to medium-velocity impact; that meant anything from a blow with a hammer or ax to a gunshot. Although their shape had been distorted by absorption into the fabric, they appeared to have hit the sofa at a slightly downward angle.

All right, I thought, standing up. Someone was about here in front of the sofa when he or she was hit or shot. Fell this way, knocking over the lamp and table. But who? And when? By whom? And why? Those were questions that no amount of examination of spatter patterns would answer. I needed to call the sheriff's department so a lab crew could go over the place, but while I was here . . .

Quickly I began to search the rest of the cabin, being careful not to disarrange anything or destroy possible fingerprints. It was a simple job—there was only one other room—and as I went I gathered shreds of the lonely life that had gone on, and perhaps ended, there.

On the bureau in the small bedroom was a single framed

photograph showing a young Margot Erickson, dark blond hair styled in a bouffant, shoulders covered in the sort of black velvet drape popular for high school graduation pictures of that era. Pretty Peggy, as Ripinsky had said they called her, smiled for the camera, but there was a tension in the curve of her lips that suggested—at least from the advantageous perspective of hindsight—a near-desperate urge to break loose from her clinging father and the small town that confined her. I wondered if today Margot felt the ensuing years had been worth their cost.

The bureau drawers contained nothing but clothing, a great deal of it unworn and some of it still in boxes from such pricey San Francisco stores as Bullock & Jones—unneeded and unwanted gifts from a daughter attempting to assuage her guilt at having abandoned her father. Hanging in the closet were the things that Hopwood actually wore—denims and khakis and a small selection of inexpensive polyester sports clothes suitable for the casinos in Nevada. The only reading material was a Bible, which lay open and face down on the single nightstand next to the metal bedstead.

I picked it up, saw that Hopwood had been reading Revelation. A phrase at the top of the right-hand page caught my attention: "And the devil that deceived them was cast into the lake of fire and brimstone, where the beast and false prophet are, and shall be tormented day and night for ever and ever."

Soothing bedtime reading, I thought as I set down the worn volume. I've never understood the appeal of the fire-and-brimstone varieties of religion; life is difficult enough without the constant specter of damnation looming over us each time we stray from some stringent and preordained creed. Perhaps it was the fact that I've never considered myself one of the righteous who would find the welcome mat spread before the gates of Saint John the Divine's envisioned holy city, but I was certain that had I lived in the vast isolation of Stone Valley, I would have sought more cheerful reading matter than his apocalyptic ravings.

I made one more brief pass through the living room and kitchen, then secured the cabin and got out of there. I'd drive to Vernon and report the bloodstains to the sheriff's department—and hope they accepted my rationalization for breaking in there.

There was a lighted phone booth outside the filling station that Hopwood used to run, so I pulled in to make my call from there rather than driving all the way to the lodge. Kristen Lark wasn't on duty; when I asked for her partner, Dwight Gifford, I was told he was on vacation. The deputy on duty wouldn't give me Lark's home number, but after some wheedling on my part, he took my number and said he'd phone her; if she wanted to talk to me, she'd call back.

I propped the booth's door open so the light would go off and waited in the darkness. Vernon was pretty much shut down by now, although Zelda's sign still glowed red against the post-midnight sky. I remembered how from the air the neon had made it look as if the lake were stained with blood, and my thoughts returned to the all too real bloodstains out in Stone Valley. When the phone rang, I started.

Lark said, "McCone, where are you? This is a Vernon number, right?"

"Right." I explained about my quick trip back here and what I'd found at the cabin.

Lark was silent for a moment. "Why'd you go out there?" she finally asked.

"It's a complicated story. I'd rather tell you in person."

"Uh-huh. And these alleged bloodstains—you say they're in the living room?"

"Yes. And yes, I broke in there. The situation seemed serious enough to justify it."

"Huh."

I waited. When Lark didn't say anything else, I asked, "Well?"

"I'm thinking. The call from the station woke me up; I've been on a back-to-back rotation, working without Dwight— bastard's off in Idaho—and I was sleeping pretty good."

"Sorry."

"Part of the job. What I'm thinking is that I want a lab crew to go over the place when it's light. I ought to get a warrant, but that's no problem because we've got plenty of probable cause and Judge Sims is always in chambers over at the courthouse by nine. Can you meet me at the cabin at, say, noon?"

"Sure."

"I'll see you then. And, McCone?"

"Yes?"

"Get some sleep yourself."

The moon was down by the time I reached the lodge. The grove lay in total darkness, the willow trees like huge black umbrellas over the cabins nestled on the slope. I left Ripinsky's Land Rover next to Anne-Marie's car and trained my flashlight beam on the ground as I descended.

Not a light showed in the cabin. I felt in my jeans pocket for the key Anne-Marie had asked Hy to give me, then got the door open and stepped inside. When I switched on the ugly overhead fixture I saw a yellow sheet on the center cushion of the sofa, weighted down by the brandy bottle. The note said, "Wake me."

That'll take some doing, I thought. Anne-Marie was a serious sleeper; she'd once told me that even as a small child she hadn't bounced cheerfully from bed. In law school she'd trained herself to catch a few winks whenever and wherever convenient—sitting in the classroom before a lecture began, on buses, even while waiting in lines. In preparation for my chore, I went to the kitchen and fixed coffee in the small electric percolator. Then I went into her room and commenced shaking her.

It was a full five minutes before I got her propped in a chair in the living room, mug of coffee in hand. Another two passed before she noticed the damage to my face. She made alarmed noises, but they were comically sleep-clogged. I related the story of my past few days as the caffeine did its work on her.

By the time I finished, she'd come totally awake. She asked me some questions about the mineral survey that Alvin Knight had falsified, then hurried over to the dinette table and pawed through the papers that were spread there. "I do believe you've got what we need to stop that development," she said. "I'll go over these patenting applications, then contact the BLM and ask what steps we should take. We may have to file suit—" Then her face fell. "Oh, shit!"

"What?"

"I forgot." She set down the file and returned to the sofa, the belt of her wool robe dragging on the floor behind her. "I'm supposed to leave here tomorrow."

"Well, won't you have to go to Sacramento to deal with the BLM anyway?"

"Yes, but I'm only stopping there to pick up some clean clothing. The Coalition needs me in Humboldt County— anti-logging protest, and some of the groups are going too far with it. We need to point out the legal ramifications to them."

"When did you find this out?"

"Around three this afternoon, when Ned finally got back from Sacramento. It was his decision to pull me off of this and send me to Humboldt; he seems to think he can wrap up the Stone Valley situation himself."

"Can he?"

She shrugged.

"Is he here now? Can we talk him out of sending you to Humboldt given this new information?"

"Doubtful. Besides, if we want something from him, we don't dare disturb his beauty sleep."

"You sound angry with him."

"Why shouldn't I be? He was in Sacramento most of the week; half the time I couldn't even reach him by phone. And then he came back here and started giving me orders like we were in the military."

"Did Ripinsky lay into him about telling Mick Erickson about the gold-mining potential here?"

"No. I think he decided that we didn't need any more dissension."

"Or maybe he had other problems on his mind." Quickly I explained about what I'd overheard on the phone extension at Alvin Knight's house.

Anne-Marie's eyes narrowed thoughtfully. After a moment she shook her head. "I can't see Hy being involved with Transpacific."

"How do you explain Knight calling him to ask where Ong was, then?"

"I can't."

"But you still don't want to believe Hy's mixed up with them."

"No. I know what kind of man he is."

"I thought I did, too. But what *do* we really know about him? There's that long blank period when he was away from Vernon—and the fact that he returned with a lot of money. Folks here may claim he was CIA, but I think that's just a romantic notion. Agency people don't make all that much. So where did he get it?"

"Don't know."

"Well, I called a contact on the SFPD homicide detail this afternoon and asked him to run a check on Ripinsky, among others. He said he'd expedite it, so I might hear tomorrow. Then maybe we'll know more. In the meantime, we have to avoid telling him what I've found out."

"You mean you do. I'm to turn over those files"—she

motioned at the table—"to Ned in the morning, and then I'm out of here."

"In a way that's just as well. I can enlist Ned in stalling any discussions and just try to avoid Hy."

"And do what?"

"I'll decide that after I meet with Kristen Lark at Hopwood's cabin."

"Shar, there may be a problem with the Coalition paying you after today. Ned's always been opposed to our bringing in an outside investigator, and now that he's in charge—"

"I'll stay anyway. It's almost the weekend."

She stood, pulling her robe tight against the chill in the room. "Dammit, I hate going off right in the middle of this! I hate the idea that the Coalition feels it can just order me here and there."

"Well, maybe when you stop in Sacramento you can talk with someone there, go over Ned's head. Besides, it won't take all that long in Humboldt county; then you can go back to headquarters and deal with the BLM."

The thought seemed to cheer her. "Maybe," she said—and yawned.

"Why don't you go back to bed?" I suggested. "You've got quite a drive tomorrow."

"I guess I'd better. What about you?"

"I haven't had much sleep in days, but I'm not at all tired. I'll have a drink; maybe that'll relax me."

She nodded and went back to her room. I had no doubt that she'd be asleep in minutes.

I poured some brandy and sipped it, but the shabby living room quickly began to depress me. It was too much like the one at Hopwood's cabin, and my thoughts kept turning to what might have happened there. Finally I took my glass onto the porch and sat on the steps.

It was after two now. A strong wind had sprung up; it rattled the brittle leaves on the overhanging trees and made their branches rasp together. I thought of the Mark Twain line Hy had quoted, about Mono Lake to the south, but equally applicable to this place: "wild, gloomy, foreboding . . . suggestive of sterility and death."

Maybe Twain had been right after all.

Twenty-three

▲▲▲

Of course, once I got to sleep I did so with a vengeance. As a result I was speeding through Stone Valley, half an hour late for my appointment with Lark, when I spied a curious sight on the stream bank. I braked, veered to the right, and drove over there to have a closer look.

Bayard, the used-up hippie, and a woman with an abundance of dark matted hair hunkered down at the water's edge, their heads close together as they tinkered with a piece of machinery. Three undernourished kids played listlessly in the dirt nearby. I glanced around for his shotgun and when I didn't see it, got out of the Land Rover and went up to them. My initial impression had been correct: the machine looked like Lily Nickles's hydraulic concentrator. I doubted she would have loaned it to anybody, much less someone as shiftless as Bayard.

As I approached, the woman twisted around toward me. Her thin face was suntanned, but with an unhealthy yellowish undertone. Curiosity flickered in her dark eyes, and she poked Bayard in the ribs. He looked up at me without recognition.

"Hey, Bayard," I said, "remember me—Lily Nickles's friend?"

Slowly he nodded.

"She loan you that?" I motioned at the concentrator.

It was the woman who spoke. "Sold it to us, along with her other prospecting gear. And now the fuckin' thing's busted."

"Sold it? When?"

"Last night before she took off."

"Took off for where?"

The woman shrugged and scratched her armpit.

Bayard glared down at the concentrator. "Bitch made us give her every cent we'd got saved from my disability, and now it's busted." He didn't sound overly angry, though; I gathered such calamities befell the pair with regularity. He thumped on the machine and tried to start it; the engine gave a feeble cough.

"Bayard," I said, "I think it needs gas."

"Gas."

"Yes, it sounds dry."

"Gas," he said again as if he'd received a divine inspiration. Without another word he stood and meandered down the streambed in the direction of their shack.

The woman watched him go, her dark eyes unreadable. "Bay ain't too smart," she said after a moment. "I knew what the trouble was, but he don't like his woman telling him what to do. You, now—that's different."

"Lily didn't say where she was going?"

"Uh-uh. But she was going for good. Otherwise she wouldn't've sold her gear. And that Jeep was packed with all her other stuff."

"How did she seem? Was she happy? Sad? Frightened?"

The woman considered, biting at the inside of her lower lip. "Oh, I'd say she was frightened."

"Of what?"

"I don't know. Only natural to be frightened out here." She glanced at the broken granite peaks that towered above us. "Me, I'm frightened all the time."

There was nothing I could say to that, so I merely thanked her and went back to the Land Rover. Instead of continuing to Hopwood's cabin, I turned uphill toward Nickles's house.

A pile of trash that hadn't been there before lay at the foot of the newly mended steps. I walked toward the house, calling out to Nickles. There was no response. When I mounted the steps I noticed that the rocker and jumble of prospecting gear were gone from the porch. Inside I found only more trash and the furnishings abandoned by the original owners. A single beer can stood in the dry sink. Nickles had taken off, all right.

Why? I wondered. On Sunday she'd told me she was going to stick it out in Stone Valley for another season. Although she admitted to being afraid of what might be happening up on the mesa, even after finding Mick Erickson's body she'd remained relatively undaunted. Between then and now what had happened to drive her away?

I hurried back to the Land Rover and drove to Hopwood's cabin.

Its door stood open, and I could hear voices inside. Lark was conferring with one of the lab personnel next to a sheriff's department van. She turned and scowled at me.

"Christ, McCone," she said, "I told you to get some sleep, but this is ridiculous."

"Sorry. I'd have been here sooner, but I stopped to talk with Bayard because I saw he had Lily's hydraulic concentrator, and it turns out she's left the valley."

"Whoa—stopped to talk with *who*, who had Lily's *what?*"

"There's an awful lot I have to fill you in on."

"I know." She turned back to the lab technician. "You got all that?"

He nodded.

"Good. I'm here if you need me." To me she added, "I don't suppose you've got any beer in that truck."

"Uh, no."

"Well, I just happen to have a six-pack." When I looked surprised, she explained, "Technically I should be off duty, and there's nobody here who'll complain. And the department isn't picky about deputies transporting their groceries in official cars."

We went to the cruiser and she got out the beers. Then we sat down on the rocks at the edge of the stream. The afternoon was hot now, but a peculiar high overcast made the sunlight watery and pale. I glanced up at the sky.

Lark said, "Gets like that when it's edging into winter. In a few weeks there'll be snow on the ground, and by Christmas it'll be so deep that a lot of the roads, including the one into this valley, will be pretty much impassable except for snowmobiles."

"What do people do?"

"Hole up or move into town. That's when we start earning our pay. People get itchy from being cooped up; tempers rub raw. We break up a lot of bar fights—family fights, too. My first homicide was a woman who cracked her husband's head open with an iron skillet. Didn't even take the eggs out of the pan first."

"How'd you get into police work?"

"My dad was county sheriff years back, and my brother's a deputy. It just never occurred to me to do anything else. What about you?"

"I trained as an investigator with one of the big security firms in San Francisco, mainly because I couldn't find any other job after I got out of college. By the time I had my state license I knew there wasn't anything I'd rather do."

"Funny how people fall into things. Let's hear what you've got."

I outlined what had happened since I'd left her office on Monday. Lark took notes on a pad she pulled from her shirt pocket, occasionally interrupting with questions. When I finished, she frowned, pulling at a short lock of perspiration-soaked hair.

"Well," she finally said, "I can't say as I'm sorry they won't be mining the mesa. And if what you say about the shenanigans with the BLM is true, there won't be any resort development, either. But as for the rest of it . . ."

"The rest is a real tangle. I wish Nickles hadn't gotten away before I could talk with her. I'd like to know what scared her off. Will you put out a pickup order on her?"

"Sure. But it would help if I knew where she might have headed."

"Sunday she told me that if she left the valley she'd go back to Nevada. I suppose that's what she did."

"Well, then, I'll request that the authorities there hold her. She's a material witness and shouldn't have left without contacting us."

I stretched out my legs and leaned back on extended arms. Most of the stiffness from my fall on Tel Hill was gone, and the mirror had shown a marked improvement in my face that morning. "What did you find in there?" I asked, nodding at the cabin.

"Just what you said we would. I won't know more until I see the lab report, but I suspect we might get a match between the stains and Erickson's blood type."

"Or they might match Hopwood's. Or someone else's, somebody we haven't even thought of."

"You're right. I'm just trying to make my job easier again."

"Keep this in mind, too: Hopwood and Erickson were family."

"Only by marriage, and you say that had pretty much busted up. Besides, I told you about the woman with the skillet full of eggs—purely a family matter."

A family matter. The words called up a hazy memory.

"Anyway," she added, "I'll put out pickup orders on Hopwood and his daughter."

A family matter. It was the explanation Margot Erickson had given me for her separation from her husband—the same explanation Mick had given his secretary, Connie Grobe. Grobe assumed it related to having or not having children, since she didn't consider Mick and Margot a family in the usual sense. But if you took into account other relatives, such as the wife's father . . .

"McCone? You woolgathering on me?"

"Sort of. How soon do you think you'll have the results back from the lab?"

"Not soon enough, given it's Friday afternoon. We're looking at next week, I'm afraid."

"Damn."

One of the lab men came out of the cabin and beckoned to Lark. As she scrambled to her feet she said, "Don't leave yet." I remained on the stream bank, sipping at the last of my beer and thinking about what sort of family matter could have caused a serious rupture of the Erickson marriage. When Lark stepped out of the cabin some five minutes later, she motioned excitedly to me.

"Look what we have here." She held up a plastic evidence vial.

As I came closer I saw it contained a bullet.

"Lodged in the wall behind the couch," she said, "and there was a faint blood spray around it. Since it's in relatively good condition—that pine is real soft wood—I'd say it passed through the fleshy part of the victim's body."

"Meaning that whoever was shot was only wounded."

"Or killed by a second bullet that lodged in the body."

"What about the shot path?"

"It's interesting. From the blood-spray pattern on the couch and the angle at which the bullet lodged, I'd say whoever did the shooting was close to the floor. That indicates he or she might have struggled with the victim, been knocked down before firing."

"Self-defense?"

"Possibly."

"What caliber is that?"

"Looks like a forty-four."

"The same as the Magnum you found in the glovebox of Erickson's Bronco—the one that had been fired."

"Uh-huh. And we haven't been able to get a registration on it." Lark looked thoughtful, then added, "Powerful weapon—too damned powerful to be used for anything but killing people. There're plenty around here. A lot of macho assholes think they need them, but it's just plain stupid to keep that kind of gun around. You've got proof of that in there." She jerked her head at the cabin.

I nodded in agreement. "I guess this rules out the cabin as the scene of the Erickson homicide."

"Yeah. What we've got here is a second victim. Just when I thought maybe my job was getting easier." Lark scowled at the vial containing the bullet. "Well," she added, "the only thing to do is go back to Bridgeport and sit on the lab people until I get at least an informal report—weekend or no weekend. Where'll I be able to reach you?"

"Willow Grove Lodge, at least through Sunday."

She gave me a thumbs-up sign and went back into the cabin.

I was driving along what used to be the main street of the town when I saw Ripinsky's Morgan idling at the far end; it looked as if he was waiting for me. When I pulled alongside, he leaned out his window and said, "Saw you coming and decided to save wear and tear on my suspension."

"I'm surprised you'd come out here in that car."

"It's tougher than it looks. Besides, a car's for driving. Why else keep one around? What's with the sheriff's people? I spotted them going this way when I was headed into town. More trouble?"

"Not exactly." Given the efficiency of the local grapevine, there was no way he wouldn't hear about the lab team going over the cabin. "They're checking out Hopwood's place. There're some bloodstains in the living room that make it look like someone met with foul play there."

Ripinsky frowned. "Jesus, I hope not. I'm not crazy about the old guy, but I've always felt a kind of kinship with him."

"How so?"

He made a quick gesture of dismissal. "Nothing I can easily explain. So where are you off to now?"

"Back to town, I guess."

"Let me buy you lunch at my place. You can fill me in on the San Francisco end of the investigation, since it doesn't look as if we're all going to be able to sit down together."

"Why not?"

"Anne-Marie's due to leave for Humboldt County any minute. When I went to town she and Ned were doing some last-minute conferring in the Coalition trailer. There was a distinct chill in the air, so I took off. What gives, anyway? Am I suddenly persona non grata?"

"The chill was between Anne-Marie and Ned, I think. She's not happy that he decided he could do without her here."

Ripinsky nodded but looked unconvinced; I could understand why. Anne-Marie had probably passed along my suspicions of Hy to Sanderman, and as I'd expected, neither had covered well.

"How about it?" Hy asked. "Can we talk?"

I couldn't keep putting him off, but I needed some time to decide which facts to feed him. Carefully chosen, they might elicit some sort of telling response without revealing very much. I searched for a delaying tactic.

"Okay," I said, "but first I need a favor. Will you show me that little museum of Hopwood's?"

"Sure. Wouldn't mind taking a look at it myself. Let's park over in the livery stable. That way we won't be climbing into ovens when we leave."

I followed the Morgan down the dusty street to a building

with gaping front doors. There was just enough room inside—amid a welter of rusted wagon wheels, trash, and an ancient wagon—for our two vehicles. After we'd left them, Ripinsky led the way along the gapped board sidewalk. In order to keep him from questioning me about my investigation, I asked about various buildings that interested me, and he replied with enthusiasm.

"That was the schoolhouse, and beyond the vacant lot is the undertaking parlor. There're still empty coffins inside, waiting."

"And over there—the one standing all by itself? Why's it so isolated?"

"The way the town looks now is deceptive. Before the fire the buildings stood shoulder to shoulder. Christ knows why it took some of them out and spared others. By all rights that one should have burned; it was the most notorious cathouse."

"They had a lot of them?"

"Fair number, as well as saloons and gambling halls. Promiseville was never as wide open as Bodie, the ghost town down near Mono Lake that's been made into a state park. But in its time there were twenty saloons, innumerable ladies of the evening, and some pretty desperate characters." He stopped, turning to look the length of the street. "What the Friends are trying to do is get Promiseville status as a historic district. We wouldn't trick it up or even restore it, but there would be government money available for preservation. If you've come up with something that will help us get those bastards off the mesa, we might stand a chance. But once they start mining it . . ." He shrugged and began walking again.

"Maybe it sounds like a waste of money," he added after a moment, "saving old wrecks like these when people are hungry and homeless. But how else are future generations going to know how things were? How are we going to know who *we* are if we don't have some sense of those who went before us?"

I could well understand his conflicted feelings. There were so many causes: feed the hungry, save endangered species, stop drug trafficking, fund the arts, find a cure for countless diseases, promote literacy, provide job training, save the environment, preserve the past. . . .

The list was endless, the proponents of each adamant that their cause should come first. And in a so-called land of plenty, there was not enough money to go around. Sometimes I pictured the country as a battleground covered with skirmishing armies of well-meaning but single-issue soldiers who would eventually wipe one another out. And all the while, the people who held the real money and power—and didn't give a damn about anything *but* money and power—watched with amusement.

I followed Ripinsky along the boardwalk, wondering how a man who spoke so passionately of saving Promiseville could have sold it out. Was I wrong about him, as Anne-Marie claimed?

The building we finally arrived at was the store I'd noticed the first time I'd come here. It had a high false front and large dusty windows overlooking the street. Its torn screen door hung loose on its hinges; the inner door scraped against the buckled floorboards as Hy pushed it open. "After you," he said.

The store of the hanged Chinese was one gloomy cavernous room. Darkness shrouded its upper reaches; odd bulky shapes lurked in the shadows. The air was musty, the trapped heat intense. I remained in the doorway until my eyes adjusted to the dim light that filtered through the filmed windows.

Before me lay a maze whose alleys and turnings and dead ends led among haphazard heaps of . . . things. When I stepped into it, I saw distinct strata: At bottom were large items—furniture, mining machinery, wooden crates and barrels. On top of these were piled household goods, clothing, tools, lanterns, bottles, crocks, and tins. A thick layer of dust covered everything.

"My God," I said, "how can Hopwood call this a museum?"

Behind me, Ripinsky gave a faint grunt of surprise.

I squeezed into one of the aisles, past an upright piano that was swathed in moth-eaten fur garments. The glassy eyes of a fox-head boa followed me. The aisle was narrow and crooked; I glanced up, fearful that a stack of browning newspapers perched atop an armoire might fall on me. After a few feet I came to a dead end at a wooden barber pole.

I retraced my steps and turned to the right, taking care not to step on a line of toy train tracks that snaked out from under a bureau. A chipped cigar-store Indian with a broken nose barred my way.

"It isn't a museum," I said. "It's a pack rat's nest—an insane pack rat."

Ripinsky didn't answer.

I made a couple more turns and finally emerged near the front of the store next to an iron cookstove heaped with books and yellowed papers. Ripinsky was leaning in the doorway, his hawk-nosed face in shadow; I could see little more than its contours and the glint of his eyes. The peculiar white light of the high desert afternoon shimmered behind him, making his dark blond curls a tarnished halo. He didn't move or speak, just watched me. Suddenly I became aware of the hush in this mausoleum of the past, was struck anew by the great silence of the valley.

My mouth went dry. I ran my tongue over my lips and stepped back until my hands were braced against the edge of the cookstove. A strange image flashed through my mind: Ripinsky and myself walking along the deserted street in that pale, watery sunlight, insubstantial as figures in an overexposed photograph. As we walked, first the town and then the two of us faded to nothing.

Ripinsky continued to watch me.

I swallowed, nearly strangling on the dryness.

He pushed away from the door frame, letting the screen flap closed behind him. Moved toward me in a loose, unhurried stride. My fingers convulsed on the edge of the stove.

Ripinsky put his hands on either side of my face and tipped it up toward his, fingers rough against my skin. His eyes fixed on mine, the fine lines around them taut. I caught my breath. And waited.

After a moment his eyes narrowed. He rubbed his thumb over the bruise on my cheek, then let his hands drop to his sides. As he turned away from me he said, "It's not our time yet, McCone."

I reached out for him, but my fingers encountered only air. "What?"

"You heard me."

I turned blindly, stumbled into a hall tree hung with dust-laden garments. Fought through them, sneezing. As I fumbled in my pockets for a tissue, I kept moving toward the far wall, wanting to put distance between us.

"McCone," he said, "you okay?"

I sneezed again, blew my nose. "Yes." I looked up at the wall in front of me, at the tattered and browning maps that hung there. They appeared to be drawings of a mine works; beside them was a fresh white sheet with similar markings. It looked as if someone had tried to copy the originals and then given up. Hopwood making souvenirs to be sold in his "museum"?

"Hy," I said, "come here and take a look at these."

He came up beside me—close, but not touching. "It's the old mine," he said after a moment. "Here's the main shaft and the various levels branching off. Hopwood must have hung them here as a display before this so-called museum got seriously out of hand."

I turned and surveyed the chaotic room. "Whatever possessed him?"

Hy shrugged. "He probably thought he was saving all this junk for posterity, but the stuff just took over."

I remembered the photograph he'd given me of the old man, pictured the intensity burning in his eyes. Then I looked up at Hy and saw the same intensity—banked now, but steadily smoldering.

I said, "Let's get out of this place."

Twenty-four

▲ ▲ ▲

I told Ripinsky I needed to make some calls and suggested he meet me for a drink at Zelda's at four-thirty. He wasn't too pleased with that arrangement, but I made it plain he had no choice. Then I took off for Vernon.

I wanted to get in touch with Bart Wallace at the SFPD to see if anything had come through on the checks I'd asked him to run. The problem was which phone to use: I could go to the Coalition's trailer, but Ripinsky might show up there before I'd finished; the booth outside the filling station was noisy and inconvenient for taking notes. Finally I decided to brave Rose Wittington's nosiness and drove to the lodge.

Anne-Marie's car was gone, and since I hadn't seen it at the trailers, I assumed she must be on her way by now. The Chevy that usually stood in front of the main building was there, and Rose was raking leaves from the tiny lawn between the lodge and the highway. I left the Land Rover next to her car and walked over there.

Surprisingly Rose didn't seem all that glad to see that she still had me as a guest. She greeted me with a frown, her tone uncharacteristically abrupt. "How come you're staying on now that Anne-Marie's left?"

"I thought I'd spend the weekend, as a mini-vacation."

"Huh" was all Rose offered as she began raking again.

"Is it okay if I use the phone?" I asked. "Credit-card call, of course."

"Frankly, I'd rather you didn't. People have been abusing the privilege, and I've decided to make it a policy not to allow the guests the use of it."

"I hope Anne-Marie or Ned didn't run up charges they shouldn't have."

"I'm not talking about them, just the guests in general."

There hadn't been any other guests, probably not in weeks, but I didn't point that out to her. "Well, I can understand why you've made that policy. I'll drive back to town to call." Halfway to the Land Rover, though, I stopped, remembering a question I had for her. "Rose, if a person needed emergency medical care for a . . . an injury, who would he go to?"

"You hurt yourself?" In concern, she peered at my face.

"Uh, yes. The scrape on my forehead feels as if it might be infected."

"You want to be careful about things like that. There's no clinic or hospital in town, and only one doctor—Gene Mahoney. He's got his office in his house over on D Street, two doors down from the Catholic church. Yellow house with a green iron fence, and there's a sign. You can't miss it."

I thanked her and got into the Land Rover. As she went back to her raking Rose looked vaguely guilty, as if she regretted refusing me the use of her phone now that I'd told her I needed a doctor.

D Street intersected with the main highway across from the Swifty Mart; at its end the white steepled church I'd noticed last Friday was awash in a sea of gold leaves from the aspens that grew in the declivities of the hill behind it. The trees were nearly bare now, their branches frail as skeletons' arms. With surprise I realized that fall was close to an end here; the air held a crispness that confirmed Lark's anticipation of snow.

A sign on an iron stanchion in front of the yellow house directed me through its gate and down a side path to the office entrance. As I stepped inside, a buzzer went off behind a closed reception window. The waiting room was vacant except for a tattered-tailed hobbyhorse that was obviously for the entertainment of younger patients. After a moment the frosted glass of the window slid sideways; a man with thinning white hair looked out at me. "May I help you, miss?"

"I'd like to see Dr. Mahoney."

"I'm Mahoney. What can I do for you?"

I crossed to the window and showed him my identification. His thin face tensed and his pale eyes became wary and knowing. He said, "What's this in regard to?"

"Earl Hopwood."

"Ah."

"Where can we talk?"

"Wait a moment. I'll come out there." The glass slid shut and shortly after that Gene Mahoney entered through the door next to it. He'd taken off his white coat, exposing a garish plaid sports shirt. It bagged on him, as did his dark trousers, and he moved as if he were a victim of chronic pain. "Please sit down, Miss McCone," he said, motioning at the U of shabby green Leatherette furniture.

I took a place on the sofa. Mahoney sat on the chair next to the hobbyhorse and immediately began fingering its bedraggled yarn mane. "I suppose I should be thankful you're a private investigator rather than from the sheriff's department," he said.

"You did treat Earl Hopwood for a gunshot wound, then?" He nodded.

"I'd expected you'd put up more resistance to discussing it."

He made a feeble gesture. "Generally I'm a law-abiding man. During my forty years of practice I've done a few things that would be considered unethical or even illegal, though they weren't to me: two abortions back before they were legalized, which were clearly cases of impregnation by rape; treatment of gunshot wounds without reporting them to the authorities when their intervention would have done more harm than good."

"And Earl Hopwood's . . . ?"

"Bad judgment on my part. I won't attempt to excuse it, other than to say I'm old and not in the best of health."

"Why bad judgment?"

"Because Earl was in an extremely agitated state and wouldn't give me any explanation of what had happened. His chief concern seemed to be that he'd lost his own gun. I should have demanded to know the particulars."

"How did he lose the gun?"

"I don't know."

"And you have no idea who shot him?"

"No, but I suppose it must have been the son-in-law."

"Why?"

Mahoney looked surprised at the question. "Well, he was killed. I assume Earl retaliated."

"Is it common knowledge in Vernon that Mick Erickson was Peggy Hopwood's husband?"

"Oh, no. When I first heard about the killing, I had no idea who the man in the lake was. But Peggy—Margot, she calls herself now—came in last night, and she told me."

"Margot Erickson came here? Why?"

"The poor woman was distraught; that's only natural. She'd lost her husband, and I suspect she knows her father killed him. Then she came here looking for Earl and couldn't find him. And on top of that she'd been badly beaten. A woman like Peggy . . . well, I doubt anyone's so much as laid a hand on her before. She wanted me to give her something to help her sleep. I thought it unwise to prescribe for her, given her emotional condition, but I did let her have one night's supply of Seconal."

"Did she tell you who had beaten her?"

Mahoney shook his head.

"Or where she was staying?"

"Why, at Willow Grove Lodge, of course. It's the only place open this time of year, and Rose Wittington was like a mother to her at one time. She certainly couldn't be expected to stay at that hovel Earl built himself out in Stone Valley."

So that was Rose's reason for not letting me inside to use the phone; Margot Erickson had probably asked if there were other guests, and when she'd heard my name had asked Rose to keep her presence a secret. But why hadn't I seen Margot's Miata? I pictured the lodge, remembered a small garage to the far left-hand side.

"Dr. Mahoney," I said, "exactly when did Earl Hopwood come to you for treatment?"

"Saturday morning, around ten."

"Was it a fresh wound?"

"It had been inflicted shortly beforehand."

"And he gave you no indication of where he might go next, what he might do?"

"No. He would barely talk to me, except to complain about the loss of the gun."

"Have you seen him since?"

"I haven't. Saturday evening I became worried about him, so I drove out to Stone Valley to check on him. The cabin was locked up."

"What was his condition when he left here?"

Mahoney considered. "Fairly good. Earl's a tough old bird."

I was silent, trying to fit these new facts to those I already possessed.

Mahoney added, "I suppose you'll have to report this to

the sheriff. In good conscience, I can't ask you not to." His pale eyes were troubled, envisioning the problems that would ensue.

I thought of another dedicated and old-fashioned doctor I'd known: the man who had brought me into the world and who, when I was young and unsure where to turn, had talked frankly with me, then written me a prescription for birth-control pills and said it was no business of my parents. He was also the one who made house calls and sat up all night at the hospital with my brother John the time he had the motorcycle accident and my folks were out of town. There are still a few of those rare professionals left— although not nearly as many as we need—who practice medicine for the benefit of the patient rather than for profit. I didn't want to be responsible for their ranks being reduced by one.

So I said, "I don't think it'll be necessary to contact the sheriff."

Mahoney let me use the phone at his reception desk, and I reached Bart Wallace just as he was about to leave the Hall of Justice for the evening. He groused a little, until I reminded him that I'd relieved him of the burden of cooperating with Mono County on the Erickson homicide; then he gladly looked up what had come back on the checks I'd requested.

"Naturally there's nothing from NCIC," he told me. "You can't expect speed from the feds. CJIS shows nothing on Hopwood, the Ericksons, or Lionel Ong. But since that's only California, there could have been something out of state. Ripinsky, on the other hand, has a long sheet going back to the early seventies. Should I start at the beginning?"

"Please."

"Conviction in Bridgeport in seventy-one. The charge"— Wallace chuckled—"was lassoing a streetlight."

"*What?*"

"Technically it was D and D. He did thirty days in the county jail and had to pay to replace the light pole."

"Good Lord. And after that?"

"Nothing until the mid-eighties. Then there's a string of arrests and convictions from L.A. County to Siskiyou, all relating to environmental protests. You want the particulars?"

"Not if there's nothing between seventy-one and then. What about Nickles?"

"Two convictions for soliciting in Sacramento in eighty-four. Not nearly as interesting as Ripinsky. But Sanderman—the one you added as an afterthought—is a piece of work."

I sat up straighter and reached for my notepad. "Go on."

"Nineteen eighty-three conviction for industrial espionage. Stole computer plans from his employer in Silicon Valley and sold them to a rival company. Did time in one of those minimum-security facilities where they take their golf clubs."

"In Sanderman's case, he probably took his PC."

"Huh?"

"Never mind. Is that it?"

"No. While he was out on bail pending appeal, his wife filed for divorce. Sanderman went after her with a gun. Didn't shoot her, but beat her up pretty bad. She filed charges, then withdrew them—probably in exchange for a more favorable property settlement."

"Anything else?"

"That's it. You want to give me a number where I can reach you if and when NCIC comes through?"

I doubted the FBI information center would do so by the end of the weekend. "Just call All Souls. If I'm not there, I'll be checking in."

After I thanked Bart and hung up, I stared at the bare cream-colored wall of the receptionist's cubicle, thinking of the fabricated life story Ned Sanderman had fed me—fed all of us. No wonder he talked so much about himself; by giving out a wealth of false and unimportant details, he could cover the damning ones. And perhaps he had good reason to cover them. Would a man who had sold out his employer also sell out the environmentalists? Would a man who had badly beaten his estranged wife similarly attack another woman?

Mahoney was somewhere behind a closed door at the rear of his office suite. I called out thanks for the use of the phone and headed back to the lodge.

Rose Wittington's Chevy was no longer in its usual parking space, and I found the main building locked. No one answered when I pounded on the door. I went to the garage and tried without success to get inside; it was windowless, so I couldn't check for Margot's Miata. Next I skirted the building and hurried downslope to Sanderman's cabin. Its door stood open, and in the living room I saw his key on the coffee table; a quick pass through the other rooms told me he'd left.

Nothing surprising in that, I thought. The Coalition's need for a man on site here was at an end; Sanderman would deal with the Bureau of Land Management in Sacramento. Still, it was strange that Anne-Marie hadn't known of his plans to leave Vernon, or that Ripinsky hadn't been told.

On the off chance that Sanderman was at the trailer, I drove back into town. When I arrived at the office park I saw that the California poppy banner had been removed from the side of the trailer, and I found its door locked. The banner had been there when I drove past earlier; apparently I'd missed Sanderman by less than an hour.

As I stood on the steps of the trailer, I saw Ripinsky's Morgan drive by and pull into Zelda's parking lot. A glance at my watch told me it was close to four-thirty. People were streaming into the restaurant; Vernon was gearing up for another weekend. With a shock I realized I'd been on the case an entire seven days.

Seven days was long enough, dammit. It was time to separate the truths from the falsehoods, and Ripinsky was a good person to start with.

Twenty-five

▲ ▲ ▲

I left the Land Rover next to the deserted trailer and walked down the highway to Zelda's. Ripinsky sat in the lounge at the same window table where Anne-Marie had waited for me the previous Friday. I elbowed through the crowd around the bar and went over there.

He smiled and stood, pulling out the extra chair. I greeted him curtly. As he was about to speak, a waitress came up with two beers. After she'd gone he said, "You have a bad afternoon?"

"Why do you ask that?"

"Because you've got two nasty little lines right here." He touched his finger to the bridge of my nose.

I jerked my head away, scowling harder. "Never mind that. What I want from you is straight talk, for a change."

Now he frowned. Sipped at his beer and waited.

"What's the connection between you, Alvin Knight, and Lionel Ong?"

"Connection? Ong's CEO of Transpacific. Knight . . . that's their supervising geologist, right?"

"I don't have to tell you who he is."

"I'd forgotten for a minute there. What's this about a connection between him and me?"

"Cut the crap, Hy."

"McCone, I don't know what you're talking about. I met the fellow once, up at the mine site when I was being given a tour by a Transpacific PR guy. I haven't seen or heard from him since."

"You spoke with him on the phone Wednesday evening, about six-thirty. I know because I was at Knight's house listening in on his extension. Knight was looking for Ong. You said you didn't know where he was, but that you'd have him return the call if he showed up here."

"McCone, you been smoking something you shouldn't?"

I leaned across the table, keeping my voice low with an effort. "Don't try to make a joke of this. Why did Knight call you?"

He saw how serious I was and regarded me for a few seconds through narrowed eyes. "Wednesday, six-thirty," he said, "I was at the Coalition trailer." Then comprehension spread across his face. "So that's who Al is."

I waited, eyebrows raised.

"I don't know where Lionel Ong enters into this, but here's what happened. I'd been there all afternoon fielding calls for Ned, who hadn't bothered to inform anyone where he was or what he was doing. Anne-Marie had just stopped by to see if I wanted to go get some dinner, and she answered the phone. It was for Ned again. She said she'd seen him on the weekend and thought he might be back soon, but maybe I knew something more specific, and then she handed the receiver to me. The guy—Al—was real insistent, said it was urgent, but I couldn't tell him anything more than Anne-Marie had. He asked me to have Ned call him, and I said I would."

I reviewed the portion of the conversation I'd heard: *He must have told you something. . . . No. He should have, but he didn't. . . . But she said she saw him— Look, I'm sorry but I can't help you. I wish I knew when he'd get here, too.*

It could fit either scenario, but I had to admit Ripinsky's was by far the more convincing—and he had Anne-Marie to back it up.

Hy was watching me. After a moment he signaled to the waitress. "You going to drink that or what?" he asked, pointing to the beer in front of me.

I shook my head in confusion, trying to readjust my thinking to what he'd just told me.

"You want something else instead?"

"White wine, please."

"Done." He moved my untouched beer to his side of the table and ordered the wine.

I turned my face away from his probing gaze and stared out the window at the lake. Twilight was coming on; long fingers of shadow reached over the water. Birds homed in on the graying tufa towers.

Lord knew it wasn't the first time I'd jumped to an unwarranted conclusion about a principal in a case, but this one now struck me as particularly hasty and somewhat paranoid. It seemed as if I had *wanted* to suspect Hy, had actually hoped to find him guilty of collusion with Transpacific. Why?

To provide a buffer between myself and this man to whom I felt strongly drawn? To remove from my life someone to whom I connected in a very basic way? Hy understood the darker side of me, the one I'd never dared reveal to George. Understood it, and neither approved nor disapproved. Accepted my violent urges and dangerous impulses because at some time in his past he had been a victim of the same.

It was frightening to feel that kinship with him. It might upset—no, forever destroy—my newly found and comfortable status quo.

When the waitress set the wineglass in front of me, I turned back to Hy. My eyes, I knew, were troubled, and apparently they told him more of what I was thinking than I would willingly have imparted. He covered my hand with his and said, "It's okay, McCone."

"No, it's not."

"Don't worry about it. We'll start over, from here on out. Deal?"

"Deal." I raised my glass and we drank solemnly.

"All right," I said, setting the glass down. "Knight tried to contact Ong. He wasn't able to, because Ong had disappeared, so he called Ned. That means it's Ned who's involved—"

"Wait a minute." Hy took his hand from mine and held it up. "Ong has disappeared?"

"Yes, either abducted or . . . oh." I stopped, confused again. "I haven't told you any of this."

"No, you've done a pretty good job of putting me off, and now I understand why."

"Hy, I'm—"

"Apologize one more time and you'll never get a second chance with me."

"Chance for what?"

He merely gave me a look—long, level, and full of possibilities.

My flesh rippled pleasurably along my backbone, and I said, "Then I guess I'll skip the apology and tell you all about it."

When I finished, Hy ordered another round of drinks, his eyes hooded, gaze turned inward. "Let me think a little bit on this, McCone." He was still considering when the drinks arrived. After the waitress departed, he said, "I had my suspicions of Sanderman from the day he got here. Nothing all that definite, but he seemed to be just going through the motions, and he was never around. Back and forth to Sacramento, generally unavailable. And the day before you got here—Thursday—when I was making one last stab at locating Earl Hopwood, I spotted Ned's car on the access road to the mine site, where it had no business being. When

I asked him what he'd been doing there, he said I must be mistaken. But all the same he was damned flustered." He paused. "Now, what about Lionel Ong? Any developments there? Ransom demands?"

"I've been monitoring the news, and nothing's been made public. A little while ago I spoke with an inspector on the SFPD about some checks I'd asked him to run; Ong's name was one of them, and I think he'd have reacted differently if anything had broken about a kidnapping."

"Not if the feds were called in rather than the police."

"I know someone who has a source in Ong's office." I glanced at my watch. Five-thirty, but as overburdened an employee as Marcy Cheung might still be at work. "I'll try to call her."

There was a pay phone near the rest rooms. I dialed the Sino-American Alliance, gave the operator my credit-card number, and was not surprised to hear Marcy herself answer. "Hey," she said, "I was hoping you'd get my message."

Damn—I'd forgotten all day to call in to All Souls! "What's up?"

"I talked with my friend Lynn—Lionel Ong's secretary—again. No ransom demands, but Ong still hasn't shown, and they're panicked over at Transpacific headquarters. The wife is flying home from Hong Kong, and the board's meeting to decide whether to go to the police."

"For God's sake, why do they have to deliberate on it? The man's been missing for two days now."

"Something to do with a big issue of Transpacific stock on the Tokyo exchange; if word gets out about Ong, it'll look like the corporation's in trouble and sink the price per share. Besides, the police require seventy-two hours before opening an investigation."

"Given Ong's influence in the city, if the family demands an immediate investigation, I'm sure they can get one going. Will you let me know if you hear more?"

"Sure. Where can I reach you?"

I thought, then took out my notebook and read off Hy's home number as well as that of the Friends' trailer. After I hung up I checked with All Souls for messages and received only the one from Cheung; Ted told me he was about to go to my house to feed Ralphie and Allie, and that I owed him five dollars for hair ball medicine. I noted it on the last page in my notebook, in the running tab I keep for small amounts due to friends. Then I went back to the lounge.

Hy had turned his chair to face the lake, propped his feet on the ledge below the window. The water was purpled now, flame from the setting sun searing its surface; the tufa towers' black reflections seemed to penetrate clear to the lake bottom. Unbidden, the line I'd read in Hopwood's bedside Bible came to me: "And the devil that deceived them was cast into the lake of fire and brimstone. . . ."

When I sat down Hy turned back to the table. Quickly I told him Cheung's news. He nodded thoughtfully and drained his beer. "Well, that situation's out of our hands."

"Yes, and there's no way we can reach Sanderman until he gets back to Sacramento—if that's where he's headed." I sipped wine, thinking about the Coalition's troubleshooter. "Hy, were you keeping a close watch on Ned?"

"Uh-huh. Like I said, I suspected something wrong about him from the first."

"Let's go over what you know of his movements for the past week. Start last Friday morning."

"He went to Lee Vining with Anne-Marie to talk with the Mono Lake Committee people. Ate take-out pizza—I think he subsists on the stuff—in the trailer; then we had our meeting. Saturday . . ." He shrugged. "First I saw of him was when he came to your cabin that night after Anne-Marie woke him so we could talk about the murder."

I pictured Sanderman entering the cabin, fresh from the shower. "Okay, early the next morning I talked with him on the dock there about how he'd known Erickson from before.

That story, along with the personal things he told me, was mostly lies."

"And Sunday afternoon he packed up his computer and went back to Sacramento because he needed to access some files."

"When did he come back?"

"Not until yesterday afternoon."

"And he was in Sacramento the whole time?"

Hy frowned. "We thought so. Anne-Marie spoke with him a couple of times on both Monday and Tuesday, but Wednesday nobody seemed able to reach him. I suppose he could have been anywhere."

Anywhere, I thought, including San Francisco, beating up Margot Erickson or abducting Lionel Ong. But what possible motive could Sanderman have for either?

"Think back to Saturday," I told Hy. "You came into town that morning, and we spoke at the trailer. Ned wasn't there. What did you do after I left?"

"Went over to the airstrip and did some maintenance work on the Citabria. Had a couple of beers with the guy who runs the place. Came back to town and picked up some groceries. I ran into Anne-Marie and one of the Friends outside the Swifty Mart. They were going up to Bridgeport for dinner and taking Rose Wittington along so she could attend her Bible study group. Anne-Marie asked where you were, and I said I didn't know. Then she invited me to come along, but I didn't feel like making the drive. I went home, and you arrived a couple of hours later."

"So this was around . . . ?"

"Four o'clock, thereabouts."

"Are you sure Ned wasn't going with them?"

"God, no. He's not much interested in socializing with people here; seems to consider us beneath him."

"Actually, it's all people he considers beneath him. He told me he greatly prefers his own company." I was silent, mentally reviewing the timetable we'd constructed. "Hy, how'd you like to do me a couple of favors?"

"Sure—what?"

"Check around town to see if anyone saw Earl Hopwood after he left Dr. Mahoney's office on Saturday morning. And then go back to the Friends' trailer and wait for me. My contact in San Francisco promised to call there if she hears anything more about Ong."

"And where will you be if I need you?"

"At the lodge. I want to check something out, and then I'm going to have a talk with Margot Erickson."

———

Twenty-six

▲ ▲ ▲

Rose's car once again stood in front of the lodge, and lights glowed behind the curtained windows of the public rooms. I left the Land Rover under a willow tree and walked downhill as if I were going to my cabin. When I reached the shelter of the grove, I crossed to the one Sanderman had occupied.

Its door still stood open, and the key remained on the coffee table. Since Rose hadn't collected it and locked up, I assumed she was unaware that Ned had left for good. I closed all the draperies, turned on the lights, and began prowling through the rooms.

Dust lay so thick in one of the bedrooms that I doubted Sanderman had set foot in there. The bathroom contained an abundance of damp towels and a lone aspirin decomposing in the sink. In the larger bedroom the bedclothes were rumpled, the hangers in the closet empty. The wastebasket contained only a menu from the take-out pizza parlor next to the Swifty Mart.

The living room showed even fewer signs of Sanderman's occupancy: a blackened light bulb on an end table, a pile of

Sacramento *Bee*s next to the woodbox. I peered into the potbellied stove; it looked as if he'd never used it. I lifted the cushions of the couch and chair; not even a stray coin had slipped beneath them. Finally I turned to the kitchen, sure I'd find nothing. Sanderman had been emphatic in his distaste for that room: "I wouldn't boil water in there; God knows what germs are lying in wait."

The room certainly didn't look unsanitary. Rose Wittington took pride in her cabins; as she'd told me when I arrived, you couldn't find cleaner rentals. But the kitchen *was* hard on the eye: the same unfortunate orange tile as in mine predominated; cabinets painted a glossy turquoise clashed violently with it and with the bilious green floor and walls. I shook my head as I looked around.

Something about the room, besides the decor, struck me as peculiar, but at first I couldn't figure what. Then I realized that the refrigerator and a metal cabinet were slightly out of position. I went closer and saw scrape marks on the linoleum where they'd been moved. I pulled the cabinet a little farther from the wall, but saw nothing behind it. I took my flashlight from my bag and peered behind the refrigerator. Nothing there, either. Then I began to examine the entire room, beginning with the walls and floor. They were scrupulously clean, but a section near the door to the living room looked even cleaner, as if it had very recently been scrubbed. Rose wouldn't have done that—she provided no maid service.

As in my cabin, the door was a swinging one whose mechanism allowed it to be propped open against the kitchen wall. I pushed it shut and looked at the section of floor and baseboard behind it. A brownish substance had seeped into the crack between the linoleum and the board, had dried and caked there, just as the blood had congealed between the floorboards in Earl Hopwood's living room.

Even the most meticulous housekeepers miss things, especially when performing a distasteful task that needs to be done in a hurry. Someone had carefully cleaned blood from the linoleum and wall here, but hadn't taken into account that the sag of the floor had permitted it to flow into the crack next to the baseboard.

Quickly I stood and surveyed the room. Assume, I thought, that the person who shed the blood was shot. Where would the shooter have stood? There, by the sink, or over there by the refrigerator. Near the end of the counter, anyway. What had the shooter—

No, Ned Sanderman. Who else? And the victim? Mick Erickson.

All right, then, what had Ned been doing in the kitchen? Getting a drink for a visitor, perhaps. And where was the gun? On him or somewhere in this room. Regardless, he stood in that general area.

I remained where I was, scrutinizing the other side of the kitchen. Then I went over there and squatted down to take a better look at the end of the counter. On the curve of the tile at about waist level was a chip. While the ceramic was cracked and marred in many places, those marks were gray with age. This chip was white—new.

I straightened, held out my hand as if aiming a gun, and measured its height against the counter. Sanderman was no taller than I; he would have held the gun at the same level.

It fits, I thought. He came in here. Erickson followed. He took the gun out, turned, and fired. But he didn't brace himself against the recoil. His hand was deflected . . . like so. The gun hit the tile and nicked it.

But why had he moved the refrigerator and metal cabinet? He hadn't needed to do that to clean up the blood. And if he'd been that careful, surely he'd also have noticed the encrustation behind the swinging door. Why else would he have gone to the trouble—

And then I remembered that Mick Erickson had been shot twice with a .22 automatic. Automatics ejected spent shell

casings. What if one of them had landed where Sanderman
hadn't seen it fall, and he'd had to hunt for it?

I leaned against the counter, considering. The medical
examiner had fixed the time of Erickson's death at around
seven on Saturday evening. The lodge was relatively isolated, and with Mrs. Wittington and Anne-Marie in Bridgeport, no one had heard the shot. It would have taken
Sanderman some time to dispose of the body, even if he'd
merely dragged it down to the lake and pushed it in. Then
he'd have needed to park Erickson's rented Bronco on the
highway near Zelda's, wipe it of prints, and walk back here.
Even if that had taken until eight-thirty or nine, it allowed
three hours before Anne-Marie had come to get him around
midnight—more than enough time to mop up the blood and
destroy any other evidence.

Yet after Anne-Marie's summons, Sanderman had taken
time to shower, and when he'd appeared at our cabin he'd
seemed exceptionally alert for a man who supposedly had
been fast abed. Alert and somewhat agitated. Why?

I thought of those spent shell casings again. There had to
have been at least two. A man who was looking for a casing
would have moved anything that wasn't fastened down; the
search would have added time to a normal cleanup. And if
he hadn't found one, it might still be here.

I began a search of my own: first in the more obvious
places, then in others that were possible but not probable.
Nothing was caught in the faded gingham curtains at the
window. The sink's drain was covered by mesh too fine for
anything larger than a crumb to have passed through. The
grease trap under the stove burners was empty. None of the
drawers contained anything but utensils. The cupboards
were bare of all but the basics. I tipped the metal cabinet
and shone my flash under it to see if there was a ledge onto
which a shell casing could have bounced, looked into the
oven, checked inside the fridge. The countertops were clear

of everything but a small electric coffee maker like the one in my cabin. . . .

I looked closer at the coffee maker. Saw that the plastic cap that usually covered the place where you poured the water was missing. It couldn't have worked too well; a lot of the water would have turned to steam.

And then I thought, Sanderman never used this, anyway. He probably didn't even know how it worked, since he didn't drink coffee or tea. Why would he have noticed this small opening?

Pulling it toward me, I tipped it slightly and peered into the cavity for the water. At its bottom nestled the gun-metal gray shell casing. A .22 shell casing, I was sure.

"All *right*," I said softly.

Without removing the shell, I set the coffee maker back in its approximate place on the counter. Turned out the kitchen light and hurried into the bathroom. Most of the towels that hung there were damp from normal use, but there were three large ones draped over the shower-curtain rod that had dried stiff, as if they'd been used with a cleaning solvent. Under the sink I found a nearly empty large-sized bottle of Formula 409.

He probably thought cleanser would destroy all traces of blood, but I knew better. A crime lab would have no trouble bringing them out.

Aware that I had no time to waste, I switched off the rest of the cabin lights, locked the door, and sprinted uphill to the lodge.

Rose Wittington didn't want to let me in. She stood behind the closed door and calmly told me to come back tomorrow.

I shouted that I wasn't going away. That I needed the phone to call the sheriff. That I knew Margo was in there, and if she wouldn't talk with me, she'd damned well have to take her chances with the authorities. And then I kicked the door.

The dead bolt turned and Rose stood before me, a sternly reproving look marring her usually pleasant features. She said, "Keep your voice down, young lady; they'll hear you clear over in Nevada. And don't you go messing up my door with those feet."

I glared at her and strode inside.

Margot Erickson huddled on one of the sofas in front of the big-screen TV, a small figure in a blue velvet caftan. The purple-black bruises stood out starkly against her ashen skin. I expected her to bolt, but she seemed incapable of further flight. She stared at me without speaking.

"I can't waste time explaining what's happened," I told her. "Just listen to my end of this conversation." Then I went to the phone and dialed the sheriff's department in Bridge-port.

Lark was still on duty. She started to tell me something about the lab report on the Hopwood cabin, but I cut her off. "Kristen, I've found out who killed Mick Erickson. How soon can you be at the Willow Grove Lodge?"

Margot started to rise from the sofa. I motioned for her to remain there.

Lark said, "Not for quite a while, I'm afraid. There's been a major pileup between here and there on three ninety-five. All our manpower's been diverted to it, and I doubt I can get through anyway. Tell me what you've got."

I related what I'd found in Sanderman's cabin, watching Margot's expression change from shock to confusion. "He left here between three and four," I finished, "possibly headed home to Sacramento, but I wouldn't bet on that."

"I'll put out a pickup order on him. You know his license number?"

I asked Rose, and she read it off from her guest register.

"Okay, I'm on it," Lark said. "Is the crime scene secure?"

"Locked, and I have the key."

"I'll be there as soon as I can."

I put the receiver down and went over to Margot. She had

drawn her bare feet up onto the sofa and wrapped her arms protectively around her knees. After a moment she ran her tongue over dry lips and asked, "Mick really was killed in one of the cabins here?"

I nodded.

"And this . . . Ned Sanderman . . . who is he?"

"You don't know him?"

"No."

I sat down next to her. "An environmentalist with the California Coalition for Environmental Preservation. He was involved with Mick and Lionel Ong in the Golden Hills project; he's probably the one who figured out how they could get hold of the land on the east side of the mesa."

She buried her face against her raised knees. "That damned project. It destroyed everything."

"Margot, I know that Earl Hopwood is your father and that you assisted on the project in some way. Will you tell me about it—from the beginning?"

She looked up again. Tears had spilled over, their wet sheen somehow rendering her bruises all the more brutal. Rose pressed some tissues into her hand, then withdrew silently to a nearby armchair and perched on its edge, eyes watchful and concerned.

Margot said, "All right, but first I want to apologize for what I did to you the other night. I panicked and didn't realize—"

"Accepted. Now tell me about Golden Hills."

"To do that I'll have to start years back, when Mick was still trying to please Daddy. Daddy's whole life had narrowed to Stone Valley and that mine; he was convinced that if he could get someone to work it again, Promiseville would bounce back like it was before. Of course that was impossible—in more ways than one—but to humor him, Mick took some samples and they showed the mine was played out. He didn't tell him the results, though, because Daddy wouldn't have believed him, anyway."

"When did he and Ong come upon the idea of making it a resort?"

"Resort?" Rose said.

I ignored her, concentrated on Margot.

"I don't know." She began twisting the tissues around her fingers. "A couple of Christmases ago Mick talked to Daddy about selling the land. He said he had a client with a lot of money that he wanted to move to the U.S. and put into mining. Daddy was ecstatic, but I didn't believe Mick. Besides, I'm something of an environmentalist myself, and I knew what modern mining methods would do to the area. But when I tried to bring that up, Mick . . . told me to mind my own business."

Rose snorted derisively.

"What happened next?"

Margot discarded the tissues and reached for a pack of cigarettes that lay beside a full ashtray on the end table. She lit one, made a face, and replied, "I don't know; I decided to stay out of it. What could I do against a company like Transpacific? How could I justify destroying my father's last dream? Besides, things weren't going well for Mick: he was horribly overworked, and the final payment to his former wife for the buyout of the business was coming due. He didn't need any more stress."

And that final payment, I thought, gave Erickson a motive beyond simple greed for wanting the Golden Hills project to happen.

"Eventually," Margot went on, "Mick realized I wasn't going to be obstructive, so he asked me to help out on the project. He'd gotten an extension from his ex-wife on the payment and was putting all his energies into getting the company's billings up. I didn't feel I could refuse."

"How did you help?"

"With the clerical things. He told me they'd decided they needed to buy additional acreage in order to mine the mesa. A man named Franklin Tarbeaux who'd filed a claim on the eastern side had agreed to patent the land and resell it to Transpacific at a good price. Or so Mick told me. I prepared the applications, consulting with the geologist, and handled all Tarbeaux's mail."

"The mail came to that Transpacific condominium on Telegraph Hill?"

"Yes. Lionel keeps the building for visiting executives and private conferences." She looked guiltily away, remembering what had happened between us outside that building, and stubbed out her cigarette. "I had a key to the penthouse and would pick up what mail arrived. Nothing ever came that wasn't related to the Bureau of Land Management dealings."

But her frequent and unexplained presence at the condo had started talk about Ong keeping a mistress there. "When did you become aware that Tarbeaux didn't exist?"

"I never knew, not until you asked me about the name and told me Mick had been carrying a second set of I.D. when he was shot. Then I began to figure out I'd been lied to."

"And when did your father find out that the mesa was going to be turned into a resort rather than mined?" That, I reasoned, had been the real start of the trouble.

"About a month ago. He'd been hanging around the mesa, all excited about the new mining venture—making a pest of himself, Mick said." She paused, seeming to listen to her words. "The man's dreams had been taken from him, even if he didn't know that yet, and all my husband could say was that he was a pest." Her gaze turned bleak, inward. I knew what she was seeing: the callous man her husband had been—or perhaps become—and the sham he'd made of their marriage.

Margot sighed and reached for another cigarette. Rose made a small sound of protest, but didn't speak.

I said, "About your father finding out . . . ?"

"Daddy wasn't much of a miner, but he knew enough to realize something was wrong on the mesa. He gained the confidence of one of the personnel and learned what Transpacific's real plans were. Then he came to the city and demanded that Mick stop the project. Mick threw Daddy out of the house. And that did it for me. I've had three husbands, but only one father. *I* threw *Mick* out of the house, told him not to come back until he did as Daddy asked.

"Of course," she added softly, "he never did."

"Your father began making trouble at the mine site, didn't he?"

"Yes. They fenced it and posted guards, but that didn't stop him." She smiled grimly. "Daddy knows that mesa inside out. There are all sorts of ways onto it—tunnels, shafts—that Transpacific couldn't begin to know about, much less block."

I remembered the old maps on the wall of Hopwood's "museum," as well as the newer half-finished one. It probably showed which of the tunnels still existed. "So what did they decide to do?"

"I guess Mick came up here to try to reason with Daddy. I suspected that as soon as I found out he was shot at Tufa Lake. Why else would he go to such trouble to make it look as if he was in Japan? He knew that I'd interfere if I found out what he was doing."

And she'd thought her father had killed her husband. That explained the almost palpable fear I'd felt at her house on Tuesday morning. "Do you know for a fact that he saw your father?"

"Oh, yes." Her features twisted, as if in remembrance of real pain. "I found out for sure on Wednesday."

"What happened then?"

She looked away from me.

"Your father showed up in the city again, didn't he?"

She dipped her chin—a small affirmative.

"He was the one who beat you."

No response from Margot, but Rose made a strange sound—half surprise, half denial.

After a bit Margot said, "He came to the city that afternoon. He'd been shot a few days before—a flesh wound. He told me Mick had come to his cabin Saturday morning and threatened him. Daddy pulled his gun on him, meaning to frighten him, and Mick took it away and shot him and then ran off."

"Did you ask him if he'd retaliated and killed Mick?"

"How do you ask your own father a thing like that?" When I didn't reply, she went on, "Anyway, he didn't give me a chance to ask. He wanted Lionel Ong's home address and phone number. I refused to give them to him; I was afraid of what he might do . . ."

When she didn't go on, I said, "And he beat it out of you."

Her "yes" was barely a whisper.

Rose moaned in sympathy and started to move toward her. Margot motioned for her to stay where she was; she crushed out the unsmoked stub of her cigarette and added, "Daddy blamed me as well as Mick for what had happened. He said I'd conspired with the rest of them against him. I'll never forget the way he looked at me . . . the hatred. . . ."

"Margot," I said, "did you try to warn Ong before you went to his house and the condominium that night?"

"No. At first I felt . . . It was like being paralyzed. This man, the one who had done that to me, he wasn't the father I'd known all my life. Mick was dead, and now the rest of my world was . . . I just stayed at home, watching it get dark. Then I snapped out of it, tried to call Lionel. When I couldn't reach him, I went looking for him, and that's when . . ." Again she looked guilty.

I asked, "How did your father seem that afternoon, aside from the uncharacteristic violence? Was he at all rational or in control?"

Rose said, "Is it rational for a good Christian to beat his own daughter?"

Again I ignored her, continued to look at Margot.

She considered. "He was functional, if you mean could he

handle himself in a way that wouldn't attract attention. He could speak normally, that sort of thing. And he didn't seem to be suffering any ill effects from the gunshot wound, except for a little stiffness. But the way he was going on . . . He was raving, spouting this biblical nonsense." She glanced apologetically at Rose. "That's the only way I can describe it."

"Has your father always been religious?"

"Not until the past few years."

Rose said, "That's when I began to interest him in my Bible study group. I think at first he only wanted to play Mr. Intellectual and show up us 'Bible-thumpers,' as he liked to call us. But eventually he saw the light."

I asked Margot, "Do you remember any of the things he said to you?"

"Oh . . ." She pushed her hair off her forehead and rested her hand on top of her head. "There was something about an earthquake. And blood. I can't phrase it the way he did, but something about the moon and sea turning to blood and the sun going black and a mountain burning."

"Anything else?"

"When he left . . . This part is vague because I was hurting and kind of in shock. He said something like, 'They will die when Christ died, on the fifth day.' Does that make any sense to you?"

I glanced at Rose. "Hopwood was reading Revelation recently, if that helps."

She stood and went to the secretary desk in the lobby, returning with a Bible. As she sat and began to page through its final book, Margot expelled a sigh and let her hand fall from her head to her side. Her eyes were half closed, her face flaccid, as if in the telling of her last violent encounter with her father she'd used whatever strength she held in reserve.

After a few minutes Rose looked up, her face pink with discovery. "Revelation six, twelve," she said. "'There was a great earthquake; and the sun became black as sackcloth of hair, and the moon became as blood.'"

I waited. Rose looked disappointed with my reaction and began scanning the pages again, lips moving silently.

I got up and moved restlessly around the room. What she'd read hadn't told me a damn thing, but Hopwood's ravings had to be connected to his later actions—to what he'd intended to do with Lionel Ong. . . .

"Listen to this," Rose said. "Revelation eight, eight: 'and as it were a great mountain burning with fire was cast into the sea; and the third part of the sea became blood.'"

So what? I glanced at Margot to see if it meant anything to her, but her eyes were fully closed now. "What about this fifth day stuff?" I asked Rose.

She gave me a look that said I must have been raised a heathen. "'When Christ died, on the fifth day,'" she quoted Hopwood. "Christ died on Good Friday. God created the world in seven days, and on the seventh he rested—Sunday."

"Friday. Today." I thought of the rest of it: "They will die." And of a phrase from the passage of Revelation I'd read in Hopwood's Bible: "the devil that deceived them."

Then I considered Hopwood, a man I'd never laid eyes on but in a sense knew intimately: a lonely man, recently steeped in biblical lore of destruction and redemption. A man who had possessed one overruling passion—and had been deceived, had had that passion stolen from him.

And I thought: *A burning mountain . . . a fire mountain . . . on the fifth day. . . .*

Twenty-seven

▲▲▲

I went directly to the Friends'
trailer and laid out my suspicions for Hy. At first he
repeated his earlier accusation that I'd been smoking a
controlled substance. But when I reminded him of the maps
at Hopwood's "museum" and the fragment of dynamite crate
I'd found on the garbage dump, he sobered and fell silent.

Finally he said, "In a way it fits with something I figured
out while I was asking around town for the old guy tonight.
He's been here all along; we've just been looking in the
wrong places."

"How can that be?"

"Think about it, McCone. Before you came up here, I
checked his cabin and asked the folks in Stone Valley if
they'd seen him. Then I concluded he was missing. You did
the same thing, and after you talked with Lily Nickles, you
assumed he'd gone over the state line for fun and games.
Even after you found out he hadn't turned up in Reno and
that he'd been seen around here by Rose and that old hippie,
we hung on to the idea that he was someplace other than
right in the area. But tonight I found out that he's been in

and out of the Swifty Mart pretty regularly, plus occasionally to the filling station."

"When?"

"The Swifty Mart three times in the past month, which is about usual for him. The filling station as recently as late last Friday afternoon, when he was inquiring about a woman in a red sports car who had come from the office park and asked directions to the tufa forest."

"So it was Hopwood who spied on me down there?"

"Guess so. He wanted to know what you'd asked the attendant, where you were headed. And he took off after you."

"Why, I wonder?"

"Well, you were a stranger in the area and had just been talking with me. I think he was keeping a pretty close watch on all of us—initially because we were opposed to the new mining venture, and later because he knew Sanderman had been involved in the Golden Hills project. That must have confused the hell out of him."

The mention of Ned reminded me I hadn't told Hy that I'd found out the troubleshooter had killed Mick Erickson. But there wasn't time for that now, and besides, something about Sanderman's motive bothered me—something I wanted to work out in my own mind first.

I said, "Hopwood must have been the one who broke into your home, these trailers, and the cabins and who checked at All Souls to find out who I was."

Hy nodded.

"It's hard to believe he could slip in and out of town like that with so few people noticing."

"Not really, when you think about it. Reminds me of these golden trout we've got in the streams here. You look in the slow-moving water where you expect them, and there they are; but if they're swimming fast through moss-covered rocks in the sunlight, you're bound to miss them."

"But where has Hopwood been staying? Not at his cabin.

And not anyplace very obvious, or the people in the valley would have spotted him."

"Earl knows every nook and cranny in the valley, and he's used to roughing it. Woman at the Swifty Mart says he's been buying a lot of camping supplies."

I thought of what Margot had said of her father and repeated it. "He knows that mesa inside out, too."

"I'll just bet he does."

"Of course, none of this proves my theory."

"There's more. While I was waiting for you, I got to thinking about Hopwood and what you found on his garbage dump. So I made a few calls and hit pay dirt with a mining-supply store down in Lee Vining. He'd been in there a few times, starting about a month ago. At first all he bought was new picks and shovels; then he needed jacks and timbers like you'd use to shore up tunnels. Struck Del, the guy who runs it, as odd, seeing as Earl's never done any hard-rock mining. Then, only a couple of weeks ago, he asked about dynamite—did Del know anybody who could help him get his hands on it without going through all the required legal rigmarole."

"Did Del steer him to somebody?"

"He says he 'may have.'"

"Uh-huh. And I'll bet the crate I found part of wasn't the only one he bought."

"Probably not."

"So what do we do now?"

"Go to the sheriff with it?" Hy didn't sound too sanguine.

I shook my head. "First off, there's a big wreck on three ninety-five. All their manpower's been diverted to it, and no one can get through. Second, if you didn't want to believe my theory, how on earth is the sheriff's department going to? They need more than what I've got to justify going out there."

"Then you better get more."

"What's this 'you'?"

"I didn't realize I was allowed in on this."

"And I know you well enough to realize I can't keep you out."

On the way to the valley we swung by Hy's house for some things we'd need. While he was inside getting them, I glanced at the clock on the Land Rover's dashboard: close to eight, not much left of the "fifth day."

Now the danger of this mission struck me. My interpretation of Hopwood's ravings was shaky at best, and the concept of the fifth day was the weakest part of it, but who knew what he had planned—and for when? I could understand Hy's reasons for wanting to go out to the valley and investigate: this was his home; he loved it, and had a stake in what went on here. But I, on the other hand . . .

He came out of the house and loaded a rope and some large torchlights into the Land Rover. "You comfortable with a thirty-eight?"

It was the caliber of gun I owned. I nodded and took the Colt he passed through the window.

Hy studied my face. "Having second thoughts?"

"Some."

"This isn't your fight, McCone."

I shrugged. "In some ways, no. But in another, it is."

He nodded. "Let's go, then. Better take this and the Morgan, huh? We might need both."

"Right. We'll leave them in the livery stable, stop by Hopwood's museum for a look at those maps. See you there." I started the Land Rover.

Once again the night was cold and the moon rode high. The landscape had that same cut-crystal sharpness. I drove along the winding, bumpy road, climbing steadily to the crest above the valley. As on the previous night, no lights shone below, and only faint security beacons marked the chain-link fence atop the mesa. But I was now acutely aware of the lives that went on in the darkness: Bayard and his family and the other desert rats in their burrows on the valley floor, the Transpacific guards in their trailers above. And an unbalanced man with a deadly purpose and a terrified hostage.

The moon shed enough light so that I could turn the headlights down to park; in the rearview mirror I saw Hy do the same. We coasted down the grade to the town and moved along the main street to the livery stable. But when we arrived there, a third vehicle was parked inside, nose pointing outward—the old van Bayard had described as belonging to Hopwood. A van painted the same yellow as the one I'd taken for the messenger service's as it labored up the hill to Lionel Ong's house on Wednesday.

I blocked the stable door with the Land Rover and Hy pulled up behind me. We approached the van cautiously, hands on our guns. I touched the engine compartment: cold. Hy opened the driver's side door and shone his flashlight inside. I peered around him.

The van contained the usual junk belonging to less than meticulous drivers: scraps of paper, torn maps, crushed aluminum cans. A crumpled gray blanket lay in back as well as some lengths of sturdy rope.

Hy and I exchanged glances. I moved around the vehicle, opened the passenger door, and leaned in for a better look. A balled-up cloth had been discarded on the floor in front of the seat. I squatted down and sniffed at it; the odor was faintly medicinal. With a tissue, I opened the glovebox. Inside rested a bottle: chloroform.

I said, "Better not touch anything." My voice sounded very loud; in the rafters above, a bird stirred in protest.

Hy didn't answer. When I straightened, I saw him leaning over the driver's seat, staring at something caught in a channel near the rear wheel well. I went around the back for a better look.

It was a pair of heavy gold links that looked as if they'd been broken off a chain. I'd seen a massive gold chain like that recently. Of course—the band of the watch Ong had been wearing when I'd interviewed him.

"Well, there's our proof," I said. "They're from Ong's watchband. The pieces of rope, the blanket, those links—and there's a rag on the front floor and chloroform in the glovebox. Hopwood kidnapped him."

"Didn't you say he may have posed as a messenger with contracts from Ong's office?"

"Yes."

"Well, here's some more proof."

I moved around the van and looked where he was pointing. In a pocket on the driver's side door was a billed cap; the words "Ace Messenger Service" were stitched in script across it. "So Ong really thought Hopwood was a deliveryman." I said. "He must have pulled a gun once he got inside the gate—I heard Ong exclaim, 'This is absurd'—marched him to the van, and chloroformed him."

"Jesus." Hy stepped away from the door. "I wish the van had been here earlier."

"Wonder where he was?"

"Who knows, with a maniac like that?"

"We'd better go look at those maps."

Our footsteps echoed like gunshots as we started down the sagging board sidewalk. Quickly we both detoured onto the soft earth of the street. In silence we approached the false front of the hanged Chinese's store. As I opened the door, trapped heat and blackness greeted me. I took the flashlight Hy held out, flicked it on, shone it around the room.

Hopwood's helter-skelter shrine to the past had been bizarre by day, but the night made it surreal. The upright piano draped in furs became a great beast with dozens of furry paws and glassy eyes. A giant's shadow spread threateningly over the far wall; my breath caught until I realized it was only that of the cigar-store Indian. I became aware of sounds: the snick of claws as rodents scampered over the plank floor, a rustle and sigh as the breeze gusted through the open door. Behind me Hy stood as if frozen. When I glanced back at him, his eyes glittered hard in the torch-light, and the planes of his face were taut. I wondered how the scene before us appeared when viewed through the filter of his own unique perspective.

I caught his attention, motioned toward the far aisle. He flashed me a wry grin and followed. The maps of the mesa hung undisturbed on the wall. I pulled down the newer drawing; Hy did the same with the tattered and browning ones. We spread them on the floor and huddled over them with our flashlights.

"Here's the main shaft," he whispered, tracing it with his index finger. "I've heard it's been sealed up for decades. This level—that's mining parlance for a horizontal tunnel—and this one, too, are long gone."

"Which side of the mesa are we looking at?"

"Near as I can tell, this map is an overview. Wait—this other one's better." He pulled a second diagram on top of it. "This level here and these two appear in that newer drawing you've got there."

"I still can't . . . This is the stamp mill?"

"Uh-huh."

"Now I see. Then this tunnel . . . level"—I traced it on Hopwood's new map—"lies near the access road."

"Probably was collapsed by the grading."

"And this one, plus the smaller one—"

"The small one's what's called a crosscut. It's at right angles to the level, leads toward where the vein of ore was located."

"Okay, this level and this crosscut are on the north side of the mesa. Any openings that Hopwood might have dug to get to them from outside would be well out of view of the guard shack and the trailers."

"So that's probably where he gained access."

"Once inside, where would he go?"

Hy shrugged. "The mesa was once full of levels and

crosscuts, as this old map shows, and there's no way of telling which are still in existence. In addition there are hundreds of stopes—excavations that extend above or below the level to where the ore deposits were. He could be holed up anywhere in there."

"Then how are we going to find him?"

"On a wing and a prayer, McCone. A wing and a prayer."

We'd gotten no farther up the slope than Lily Nickles's deserted house when I identified something that had been bothering me since we'd left the Chinese's store. I motioned to Hy, and we went onto the shelter of the porch.

I said, "I'm worried about those people on the mesa."

"The Transpacific guards?"

"Yes. That's at least three lives—"

"Bastards knew what they were getting into."

"Did they?"

". . . Not this, at any rate."

"Hy, if something goes wrong, if this fifth day nonsense isn't so nonsensical after all—"

"Not our problem. Besides, we don't have time—"

"How would you feel knowing you could have gotten them off there and didn't?"

His eyes flashed angrily in the moonlight as he swung his glance toward me. "This is coming from someone who has admitted to wanting to blow two people away?"

"I had good reason. Besides, as you told me, what counts is that I didn't."

For a moment he didn't speak. Then, "Oh, hell. We'll get them off of there. Come on." He started toward the steps.

"You go."

"What?"

"I suspect they'll listen to you better than they would to both of us. If they have a communications setup, you can notify the authorities about Ong. If not, have one of them go to town and do it."

"And what will you be doing in the meantime?"

"Trying to locate the entrance to that tunnel. You can catch up—"

"No, McCone."

"Yes, Ripinsky."

We matched glares.

Hy said, "Not twice in one lifetime."

"What?"

"You are the same goddamned stubborn annoying kind of person as my late wife, and one man doesn't deserve this kind of grief twice." He threw his arms out in exasperation. "You win—I'll go get them off of there and catch up with you. But I warn you—fuck up and get yourself killed, and it'll be doubly your loss."

"Why?"

"Because, McCone, then you'll never get to find out how good we could be together."

Without giving me the chance to reply, he went down the steps and moved away toward the access road.

Twenty-eight

▲ ▲ ▲

When I could no longer see
Hy, I started down the porch steps, but the way the moonlight bleached my already pale tan jacket made me pause.
Under it I had on a burgundy sweater, dark enough to be
unobtrusive, but too lightweight to keep out the cold.

I set down the torch and rope I carried and went into
Nickles's house to see if she'd left any clothing that I could
wear in place of the jacket. The rooms were pretty much
stripped bare, but on a hook behind the kitchen door, where
she'd probably forgotten it, hung a heavy black wool shirt. I
traded the pea jacket for it.

I'd put Hy's .38 in the deep pocket of the jacket, but the
shirt had none large enough to accommodate it. Since I'd
need both hands free, I shoved it through my belt on the
right side, far enough toward the rear so it was out of the
way but still within easy reach—not an arrangement that
pleased me, but the best I could come up with. Then I went
outside, draped the rope around my shoulders, picked up
the light, and set out for the north side of the mesa.

As I walked I became increasingly uneasy. The overwhelming silence, the moonshot darkness, the stark landscape that afforded little cover: all were serious handicaps. Add to them the fact that I didn't know the terrain and had little clue to where the entrance to the tunnel might be; the presence of a deranged man with a hostage and a good quantity of dynamite; the uncertainty of the armed guards' reaction to Hy's arrival—it all made a grim picture. I decided not to think about it, to concentrate on the immediate, practical details.

Be careful where you step. Watch for figures in the shadows. Use all your senses—plus your intuition.

I reached the end of the twisted iron skeleton of the stamp mill. Skirted it and began climbing.

Focused as I was, disturbing emotions intruded: at first a tug of home, a longing for familiar places and people. Then a flood of yearning for George and the pleasant existence we normally shared. My last words to him replayed in my mind: "We'll talk." What if I didn't survive this and that talk never took place? How would he reassemble the fragments of a life that less than a year before had been badly shattered?

Yearning turned to guilt, not only toward my lover but toward the others I cared for. And guilt turned to fear. Only normal to be afraid, I told myself.

But under these feelings I was aware of others not nearly as acceptable. At first they were manifested as physical sensations: my skin tingled; subtle odors smelled sharper; faint sounds were amplified; my sight was honed fine. Then I felt excitement rising and flowing through me, a stronger rush than that from any drug. Its effect was as close to euphoria as any I'd experienced.

Danger, I now realized, was the thing that brought me fully alive. Conquering it and my own fear was what gave me a reason for going on in the face of an increasing sense of futility. That was the real truth that I kept from George and the others, who would have found it a shameful addiction. And that was what Hy had intuited and accepted.

I pushed these thoughts down and allowed the rush to fuel my climb up the mesa.

The night was so still that I could hear voices up where the guard shack was. Voices shouting, but nothing more. Did that mean Hy had persuaded the Transpacific crew to abandon their posts? Or were they shouting at him to get off there?

After a few minutes the voices became fainter. I looked up, realized I could no longer see the security beacons, judged I'd reached the far north side. The mesa here was bounded by a boulder field, its rocks larger and more sharply fractured than those by the stream. The granite underfoot was worn smooth. I shone the light down, saw signs of a trail, and began to follow it.

It climbed steadily upward, then looped toward the east and disappeared. I retraced my steps, looking for marks in the dust. There were some—made by my feet. And then there was an overlapping of the tracks, more than I'd made.

I trained the torch's beam on the upward slope. No opening there, nothing but sheer granite and a cairn of tumbled rocks. I moved closer, examined the placement of the stones. Somehow they looked too artfully arranged.

Going even closer, I shifted the light to my left hand and slipped the Colt from my belt. Edged around the cairn. It didn't actually touch the wall; there was a space behind it about two feet wide. And beyond that a ragged A-shaped hole perhaps a yard high.

Quickly I flicked off the torch and moved into the small space. Listened. Heard nothing. After a moment I crouched down and peered into the hole. Total darkness. I felt around on the ground and found a pebble, tossed it through the opening. It skittered noisily off what I supposed were rock walls and floors. I waited until the sound died away into silence.

Finally I turned the light on again and shone it through the opening. Inside lay a low, narrow tunnel. The gashes in the rock were fresh and raw. The tunnel extended perhaps eight feet, then opened into a larger space, where the torch's beam fanned out on more rock.

I bit my lip. Straightened and considered. By now Hy would have those men off the mesa—if they had agreed to leave. How long before he caught up with me?

A long time. Maybe not at all.

"Dammit," I whispered.

I have few phobias. I used to be afraid of birds, but I've mellowed to the point of being able to go inside the aviary at the zoo. Spiders, heights, wide open spaces—they're fine with me. Lock me in a closet and I'll amuse myself for hours. But the one thing that I can't abide is the thought of crawling through a constricted space. Like that tunnel.

Well, I told myself, that's just too bad. What you've got here is a tunnel that needs crawling through.

I replaced the gun in my belt, pushing it farther back so there would be no pressure on it. Went back around the cairn and arranged some rocks as a marker for Hy. Then I got down on my hands and knees and pushed the torch into the opening. Took a deep breath and wriggled in after it.

The tunnel slanted downward. I inched along, pushing the torch, trying not to think of the walls that pressed in on me. A couple of times the rope caught; I yanked it free. The last few feet were so sharply canted that I all but fell into the larger chamber. The torch rolled away from me, its beam hopping in a chaotic dance across the gouged and scoured rock walls. I righted myself, grabbed it, shone it around.

The level I'd reached was a good seven feet high and almost as wide. Its walls were interrupted by deep excavations—stopes, Hy had called them—that showed where the ore had been removed from a vein. The floor was worn smooth by feet and time, and the light reflected off it as if it were wet. Seven hundred yards ahead, the level curved into blackness.

I took the rope from my shoulders and made a loop at one

end. Fastened it around a jagged projection at the foot of the farthest stope. Then I wrapped the rest of it over my arm and moved close to the wall. Turned off the torch and felt along, uncoiling the rope as I went. When I reached the place where the wall curved, I stopped to listen.

No sound at all. Merely a deep dead silence that must have extended to the earth's core.

But there was something . . . No, just my own breathing. I held my breath, became acutely aware of the beat of my heart, and then started around the curve. Stopped again, thinking I detected motion. And then I heard a sigh.

It came from ahead and to the right. I let out some more of the rope and edged along. The floor slanted, leveled out again. The sigh was not repeated.

I wanted to use the torch, but I was afraid of who might be waiting in the darkness. The dark was my handicap, but also my protection. I kept going, realizing I was about to run out of rope. My sense of distance was lost. Time had become elastic. Reality was a memory.

One sliding step. Another. A few more yards of rope left. Another step, hand on the icy rock. When the rope ran out I'd have to turn on the light to avoid losing my bearings here in the black bowels of the mesa. . . .

My foot bumped against something soft. Another sound came: this time a recognizable moan of protest.

I switched on the torch. Lionel Ong lay almost at my feet, swaddled in layers of gray blanket.

At first I thought he must be semiconscious, but as I bent to check, his eyes flew open, glazed with terror. I moved the blankets, saw he was tied in a fetal position, wrists lashed to ankles. A dirty gag bit into his mouth; blood had caked around its edges. He jerked his head toward me, and I heard the bones of his neck pop from tension.

Earlier I'd taken my Swiss Army knife from my bag and stuffed it in the pocket of my jeans. Now I dug it out and cut

Ong's bonds. He remained still as I sawed through the knot in the gag. Remained silent after I removed it.

I motioned for him to keep quiet and helped him to a sitting position. He began to flex his fingers. Holding the torch aloft, I examined the chamber around us. It appeared to be a crosscut between the level I'd come along and a parallel one. On the wall was a single candle in a crude metal holder, wax dried in multicolored rivulets on the rock below it. That was all, besides Ong and his cocoon of blankets.

Ong had begun to massage his wrists and ankles. His mouth worked as he passed his dry tongue over his cracked and bleeding lips. I crouched close to him, put my mouth to his ear. "What has he got planned?"

Ong's reply came out a croak. He shook his head and grimaced as he tried to work up some saliva. It was a minute before he could speak. "Blow it up. Charges down here. On top, too."

"Where is he?"

"Checking them. Then intends to move me closer."

My skin prickled, and I straightened. "We've got to get out of here."

"Can't walk—numb."

"Yes, you can. I'll help you."

I grasped him under his arms and pulled, got him upright, and then he sagged against me.

"You have to help," I told him.

He nodded, gritting his teeth as he tried to put one foot in front of the other.

Sound in the parallel level: footsteps, and no attempt to conceal them.

Ong flinched. "Him!"

I began to drag him toward the other level. He lurched sideways, and we both crashed against the wall.

As I pushed Ong off me, light blossomed in the far level. A man appeared at its entrance.

He bore only the most superficial resemblance to the photograph of Earl Hopwood. His gray hair straggled wildly about his head; flesh fell in turkey wattles from his neck; the furrows of his face were like the striae of the rock around us. The eyes were how I identified him: black and burning with spits and flares of colors that seemed part of an alien spectrum. Colors of another world, where the sea and sky became as blood, the moon black as sackcloth.

I shoved Ong away from me and reached for the Colt. But by the time my fingers touched its butt, I saw Hopwood had a weapon leveled at us. I let my hand fall to my side where he could see it.

For a few seconds none of us moved. Then Hopwood looked from me to Ong and said, "The whore and the deceiver."

"Mr. Hopwood." My voice sounded weak and tinny. "I've just come from your daughter. Margot is waiting for you at Willow Grove Lodge. She wants to see you."

"I have no daughter named Margot."

"Peggy, then."

"Margaret, like her mother."

"Yes, Margaret. She's waiting. Won't you come with me?"

The gun in Hopwood's hand wavered. I glanced at Ong, saw he was crouched on the ground. Would he be of any help?

Hopwood steadied the gun. "She will come here in time. To be cleansed of her deception. All things will be made new."

Christ, I thought, he's really flipped out. I can't reason with him.

I glanced at Ong again. He hunched lower now, arms wrapped around his midsection. No help from that quarter.

The Colt weighed reassuringly against my right hip. I said, "How will all things be made new?" and brought my arms behind me, like an attentive Sunday school pupil.

Hopwood's mad eyes seemed distracted. Again his gun

wavered. I calculated the distance I would have to spring to get hold of it.

But he steadied it once more. "First the mountains and rocks must fall."

My fingers touched the Colt's butt.

"And the star that is called Wormwood."

I began to slip it from my belt.

"Many men died of the waters, because they were made bitter."

The revolver's cylinder caught on my waistband. I couldn't free it unobtrusively.

I shrugged, using the motion to pull the gun free and said, "The waters of Tufa Lake have always been bitter."

"Be still, mother of harlots!"

I held the Colt behind me—ready, seeking my opportunity. Watched Hopwood, who watched me, strange eyes flashing their alien colors—

And then Ong decided to be brave after all. He sprang upward and leapt at Hopwood, hands reaching for his gun. I brought the Colt up. Saw a blinding flash. Felt rock fragments pepper my skin. As I dived to the ground, the sound of the shot echoed and reechoed.

Ong was down, too. I rolled, grasped the Colt in both hands, squeezed off a shot at Hopwood without aiming carefully. It missed, and he pivoted and dashed into the level behind him. I heard his footsteps, running away deeper into the earth. Running toward his dynamite charges.

Ong pushed up from the ground; he hadn't been hit. I grabbed his arm, dragged him toward the parallel level. He stumbled. I yanked him harder.

"Come on, dammit! He's going to detonate—"

Ong got his legs under him and ran with me.

I'd left the torch on the floor of the crosscut, and when I searched for my guide rope, I couldn't find it. Ong was blundering through the darkness in front of me now, breath sobbing. I followed, stumbling and going down on one knee, caroming off the wall and slamming into his back. He fell. I pulled him up and dragged him some more.

Ahead then I saw a pinpoint of light. Heard voices. The pinpoint enlarged: the access tunnel. People outside to help us.

I shoved Ong into the small space. He balked, so I shoved him harder. Ong scrabbled forward, momentarily blocking the light. I crouched and dived in after him. Rock scraped my skin. Ong's foot kicked out and grazed my forehead. And then a rush of fresh air and Hy's voice, louder than the others: "Easy, easy."

I clutched the lifting arm. "The dynamite's about to blow!"

"Christ!" It was Hy's arm. He pulled me to my feet, grabbed my hand. "Come on!"

I ran with him, stumbling and panting. Around us were the sounds of other running feet and figures blurred by the darkness. My breath came hard; pain seared my side. The beams of flashlights bounced off fractured granite; rocks clattered and rolled; a man's voice cursed furiously.

I stumbled again, lost my grip on Hy's hand, pitched headlong. He caught me, rolled with me. We came to rest on hard, level ground. Nearby I heard the sound of water.

I lay still, panting. Hy leaned over me. Between gasps he said, "You damn near doubled your loss, McCone."

I looked up at him. His face was grim; wild curls hung over his sweat-slicked forehead. I sat up, smacking my own forehead against his chin.

Hy pulled back. I saw we were on the lower slope, not far from the stream. The mesa loomed above us, security lights ablaze.

"Hopwood," I said. "He's in there. We've got to stop him!"

"Nothing we can do. We'll have to let him blow it up."

I tried to get to my feet. Hy yanked me down.

I said, "We can—"

"No way."

"I could—"

"You go back there and you've got even more of a death wish than I do."

I looked into his eyes, then back toward the mesa.

Death wish.

It takes many forms: the needle and the bottle; mountain climbing in avalanche time; games of chance when you know the deck's stacked against you; wild car rides at night. For whatever reasons, the private hell that Hy described his late wife as saving him from had probably embodied a death wish. As did my own addiction to danger. . . .

Many forms, but this wasn't one of them. "No," I said, "it's not that strong in either of us."

I looked away from the mesa. Allowed him to help me up. When standing, I noticed Ong several yards away, being supported by two other Asians.

I thought, I hope he gives you a fat bonus for this, you poor bastards.

Slowly we moved down the slope, a ragged and wounded little army, following the streambed toward the town where so many dreams had died. As we reached the first building, I heard a helicopter overhead, glanced up at it and then at Hy.

"Sheriff's department," he said. "The guards found one of Hopwood's dynamite charges up top and radioed Bridgeport before they evacuated."

The helicopter circled, darting and dipping as its pilot searched for a place to put it down. Then I heard a low rumbling deep in the earth, felt a tremor like the beginning of an earthquake. It gathered in volume and momentum.

A series of bangs, violent but muffled.

I jerked my head toward the top of the mesa in time to see the burst of fire. And then the moon and sky became as blood.

Twenty-nine

▲▲▲

Hy and I arrived at Bridgeport in a Highway Patrol helicopter. The county choppers had been used to evacuate the Transpacific personnel, Lionel Ong—who by then had proclaimed himself savior of the day, in spite of his heroics almost having gotten both of us killed—and Bayard and his family, whose shack had been set afire by falling cinders.

By the time we left the valley, the conflagration on top of the mesa had almost burned itself out; planes were spreading retardant in a firebreak along the main street of Promiseville. Several buildings had been lost, their tinder-dry wood perfect fodder for wind-whipped sparks; Nickles's house (along with my pea jacket) was among them. As we watched them flare and collapse upon themselves, I saw pain on Hy's face, but when I spoke to him he turned away, pretending indifference.

Beyond halting the spread of the flames, the rescue crews had little to do. Except for Bayard and his brood, the desert rats had scattered. The crews would attempt to locate Hopwood's body, of course, but I seriously doubted they'd

313

find any trace of him. Even from the valley floor, the force of the explosions deep within the mesa had sounded too violent not to cave in what remained of the fragile old mine workings. In a way, I supposed, the mesa would be a fitting burial cairn for the man to whom it had become the symbol of Armageddon.

Lark met us at the door of the county sheriff's building. She was wired, crackling with nervous energy, and the first thing she said to me was, "Sharon, you look like hell."

"Thank you."

Her freckled face flushed. "Didn't mean it that way. Ladies' room is down the hall there. We'll be in the first interrogation room."

I followed the hallway, used the facilities, washed my face and hands. There were fresh scrapes on my forehead and cheekbones; my hair was tangled and snarled. I still wore Nickles's wool shirt, but dirt covered it and one sleeve was half ripped off at the shoulder.

I'd rescued my bag from the Land Rover before they evacuated us from Promiseville, and now I extracted my hairbrush and set to work. After doing what I could with my long mane, I bound it at the nape of my neck with a rubber band I found on the counter. Then I leaned forward intending to study my fresh facial wounds, but the room seemed to tip. Gripping the washbasin harder, I waited for everything to right itself. When it did, I observed that my face had turned the color of cold, congealed oatmeal.

I filled the basin with cold water and splashed my face and wrists until I felt better. Only a little more to get through, I told myself as I dried off, and then you can go home and never come back to this horrible place.

I found Hy and Kristen in the interrogation room, drinking coffee. He'd freshened up, too, and his wild curls were slicked down; a drop of water glistened at the tip of his stubbled chin. I accepted a cup of coffee, but immediately set it aside; the acid had started my empty stomach roiling.

Lark taped statements from both of us, then shut off the recorder and tipped contemplatively back in her chair. "Squares with what the Nickles woman told Washoe County," she said.

"They picked Lily up in Nevada?" I asked.

Kristen nodded. "Reno. You were right about her taking off because she'd seen something—Hopwood, hauling a case of dynamite up to that tunnel he made into the old mine. Seems she got curious again, went looking around, and spotted him. She figured something big was about to come down, so she split."

"A good thing, too," I said. "Her house was one of those that went."

"Maybe it wouldn't have burned if she'd told someone what she'd seen," Hy said.

Lark righted her chair and stood. "Well, that about wraps it up. Damned shame, all of it. Damned religious nut case. That's the trouble with these zealots: everybody's got a cause, and to hell with everybody else."

"Sometimes people become nut cases like Hopwood because they just get pushed too far," Hy commented.

She looked severely at him. "That's no excuse. And I'm not just talking about folks who think they've got an open line to God. You environmentalists aren't much better."

I would have expected him to become angry, but he merely shrugged and set his empty coffee cup on the table. "Better to have a cause than to go through life passionless and uncaring."

"That's all well and good, but you've got to exercise a little reason."

"Reason's all right up to a point. But what're you going to do when nobody will listen?"

It was a stalemate. I interrupted them. "Kristen, what about Ned Sanderman?"

Her face lit up, as if she'd just realized she had the perfect present for me. "He's right here in the next room. Son of a bitch walked in about three hours ago, gave himself up."

"What did he have to say?"

"Not much. As soon as we read him his rights, he got seriously uncooperative, demanded a lawyer. Only one available was Tom Lindsay, our local shyster. He's with him now, and Sanderman isn't saying a word, but at least we've got him."

"Can I see him?"

"Sure." She motioned for me to come with her. "But if you're thinking you can get something out of him, forget it."

Sanderman and his lawyer sat at a table in a room similar to the one we'd just left. Under the glare of the neon, Ned looked tired, scared, and somewhat sick. The lawyer, Lindsay, was a fat man in a teal blue suit with a dusting of dandruff on its shoulders. He looked like the kind of attorney who inspired jokes about no skid marks.

When Sanderman saw me, his eyes widened and he started to get up.

Lindsay motioned for him to sit down. "Detective Lark, we've been waiting for some time now. Are you—"

I stepped forward. "Counselor, I'm Sharon McCone, private investigator employed by Mr. Sanderman's organization."

Lindsay ignored the hand I offered. "If you're concerned about your fee—"

"I'm concerned about Ned, Mr. Lindsay." I pulled out a chair and sat. Lark leaned against the wall behind me, arms folded, eyes faintly amused.

I turned to Sanderman. "How are you?"

He shrugged.

"Why'd you turn yourself in?"

Lindsay said, "I have instructed my client—"

I glanced at him, not bothering to hide my distaste. "Why don't you just be quiet? I'm trying to help your client."

Lindsay sputtered. "Detective Lark, I protest this—"

"To put it less politely, Counselor—shut up. Your client isn't guilty of the charges. He didn't kill anyone. All he's guilty of is improperly disposing of a body."

Lark made a surprised sound and pushed away from the wall. "What are you talking about, McCone?"

I ignored both her and the lawyer. Said to Sanderman, "That's true, isn't it?"

Looking relieved, he nodded.

"All right," Lark asked, "if that's so, who *did* kill Mick Erickson?"

"I don't know for sure, but I'd guess it was Earl Hopwood. Ned?"

"Yes, that's who did it."

Lindsay was staring at me, his fat mouth pursed, his jowls pouched in disappointment. I supposed he was mentally watching an extortionary fee slip away.

Lark asked me, "How do you figure that?"

"The more I thought about Erickson's murder, the more I realized Ned didn't have any motive to shoot him. Even though all the physical evidence pointed to him, there was no reason for him to quarrel with or kill his co-conspirator."

Lark turned to Sanderman. "Are you willing to make a statement?"

"That was why I came back here in the first place. But when you said you were charging me with murder—"

Lindsay said, "Now just hold on here—"

Sanderman interrupted him. "Is it possible to fire my lawyer at this point?"

"What? What?"

Lark smiled. "Maybe you better keep him—if he promises to stay quiet. I'll go get a tape recorder while you think it over." She hurried from the room, nearly sparking with nervous energy.

Lindsay said to Sanderman, "You're being a fool."

"If you want to stay here, keep quiet."

"I want it on record that you're doing this against the advice of counsel."

"Good. We'll put it on the tape."

Lark fetched the recording equipment, and Ripinsky followed her in, shutting the door behind him. When she had it set up and had made a preliminary statement, she said to Sanderman, "Will you tell us in your own words what happened last Saturday evening?"

Ned ran his tongue over his lips and glanced at the recorder. He wiped damp palms on his blue-jeaned thighs and began to speak. "It started around six o'clock. Mick Erickson arrived at my cabin at Willow Grove Lodge to talk about the problem with Earl Hopwood."

Erickson, Sanderman went on, told him that he'd been staying in one of the trailers at the mine site for the past few days and had twice met and attempted to reason with his father-in-law at his cabin in Stone Valley. Hopwood had been difficult to reach because he was no longer living there but camping out somewhere while he continued his harassment and vandalism at the Transpacific property. On the second occasion—that morning—they quarreled and Hopwood pulled a gun on him. Erickson took it away from him, accidentally inflicting a flesh wound.

"It shook Mick up a lot," Sanderman said. "He liked the old man and never intended to hurt him. And he was afraid of what it might do to his chances of reconciling with his wife. But it had also given him the idea that it might be necessary for Hopwood to, as he put it, meet with an accident. Anyway, we kicked that idea around for a while, but neither of us was really for it. I was nervous, though; it would have destroyed me with the Coalition—with the entire environmental movement—if the deal had fallen apart and they had found out that I'd sold out Promiseville."

"Why did you do that?" Lark asked. "Money?"

"Yes. A lot of it."

Behind me, Ripinsky hissed.

Sanderman glanced at him. "It wasn't for myself, though—it was for the Coalition. Transpacific made two substantial cash payments to me, which I donated, and they promised a much larger one once construction began on the project. Some people"—he threw an accusing look at Hy—"don't realize the costs of running our campaigns. The administrative expenses alone . . . Sometimes you have to jettison one cause in favor of a more worthy one."

Ripinsky remained silent, but I could feel his rage building.

"Go on with what happened that evening," Lark told Sanderman.

"We'd been talking for about an hour. Somebody knocked at the door and I went to see who it was. At first I thought he was one of these mountain men—wild eyed, unkempt—but Mick came forward, called him 'Mr. Hopwood.'"

Sanderman had also thought Hopwood drunk, although he'd soon realized he was seriously unbalanced. He and Erickson quickly took up their quarrel where they'd left off earlier, and soon Hopwood was reeling around the cabin, raving and making strange accusations.

"What kind of accusations?" Lark asked.

"Archaic-sounding things, like he was quoting Scripture. He called Mick a deceiver and a fanged serpent. Said he was a servant of Satan."

"Was Mr. Hopwood armed?"

"No, Mick had kept his gun after he shot him, locked it up somewhere."

"Go on."

"Things were seriously out of control. Hopwood ran into the kitchen. Mick went after him, yelling something about knives. Then there was a shot. Mick started to fall. Another shot, and then Hopwood leapt over him, carrying my twenty-two, and ran out of the cabin."

"Where did he get the twenty-two?"

"From the refrigerator. It's a good hiding place."

"How do you suppose Hopwood knew it was there?"

Sanderman looked blank.

I motioned to Lark. She frowned, switched off the recorder. "What do you want to tell us, McCone?"

"I think Hopwood saw the gun when he broke into the cabin right after Ned came up here."

She nodded, looked back at Sanderman. "Was it in the fridge the whole time you were staying there?"

"Except for one time when I went back to Sacramento."

"Okay." She restarted the recorder, recapped what we'd said. "Now, Mr. Sanderman, what did you do after Mr. Hopwood ran away?"

"Went to see if Mick was dead, of course. He was. Then . . . for a while I couldn't do anything. Finally I realized I had to get the body out of there. If I called the authorities, it would all come out and I'd be ruined. It was awfully difficult; he was heavy, and I couldn't move him very far. Finally I just dragged him down to the lake."

Ripinsky made a disgusted noise. I knew how he felt; it hadn't helped that Sanderman had spoken in a self-pitying whine.

Lark kept her expression neutral. "And then?"

Sanderman sighed, as if the effort of recounting it made him weary. "I drove the Bronco he'd been renting into town and parked it on the highway. Walked back and started to clean up the blood. There was a lot of it, so I went back to town for some cleaners. While I was scrubbing the floor I realized I couldn't locate one of the spent shell casings from the gun. I looked everywhere, but I never did find it."

After a moment Lark asked, "Is there anything else you'd like to tell us?"

Sanderman shook his head, eyes closed.

Kristen switched the recorder off. "Mr. Sanderman," she said, "I'll tell you right now in the presence of your attorney, this doesn't look too good for you. Your story's uncorroborated. You admit the weapon was yours, and now you can't produce it. Why should I believe you aren't conveniently pinning this crime on a man who's dead and can't contradict you?"

I said, "Because he doesn't know what happened in Stone Valley, doesn't know Hopwood's dead."

The startled look on Sanderman's face confirmed that.

"Besides," I added, "Hopwood had the twenty-two with him in the mine tunnel."

Lark stared at me, unblinking. Her expression said she didn't believe me. "You saw the gun, McCone?"

"As I stated earlier, Hopwood fired at Lionel Ong and me. It was a twenty-two automatic. If you run a check, you'll probably find that Hopwood didn't own one."

"You didn't mention the type of gun in your earlier statement."

"I didn't think of it. It didn't seem important."

"And now it's buried under tons of rubble with Hopwood."

"I guess so."

Lark regarded me steadily for a moment. "You'd testify to that?"

"If I had to."

"Sanderman," Kristen told him, "you owe McCone a big one."

Quickly I flashed him a look that said, *Don't thank me.* As Lark began packing up the recording equipment, I wondered why I'd come to Sanderman's aid. I had no idea what kind of gun Hopwood had held on Ong and me in that tunnel, couldn't truthfully testify to what I'd said. But I believed Ned's story and wanted to help him. *Why?* I didn't like the man one bit. He was a type we're seeing more and more of: passionless, programmed opportunists who will cheat and lie and—yes, if they can get away with it—murder, not for personal gain but to further a program.

Not a cause, a *program.* Not something they deeply believe in, but an agenda that is merely an exercise in management skills and control. I dislike that bloodless kind of individual, and, more important, I fear them all. They are the ones who someday will sell out the world if it means they will win at their own particular intellectual games.

So why help Sanderman?

Perhaps because under all his lies and self-serving statements I'd sensed a smoldering of humanity. Because under the false things he'd told me there lurked a trace of truth—and pain. I remembered his face when he'd told me that all his life he hadn't related; I heard the hollowness of his voice when he tried to speak proudly of his self-imposed isolation. As I'd told Hy that night when we drifted together on the lake, maybe there was *something*. Maybe there was hope for Ned Sanderman. . . .

Lark said to me, "Chopper's about to take a run down to Stone Valley. If you two hurry, you can catch a ride to Vernon."

I glanced at Hy. He nodded and stood. I followed suit, not looking back at either Sanderman or his attorney. Lark accompanied us to the door.

"Sharon," she said, clasping my hand, "I owe you, too. Plenty."

"Maybe someday I'll need to call in the debt. Who knows?"

"In the meantime, you come back up here. We'll go fishing, hell around in the bars, whatever. Okay?"

"Okay," I said, knowing I never would.

On the way out of the building I glanced at Hy. His jaw was bunched with anger—whether at Sanderman or at me for backing up Ned's story, I couldn't tell. He asked, "Now what?"

"I want to go home."

He nodded, didn't protest. "I'll fly you to Oakland."

Back at the Vernon airstrip, I called Hank and asked him to meet me at General Aviation in Oakland. Then I sat drinking a Coke with the owner while Hy gave the Citabria its preflight check. I hadn't wanted to return to the lodge for my things; too many questions would be asked, and I couldn't bear to face Margot Erickson yet. Hy said he'd tell Rose Wittington to ship my bag down to the city.

Dawn was bleeding over the eastern hills as we took off. I watched the lake staining pink, took a last look at the alkali plain and the cones of the fire mountains to the south. Then I dropped into an uneasy sleep.

Even after I woke somewhere over Livermore, Hy and I didn't speak. The intimacy between us had vanished, it seemed. It was as if the danger we'd faced together had allowed it to flower; in the less fertile soil of safety, it had withered and died.

When we taxied into a visitor's space at Oakland, I saw Hank leaning on the chain-link fence near the General Aviation terminal. His sleepy face and wind-ruffled steel-wool hair spoke of the familiar comforts of home. Wordlessly, Hy got out and helped me from the plane. Then he turned away to hook the wings to the chains on the tarmac.

I waited. He moved around the Citabria. "Better go now," he said. "Your boyfriend's waiting."

"He's not my boyfriend. He's my boss, Anne-Marie's husband."

"Whoever."

Stung, I turned and started toward Hank.

"McCone."

I kept walking, then glanced over my shoulder. Hy stood next to the plane—double-luck two eight niner—left hand resting on its high wing. "Yes?" I asked.

He gave me a long, solemn look and leveled his right index finger at me, as he had on the day I'd met him. "Glad you didn't say good-bye," he told me, "because it hasn't even begun with us yet."

Afterword

▲▲▲

he yellow roses continued
to arrive at my office—one every Tuesday morning, with
never so much as a card. They brought visions of gnarled
tufa towers and ice blue water, of alkali dust devils and
fractured stone. And on those occasions when I couldn't
block the memory, I also saw a flaming mountaintop and
ashes settling over a town where—now—everybody's
dreams had died.

Our winter was a wet one for a change. Soggy gray days
naturally depress me, but this year my moods sank deeper
and lasted longer. The story of what had happened in Stone
Valley remained in the news for weeks; as I'd expected,
Lionel Ong set out to gain maximum mileage from his
self-proclaimed heroism. The Coalition put a stop to that,
however, by holding a press conference and baring the
details of Transpacific's dealings in Mono County. With the
cessation of the media coverage, my life regained a semblance of normalcy.

George and I put off the talk we'd promised each other.
After my return from Mono County a haze of questions that

324

he'd rather not have asked and I'd rather not have answered filtered between us; even our good times were blunted by excessive politeness and caution. We drifted, unsure of our destination, as Hy and I had drifted in the boat on Tufa Lake.

For Thanksgiving we threw a big dinner party at George's place; unlike in the days before I'd gone to the high desert, we felt more comfortable in a crowd. Three of his colleagues, most of the folks from All Souls, and several other friends attended. The cleanup took an entire day.

In early December Ned Sanderman pleaded guilty to and was sentenced for improper disposal of a body and failure to report a homicide, thus relieving me of the need to return to Mono County for a trial. My feelings about that were strangely mixed—and briefly I wondered why.

Around the same time Anne-Marie returned to San Francisco and announced that in the future she'd be working with the Coalition from her home. An elated Hank organized a chili cook-off in her honor, at which we charitably allowed him to claim third prize.

Before the holidays I got Lily Nickles's address in Reno and sent her a new Pendleton shirt to replace the one I'd ruined. In her thank-you note she said she'd gotten scared by the AIDS epidemic and opted for a straight job. If I ever needed my sensibilities ruffled, however, I was to look her up; she still behaved "pretty damn shocking."

And George and I continued to drift. He asked me to go to the Bahamas for the holidays, but—in light of the recent upheaval—I felt obligated to visit my family. George didn't act terribly disappointed and decided to go alone.

After the usual festivities in the city, I flew to San Diego on Christmas Eve and, with initial reluctance, spent it with Ma and That Man at their new home in the retirement community at Rancho Bernardo. Melvin Hunt proved to be charming, and seeing Ma so happy laid most of my reservations to rest. However, when I coyly asked her if I should shop for a dress to wear to a wedding, she told me I was crazy if I thought she would remarry at her age. On Christmas Day, I met my brother John, his kids, Charlene and Ricky and their brood, plus half the Savage backup musicians at the old family home, where we fixed dinner for Pa. He was in fine fettle and didn't venture near the garage all day, so the last of my reservations joined the others.

In January Rae received her private investigator's license from the state of California. We all celebrated at the Remedy Lounge, and as she and I touched glasses after one of the toasts, I realized that the distance between us had begun to narrow.

In February George again asked me to move in with him, but I sensed the proposal was a halfhearted gesture at best. By now we'd drifted so long that neither of us really believed we had any destination. When I said no, he seemed relieved. At the end of the month we finally had the long-delayed talk; its upshot was a promise to remain friends—one we've thus far kept.

In early March Hy Ripinsky was arrested for disorderly conduct at an anti-logging demonstration in Siskiyou County. Charges were later dropped.

And a single yellow rose continued to arrive every Tuesday morning.

On one of those mornings, when the weather page of the paper told of the spring thaw, I threw a bag into the MG and drove southeast and over newly opened Tioga Pass to Tufa Lake—going back after all. It was time to find out how good Hy and I would be together.